T0146632

YOU LOVE HIM OR YOU HATE HIM:
READERS RESPOND TO DAVID NOWEL'S
SPACESTATION ARK

"Dave, I never told you this before, but I've been reading your book and it's great"
>-A 31-year-old woman the author has
>been infatuated with for five years

"I gave the book to my sister, warning her that the author had a screw loose. She really liked the book, but then, I never really liked my sister."
>-A loyal 10 year-old friend of the author

"God, I really love the chapter about Hector- something every working woman should have."
>-A tall, beautiful business associate of
>the author who has Amanda's legs.

"It's the most disgusting thing I have ever read: pure trashy pornography. What in heaven gave you the opinion that you could hand stuff like that out to an employee."
>-the author's former business associate

"My God, you really are a writer!"
>-The real Philip

"That last guy had to be on LSD when he wrote that stuff. Wow! It's the greatest stuff I've ever read."
>-A 17 year-old fan.

"I don't care if your book does become a bestseller. I'll never read that shit."
>-The author's ex-boss

THE YEAR: 2010

A NEW NATION

A NEW SOCIETY

SPACESTATION

ARK

DAVID J. NOWEL

Trafford rev. 08/27/2015

 www.trafford.com

North America & international
toll-free: 1 888 232 4444 (USA & Canada)
fax: 812 355 4082

In memory of and dedicated to my grandmother, Jawiga Nowel. And to her children, especially her son, my uncle, Simon Nowel. It was the money my uncle left me that made this printing possible.

In special recognition of my final editor, Donovan Coons, a recent creative writing graduate of California State University, Long Beach. He stuck with it and finally pulled everything together.

Also, thanks to all those people I met in the last ten years who encouraged me. And thanks as well to those who weren't so supportive but listened to what I was trying to say.

CONTENTS

PLEASE BE ADVISED THAT CHAPTERS INDICATED BY 🐾 CONTAIN EXPLICIT SEXUAL THEMES, THAT MAY BE CONSIDERED OFFENSIVE BY SOME READERS. PLEASE USE YOUR OWN JUDGEMENT.

SPACESTATION

ARK

PROLOGUE

KEIKO

MEANWHILE, BACK ON THE ARK

From his isolation cell on board the Ark, Alex Abramawitz looked down on the tiny blue and white sphere of his home planet Earth. He saw the ponderous continent of Africa, its enormity dwarfed by his perspective from space, as if it were a miniature elephant's ear shrouded by inconsequential puffs of cotton. Alex wondered if space travellers, perhaps ten thousand years ago, might have gazed at Earth from a similar orbit over the planet. If they had, he could see why they might have chosen Africa for a landing pad: something about its shape had an almost magnetic pull. In Alex's mind, the African continent possessed a deep significance. It was the hothouse from which man had first flowered. And he imagined how, after the first extra-terrestrial visitors landed, their seed might have commingled with indigenous species. Humankind's advanced and sudden origin in Africa was easily conceivable from a spacecraft hovering a hundred miles above the surface of the planet.

He saw the Atlantic Ocean and the beginning of the bulge in Africa's side that had once been a part of South America. From there, Africa's boundaries rolled up and over the Strait of Gibraltar and headed straight east, jutting out into the Mediterranean sea only to barrel back down into the irregular trapezoid of Saudi Arabia and the narrow-waisted Red Sea. He saw the Indian Ocean, the landmasses of Southeast Asia and the white, swirling clouds that quilted themselves together over northeastern Australia, New Guinea and the Great Barrier Reef.

To the south, like a gelatinous silver cap, icy Antarctica spread itself over the bottom of the sphere, and it was the image of this frozen land that most captivated Alex. He looked forward to the day when the Ark would develop machinery to recover the solidified water reserves of the barren South Pole. To the inhabitants of the Ark and other space stations, water was a more precious commodity than gold or silver. As human colonization of space expanded further and further beyond the immediate orbit of the mother planet, water became the most difficult resource to transport to these new pioneers. When Alex thought of the naysayers who had told him it could never be done, he smiled. Soon, he knew, the Ark would have the technology in place. They would be able to supply every space station and space settlement from the Ark to the Moon Base to the future colonies of Mars and beyond while still managing to maintain enormous reserves.

This image of the Earth never failed to spark Alex's imagination. If only his high school geography teachers had used a globe like this, he told himself, he might have been a little more interested in what was going on, his talents might have been recognized sooner. To Alex, school had been a necessary inconvenience. His ideas about a future in space had been laughed at and his concentration on writing his books made the study of more mundane subjects impossible. With the Earth hovering meekly below him, Alex believed himself to be successful. His ideas, his dreams, had been turned into reality by the force of his own persistent will. And better yet, his vision of the world had improved the lives of tens of thousands of others who looked to him for new visions and guidance.

If world leaders from past eras had been able to see the world as he did, Alex wondered if their ambitions might have been checked, if the horrors imposed by Hitler and other dictators might have been mitigated by this humbling image. Too many atrocities had been committed, Alex thought, because men in power hadn't been able to see the big picture. To the Romans, the Earth had revolved around the thin finger of Italy and the Mediterranean sea. Would they have acted differently if they had been aware of the huge expanse of the planet they were spinning around on? And if they had understood the infinite nature of space? Would that knowledge have altered their decisions? Someday, Alex believed, his great-grandchildren would look back on their home galaxy from some now-distant galaxy and marvel at how little their ancestors had been aware of.

Alex called out some small adjustments to the computer and the Ark's satellites fed his monitors an image of the small African village he and Keiko had visited less then a thousand achievements ago. She had been so happy talking to the children who lived there. As she stood among them dressed in native garb, they had looked at her with awe. On the Ark, Keiko was often considered a recluse, a weakling, but in Africa she carried herself like a professional actress. Every word she spoke suggested music, her voice ringing out like the chords of a plucked harp. Her ability to empathize with anyone she met made her an irresistible force. The people of the village had been hypnotized by her, unable to take their eyes from this diminutive woman who radiated goodwill and peace.

"On the Ark, the moon and stars are so close you can touch them!" she had exclaimed. She told the villagers about spacewalking, about how they could see the whole Earth from the Ark. They laughed when they heard about weightlessness. It was impossible, a little girl said, to float up from the ground like a bird. But Keiko convinced them it was true. "It's like watching a feather in reverse," was the way she described it.

Alex could not remember a happier time in his life. His memories of the trip warmed his heart. His mind was often filled with thoughts about Keiko, about how much she had done for him. They had come so far together that he couldn't imagine a life without her.

Over twenty years ago, against the advice of every person he knew, he had fought for and won her release from Camarillo State Hospital for the Mentally Ill. Doctors had diagnosed her as a manic-depressive, paranoid schizophrenic. At the time, she was twenty-four years old, and Alex had been taken with her vulnerability, her innocence. But as Alex remembered her among the children of Africa, it seemed to him that she had not changed. Now that she was forty-eight years old, she still possessed her magical aura of youth. She was more comfortable with a circle of young people than she would ever be with her contemporaries on the Ark.

Her openness to other cultures made Keiko the ideal touring companion for Alex when he went out on Ark business. Although the Ark's educational computer systems had allowed Alex to learn the basics of over fifty languages, Keiko had been able to master more than one hundred, including many of the regional and local dialects spoken in small villages and remote areas. Alex had come to rely on Keiko during these promotional tours and she, in turn, had learned to instinctively rephrase Alex's sometimes cumbersome declarations about the Ark into colloquialisms their audiences would understand.

The most common question asked of them was, "What is it really like on board the Ark?" Even though this should have been a simple question to answer, Alex found it difficult to respond. He answered by telling them that the Ark was a huge platform in space, but that didn't seem to properly enlighten them. When he told them it was a space station, only a few more faces seemed to light with understanding. He generally found himself unable to describe the grandeur and diversity of the Ark. "Imagine the fanciest hotel you have ever seen: the Biltmore in Los Angeles, the Algonquin in New York. Imagine the palace of a king. Some sectors of the Ark look like that. Other sectors make you feel like you are right in the middle of the universe looking out. Everywhere you go," he told them, "it's different." When Alex finished his speech, however, the people turned to Keiko, expecting her to be able to translate this strange man's enthusiasm into images they could understand.

Alex and Keiko's tours of Earth, which visited the most overcrowded and prosperous cities of the world as well as the remotest settlements, had made the Ark the most popular tourist destination in the history of humankind. Many people who came for the thrill of a journey into space decided to stay once they saw the possibilities offered by a life in space. Their messages home convinced tens of thousands more that they should also emigrate to the Ark. The Ark, like the United States in the late nineteenth century, was hungry for more citizens and everyone willing to be naturalized to Ark citizenship was welcomed.

Newly christened Arkians found their ways of life radically changed. A former rice farmer from Cambodia found himself trained to work on computer information systems. A factory laborer from Cuba became one of the Ark's leading economic analysts within a year; with the aid of teaching computers, she advanced from an elementary school background to post-graduate status in less than six months.

Alex marveled at how the Ark had changed in just fifteen years. In 2005, the ship had been a simple platform of interconnecting tubes and chambers. Some of the portals had been so small, he had barely been able to squeeze his body through the crawlspaces. They had not been able to simulate gravity and life on the Ark had been an ongoing spacewalk.

As technological innovations caught up with Alex's conception of the Ark, however, it was only a short time before superplastics and zero-gravity building techniques were utilized on board. Alex oversaw the rapid construction of huge living areas, public facilities, office buildings, laboratories and recreational complexes. Within seven years, the Ark already closely resembled the Earth's most bustling metropolises. Transparent walls had been manufactured to allow for clear vistas of the solar system. In some places, Arkians were able to walk out onto nearly invisible platforms, enveloped on all sides by the vastness of space.

What had most astounded Alex was the amount of opposition and resistance his plans for the Ark met with. No one wanted to listen to him, and those who did told him his ideas were impossible to put into practice. Humans, Alex had soon discovered, were not interested in pushing themselves to the limits of their potential. They were afraid of change, were unwilling to listen to people who wanted to upset the status quo. As a young man, his mother had been fond of telling him, "Curiosity killed the cat," every time one of his odd ideas about people in space met with derision. People were afraid of new discoveries, Alex came to realize, but they were perfectly willing to enjoy the fruits of the labor of men who struggled to make their dreams come true.

In the 1960s, Alex's parents took him to the New York World's Fair. He was captivated by a General Motors' exhibit showing a modern city that could be built on the ocean floor. By the turn of the century, the engineers predicted, such cities would be commonplace. Most people who saw the exhibit dismissed the idea. "Impossible," they said. "Impractical." They had been right about impractical, thought Alex, but they never would have imagined that it would be easier to live in space than to try and build an underwater civilization. The space solution, besides overcoming the many engineering problems associated with cities in the ocean, also allowed for new space stations to develop without specific national identities. Space was a wide-open territory and, for the moment, no one power could claim autonomy of any particular region of the heavens. More than two dozen countries operated space stations, but none of them dared to declare themselves in possession of the solar system. The Ark, with its own citizenship, was the closest thing to a new nation in space.

The pioneers who came most readily to the Ark were people like the African villagers whom Keiko and he had talked to. As their aboriginal way of life grew more and more difficult to maintain, the Ark offered a new start. The formerly impoverished peoples of Africa and Southeast Asia who found success and wealth on the Ark now redirected their capital to their countries of origin. The Ark had singlehandedly revitalized many of the Third World's most ravaged nations. Alex wondered how many of the African villagers he and Keiko had talked to would end up actually emigrating to the Ark. Those who did would find their lives transformed. Some would not be able to adapt and would ultimately return to their villages, but those who stayed would be involved in creating a new world, a new society. Alex loved thinking about the opportunities available to those ambitious souls who came aboard.

Alex hated to think that his trip to Africa with Keiko might have been their last journey together. He was getting older and space travel was beginning to take its toll on his body. The massive doses of radioactive sunlight he received on the Earth's surface increased his risk of contracting cancer, and each time he returned from such an excursion he found himself spending longer periods of time in quarantine, ridding his body of the toxins, molds, fungi and communicable diseases he had been exposed to in the unfiltered environs of Earth. Although he despised spending time away from the frenetic Arkian social scene, he knew that the Ark's hermetic environment could not risk an infected person roaming about. Keiko's health, too, as much as it seemed to be improved by her happy times with people on Earth, grew more fragile as she aged. He thought the unsettling shock of travelling between such vastly different cultures might be contributing to her increasing emotional instability.

In addition to his health concerns, Alex was beginning to find himself unnecessarily flustered by his return visits to Earth. After only a few days on the planet, he missed the comforts of the Ark and was afraid that having gone off his computer designed diet, he was putting himself at risk of heart attack or some disease. He missed the machines that made his life enjoyable, that allowed him to be his most productive. Furthermore, he found that he was getting tired of having people gape at him as if he were some kind of freak. He realized that his completely bald body—shaved to facilitate entry into the Ark's ergonomically molded plastic space suits—and his pasty skin shocked people, but he fervently disliked the comments that he overheard: "Grub." "Looks like he's dead." "Albino."

Yet he knew that his job as lead pitchman for the Ark would never be finished. No matter how many video and computer-assisted presentations were made, the people of Earth still loved to be sold to by a flesh-and-blood human being, and Alex and Keiko were the most successful sales team the Ark had. Even so, Alex regretted that they would never be able to really express the miracle of the Ark in a sales pitch.

Until one actually stood on one of the Ark's observation decks, it was impossible to imagine what it would be like to live in space. From the Ark, the Earth looked like a tiny blue and white ball, its continents like the pieces of a jigsaw puzzle.

Alex's time on board the Ark reminded him of his first years in California nearly forty years ago. The people had been open and friendly. Strangers said hello in coffee shops. Everyone he talked to felt like they were experiencing a new world for the first time. California was like no other place in America: the geography was strange, the climate oddly benign, and the culture developed a similarly iconoclastic bent. The Ark was the new California. Everyone was embarked on an adventure. They were making history, starting their lives from scratch. It was a new, wide open country and Alex reveled in it.

Alex heard the muffled swooshing of a door opening behind him. It must be Keiko, he thought, as he had programmed the computer to open the door only for her. When he turned to face her, however, he was surprised by what he saw. She was dressed as if she were planing to attend one of the Ark's grand balls. She wore a platinum wig over her long, jet-black hair and blue contact lenses over her dark brown eyes. Alex was struck by how naturally the light-colored wig matched Keiko's Japanese complexion, how beautifully her artificially bright blue irises flashed from under her heavily made-up eyelids. She had painted on lines of thick mascara that traced an elongated curve from her eyelids to her temples, lending her the appearance of an ancient Egyptian goddess. Above each eye, deft lines of red paint highlighted her wild mascara and were echoed by similar splashes of color on her earlobes and lips. A single, large ruby dangled from her left ear, and her right ear had been pierced several times with matching ruby studs. Other rubies had been placed in the corner of each eye with cosmetic glue and from an Indian-style piercing in her left nostril, a garnet flower blossomed.

Alex was most curious, however, about a delicate gold ring which appeared to pass through the septum of her nose.

This ring matched a thin chain looped around her neck. From this exquisite necklace hung a diamond-shaped, gold medallion with four small rubies inset into each corner of the pendant.   Carved into the amulet was an inscription in Keiko's bold hieroglyphs that read: "Alex."

A smile passed over his face and Keiko let out a sigh of happiness to see Alex pleased. She placed her arms around him and hugged him tightly to her. "I love you so much," she said loudly. "I want the whole universe to know. I want everyone to know that I love you." She released him from her arms and stood before him. "Alex, let me tell the whole universe that Keiko loves you."

He continued to smile at her, but he was troubled by her sudden gregariousness. How many other nights had she been like this? He tried to remember, but couldn't come up with an exact number. After months of denying him physically, she would suddenly change, coming on to him so strongly that his stomach almost turned. He was long past feeling any kind of physical attraction for her. He wondered if she had taken some of the Ark's potency elixir to boost her libido.

"You are so handsome," she told him. "Your body is so strong. I love your soul. Let them know that Keiko is in love with you. I am yours forever."

She would continue with these accolades, Alex knew, until she had so greatly aroused herself that she would be able to give herself an orgasm without him having touched her. After she climaxed, she would fall asleep in his arms, waking up the next morning with no memory of what she had done. Her troubled mind blocked out any past experiences that might disturb her, and her schizophrenia had so confused her sexual drive that any kind of sensual contact made her laden with guilt. As a general rule, on the rare occasions when she was aroused, she could not stand to be touched.

The first time this happened with Alex, she became so despondent that she attempted suicide and Alex had been forced to return her to the care of the Camarillo State Hospital. Now that she dozed with her head in his lap, he thought about their past together, how many years they had spent linked by an undescribable spiritual bond. She was neither his wife nor his girlfriend, but she had stood by him through a series of marriages and tangled relationships. He was her protector, keeping the real world at bay, and she was his spiritual guide, offering his soul comfort, assuaging his ego.

He first met her at a cocktail party in California. A friend of his named Terry Hotchkiss owned a sizable house in an exclusive area of Laguna Beach. After a series of numbing conversations with some extremely dull partygoers and an agonizingly unexpected encounter with his ex-girlfriend Annette, Alex had decided to become invisible, to talk to no one. He just wanted to sit in a corner, sip his beer and watch the other guests making fools of themselves. They're all playing make-believe, he thought, just looking for excuses to have a good time.

After spending nearly an hour vilifying every person who passed before him, he stood up to leave. He had had enough. His own cynicism was becoming tiring. But just as he was about to make a rather obvious and nonsensical excuse to Terry, a young woman walked into the center of the room. Alex found himself unable to look at anyone else, including Terry, who continued to make small talk with him. It was as if a spotlight were shining on this young woman. He could see nothing but a radiant white aura. When she walked past him, however, he was able to see her face clearly. She was stunning, her nearly androgynous Asian features perfectly formed. But something other than her beauty troubled him. She couldn't have been older than thirteen, he thought. My god, I'm ogling someone's child.

Before he had time to collect his thoughts, he realized that she was standing in front of him, asking him a question. The din of music and conversation, however, made her small voice inaudible. She repeated herself. "Hi, I'm Keiko. We came from Long Beach. My girlfriend works with Terry." She indicated a young woman a few feet away. "What's your name?"

She spoke with a strange accent. Alex found himself so

disquieted that he was unable to answer her. "You're from Long Beach," he said lamely, "but you sound like you're from England."

She laughed at this. Alex felt like an animal caught in the headlights of a rushing car. What is wrong with me, he thought. I'm an old man. I'm nearly fifty years old. I'm supposed to be able to handle situations like this.

"I lived in Germany for quite some time," she told him. "Everyone who speaks English there learns to speak from teachers who speak with British accents. We listen to the BBC for news. I guess I still tend to speak English like the Germans do, with a British accent."

After a while, Alex managed to tell her his name and she told him about herself. She had been awarded her Master's degree in German from the State College in Long Beach, but now she was focusing her studies on metaphysical philosophy and Eastern spiritual methods. Alex found himself unable to make any kind of intelligent comments on the subject of Eastern philosophy—to him it was all a concoction of swamis and bronzed Buddha's bellies—and despaired to see her losing interest in the conversation. When he mentioned he was a writer, however, her eyes lit up.

"Really?" she asked, surprised. "I would love to get a job as a reporter. Do you think you could help me?"

He told her that he was a novelist, writing books about space travel. That meant he wouldn't be able to help her find employment, but he went ahead and told her about his vision for the Ark, his ideas about humanity's new life in space. Alex was gratified to find her interested in his ideas.

"I think it's fascinating," she said.

"In my book," he told her anecdotally, "the space station tries to save Earth from a group of terrorists who are planning to detonate an atom bomb in New York City."

The immediate change in Keiko's appearance startled him. "Oh, no," she gasped. "Please don't write about that. If you do, it's sure to happen."

Something about the wild look in her eyes told Alex she wasn't joking, but he tried to laugh her comments away. "Oh, yes, the infamous copycat syndrome."

"No!" She grabbed his arm and looked him directly in the eye. He felt like he was talking to a child who had just woken up from a nightmare. "I'm serious. You mustn't write about it. Promise me."

To placate her, he agreed. "All right, I won't," he told her. He was intrigued by her suddenly emotional response to his work. After they finished their conversation, he asked for her telephone number and she gave it to him without hesitation. He left the party in a state of confusion. Obviously, she was not thirteen. She had to be at least twenty-five. But he was forty-nine. Did he really want to get involved with a woman so much younger than he? And what about her sudden mood swing? That was more than a little odd.

After struggling with the question all night, he decided he would call her. He was surprised, however, to hear her discouraging him from any further contact. "You're too intense for me, Alex. I don't want to get involved with you," was what she said.

He didn't understand. "Are you seeing someone else?" he asked.

"Not really," she told him. "But that's not the issue. I don't like whatever it is you're writing about."

"But it's fiction! It's make believe!" he retorted.

"But you believe everything else you write about," she said. "You believe in space stations and flying to other planets. Are you trying to tell me you want the part about your spaceship to come true, but not the part about the bomb? I don't think you can have one without the other."

Alex believed her logic to be perfectly ridiculous, but his desire to remain on her good side drove him to admit that he had never thought about his books the way she had.

"People your age never think about things that way," she scolded. Do you know what it's like to be born into a world in which every day might be your last? The news on TV reminds us every day that Armageddon is just around the corner. I've spent most of my life wondering just when someone's actually going to use the bomb."

"I'm sorry," he said. "I didn't know." Alex realized that his generation hadn't been born under the shadow of the bomb. How frightening it must be for a child to have grown up with the knowledge that adults were foolish enough to risk the future of the whole planet. It only took one slip and everything would end. Only a child or an insane person could tell how close we all were to the edge.

Alex felt that he had to convince Keiko that he was on her side. He asked her to let him mail her some of his work. He wanted to show her about his vision for the future, the peaceful future of humankind. She agreed and said she would call him after she had read his story.

He sent her his manuscript after removing the part of the story about the terrorists. She called him a few weeks later and asked to see him. Soon they were spending every day together and Alex realized that he was in love with her. But despite all the time they spent together, Keiko refused any kind of intimate physical contact. Occasionally her mood swings caused Alex inordinate amounts of anxiety, but he believed that as Keiko grew closer to him, she would lose her inhibitions, display fewer signs of her illness.

On one disastrous occasion, however, Alex decided to take Keiko to a performance of the L.A. Symphony for her birthday. He paid over a hundred dollars for the tickets and made reservations at Spago weeks in advance. But when they arrived downtown, Keiko panicked at the sight of so many people. She demanded that he take her home immediately. Alex tried to persuade her to stay, but realized his pleading was futile and turned the car around. In the jam of cars, however, Alex missed the freeway onramp, which made Keiko more frantic. As they crept down Broadway in search of a connecting street, Keiko began to weep. She told Alex she felt like she was going to die. To make matters worse, when they found the freeway, construction slowed traffic to a standstill.

"I'm sorry, Alex," was all she could say through her sobs. "I'm so sorry."

On New Year's Eve, 1985, almost ten months after their

meeting at Terry's party, Keiko came to his house for dinner. After a midnight celebration with champagne, she asked if she could spend the night and he happily led her upstairs to his bedroom. He lay beside her in bed, quivering with desire. They were both nearly naked, but Alex knew that he could not be the one to make the first move. If he did, she would run even further from him. He waited for what seemed like hours, but she did nothing. When he reached over to touch her face, she pushed his hand away. He fell asleep feeling rejected, wondering if they would ever be able to have a normal relationship.

When he woke, she was gone. The only indication of a reason for her departure came when he went out to get the morning paper and found a note she had left on the door. She must have come back early to leave it. He hurriedly opened the small envelope. Printed on the front was an etching of Mahatma Ghandi. The caption read:

> *"I know the path. It is straight and narrow. It is like the edge of a sword. I rejoice to walk on it. I weep when I slip. God's word is: 'He who strives never perishes.' I have implicit faith in that promise. Though, therefore, from my weakness I fail a thousand times, I will not lose faith."*

Inside the card, she wrote:

Dearest Alex:

I remember all that you told me Sunday a.m. in the hope that I can meditate on it and clear it up. Certain patterns are hard to break. I will make an effort not to be so irresponsible. I should not lead you on. I know how you must feel. If I were you, I wouldn't get so mad, though. It really hurts you inside. Take things a bit lighter. Sexually wise, I do not know where that is going. I will try to be better with you in regards to that. I do love to kiss and play with you, but sex itself goes deeper.

> *We'll talk about it. I somehow feel as if we will be*
> *reliving last night forever. Alex, I do really care for*
> *you. I really, truly think you are a great man. I*
> *will do better to try to support you.*
>
> > *My love is with you,*
> > *Keiko*

He decided to call her immediately. He told her that he understood. He would expect nothing of a sexual nature from her. After that, they spent their days together platonically, walking along the beach, talking about their childhoods, their plans for the future, the day-to-day events of their lives. She brought him books he had never read—Schoepenhauer, Nietzsche, Tolstoy—and they spent long evenings discussing them. Alex continued to work on his books, with Keiko typing the manuscripts and helping him with editing decisions. Violence as a plot element, however, was out of the question. Whenever he felt the need to show some real grit in his stories, he hid them from her, unwilling to submit them to her pacifist revisions.

He noticed that she became more and more possessive of him. When a strange woman was near, she instinctively put her arm around his waist. He knew that she was afraid of losing him. Yet on one night, Alex called her apartment, expecting to find her there. He called until one o' clock in the morning but there was no answer. The next day when he questioned her over the phone, he discovered that she had been out on a date. She said it meant nothing, but he was outraged. He could hardly believe his own jealousy. She cried and asked him to forgive her, but he hung up abruptly after telling her he was tired of waiting for her. He didn't want to see her anymore.

That night, she came to his house and immediately fell into his arms. She practically dragged him up the stairs to the bedroom. "I want that big cock of yours inside me," she told him. "I want you to fuck me, Alex. Stick it deep inside of me." She thrust her hand into his pants and squeezed his cock, pushing him back onto the bed. They made love in a wild frenzy. Keiko told him she had never been happier.

But again, he woke to find himself alone. This time, however, instead of leaving him a note, she left him a copy of a story she had written. He had not been aware that she was writing stories and was surprised to see the bundle of pages before him. But soon after he began reading, he found himself engrossed in a remarkable documentation of Keiko's inner life.

Alain

Outside the warm air gushed through the trees as if a thunderous roar of emotions would pour out of the mouths of the rain gods. The time was ripe for such a display of power amongst the heavenly ones—as was the time for Francesca to appear in the living room at Alain's place. She walked in as if she herself were a rain goddess. The brown and red dress fit her exceedingly well as it revealed her cleavage and round, firm bosom in a manner that Alain had only dreamt of in his fantasies of nude beauties surrounding him and slowly caressing his thighs and buttocks, until the two most beautiful ladies made love with him for many hours. And now here appeared Francesca after losing twenty pounds and exercising most everyday so that her body was transformed into that of a Venusian goddess. She felt thrilled with her new body and Alain sensed her excitement. Alain missed her very much. She had been away on a teaching sabbatical overseas. Without words, however, they knew that this was the time to retrieve the past year in a way that most people would not contemplate, much less consummate.

As Francesca entered the living room, Alain had the chance to watch her and he caught hold of every single curve, movement, reaction and emotion of love and warmth which Francesca so gracefully carried until she softly sat down on the sofa. Her calves were smooth and muscular and the heels she was wearing positioned her feet in such a way as she was sitting that Alain commented to her on just how absolutely beautiful she had made herself that evening. It was a tremendous compliment to her and it made her feel like a bona fide princess, a princess that she had always dreamt of becoming. Alain assured her that with her graceful manner it was indeed possible to envision such a reality! It was some merry-making, perhaps, but it certainly provided Francesca with some genuine escapist fantasies.

Then Alain joined her on the sofa, in order to get an even better view of the beauty beside him. The dress clung tightly to her thighs. He could only stare. Her long, sinewy fingers played on top of her left thigh, and covered her small, tight stomach and pubic area. Francesca had been quite animated when she arrived, but now she had calmed down and became extraordinarily quiet and doelike, in contrast to her tigress persona. The gentle look of a doe calmed down her intense features and flooded her eyes.

Francesca lifted her face and pressed her lips to his. For an instant he was utterly still. Then his warm, wet tongue was caressing her lips and she was opening her mouth, inviting him inside, kissing him with unbridled passion. As they kissed she unbuttoned her dress. Then she pulled away from him and let the soft, faded garment fall from her shoulders. Alain stared at her, his dear face troubled, his blue eyes cloudy. God, she thought, he is so handsome! She unbuttoned his shirt. When she had undone the last button, he took her wrists and held them down at her sides.

"You really are beautiful," he said, blushing as he gazed at her naked body. "There's nothing that would give me more physical pleasure than to make love with you. I really mean that."

She didn't give him the chance to talk himself out of anything. She pressed her finger to his lips, forcing him to be silent. Then she backed away from him, maintaining his gaze all the while, and plopped down onto the end of the couch. He opened his mouth to speak, but she hushed him with the threat of leaving if he said a word. As he stood there staring at her, a perplexed look on his face, a bulge in his pants, she parted her legs and started stroking her inner thighs.

She sat up straight on the couch and lifted her feet, planting them on the cushions. Her knees were way up and her legs were spread open so that her private parts were exposed. She held open her lips with one hand and with the other she began playing with her clit, tapping the little trigger with just the tip of her finger. Then there was the sound of his zipper opening. He was stepping out of his pants and undershorts at the same time. His cock, long, thick and hard popped out of his clothing. She cupped his buttocks in her hands and drew his groin close to her face. There was the subtle but unmistakable masculine scent of his cock and balls. She rubbed her cheek against his cock, then against his silky, distended testicles. He was groaning from deep in his throat. Suddenly he placed his hand on her face and he pushed her face into his cock.

"Suck, baby," he muttered.

She gulped him down, drawing all but an inch or so of his magnificent cock into her mouth. He grunted with pleasure, his hips undulating as she pressed his groin into her face. His buttocks were taut in her hands. She kneaded them vigorously, sucking his cock just as vigorously, until his shaft was throbbing in her mouth.

Gasping with passion, she straddled his groin, took his cock in her hand and guided him into her.

"Oooh, good," Francesca hissed. She began to move up and down, riding his erect penis toward her climax. Her hair was strewn out over her shoulders and back, her giggling breasts rose and fell as she moved with him. He pushed his cock all the way into her so that it filled her pussy completely. While he was fucking her he kept kissing her breasts and neck and running his fingers through her hair. He began to rock his body against her faster and faster, and he put his hands around her hips and pulled her down on himself. He was breathing harder and harder and both of their bodies were covered with perspiration. She cried out as her body responded to his with an echoing vibration that shook her entire form. It didn't take either one of them much time to come. For one brief moment they were hurtling together through another universe, where nothing existed but the purifying pleasure of two loving bodies joined in orgasm.

Then they slumped down on the bed exhausted and totally relaxed. There was complete silence, with no sound but his heavy breathing and Francesca's quieter, more regular sighs.

"Sweetheart?" she said.

"Yes," he whispered.

"Are you happy that I'm back?"

"I sure am."

They would just lie there panting on the couch, bodies

drenched in perspiration and sexual elixirs, until they gradually drifted into a deep, contented sleep.

Alex was touched by the story, moved by the sensual if sometimes stilted prose written by a woman whom he had considered frigid. Beneath this story, however, was a copy of a second, shorter tale, in which Alex learned of her fears.

Dragon's Comeuppance

You appear, suddenly, in the house, all two hundred pounds of you. Are you here to attempt to break my powerful will and so swallow me whole, as if I were a hurried suppertime plate of meats? But I know from whence you come and I recognize your angry countenance, sizzling with lust and power to break me into tiny pieces, never to survive the quicksand pits you lay before me so very subtly. It is your sly ways which mean to trick me into subservience to your sensual desires which reek of sharp aromas and fearfully treacherous adventures which I so desperately want to understand without plunging headlong into your abysmal pit of woe and fears unimaginable. Is this possible? I dare to say that it is not. My meekness can never penetrate your thick-skinned hide. Your inky black eyes peer out of deep sockets. The curtain is drawn back and through the pains I fathom your existence to be that of a warrior forever unable to express freedom of the heart or love in any form. The nostrils and tongue jump out in an attempt to swallow me and smoke me into your jaws of sharpened fangs. To keep myself sane while encountering your jealous and cunning ways is to be the accomplished tightrope walker, precariously perched upon a strand of nothing, balancing, as if this were something quite ordinary. Your reptilian armor is a wire brush roughing against my shins as I climb upon your back and hang on for my dear life as you roar so loudly to the heavens and spurt fires and uncontrolled emotions into the clouds, scaring away all creatures for hundreds of miles. My fright is without bounds as the skin on my fingers bleeds profusely, but goes unnoticed by me. I am too busy keeping myself in the saddle! My ragged clothing hangs on my skeleton-like figure as I grasp for my breath and pray to the spirits of light to save me from this dreaded beast lest I be swallowed whole and vanish from this blessed earth.

Alex read the story again. He sadly thought of how she must of thought of him as he made love to her. He was the two hundred pound dragon.

BOOK ONE

AMANDA AND THE ARK

CHAPTER 1

TRAVEL

In most situations, Vladimir Susoeff passed easily for an American. His full head of dark brown hair and athletic body gave most people the impression of a former high school athlete. Not quite six feet tall, his body's strength came from his compact, Slavic stature. His open face and pleasant, friendly manner put others at ease, but his dark eyes, sunken into bony sockets, occasionally flashed with a coldness that suggested the power and authority he possessed. There was no mistaking his decisiveness, and his ability to command had served him well.

Yet there was a subtly feminine quality to all of his actions. Although these traits were imperceptible at first, those who took time to observe him noticed a delicacy in his walk, a languid flair to his mannerisms. He took very small, careful steps, making little sound, unlike his colleagues who roughly dragged their boxy Russian dress shoes over the tiles of the laboratory. When he spoke, he gesticulated dramatically, energizing the conversation with increasingly rapid and fluid movements of his hands. His fingers seemed to draw his words into the air. Watching him engaged in a debate about science or politics was like watching a ballerina laughing her way through a simple folk dance.

Standing impatiently in the experimental room of the Russian space station, Vladimir waited for the results of his latest experiment. Although he was anxious to see the figures, he was more concerned about his family life, the life he left behind for months at a time so that he might serve his country in space. He missed Thasha, his wife, and his children, and he hoped that the successful conclusion of this test would bring him closer to another meeting with them.

Lately, he had spent a great deal of his time thinking about his life on Earth. He ached to be back on the planet where he had been born, longed to re-experience the places and people of his youth. The present course of his ESP experiments, however, had helped to relieve some of his homesickness, and he no longer felt like a castaway stranded in space. There was hope now. He could see the potential to eliminate unnecessary travel by using ESP.

Research into ESP travel had been initiated by Russian scientists because the Russian space program had always emphasized longer and longer orbiting periods for their cosmonauts. While the United States focused on intermediate space shuttle launches, Russia strove to perfect techniques that would allow cosmonauts a "recreational period" during their almost unendurably prolonged space shots. Because the Russians' orbiting capsules were so small and ill-equipped, the cosmonauts were unable to move uninhibitedly or leave the capsule for what the Americans called a space walk.

Early experiments into ESP travel involved placement of electrodes onto the forehead of the subject, a simple electroencephalographic procedure. Gradually, researchers moved from merely reading brain waves to stimulating particular regions and lobes of the brain with minute electrical charges. At first, they discovered that they could artificially stimulate "warm" or euphoric states within the subject's mind. This was followed by the mapping out of memory banks, where past experiences were stored. The smell of strawberries could be triggered in a subject whose nose had been stopped up. A blindfolded man suddenly saw his childhood home. A woman heard her grandmother calling her name.

The first real breakthrough, however, came in an entirely unexpected manner. A young man had been wired into the triggering mechanism and they listened to him describing a day he had spent ice skating. He had been with his girlfriend, he told them, he could smell her perfume. They watched each other skating, moving slowly around in a large circle. At the center of the lake, boys were shouting and playing with hockey sticks. These were the normal recollections of a subject under the control of the encephalographic triggers.

At this point, however, the scientists changed the scope of their inquiry. They wanted to see if they could get him to feel the cold, as physical sensations could not yet be stimulated with regularity. They continued to ask the young man what was happening as they increased the amount of electricity being fed into his brain. Suddenly, one of the researchers shouted, "Look out! Oh, God, there's a hole in the ice!"

The subject, who could not hear the man, continued to describe the events of his day: "As we skate, I notice that the ice to the left of us is beginning to crack. I think one of the boys is in danger of falling in, but then I think that we, too, might fall in."

The subject's voice remained constant and steady, but the other man's face was wrought with terror. His eyes were closed tight, but his body jerked with spasms as if he were running in a dream. "They're going to fall in," he shouted. "Stop them."

The other researchers immediately stopped the test and the man fell to the floor, gasping. "I saw them," he said. "I saw them skating."

Thus the Russians became the first nation to artificially stimulate ESP events. The EEG researchers joined the existing KGB-controlled ESP department and it would be years before the United States even had a clue as to what was going on in the Russian laboratories.

Current research into ESP could only be performed in the unique vacuums available in Zero-G conditions. As he waited for his colleagues to remove him from the web of electrodes spun around his head, Vladimir thought about how much he longed for the Russia of the past, its government, its people, and even for its time under Communism. He had earnestly believed in the great experiment of Communism and still clung to the notion that it might have succeeded if it had not been for the megalomania of Stalin or the interference of the old world countries. The United Russian States, as the western Soviet Union was now called, had accomplished many great scientific achievements, discoveries he had often witnessed personally aboard the space station. He was convinced that his current work would be another success in a long string of successes. In the future, he thought, I will be able to sit down and talk with my wife and children every evening. I will travel hundreds of thousands of miles to sit at their dinner table. I will travel in my mind and so will every other person aboard this floating platform.

In spite of all the advances he had made, one minor problem still aggravated him. He was increasingly annoyed by the preliminary procedures necessary to conduct the experiments. The flat scrape of adhesive tape being pulled from the electrode pads was like fingernails on a blackboard to him. Assistants' fingers daubed chilling spots of conductive gel onto his skin. Finally, the adhesive electrode pads were applied to his head and torso, hundreds of them concentrated on his scalp. In order to regulate his body's responses, his forearm was pierced with needle-thin tubing leading to a small black tank which dispensed intravenous solution. To control his body's reaction to subconscious stimuli, his arms were strapped to the chair.

He hated the feeling of being restrained by the paraphernalia of his experiments. How ironic and tediously human, he thought, that the very research that might set the mind free must also tie up the body. He felt more like a robot than a man as he sat in the chair, waiting for the experiments to begin. He was never quite certain when his colleagues actually started the tests, as they did not notify him when they began. Without warning, he began to see images of his past, but he could not tell if he was conscious or asleep. Within moments, however, he was no longer concerned about the state of his body. He was too caught up in the experience.

During a previous experiment, he had dreamed of his childhood and his adolescent adventures with Thasha. He saw his parents' farm, the old tree he had climbed as a child, the brook that ran by the house. He enjoyed the revival of old memories as much for the experience as for the recollections they triggered when he was finished with the tests. Memories of his youth brought on reminiscence of the brief time he had spent with the American writer Alex Abramawitz. Although he had met him only once, nearly a decade ago, their conversation was indelible in his memory. Abramawitz's writings had initially been well received by the Russian scientific community because the scientists perceived that he was sympathetic to their nationality, but his continuing favor was due to the visionary essays that had conceived of and then led to the construction of the Ark, a multinational space enterprise. As far as Vladimir could tell, he and Alex had nothing in common except that they both lived and worked in space, yet he felt that Alex was akin to a long lost-brother. Somehow there was a strong affinity between them. Lately, he had been feeling a strong urge to contact Alex, to visit him on the Ark, but for some unknown reason, he had resisted this impulse.

He admired the people who lived on the Ark, and he envied the technical advances they had made on their space station. The Russian station could not compete with the advanced technology and gargantuan funding of Arkian research and at this point it was unlikely that upgrading the Russian facilities would do any good. An entirely new station would have to be built if the Russians wanted a national vessel that could vie with Space Station Ark. As it was, the Russians had invested heavily in the Ark's international company, and if not for this investment, Russia would not have outpaced the United States so readily during the last decade. Lack of American foresight had reduced the most powerful nation on Earth to a minor role in space.

Despite fears that Russia would collapse after Communism fell, the expanse of Russian natural resources allowed the nation to fulfill the historic role hoped for by Peter the Great and Alexander II. For the first time, Russians, without fear of English, German or French interference, could advance on their own course. Investment in the Ark and the investment's subsequent returns set the country off in a new direction. While American fighter planes were superior to anything the Russians would ever have, their control of Earth's skies would matter less and less as space technology, travel, and business became more and more important.

Why, Vladimir wondered, did so many other nations think of Russians as backward, inferior, when history proved over and over again that the Russian and other Slavic people had overcome the most horrible obstacles to succeed? He believed he belonged to a superior race of people who only wanted to be left alone to enjoy the vast wealth of their motherland. It was obvious why the Americans, who lived on their island of wealth and self-satisfied smugness, could not understand the Russian mindset. The West still didn't understand the nature of the threat Mongol and Muslim factions posed to his people.

Since the breakup of the Soviet empire and the creation of new governments in Siberia, Adzerbaidhan, Irkutsk and other border regions, Western Russians had been forced to seek stability in reunification with the rest of Europe. These alliances furthered tensions between the innumerable small factions of cultures and nationalities that had formerly been glued together in Stalin's authoritarian collage. At present, Russia was using its European contacts to ensure military capabilities against an invading force. If Russians had to defend themselves against disgruntled former Soviet states, they would.

Time and time again, Russian ingenuity had triumphed over supposedly better armed and more sophisticated armies. When it came to aircraft, for example, Russian fighter jets, unable to approach the technological advantages of the American planes, relied on Russian ingenuity. They cost one hundred times less to build and they were easier to maintain. Function and practicality were the foremost considerations in Russian weaponry. For this reason, Russian tanks had outperformed the purportedly superior German Tiger Tanks in the Second World War. But still, the world assumed that the Germans and Americans led the world in arms technologies. If one considered only the amount of money spent and the gadgets on board, perhaps this was true. But when it came to performance, Russian troops could rely on the munitions provided by the motherland.

Vladimir knew that for all their misconceptions, the Americans understood at least one important element of the Russian character, a trait that both Napoleon and Hitler had underestimated. The Russians, like the Americans, were a multinational people, and, despite their differences, they found a common cause in defending their soil. Russians would fight like hell to repel an enemy who dared to claim the motherland for their own. The homogeneous Europeans and Asians would never understand this, even though it was a European scholar, Alexis DeTocqueville, who had first contemplated the effect of multiculturalism on a nation.

Even the women of these two giant nations were trained to serve in the military. Only the Israelis could boast of similar patriotic service. Vladimir believed that this was another sign of Ameri-Russo understanding and respect. But, tragically, neither country had really foreseen the role space would play in the future of humankind, creating a power vacuum that continued to disrupt international relations. In only twenty years, the Ark had grown from the seed of an idea in Alex Abramawitz's writings to the most powerful presence in space, an entity with wealth far surpassing that of the past superpowers. Funded by multinational investors, the Ark was born of a spirit that ignored national origins and focused solely on profit and efficiency. Matters of state only got in the way.

Even so, the Ark's initial development had depended entirely on the support of world politicians. Had they not nurtured this project, it might never have flown. Vladimir wondered if world nations would have funded the Ark so generously if they had known how rapidly it would supersede them, and how heavily they would have to rely on the economic support that the Ark now provided. The Ark was to the modern world what the United States had been to the

20th-century world, providing innovative outlets for capital and new sources of business. It had taken the United States nearly two hundred years to consolidate its economic and political power. The Ark, from the moment it was conceived to the present, had only needed twenty. And while the United States had shown the world how to produce new goods and services, the Ark offered an entirely new kind of product: a new understanding of human potential.

The Ark made most of its money by modifying people, making them more productive, more efficient. The idea that humans were finally going to live up to their potential was the economic currency of the 21st Century. The Ark set out in search of this new humanity by rethinking and reconstructing every human convention. A new world required a new philosophy, and the Ark sought to provide people who could succeed in space. With teaching machines, the Ark could make anyone a genius. New medical techniques offered longer, healthier lives. All of the new technology discovered on board the Ark was developed immediately for consumer applications. The bureaucracies that frustrated research on Earth were forgotten on the Ark. The revolutions and wars that humans had previously required to make major changes on Earth had vanished. On the Ark, education was simple, achieved before a child had even been born. New ideas were introduced with ease. People did not resist the advances science made toward discovering the true nature of humankind.

The inhabitants of the Ark became supermen and their newfound powers benefitted all of the nations of Earth, especially the most underdeveloped. The peoples of Asia, India and Africa made up the majority of space pioneers. The Third World conditions into which they were born meant they had nothing to lose by heading out into space. The joint ventures they began with their former countrymen were now rapidly turning the Third World into the First World. The traditions of the Old World had been broken. The Ark had achieved what seven thousand years of civilization had been unable to.

Chapter 2

The Experiment Works

Vladimir felt the muscles in his body begin to relax and he sank back into the chair. Visions of Alex Abramawitz kept flashing in his head, images Vladimir remembered from his conversation with the renowned writer, and from frozen portraits from book dust jackets and magazine articles. He heard Alex's voice and he saw his own back, hunched over, leaning in close to Alex, who sat on a black leather and chrome couch. As he responded to Alex, he thought his voice sounded strange, unexpectedly thin. He felt as if he might faint.

As always, the first few moments of transition into the ESP state were disorienting. He now saw himself walking down a corridor. He felt like a man watching himself on videotape for the first time. He was still conscious enough to note that the experience was unlike his previous tests. Watching himself walk, he decided that the man he was watching didn't look or sound like himself. Perhaps, he thought, they were trying a new pharmacological enhancer. Or perhaps they were reversing the experience on him. It was entirely possible that he was seeing with another person's eyes. Whose point of view is this, he wondered? He tried to get the images to reveal their point of view, trying to impart his will into the simulated experience.

Before he was able to notice any effect, he realized he was now back in his own body, talking animatedly with Alex about automobiles and American culture. Although he couldn't see him, he heard Alex say, "Think about the car. Everything about it screams big business. What do you need to sustain cars? Oil and gas, steel, rubber. Who are the

companies who own everything? G.M., Ford, Exxon, Shell.
They've owned it all for a hundred years and they'd like to
own it for hundreds more. All of these huge corporations are
just exploiting people. Companies like these used to be the
driving force behind the American economy, but now they're
archaic. Their manner of competing in the marketplace is the
equivalent of the legal system settling disputes with duels or
Old West high noon shoot-outs."

Vladimir now saw Alex sitting directly in front of him.
He was completely immersed in the simulation. Alex's eyes
remained level, gazing into Vladimir's, even as he made his
most emphatic points.

"These car companies only exist for the benefit of other
big businesses: petroleum, insurance and medicine. Do you
know how much Americans pay for their auto insurance?"
Vladimir shook his head. "Some pay up to four thousand
dollars a year! And there's no way for anybody, I don't care
how good their driving record is or what kind of car they
drive, to pay less than two thousand dollars. When you add up
all of the taxes and hidden taxes, like insurance, that the
American people have to pay for, it probably adds up to
something like eighty percent of everything they earn. It's
ridiculous! The American people think they're not living in a
socialist state, but I'm positive that they pay more in taxes
than the Russians or any other country in the world. They're
just so used to having to pay this fee and that fee, and meeting
the standards of this or that law and regulation that they
don't even notice what it is they're paying for."

Vladimir was distracted for a moment by Alex's finger,
thrust up into the air after his last parry at the bulwark of
American capitalism. He lowered his eyes to meet Alex's just
as the writer began speaking again. Alex continued his
harangue in a whisper, as if the room, which held no other
occupants, were bugged.

"Vladimir, listen, all systems, all governments, all
corporations, have their own way of distorting the truth. The
government passed a law requiring everyone to buy auto
insurance. And who wanted that? The citizenry? No. The

insurance companies poured hundreds of thousands of dollars into a campaign to have that law passed. Now people are supposedly protected against accidents, thefts, and lawsuits. But what about all the people who can't afford to drive now? They've made criminals out of people who don't have an extra few thousand dollars to pay the insurance companies. And to make matters worse, these companies that now have government laws requiring citizens to buy their products no longer put any money back into the community. Instead of employing more people to process claims and applications, the corporations bought computers and fired the people who didn't have the education to use them.

"And instead of reinvesting their money in ventures that would create jobs for the people they left unemployed, the insurance companies plowed their money into real estate developments and bonds and securities. The money flowed from the banks out into these useless investments and then back into the banks. The bonds and securities are just paper and speculation. And Houston, Los Angeles and New York are all filled with office buildings nobody wants or needs. Nobody's produced any jobs or inventions or anything really important.   All the money generated by the laws of government went to bolster the wallets of those who could already afford everything they needed."

Vladimir groaned, trying to free himself from this conversation, not wanting to have to think about Alex's sometimes overwhelming political discourse. He imagined himself pushing the image of Alex from his head and slowly Alex's still-speechifying visage grew dim and grainy, like a weak holograph. When Alex was almost gone, he found the writer's place taken by Thasha. She sat exactly where Alex had been, with her legs crossed in the same position.

The room dissolved and he found himself standing in his mother's kitchen in the family farmhouse, but Thasha hadn't followed him there. Outside the window, he could see the stream frozen over. He was seventeen years old. He walked to the front door and opened it onto a plain of snow, perfectly white, interrupted only by a few dark and ice-blanketed trees.

The wintry steppes stretched out for miles from his parents' front porch. He could feel the bite of the cold air in his chest as he inhaled. He thought he could smell the air, scrubbed clean by the still falling snow. Snowflakes fell on his face and he opened his mouth to gulp at the drifting particles. Each nearly invisible crystal tasted fantastically sweet on his tongue. Some melted on his cheek and collected in rivulets in the creases around his nose and mouth.

He walked to the oak tree that stood just outside the front gate. In spring his mother planted a small flower bed in front of the house and vines would creep over the top of this low fence, blooming in subdued purples and yellows. The tree was the tallest object visible on the plain, rising many feet above the barn where the animals could be heard rustling. Vladimir placed his hand on the tree's massive and frosted trunk. He thought about the enormous roots that twisted their way into the soil beneath the covering of snow. In warmer months, they stood out from the ground like the veins on the back of his hand. He sheltered himself from the wind behind the trunk and found he could not see around its girth without taking a step to the side. Pieces of rough bark scraped at him through the folds of his winter coat and he winced as if they were fingers of ice jabbing him in the ribs. He automatically turned up his collar to thwart the wind, adjusting his hat so that its brim was nearly into his eyes, its wool flaps lying over his ears.

He sensed that he was waiting for Thasha and was suddenly struck by the certainty that she would come. He told himself he must be re-experiencing one of his past trysts with her. He looked out at the winter fields and it seemed as if nothing were moving on the steppes. But, as if to prove this an illusion, he became aware of the sound of running water: the brook was still flowing under a sheet of ice. The snow muffled every other sound, and for what seemed like an incredible amount of time, he heard nothing but the stream, his own steady breathing, and the rustling of his clothes. Inside his coat, the air seemed heavy and sleepy. I must be freezing, he told himself.

Behind him, on the other side of the tree, he heard the first dull crunchings of Thasha's approach. His heart began to pound rapidly in anticipation of seeing her. In winter, they were assured of privacy in the empty fields, and Thasha could cross the frozen brook with ease. Vladimir moved around the tree trunk so that he could watch Thasha without her seeing him. Slowly, she pushed her way through the inches of snow with her head down, concentrating on her movement. He thought he could see her breath wisping out from under the bristles of her fur hat. When she had almost reached the tree, he called out to her and she looked up, cheeks red from the cold and exertion. The rest of her face was as white as that of a porcelain doll, and from that perfect complexion shone the light of her brown eyes.

Vladimir stretched his arm out to her and she nestled in his arms. He pushed back her hat from her forehead and dusted the snow from her face. His tall frame leaned back against the tree and he felt the heat of her body pressing into his. Her fur hat felt soft and warm against his cheek as he moved his face down to hers. He wondered at the beauty of her soft brown eyes, which were almost yellow among the green and copper flakes of her irises. The vapor of their breath blended together into small puffs of steam that floated up into the branches of the tree.

Sheltered by the tree and secluded by the formidable cold, they felt as if they had been separated from the rest of the world. Their love for one another was like a physical presence, an individuated force that only they could understand. This was not, Vladimir was sure, merely a childhood romance. As they laughed and talked, Vladimir believed that he was going to spend the rest of his life loving Thasha, and the clarity of that vision was matched by the lucidity and alertness of his mind. It was as if their presence under the tree had sparked an incredible energy, an energy of love, passion and creation. For a brief but wonderful moment, they had transcended the fields around them, risen above the surrounding farms and flown away from the cares of the Earth. All he could feel was the warmth of their bodies, clinging to one another, and he wondered if he was dreaming.

Within a moment, he was awake and the lights of the laboratory were in his eyes, the faces of the other scientists peering down at him. He had been asleep for less than a second. The electrodes were being peeled from his face and scalp, the monitors were being scrutinized for information about his physiological changes during the trance. During his debriefing, he related to his colleagues how vivid the sensations of the simulation had been, how clearly he had seen the snow, the smell of the air, the intensity of his emotions. The other researchers were pleased with the results, but he could see they did not share his vision. They thought his experience had been nothing more than a conglomeration of impressions stimulated in his brain by their manipulation of the electrodes, but Vladimir believed his conversation with Alex had to be something more. He had never held that discussion with Alex, yet it had to be more than a fantasy created from nothingness. He remembered smelling Alex's cologne. That had to be real! He knew his mind could not have created all of the details he had seen and felt. His memories of Thasha had never been like this in earlier experiments. Even the concepts that Alex had talked about were new to him. He could not have summoned all this from the ether. He was sure that at some point he had been reading their thoughts in the present. After all the setbacks and discouragement, he was finally successful. All of the minor discomforts he had suffered had been worth it.

As he neared the end of the debriefing, he was notified of an urgent call from Thasha. The aide sent to call him to the phone apologized for interrupting the meeting but said that she had been in a nearly hysterical state, fearing that he had been injured. She was demanding to speak to Vladimir immediately.

Vladimir sat down in front of the videophone screen and punched up the channel on which his wife waited to talk to him. After a few lines of static rolled by, her faced materialized before him. She was older than the vision he had seen just an hour ago, but her brown eyes still shone with the light and beauty of her youth, her skin still had the same creamy quality. In place of snow, however, tears glistened on her cheeks and she spoke in tense sobs.

"Oh, Vladimir, I'm sorry."

"Sorry for what?" he asked her, not caring that he had been interrupted. He only wanted to know what had been troubling her. Could it be, he thought, that his trance had triggered her thoughts of him?

"I don't know. It's crazy." She couldn't look directly at him. "About an hour ago I became totally preoccupied with thoughts of us when we were young. I even saw us together under the tree at your parents' farm. I haven't thought about those days for years and suddenly it seems as if it just happened yesterday. It seemed so real. And for the past hour I haven't been able to do anything but think about you and worry that something might have happened."

A huge smile spread over Vladimir's face. He was right. The experiment had worked. "What else happened, Thasha? Tell me everything."

"I kept seeing a stranger with us. A man named Alex, who I've never seen before. I don't know who he was but something about the whole thing made me think you might be in danger." She shook her head and wiped the tears from her face.

"I'm perfectly all right," Vladimir reassured her. He wasn't quite ready to tell Thasha everything about the experiment and he tried to suppress his smile. "I, too, was thinking of those beautiful moments, Thasha, and I miss you. But everything is normal and going on as usual. Our same boring routines."

"Vladimir, I miss you so much," she gasped, about to begin crying again. "I can't wait until the month is out and I can see you again."

"Don't worry about me. There's no danger here at all. They take good care of me."

Thasha began to smile and Vladimir beamed back at her. "I feel I can't say any more. It feels like the whole world is listening in on us." She always complained to him about her fear that spies might be listening in on them. In many ways, people of Vladimir's generation still lived in Soviet Russia.

"This channel is secured," Vladimir told her.

"Promise me that you'll call me if you think about the old oak again. I feel so close to you, even with you floating around out there. Will you promise?"

"I promise."

"Goodbye. I love you." There was a pause and the screen went blank.

Vladimir continued to sit before the darkened screen, amazed at how suddenly the screen could be filled and then emptied of his wife's image. He pondered the manner in which she had so recently filled his own mind as he fell under the spell of the electrodes. Just as suddenly as she had vanished from the telescreen, the spell had been broken and the images of their past time together had been flushed from his mind. Vladimir thought about the other scientists and considered telling them of Thasha's experience. But he knew they wouldn't believe him without hard evidence. Thasha's story would only be anecdotal to them. He knew he had to press on with the experiments.

What concerned him, however, were the continuing associations his mind was making with Alex Abramawitz. And there appeared to be some kind of danger coupled with Alex's appearance, a danger even Thasha had noticed. He wondered what the danger meant. Should he feel threatened? He would have to wait for the next series of tests and concentrate harder on learning something new.

Because of his conviction that his ESP experiment had been successful, Vladimir was not surprised by the mission assigned to him in his newly arrived orders. He was to take a two week leave and meet with Alex Abramawitz aboard the Ark as soon as possible. There was no explanation as to why he was to meet with the American, but the orders called for top secret confidentiality on all matters of the assignment. I knew there was reason for my visions of Alex, he told himself. A detachment of research aides escorted him to the next shuttle with military brusqueness, the intensity and urgency of their actions leading him to believe that his meeting with Alex had more than scientific significance.

Two of the aides accompanied him on the short flight. Wondering about his approaching reunion with Abramawitz and excited to take his first steps on board the Ark—a ship with amenities and luxuries he had been hearing about for years—he lost track of time. The thud of landing gear on the transport docking platform of the Ark seemed to come only moments after he first heard the engines of the shuttle roar behind him. A shivering hiss of air could be heard outside the shuttle as the airlock was pressurized. Once the landing bay had reached a state of equilibrium, an aide opened the shuttle's airlock door. Vladimir was dumbfounded by the appearance of the man who stood in the corridor before him.

Dressed in the tight-fitting, blue work smock of the Ark's crew, Alex appeared thin, muscular and handsome, the keen intelligence of his eyes flashing with the energy of a young college professor. Although he knew Alex was well into his seventies, Vladimir thought the man standing before him was well shy of fifty. Unsure of what he saw, Vladimir checked the man's insignia: white specialty training stripes denoting medical service decorated each sleeve, over his heart the hieroglyphs A. Abramawitz stood out in red. Opposite the name, which made Vladimir wonder if this might be the writer's son, were lines of decorations and ribbons, identifying the wearer as a master of engineering, spaceflight, spacewalking, welding, electrical engineering, law, medicine, chemistry, communications, photography, nuclear physics and toxic materials, among others. If this was Alex's son, thought Vladimir, he was every bit as talented as his father.

Alex smiled broadly at Vladimir and extended his hand to welcome him. He could see that Vladimir was having trouble recognizing him. After all, it had been many years since Vladimir had first met him and his physical appearance had changed considerably.

Vladimir moved to shake hands and tried to generate a tactful plan to ascertain the identity of this welcoming party. As his hand touched Abramawitz's, he was pulled not only into the firm clasp of a handshake, but the tight embrace of a Russian-style bear hug.

"Welcome, my friend," Abramawitz said to him in Russian. The voice was unmistakably that of the writer Vladimir had met many years ago.

"Is that you, Alex?" he asked in English, his heavy accent making the words sound leaden.

"Of course, my friend. You don't recognize me, do you?" He tightened his arms around Vladimir. Vladimir wondered about the rejuvenation techniques they must have developed on the Ark to make the elderly writer look so young. But wrapped up inside of this man's arms, Vladimir felt comfortable and secure, reminding him of his recent ESP experience with Thasha. The thought of that embrace, coupled with this sudden reunion with the man whose memory had so preoccupied him over the past few days, gave Vladimir such a strong, undescribable feeling that he was unable to speak. He thought to himself, this is not the hug of an American, it a true, traditional Russian greeting. As they relaxed their arms, it was as if a magnetic force between them made breaking the embrace difficult.

Alex had not stopped smiling. "Vladimir, I have so many surprises to show you. Some of them are good, some not so good, but we will have time to discuss them all." He clapped Vladimir on the back with a resounding thump. "I am so glad to see you again."

Vladimir could only nod his head, as if to say, "Yes, it is good." He was still confused by the unexpected intensity of his feelings. Perhaps, he thought, the connection that had linked him to Alex a few nights ago had not been entirely broken by the end of the trance. It was certainly possible that Alex, with the advanced technology available aboard the Ark, might even be able to read his thoughts. As they walked along corridors leading into the interior of the Ark, Vladimir tried to pry into Alex's mind, but was not able to. As a representative of his government, he felt he was at a distinct disadvantage.

Vladimir spoke softly, in broken fragments of English. "Alex, I cannot tell you how long I looked forward to this visit. I have had many thoughts of you for many weeks, and something tells me this is the last time I will come to visit you here in space." The deep, husky quality of Vladimir's voice was colored by an unmistakable sadness. "I think we have so much to talk about."

"Yes, my friend, yes." Alex smiled again and threw his arm around Vladimir's shoulders. "We will talk and talk. But I think first, perhaps, we will start with a little bit of what we Arkians call super vodka."

Vladimir answered his smile, "I have heard about this vodka. It feels like I haven't had a drink for a long time."

Alex turned a corner, leading to the community room they would use for their drinking and discussion. On the Ark, individuals did not have permanent private quarters. Sleeping rooms were rotated on a regular basis to allow for intermittent naps and recreation facilities were requisitioned and then assigned by a central computer. Each recreation room was designed for a multitude of functions, kept immaculately clean and decorated with clever machines that adjusted the accommodations to suit the taste of the inhabitants.

The floor and walls were upholstered in a soft but resilient material that resembled fine carpet. The interior was lit by a system of fiber optics, controlled by oral commands directed to a resident computer. These optics also controlled the color of the walls and floor by illuminating the neutral material with different hues of light. The computer adjusted both color and light levels after sensing the mood of the occupants and altered the environment accordingly. A group of political officials might find themselves in a strongly lit, ivory and brown room, while a child at play might see dazzling pinks and wild orange. Lovers in search of privacy would find the room steeped in velvet red, only a dim quaver of light emanating from the optical diffusers.

Each person aboard the Ark had their voice fed into the computer, where they could be instantly recognized by any terminal. Stress level, emotional state and the nature of an individual's visit were detected by analyzing vocal patterns with a computerized sensor that scanned for variations in pitch, volume and diction. As Alex explained the functions of the room, the walls undulated from soft blue and violet to purple and green.

Almost invisible seams in the walls and floor indicated various furnishings and recreational equipment that could be summoned by a verbal command. Vladimir wondered what Alex might call up and checked to make sure he was not standing on top of something. As he looked down at his feet, he noted how thick and spongy the carpet felt. Despite the current austerity of the empty room, it possessed an air of elegance. Looking to the back wall, Vladimir thought the room looked much larger than it had when he first walked in. And it was true, the room did seem to be larger. The computer manipulated the lighting to give the appearance of great depth or intimate coziness, depending on the occasion.

"Well, guess what I am thinking of," said Alex. "I think I know your favorite color." Almost immediately, Vladimir noticed the walls and carpet taking on various shades of red, as if the room were decorated in rich, royal fabrics. A wall panel slid open silently, revealing a huge aquarium filled with exotic fish. Their brilliant, sometimes fluorescent colors were reflected onto the ceiling. Vladimir estimated that the tank must be at least thirty feet long and ten feet high. Octopi, seahorses, corals and anemones populated the clear salt water. The aquarium, filled with specimens difficult to keep alive in Earth aquariums, was a typical Arkian luxury.

Vladimir stood mesmerized by the aquarium. He had never seen such fish in anything but magazine articles and encyclopedias. Fish native to Russian waters were rarely this brightly colored. Alex proudly exclaimed, "There are many aquariums on the Ark. Some of the smaller aquariums are populated with fish we have bred specifically for life in zero gravity. Some of the fish you see here were mutated specifically for their unusual colors." Alex's tone grew gentle as he made a small confession, "Seeing new life forms emerging from the barrenness of space makes us feel a little more at home. In another quadrant of the Ark, we have some huge tanks, populated with whales, dolphins and large species of Earth fish. When I'm surrounded by all of this water, I feel secure. I think it creates a womb-like serenity."

For Alex, water played an essential role in his sense of karma. He believed that his family tree could be traced back to the Vikings, who inhabited the coastal regions of Northern Europe. His obsession with the ocean had prompted him to design the Ark with a large number aquariums and research centers devoted to an increased understanding of the ocean. Despite the beauty of the replicas he had designed and installed, he missed the effect of standing on the shore, witnessing the powerful crash of surf on a beach, the seemingly endless expanse of water that stretched out to the horizon. Even the advanced technology of the Ark could not replicate his memories of the ocean, and he often felt homesick for his former, Earthly life when he had always lived in close proximity to the sea.

Alex spoke a few words to the computer and the room was immediately filled with elegant furniture. Other apertures in the wall opened to reveal holographic vistas of mountain ranges. Vladimir identified Mount Blanc in one and almost believed that he could step through the opening into a bank of snow at the foot of the mountain. Behind another wall of glass was a terrarium filled with fantastic cacti, lilies and other flowering plants. The plants resembled species found on earth, but Vladimir assumed all of these had been produced in the Ark's biotechnology laboratories.

Alex gestured toward two large, leather armchairs seated across from each other. A small table, constructed of a clear, glassy material, sat between them. Vladimir made his way to the closest chair and sat down. Immediately, he felt the chair fluctuate as it adapted to his body. He felt the panels of the chair moving to support his back and sides, cushion his neck and head. After the initial changes finished, he detected a slight vibration emanating from the chair into his body. It was like the soft touch of a woman massaging his body with delicate brushes of her fingertips.

Alex reached into a nearby cabinet and removed a flask constructed of an extremely thin, clear substance. It was filled with a transparent liquid that seemed to reflect the reddish color of the room.

"Straight up, Vladimir?" he asked.

Vladimir nodded in assent and watched Alex pour a large amount of the liquid into a glass that matched the flask. Accepting the glass, he immediately raised it into the air, saluting Alex and gulping down the contents with one graceful motion. Alex, not waiting for Vladimir to finish, did the same. He collected his guest's glass and poured two more drinks of equal size. This time he saluted first and managed to finish moments before Vladimir. Both men let out sighs of exhilaration as the drinks sent instantaneous streaks of heat through their bodies. Vladimir wondered for a moment if this "super vodka" was made from alcohol or from some synthetic compound. But as the warmth of the drink continued to pass through him, he grew less concerned with its origins. On Earth he had rarely tasted vodka this good. He was a fool to quibble about the source of such great satisfaction.

He felt the drink loosening his tongue and decided not to

restrain himself. He wanted to get to know Alex on a personal level. He looked directly at Alex and said, "Tell me, do you have a woman?"

Alex grinned into his empty glass. "Yes, I suppose there is a woman who I think of as my companion. We've been together for more than thirty years." Alex's smile turned almost into a frown, his words coming slowly. "The funny thing is that she's not like most of the women here on the Ark. It's ironic that this station, which in many ways I created, is home to so many women who live their lives the way I hoped they might, but the woman I care most about has never been able to accept our innovations."

"I am not sure what it is, exactly, that you are saying."

Alex smiled weakly, his eyes still cast down. "Well, the problem, I suppose, in a manner of speaking, is . . ." he paused for a moment, ". . . sex."

Vladimir let out a hearty laugh. "Sex?"

"She thinks sex is only for animals. It's primitive, an indulgence that is below her. She's terribly nervous in bed."

Vladimir found it odd that he was talking so intimately about the love life of one of the world's most renowned writers. Still, he pressed on, eager to talk to Alex about almost anything. His orders didn't ask him to return for two weeks. As Alex had said, they had plenty of time to talk. "What is her name?" he asked.

"Keiko."

Vladimir had trouble believing that a man would stay so long with a woman who did not satisfy him. He looked at his empty glass with disbelief.

"I know what you're probably thinking, my friend," Alex told him. "And believe me, I wish it could be different. Once, a long time ago, I abandoned her. But I don't think I could ever leave her again."

"Why not?"

"I fell in love with her the first time I saw her. She was at a party in California. When they introduced me to her, all I could see was a beautiful woman. She was so exquisite I couldn't stop looking at her. She moved like no other woman

I had ever seen."

"She sounds like a dream that was too good to come true."

"You are so right, my friend."

"Tell me about her."

"Yes. I will tell you." Alex stood up from his chair and reached for Vladimir's glass. "But first, we will drink again, no?"

Vladimir smiled and surrendered his glass. He could tell he was going to enjoy spending time talking to Alex.

Alex and Vladimir spent the next half-an-hour taking small gulps from their drinks, occasionally replenishing them as Alex told the story of his life with Keiko. Even after their horrendous sexual experience, Alex, convinced that he loved her, asked her to live with him and she accepted. They traveled around the country together, first as platonic friends and then as lovers. After a while they found that they rarely spoke to one another when they were alone, finding they could communicate just as well without saying anything. It was Alex's first hint that Keiko possessed an extraordinary ability.

In Keiko, he had found a woman whose innocence never faded, and her childlike hopefulness inspired him to work harder on his plans for the Ark. She held deep compassion not only for humankind, but all living things. Some days he came home to find her weeping, distraught about the death of a cat in the street or the wilting of a flower in her garden. At first, Alex was touched by these sentimental outbursts, but within a few years, her crying spells escalated and he was no longer able to comfort her. She would weep for hours, intermittently shouting and screaming at presences that Alex could not see. The increasing number of these spells wreaked havoc on what little sex life they had. Keiko referred to herself as a whore after any kind of intimacy and soon even the slightest physical encroachment on Alex's part was met with crying and expressions of disgust.

Alex insisted that Keiko see a doctor for professional treatment of her schizophrenia. Lithium was prescribed to balance her mood swings and Alex tried to monitor her behavior for any signs of relapse. For a while, everything went well, even though sex remained out of the question. But as work on his writing and lectures increased, Alex was less and less able to keep a close eye on Keiko. At one point, she had grown so frightened that she was unable to travel with him and he returned from a weekend conference to find her hospitalized. She had slashed her wrists and taken all of her two week supply of lithium.

Keiko was again committed to the asylum in Camarillo, from which she called Alex frequently. He despaired when he heard her pleading voice surrounded by the moans and disquieting shouts of the other patients. She begged him to get her out but the doctors insisted that she stay. After five years of treatment, she was released on a conditional basis. Since that time, Keiko had remained troubled but stable. Alex, though he had married and spent time with other women, still loved her as much as he ever had. In fact, it was his continuing concern for Keiko that broke up his second marriage to a woman named Wendy.

"Even though she has had so many troubles," Alex explained, "everyone who meets her loves her. She has such an incredible empathy for life and I suspect it has something to do with her schizophrenia. She's almost fifty years old yet she remains childlike, innocent. And the crazy thing is that despite this exterior quality of naiveté, she is incredibly smart. She spends all of her free time studying. She even helped me write my first book."

"She did?" Vladimir was surprised at the revelation that a book that had so influenced his life had been written by two authors.

"Yes, and, unfortunately, I think my ideas about the destruction of the world contributed to her illness. She became obsessed with Armageddon. She hasn't been able to develop a normal adult's callousness to the destruction of life. I still try to insulate her from that kind of talk."

"So," Vladimir asked, "what is your life like now?"

"I know it sounds strange, but I think we relate to one another now as father and daughter, sometimes as brother and sister."

"And never as lovers?" Vladimir thought this was one of the strangest love stories he had ever heard.

"Well, when I said that the biggest problem we had was sex, that wasn't entirely true. We do have a sex life. Whenever she thinks I'm straying too far, staying away on trips too long, not paying enough attention to her, she opens up sexually."

"And what does that mean?"

"Vladimir, I must tell you, there is nothing like having a schizophrenic lover. I swear. I never know what she's going to be like. When she decides she wants to have sex, she always has a new surprise for me. Things that go far beyond any of my fantasies. Her mind, troubled as it might be, also has an amazing propensity for creative sexuality."

Vladimir tried to imagine himself being involved with such a woman and had difficulty in doing so. His life with Thasha had always been relatively stable. Their sex life was enjoyable, if not always the most passionate. Like many men who spend a great deal of time alone and away from home, Vladimir had often comforted himself in the arms of other women, but he was glad to be able to return home to a loving wife and family. He did not know if he could deal with the manic ups and downs of a relationship with a woman like Keiko.

After a few moments of silence, Alex began talking again. "There is also another aspect of Keiko that I only hinted at before." He paused to take another drink. "She has amazing extrasensory powers. When you meet her, she will probably hypnotize you within a matter of seconds. You won't even notice it at first, but soon you will feel an empathy emanating from her unlike anything you have ever felt before. I have seen her move people to tears when she talks. And she doesn't do it intentionally. Her heart, not her head, moves her to try and help everyone around her. She expends so much energy trying to connect to people that she exhausts herself. After being in public, she often has to rest for days, trying to get back her strength."

Alex's eyes were glassy with almost-cried tears and drink. "I tell you, Vladimir, she is absolutely the most beautiful woman in the world . . . physically . . . spiritually. I can't imagine living without her. Taking care of her, protecting the fragile child in her is more like a joy than a burden. Some people find that hard to understand. She projects such a strange image to people that they can't believe she is such a good friend. Sometimes she's resilient, but other times I think she finds life unbearable. The love I give her is a poor substitute for a perfect world."

Vladimir began to see why Alex was so concerned with reshaping humankind, why he pushed himself so hard to realize human potential. In addition to his scientific and philanthropic interest, his love for this woman pushed him to try and eradicate evil. Like Vladimir's experiments, which he hoped would bring him closer to his wife, Alex's writing and inventions had been inspired by a romantic ideal, by love for a woman.

Dreamily, Vladimir remarked to Alex, "It is wonderful what a woman can do for a man."

Alex, not entirely understanding his companion, seemed to snap out of his lovesick funk. "You must have heard about the women on the Ark. Have you?"

"What is there to hear?"

"I thought everyone was talking about our women: how they look, dress, act and work like men. That's the image almost everyone has of them." Vladimir remembered seeing pictures of women dressed in uniforms identical to Alex's. He had read that they worked in every sector of the Ark, in every occupation: from machinists to athletes to surgeons.

Alex continued, "Well, I admit they look a little tough when they're in uniform, but when you see them at one of our dances, every woman on this ship is as beautiful as Aphrodite herself." Vladimir wondered that a man who had so recently spoken lovingly of his companion could now be fixated on the sexual attractiveness of women he didn't even know. Vladimir never reveled in the beauty of his mistresses, feeling that it somehow further denigrated his relationship with Thasha.

"I tell you, Vladimir, on the Ark the most masculine women in the history of humankind become the most feminine, the most exquisite things you have ever seen. There has never been anything like it. You probably wouldn't recognize your own wife if you saw her in one of our ballrooms."

Alex got Vladimir another drink and they smiled drunkenly at one another. The Russian's moral reservations about Alex's stories began to fade and he found himself wanting to hear more. Alex opened a fresh decanter of vodka and began to describe the Ark's most anticipated social event.

"We play a game that Americans call spin the bottle." He made a wavering ellipse with his forefinger to illustrate. Vladimir nodded to show that he understood. "Only it's an adult version. You dance with a person selected by a random spin, and the beautiful part is that a computer allows you to see an image, a computer-generated picture, of what your partner is thinking. And everyone is masked. You have no way of knowing the identity of your partner. People work for weeks reshaping their bodies so that no one will recognize them at the ball.

"And it's fantastic. People's fantasies appear, as if they were in a comic book, over their heads in little balloons. As you dance with a woman, you see exactly what she is thinking about. If you hit it off with her, you can watch as she seduces you in her mind. Soon, your imagination is reacting and she can see it happening above your head. It becomes an interactive fantasy. You never actually touch one another, except when the dance calls for it, yet you live out this vicarious image of your own fantasy. Amazing. One of the best applications of our ESP and computer technology.

"You might dance with a half-dozen different women during the course of the ball, but at the end of the night, the computer pairs you off with the person you're most compatible with. One night, I was matched with this absolutely gorgeous woman, a German. We left the ballroom and made love for hours. Do you know who she was?"

"I have no idea," responded Vladimir, chuckling to

himself. He saw a blonde, Nordic princess bowed back in his arms.

"Keiko."

"What?" Vladimir burst out laughing.

"I had no idea it was her. Not even after we had sex. She had changed her appearance completely. Blonde hair. Blue eyes. She spoke fluent German. An amazing masquerade for an Asian. Later she told me she had spent a month reshaping her body in the Ark's body sculpting machines in order to fool me."

"Your friend does many strange things like this?"

"I wish it happened more often, but sometimes she just lets go of her inhibitions and I see a side of her that I thought had been locked away years ago. She spends so much time trying to empathize with others that she ignores herself. I think her fear of her illness makes her afraid to let go. She equates letting go of her emotions with loss of control over her schizophrenia. The wildness, the abandon of sex is so close to the primitive edge of human experience that she thinks she can't tell the difference between ecstasy and insanity. I try to reassure her. I try to help her, and in turn she supports all of my work. Helps me to make the right decisions. Is totally unselfish. She loves everyone, like a saint."

Alex had the vague suspicion that, under the influence of the vodka and Vladimir's presence, he was beginning to ramble a little more than normal. The synthetic liquor was a delicacy reserved for only the most important foreign emissary and Arkian celebrations and it had been quite some time since he had last indulged in its intoxicating spirits. He steadied himself, however, and pressed on in his description of Keiko.

"But like a saint, she is sometimes a bit of a prude. Every time she loses control, she feels terrible. After our night together at the dance, she was obsessed with the notion of repenting for her wicked acts. She showed me her diary, filled with entries enumerating her sexual fantasies. I couldn't believe she had written them. Why are you showing me these? I asked her. She told me she had to in order to atone for them. She tries to divorce her sexuality, her carnal nature, from what she perceives as the purity of her love for other people. In her mind they are separate and unequal."

Alex sat still for a moment and then put his drink down. "Well, perhaps another day we will talk about your love life?"

"I do not think it is as exciting as what you just told me."

"But you love your wife?"

"Very much. I miss her much when I am on a mission."

"Speaking of your mission," Alex said, "may we talk about that now?"

Vladimir sat forward and tried to clear his head. Was Alex aware of his work? He never imagined that he might take an interest. But of course, it was Alex's driving passion to know what was happening in all areas, to synthesize disparate systems into a functioning whole, the same kind of synthesis that led to the creation of the Ark.

"Yes," Vladimir responded, hoping he would be alert enough to remember what was said. "I would very much like to talk about it."

"I've been following the work you've been doing." Vladimir's heart leapt. Alex Abramawitz, looking over his shoulder! He felt honored. "I hope you don't mind, but I think we've made some advancements here on the Ark that might be of use to you. Some of what we've done has been inspired by your work with ESP and direct electrode stimulation."

"Really?"

"What we've done in the consumer sector is to implant electrodes into the temporal regions of the brain so that operators of telephones, radios and other interactive telecommunications equipment don't need to use microphones or headsets. The electronic impulses are picked up directly from a synapse bundle and relayed to the equipment. This allows for freedom of motion while maintaining contact. A second set of implants in the occipital area has enabled us to display images and other visual data in the mind of the implanted individual. Equipment operators see statistics and other information without having to refer to a monitor. It's saved our clerical workers and mechanical engineers, among others, thousands of hours of work time. We also offer the implants as entertainment devices. Movies without screens, perceived in three dimensions! Its more than cyberspace and virtual reality ever promised."

Vladimir had no idea research had progressed so far on the Ark. He mind reeled at the thought of how far the Ark had come and the stupor of his heavy drinking was not wearing off fast enough for him to catch up. "Incredible, Alex. Incredible," was all he was able to say.

"Think about this, Vladimir. I've heard that you despise the prep time for your experiments. This means that you can have the electrodes implanted permanently. No more wires sticking out. They could work on you remotely."

Vladimir hadn't even considered that possibility. "No more wires," he muttered.

Alex moved over to Vladimir's chair and crouched down next to him. His joviality had been replaced by a grave expression. "Vladimir, I felt you communicating with me the other day. I know how far you've gone with the experiments, even if your own people don't realize it. I brought you here to tell you because I want you to work on a project for me."

"What is it?" Vladimir's fuzziness was dissipating rapidly.

"It's personal."

"Personal?"

"A personal favor. I want you to use your new techniques without telling your government about how far you've come."

For a moment Vladimir considered what this might mean. Would he be betraying his country? Giving up secrets to the Ark that might be used without himself or his country receiving credit or profit. Before he could answer, Alex spoke again.

"You know, Vladimir, that I have always been a great admirer of Russian culture."

"Yes." Vladimir was slow to respond, still thinking about what Alex was asking him to do. "I have read everything you've written."

"Good. And there's a reason for that affinity."

"A reason?"

"Yes. One of the first books I read outside of the medical field was a history of Napoleon's campaign in Russia."

"That's the reason?" Vladimir was growing increasingly anxious about Alex's request. Alex continued as if he had not heard the question.

"Napoleon launched his invasion from the river Niemann in Poland, and for some reason that fact always stayed with me, even though I'd never heard of the Niemann before. But years later, when I was in my late thirties, I discovered that my grandparents lived less than fifty miles from that river in an area that constantly changed hands between the Russian and Polish governments. My grandfather left Poland because his family didn't want him drafted by the Russian army. They believed they were Poles and didn't want to serve under a tsar. So he and my grandmother made their way to the United States, to a place called New Britain in Connecticut. This was in the early 1900s, around the time of the Russo-Japanese War."

"And what does that have to do with my experiments?"

"I'm getting to that part. After the first world war, my grandfather wanted to return to what was left of Poland to reclaim his estate, but my grandmother hated the old country. She had been a peasant and had nothing to return for. She told me that once the family's horse had been sick and they all took turns hitched to the plow to turn the soil. When I was young I believed her. She could lift me out of bed even when I was sixteen years old. Strong as a horse."

Vladimir laughed at the old world anecdote. "My grandparents, too, are from that area of Russia. I used to visit the Niemann often."

"So much the better!" Alex had a look of supreme delight. "This may help both of us."

"What is it you want me to do?"

Alex stood up and held his head close to Vladimir's. "I know you're reliving the past in your experiments. I want you to use one of your test runs to try and verify my ancestry. I want you to go further back."

"What's so important about them? I don't know why you need to use me?"

Alex grew more and more animated as he spoke. He moved away from Vladimir's chair and began to move about the room. Vladimir had to sit up in order to keep him in view.

"I have done quite a bit of informal research into my ancestry. I have used hypnosis and meditation to regress back into the past and I feel certain that my grandmother was a descendant of the Vikings. Probably some time in the eleventh century, about the same time as the Norman conquest, a clan broke off from the coastal group, possibly interacting with the Tartars or some other tribe of oriental marauders passing through northern Europe. When I was a young man in the Navy, I used some archaic books in a Charleston, South Carolina, library to identify my racial characteristics."

Vladimir was surprised to hear this. "They have such books in America?"

"In the 1650s," Alex explained, "Charleston was a booming metropolis, but sixty percent of the population was black. Masters often raped their female slaves, requiring a codification of racial makeup to determine citizenship and bloodlines. Like the Nazis, a great deal of attention was paid to classifying facial and cranial characteristics to determine racial background. There were pages and pages of detailed illustrations of nose types, ear types, earlobe types, eyes, everything."

"So what did it tell you?"

"As I compared myself with the images, I realized that I had many Asian features. My supposedly Eastern European background was linked not only to Northern Europeans, but to the people of Asia Minor. I know that Keiko's grandparents are Russian and Japanese. So somehow, somewhere, I believe I am related to Keiko. You're related to Keiko. If your grandparents are from the Niemann River area, I'm probably even related to you. I have no evidence, but everything points in that direction. I want to see if you can push yourself far enough back to verify my hypothesis."

Alex stood over Vladimir, placing his hands on Vladimir's head. "Somewhere in your memory, programmed into your protoplasm, your DNA, lies a memory that's going to help me. A memory that only you can retrieve."

"Why don't you conduct your own experiments? If this memory you are speaking of is programmed into me, it must also be programmed into you."

Alex removed his hands from Vladimir's head. "We've duplicated your procedures, but apparently you are the only subject with the natural sensitivity to make the experiment work. You have more experience than anyone in the field and I cannot duplicate your innate ability."

Vladimir felt a warmth like that of the vodka creeping over him. Could all of these pieces really fit together? Or was it preposterous? He didn't want to doubt Alex, but it seemed unlikely that his experiments could prove such distant interrelationships. Still, the idea of finding out appealed to him. Alex's visionary work with the Ark had seemed ludicrous at first. He had been laughed out of corporate boardrooms across the world. But now Vladimir sat in a chair in a room aboard the Ark, the same project the Earth's leaders had scoffed at. It was possible, he supposed, that he and Alex were related. It couldn't hurt to use one experiment to try and discover what Alex was looking for.

For several minutes, neither man had spoken. Finally, Vladimir responded, "I will do it. I will try to find what you are looking for."

Alex clasped his hands together. "I am so happy to hear you say that. I was sure I could count on you. I tell you, Vladimir, this goes beyond just my own knowledge. If we can prove this, it will be a testimonial to the brotherhood of man. It will prove that the people of earth are all one race, that superficial characteristics are meaningless." He reached out and took Vladimir's hands. "So many of us have forgotten, have ignored how important we are to one another."

Alex suddenly changed tack. "Do you know why, when I wrote my book, I included a passage describing the necessity for building the Ark?"

"I thought it was a story, perhaps from the Bible. You said you wanted to build the Ark as a museum of our culture, of humanity, in case of an atomic war. I believed it was like a fairy tale."

"Well, it was based on that, but it means more to me. Geopolitics are steering the world straight into a terrible disaster, one that the Earth may never survive and that politicians may not be able to avert. I want to find evidence that offers people a reason to keep moving forward, instead of destroying themselves. We, as clever animals, always feel a need to change things. We outgrow our surroundings, always looking for the next horizon. Perhaps we have outgrown earth, so we look elsewhere in the cosmos for something new. We want to move forward, but we often misstep."

"You think the war is unstoppable?"

"Sometimes, yes. And that's why I want this, to give hope to those who are left behind, so that even on a broken planet filled with terror, radiation, the detritus of war, there will still be human dignity, a hope that humankind is moving forward."

"Alex, even if I find what you are looking for, how will you tell others about it? All of my work is classified. You cannot publish the results."

"My friend, if there is a catastrophe similar to the one I predict, classification of research will no longer be the priority it once was for your government. Assuming there is any security left in the scientific sector, it is likely that you will be able to take advantage of an unstable situation."

"The chaos of Armageddon? Is that what you're talking about?" Vladimir found it hard to believe that Alex could discuss the near annihilation of humankind with such unflinching pragmatism.

"A nuclear war must be looked at objectively, no matter how destructive it is. From our vantage in space, we can save people if we are successful. We have no national alliances to bind our response. That makes us the only entity able to offer neutral aid to a planet suffering horribly. We will be the only hope! And for that reason, we must be successful. The knowledge you bring me will be the first step in restoring humankind."

Vladimir took another sip of his vodka, considering everything Alex had told him. His mission to the Ark was asking more of him than he thought he could give.

CHAPTER 4

EVEN FRIENDS ARGUE

As Vladimir considered the ramifications of an unauthorized release of research data to Alex, Alex himself, adrenalized by his vision of world harmony, soliloquized on the social advances of the Ark. Vladimir watched him with numb suspicion. Why should he play a role in this man's version of world history? He wanted to believe Alex, to trust in him, but he sensed danger in taking the risks of a revolutionary. Although Alex had never toppled a government with guns or explosives, the Ark's economic and social influence made the governments and law enforcement systems of Earth look like anachronisms. Would he be betraying his country to pass information to Alex? What if he was caught? He felt certain there was little chance that anyone would notice that he had changed the scope of his experiments or that they would see any significance in such changes. But there was always the possibility. He hated to think of how that might affect his career, his family, his position. Alex, misunderstanding or paying no attention to Vladimir's contemplative state, continued like an impassioned lecturer.

"Since I've been in space, I've realized how completely limited our social and sexual choices were on Earth. A man only had a few options: marriage, cohabitation or dating. Anything else was considered immoral or, as it turned out, physically dangerous. Everything was unsatisfactory in one way or another, too much commitment in marriage, too little stability in dating. Really exciting sexual relationships simply weren't available. After going for years without having sex, I realized someone had to change the rules. Perhaps we've made a few missteps on the Ark, but I think we've opened people up to some of the more interesting possibilities of human sexuality. Sex is more than marriage, the biological clock and reproduction.

"I saw how addicted people became to anything that they thought made them feel better: drugs, sex, food, alcohol, gambling, movies, sleep, work, pain. Comfort became their addiction, to feel like they belonged to something. People were trying to find themselves in the conventions of the societal framework, rather than trying to discover themselves in the context of something new. Perhaps you never heard of it, but in the 1980s American presidents declared a "War on Drugs" that did almost nothing to stop people from using drugs. People became inundated with ridiculous phrases like "Just Say No," "Say Nope to Dope" and "Hugs not Drugs." They were just platitudes invented by copywriters to sell the War to the suburbs and the people who generated tax dollars. But the mistake the government made was in trying to make all drugs out to be evil. They never tried to elevate the consciousness of citizens to see that some drugs could be used to benefit society. Sure, drugs could become addictive, but most people were never taught how to control that impulse. It's the same with food. Every single person on earth is hooked like a fish on the most addictive substance ever invented and they don't even realize it!"

Once again, Alex's finger was thrust into the air in a flourish of oratorical triumph. Vladimir considered the lunch of meat, potatoes and bread he had finished just before he received his orders to meet Alex. Was that an addiction? Were grains and tubers the opiates that Marx never suspected? He couldn't resist interrupting, "A potato a drug? Is that what you are saying?"

Alex's eyes came back into focus and he turned his head toward Vladimir. "Food is the worst addiction man has ever faced. The world's governments know it, but they allow it to continue because of the profits to be made, the power to be had by controlling food supplies. A silo filled with surplus grain is every bit as powerful as a silo filled with a nuclear warhead. It used to be that people understood the value of food. They had to farm their land, grow crops. If there were drought or the crops failed, they might go hungry or lose their land. But now the terror food can inspire in people is cloaked in its ready availability. Only the few Westerners who have witnessed an African famine know the consequences of starvation. But in America and Europe, people see food as a source of recreation, like the Roman forum and gladiator battles were to the elite of the first western empire."

"Many of us in Russia think that it is you on the Ark who are decadent," Vladimir responded.

"But don't you see the positive results we've gotten?" Alex cajoled. "Can't you see how far we've come?"

"I see that your science has made great leaps forward," Vladimir conceded. "But I have not seen how your people are so much happier."

"Have you ever met someone who lives here?"

"Only you. We rarely come in contact with people from the Ark. You are only computer interfaces, business conducted through terminals, never in person. I was surprised that you knew about my experiments. I never think of you people looking into what we do."

"Of course we're interested," said Alex. He wondered at the perception outsiders had of his floating society.

Vladimir pressed on, determined to find out exactly how Alex knew about his ESP work. "I am still wondering, my friend, how you knew about my research. It is classified top secret."

Alex's cockiness returned. "It didn't take much, I have to tell you, to understand what you were doing. I've known where Russian science has been headed for decades. Consider Pavlov's experiments in conditioning, followed by Russian insistence on funding research on the mind and pharmaceuticals all through the Cold War. Then add in your papers on ESP. It's not hard to follow the general plan."

"And was I that obvious?"

"It really doesn't have much to do with you. I saw the beginning of these experiments before you even thought about working in the field. In 1953, I was working in a neurophysiology lab where a brain cancer patient, during an exploratory operation, had various regions of his brain stimulated by doctors. It turned out his brain was like a recording machine. He remembered passing incidents that most of us forget, symphonies and conversations he heard as a child that he now recalled with perfect clarity. That discovery was entirely accidental, but even then we believed that if we could find a way to map out the brain, we might be able to treat human memory as a library, able to access any information at will."

Vladimir rose from his seat and walked resolutely to the liquor cabinet where he began pouring himself a drink. Alex called out to him. "Vladimir, might I entice you to sample some of our synthesized drugs."

Vladimir waved the invitation off as if he were swatting a fly. "No, I enjoy my vodka. It is all I need. I get enough chemical and electrolytic compounds in the experiments. I have taken enough mind changing drugs to last me for a while." Vladimir noticed that Alex was smiling at him like a parent humoring a child. "But don't let me stop you. A Russian is nothing if not tolerant of his host." He couldn't resist adding, "Especially when he is a guest of a tolerant man like yourself."

Alex chuckled to himself and crossed the room, commanding another cabinet, filled with brightly colored flasks, to reveal itself. Alex explained that each color—black, electric blue, red, yellow—represented the mood that the drug elicited. Dark colors brought on dark moods, culminating in a tragic but cathartic experience. The lighter flasks were filled with euphoric substances, bringing on varying intensities of happiness or joy. The deepest, darkest colors had a tranquilizing effect. After mulling over the contents of the cabinet, Alex selected a neutral yellow bottle and filled a small glass from which he sipped slowly.

As their conversation continued, Vladimir watched Alex to see if any change came over him after imbibing the drug. The effects revealed themselves slowly at first, with Alex displaying an increased alertness and even faster speech patterns than Vladimir had seen before. After five or six minutes, the stimulants turned Alex into a man possessed. He began to speak Russian clearly, using more and more idioms. Alex's normal willingness to discuss one aspect of a problem in detail became exaggerated and as Vladimir continued to sip from his vodka, he had difficulty keeping up with the variegation of Alex's discourse. When Vladimir spoke, Alex interrupted him almost immediately, able to relate in detail exactly what Vladimir was going to say, and then elaborate on the ideas and philosophies that had brought Vladimir to his way of thinking. After several such demonstrations, he realized that Alex was picking his mind with unfailing accuracy.

"My friend," Vladimir said, "I think it is becoming increasingly unnecessary for me to speak. You seem to know exactly what I am going to say." Alex responded with a gleeful look, but Vladimir remarked petulantly, "I think you have given yourself a slight advantage."

"Advantage, yes," Alex said playfully. "But remember, I offered the advantage to you first." For the first time in an hour, he sat down. "I propose an experiment. You just sit there and think for a while, and then we'll see what I have to say about it. Why don't you begin by thinking about what my mouth is doing?"

Vladimir glanced down at Alex's mouth and a chill ran through him. His lips had not moved. "What is it?" he asked Alex, and just as suddenly realized that he no longer had to speak to communicate with the man who sat across from him.

He heard the response, "What do you think it is?" Alex smiled serenely.

As he marveled at this development, he was overwhelmed by an urge to urinate. The need to relieve himself came so strongly he was sure Alex had suggested the urge to his body. As if in answer, a portal slid aside revealing a sizable restroom. He left his seat and entered the room, the portal sliding closed behind him. He began to urinate.

While still in the act, he wondered about the Ark's waste disposal system and was suddenly inundated with visions of blueprints with sewer lines highlighted, flow directions notated. As if in a computerized tutorial, he saw the Ark's treatment facility separating the water from waste and directing the scarce liquid into a drinking water reclamation system. The remaining organic film was broken down with bacteria, which in turn fed algae, harvested by Ark nutritionists. The algae, fortified with chemical agents, was processed into the food supply and transformed into the paste-like substance consumed by the Ark's inhabitants.

When Vladimir emerged from the bathroom, Alex stood near a table holding a palette of snack foods derived from the paste. "Care for a snack?" he asked. Vladimir looked over the regimented display of what appeared to be an appetizer plate of carrots and celery, potato chips and thinly sliced meats and crackers. His thoughts immediately cast back to the demonstration he had just envisioned and he blanched momentarily, but sampled a few anyway, finding they tasted exactly like the food they mimicked.

"Delicious," he said, taking a handful of synthetic snacks with him.

Alex spoke in Russian, "As long as you're dining with me, perhaps you'll oblige me in sampling one of our newest products. It tastes, at least we think so, exactly like champagne. Why don't we see if we can taste the difference?"

Alex produced a pair of exquisite crystal glasses, obviously manufactured on Earth. Up until this time, the containers they had used were made with a glass-like film, indestructible unless exposed to certain light waves. Dishes and glasses made of this substance were sanitized by disintegrating them with light-frequency generators and then remodeling the recycled material. Cleaning normal glasses and dishes on the Ark required far too much water for the Ark to expend on cleaning up after meals and real glass, they had discovered, took on some alarmingly dangerous qualities when utilized in Zero-G.

"These pieces date back to the nineteenth century," Alex explained, holding the glasses to the light so that the cut crystal cast splintered webs of reflected light on the walls.

"They're from my own collection, but anyone on the Ark may use them for special occasions."

Vladimir accepted one of the glasses, now filled with the synthesized champagne. "This is very generous of you," he told Alex.

"We have a communal collection of valuable items that everyone shares. Unfortunately, several of the glasses from this set have been broken, so I'm afraid we won't be able to live up to Russian tradition by tossing them to the floor and grinding them under our heels."

They laughed more than they should have at Alex's joke and then lifted their glasses, Vladimir offering a toast. "To new friendship and new discovery," he cried.

Alex answered, "*Nosdrova!*"

Vladimir immediately felt his body respond drunkenly to the champagne. He felt his way to his chair. "Excellent champagne," he declared, taking another sip, and chasing it with a handful of crackers.

Oddly, the initial jolt of the champagne subsided and he soon felt as lucid as he had upon arrival. "This is strange," he remarked, noshing on some of the synthetic meat from the plate.

"Not feeling quite as tipsy as before?" inquired Alex.

"No. This is how this champagne is supposed to work?"

"No," Alex explained eagerly, still excited about showing off the Ark to his friend. "It's the food you're eating. The nutritionists have formulated this food to absorb and counteract the effects of alcohol. If you eat enough, you'll go from stone drunk to stone sober."

"This is a good prank."

"It's not a prank. We've worked on these for a long time. As I told you we're trying to free our citizens from the effects of addiction, both to alcohol and food. We've developed these to countermand the cravings alcohol sets up in some of the people on board, the people who under normal conditions might become alcoholics."

"But for a guest, Alex? Is this how you should treat me, a Russian?"

"I know it must be hard for a Russian," Alex said with mock concern. "Perhaps you could eat a little less."

"Perhaps you could bring me some real food and drink?" joked the Russian and the two men roared with laughter, at this point willing to laugh together for any reason.

Alex shook his head, trying to clear the tightness of laughter from his throat. "Tell me, how is your wife, Thasha, and the old oak tree?"

Vladimir, no longer stunned by Alex's revelations, took a moment to reflect on what the Ark's advances meant for his work, how trivial his experiments must seem. The idea of Alex being a part of such a personal moment as his wintry recollection of Thasha angered him.

Alex answered his thought. "Don't worry about that, from now on you will know what I know."

Vladimir covered his head with his hands, "You must stop this. Does anything I think escape you."

"No."

Vladimir rose unsteadily from his seat, and took a drink from the bottle of vodka. He swept aside the glass of champagne, upsetting the tray of food. He pressed his face close to Alex's. "I am tiring of these games. I like to drink vodka, but you think I am an alcoholic. I like to eat and you give me crap, literally!"

Despite his confrontational manner, Alex was gladdened to see his friend sparked to defiance. His self-control diminished, he was lashing out at the daunting future the Ark offered a man not participating directly in the Ark's program.

"This newfangled ship. These drugs. Do you think this is human?" Vladimir demanded. "This Ark? Do you really believe in all this?"

"Do you really believe in Europe, in Russia? In what is happening between all the hundreds of little nations down there? Is that human? Black skin separated from white. Eyes turned up warring with eyes turned down. Blue eyes at odds with brown eyes. Nations at war is all I see. Nobody wars here."

"I still do not see why it has to be as you have made it."

"Vladimir, people have to break from the old ideas if they want to move ahead."

Vladimir's face twisted in a grimace, mirroring the conflict inside of him. Something told him that Alex offered a horrible, manipulated future for humankind. But his vision of peace, the comforts achieved by the Ark, were irresistible. Vladimir saw himself dressed in the blue uniform of the Ark and he felt faceless, imagining that wearing the uniform necessitated a loss of identity. His eyes closed tightly. He had forgotten that the man who challenged him to accept this new version of society stood only a few feet away.

"I understand," Alex said softly.

"How can you understand me? You're living up here, isolated from the rest of world. Why is this real? Why is this the future? Men continue to live and die on earth and you're up here making hors d'oeuvres out of piss water. You can read my mind, but I think you cannot see my heart."

"Vladimir, on Earth, men continue to live out lives dictated to them by governments who read their minds, but they don't have to do it with ESP. Governments know what men want: a job, food, a good time every few days. So they give it to them. What the governments ignore is the heart. Freedom, power, the ability to be who you want to be . . . none of that is granted by the government.

"The Americans take over Latin America. The Russians take Eastern Europe. The Nicaraguans take up arms to install their own government and the Russians start freeing their little satellites. New governments are installed and they promise everything, but nothing ever changes. Were the *Sandinistas* right? Was Samoza better? It doesn't matter, because the hearts of men were still ignored. In space, we have formulated a revolution of another kind. This is political upheaval. It's the chaos of people looking for themselves in another context, of people reinventing humanity, mapping out a better future.

"On the Ark, there is a government in which everyone participates. Every person on the Ark has a chance to act as president. Every man has the right to learn any trade and practice that trade. Skills are interchangeable. Computers can help anyone learn almost anything. On Earth, no one can get enough power, it's another addiction. People can't get enough of anything and they kill one another to get more. They'll kill themselves pursuing something that will never satisfy them. Everyone on the earth might as well be numb with heroin."

"Do you really believe that?" Vladimir asked, his head resting forlornly in the cradle of his hands. The Ark's government sounded like anarchy, its social programs like a utopian impossibility. The dispensation of new products on the Ark seemed like a mockery of the former Soviet central distribution system.

"The whole point of living here on the Ark is to free people from themselves," Alex insisted. Freed from addiction to sex, sleep, power, food, drugs, everything. No loneliness, no poverty. Nobody feels useless. Everyone achieves what they can."

"Do you think you have the answer for all these people?"

"If you mean 'why we're here' or something like that, I don't think there is a real answer. At any rate, we're not to the point where we can even think about addressing those issues. Aboard the Ark, people experiment with so many different philosophies, I think there's hope we'll come up with some interesting new ideas about the meaning of life, but I think it's unlikely that any one person will find one answer. If it's there to be found, our differences will help us find it."

"We have those same differences on Earth," Vladimir pointed out.

"Yes, that's true," said Alex, "But usually you end up killing each other for those differences before you can learn anything."

"Sometimes you talk about us as if you were another species, as if you were no longer men," Vladimir said, indignance rising in his voice.

"I'm sorry if I sound that way." Alex remained unperturbed by Vladimir's anger. "But we've made so many changes in the way we live, sometimes it feels as if we've completely broken with the rest of humanity. Look at our love lives. Institutions like marriage have been completely restructured. Some people choose traditional marriage, other people make contracts, renegotiating them when they feel a need to." He asked Vladimir directly, "When you're on earth with your wife, are you always satisfied with your marriage?"

"Almost always."

"Then you are the rare exception. But even so, I don't think you're being entirely honest. You're not happy when you're up here, so far away from her. Is that the kind of life you want? Is that fulfillment?"

Vladimir began to weep, the tears showing bright tracks on his hands when he wiped his face. He missed his wife. He missed his children. He missed Russia. Alex took Vladimir's hands in his own, knowing that his utopia would never be able to replace Earth for a man like Vladimir, a man strong enough to be honest with himself. He tried to raise his friend's spirits.

"Let's turn away from all this talk," said Alex definitively. He placed his arm around Vladimir's shoulders. "I'm not trying to convert you. All I want you to do is understand what it is we're doing here. If you can't help me try and take the next step that's up to you. If you can't, I understand. But I have to tell you, I have intelligence reports that indicate a great international conflict is likely to occur within the next two weeks. I need your help, if you'll offer it, to keep a lid on things."

"So," Vladimir replied with thinly veiled resentment, "You play God with the world, too."

Alex replied in an unusually jaded tone, "When I have to, I do what I can to insure the stability of our lives aboard the Ark. Until we are completely self-sufficient, it is imperative that Earth's governments maintain some semblance of peace."

"Is the Ark all you care about?"

"Of course not. I thought you knew that. I want us to work to avoid disaster for the people left down there. And I'm making our position perfectly clear. We are neutral, but we're not going to allow anyone to jeopardize our autonomy. I am sending a mandate to all Earth nations, telling each government that we won't tolerate any communications satellites to be tampered with—no matter what country they belong to—nor will we allow any magnetic impulse systems to interrupt our transmissions. Computer links and electronic communications must remain operational at all times."

"Why all of this focus on the communications systems. They don't have anything to do with the Ark. Nobody's going to allow you to declare every satellite off limits."

"First of all, my friend, the satellites are the only systems we can adequately protect from our orbit. If international tensions rise, they must be viable to allow for diplomatic communiques to be transmitted. I believe that the events likely to transpire will be of such a nature that a nuclear war may be initiated if the superpowers do not understand what is happening."

Alex leveled his gaze at Vladimir, noting the attention he paid to every word being said. Alex could tell the Russian still struggled with the Ark's program, but he knew he could count on him to work diligently to forward the cause of peace.

"The bottom line, Vladimir, is that it is up to those of us in space to save those on earth, and that means we must consider ourselves allies. We have the means to force that alliance if the need arises, but I would prefer to have your cooperation. We will be working with you and your people as well as the American station. But Russian involvement is crucial to us, even more so than American aid."

"You want us to work with the Americans?" Vladimir was incredulous.

"If there is a war, the Ark will remain neutral, and we expect both the Russian and American space stations to do the same, no matter what happens on the ground. The war must not take place in space."

"Is it possible to control our government's commands?"

"Your governments will not risk destruction of such valuable assets. They know we have the means to do it."

Vladimir was startled by this revelation. "I didn't realize the Ark was authorized to carry weapons."

"Of course we are not authorized to carry weapons, but our offensive strategies don't involve conventional weapons. This will be a war fought with technology, with computers. I think even your limited time aboard the Ark should have shown you what we might be capable of. You'll be here for a while. Take a look around. Tell your superiors that we aren't to be trifled with. By placing the comm satellites under our protection, we ensure that no one can interfere with us. Our defensive, neutral position allows us liberal scope to take intercessionary action in order to protect ourselves."

"Alex, I told you I will help you, and I will live up to my word. I do not know how you intend to use my work to avert this disaster you think is going to occur, but I will do what you ask."

Alex threw his arms around Vladimir, hugging him. "We are brothers, you and I. Occasionally, I think there is a destiny that calls us to act in a certain way, and I feel certain our meeting was not a coincidence. I propose that we now put all of this behind us. The next few days will be very busy and we should enjoy ourselves while we can." Alex removed another flask of vodka from the cabinet.

"A Russian knows when to talk and when to drink, my friend," exclaimed Vladimir. The two men laughed together, their common goal and time spent together a strong bond between them. They would continue talking and drinking for several more hours.

CHAPTER 5

BRING IN THE GIRLS

Bobbing drunkenly back and forth, Alex and Vladimir grunted semi-intelligently, holding on to one another for support. Alex nearly lost his balance as he attempted to execute an oafish slap of Vladimir's back. Succeeding in hooking his arm around the burly Russian's neck, he hung on for support. Meanwhile, the shoulders on which he leaned began to shake with spasms; Vladimir was weeping.

"That is okay, Alex. It is okay," he blubbered in a coarse accent.

"What's okay?" Alex had no idea what he was talking about.

"I had to argue with you, my friend," he explained. "That is the way I am, a Russian. Our books, our music, every Russian loves the motherland. Even up here in space, I love her more than anything." Pausing for a moment to take another drink, he grasped Alex's head between his hands and looked the writer in the eyes. "We have gotten all bullshit out of the way. Man to man, no?"

Alex, still not quite sure what it was his friend was talking about, agreed, "Man to man. Right."

Vladimir clumsily patted Alex's cheek and leered, "So, we are having ourselves a very good time, no?"

"A good time. Oh, yes."

"Then tell me, my friend, where are the women? I demand that you bring out some women!" Vladimir was shouting.

Alex slipped his head out of Vladimir's hands and leaned against one of the chairs. "Women?"

"Of course, there must be women!"

Alex toyed with him. "Our women are nothing like you've ever had before. I'm not sure you can handle it."

Vladimir's eyed flared and he spread his arms out like a menacing bear. "I am Russian. Strong! With Tartar blood roiling wild in me. Give me two, three, a whole army of women. I'll show you what I can handle!"

Alex responded with equal vigor. "An army, yes." He reeled to the corner of the room and barked into an invisible comlink, "Genie."

A roughly seductive, female voice replied, "Yes, Alex."

"Please explain to my friend here how he might find a suitable companion for the remainder of the evening."

The corner wall slid away to reveal a large screen flanked by an imposing console. The voice addressed Vladimir coyly. "If you would be so kind, sir, to allow me a moment of intimacy." An anodized cylinder emerged from the console at chest level. Before Vladimir could figure out what he was supposed to do with such a small aperture, the computer asked him for a breath sample.

Alex, like a boss lauding his secretary, spoke proudly of the Ark's technology. "Genie here is our most advanced computer, updated with our latest experimental technology."

"You put so much into a machine for love?" asked a bewildered Vladimir.

"It's the best place to try our latest programming. If something goes wrong here, the worst that can happen is a bad date. Genie is almost to the point where she has artificial intelligence. When we've gotten all the bugs out, the same program will be used for applications on our other computers."

"Why the breath sample?" asked Vladimir.

"Genie analyzes for hormones and other physiological characteristics. The love of your life is probably based in large part on pheromones, biological attractors. Genie can also identify almost any communicable disease, including STDs. Almost everybody uses Genie as the first stage of medical care. If you've got a cold, Genie can identify the strain of bacteria or virus. It's all in the breath sample."

"How did you develop such a program?"

"In the 80s, I started selling primitive versions to American corporations to measure the level of toxic chemicals in expired breath. Advanced programs are still being used for all biological monitoring in American and European industry. I developed programs to track human metabolization with the same kind of program and now all of the Ark's nutritionists use the computer in order to perfectly balance each person's diet. Babies in our nursery rarely cry because the feeding machines dispense exactly what they need before they've even realized they're hungry. Genie even scans for allergies and ensures that each individual receives a hypoallergenic diet.

"The Israelis developed a similar technology for anti-terrorist applications. Computers analyzed the residue of a solvent shot into a suspect package, maybe a suitcase. If there were any explosive materials in the container, traces could be detected in the escaping air, carried by the solvent. They went so far that they even injected solvent into the tires of cars entering and leaving secured areas. When cars tried to leave an area inhabited by suspected terrorists, they would reanalyze the tires. Any change in the concentration of solvent in the interior of the tire was an indicator that the tires might be carrying explosives or smuggling contraband."

Alex couldn't judge by the look on Vladimir's face whether his friend was unconvinced or simply incoherent. "Maybe you don't believe everything I'm telling you, my friend. But if you blow into that tube, Genie's going to get you whatever you want."

Vladimir, still unconvinced that his breath had anything to do with sex, decided to humor Alex and blew into the tube with gusto. After the sample had been collected, the computer began questioning him about various body types by projecting faceless holographs of women with changing body parts: long legs, large shoulders, short torsos, high foreheads, small or wide hips, muscular or voluptuous derrieres, long hair or bobbed. The bodies before him were unclothed. Vladimir called out his preferences in rapid bursts of "Yes, yes," or "No! Never."

As the body types narrowed down, facial characteristics

began to appear: thick or thin lips, almond-shaped or wide-open eyes, blue or brown eyes, dark or light skin. Women from every part of the world began to appear before him. At this point, the images were no longer types, they were clearly holographs of real women, sampled by the computer. Vladimir marveled at the variety of women living on the Ark. As the image of each woman hovered before him, he could smell the woman's perfume, hear the rustle of her clothes. He was asked to comment on each woman's image, and the computer informed him that his voice was being analyzed to measure levels of excitement.

Finally, the women were dressed in different types of clothing, some so bizarre that Vladimir decided they must be costumes that excited some people sexually. Several of the women had their bodies completely covered in tattoos, the patterns interlocking like an intricate tapestry. Vladimir emphatically shook his head, crying, "No! No!" to these women.

The last image blurred away and Genie's voice addressed him, "I have selected fifty available women. Would you like to choose from the entire pool or shall I select a narrower sample for you?"

Vladimir hopped about with excitement. Fifty women, all guaranteed to be compatible with him! He found it difficult to believe. He made a grand gesture with his arm, like a sultan addressing his court, "Bring them all! This is a party! I will judge your taste for myself." Vladimir looked at Alex and saluted him crisply.

Alex nodded his head in approval. "Genie! You heard my friend."

The computer responded. "Alex, I will invite all fifty to meet with our Russian brother. However, I have chosen three women who will be considered your exclusive dates."

"Only three?" Vladimir intoned ironically.

The computer continued to process information for a few more moments. Soon, however, full holographic images of three women appeared before him. The computer named each woman: "Barbara, Katerina and Luz." Vladimir marveled at the beauty of each of them. They were not models or some other distant abstraction. They were beautiful for an unfathomable reason that Vladimir could not yet comprehend. It was something about the way the Barbara stood, something about the laugh lines around Katerina's mouth that made them stand out. For Luz, it was the intelligence that was readily apparent in her eyes. Their faces were like beacons that drew him to gaze at their features. Symbols below each image related personal interests and biographical information for each woman. Vladimir saw that all three of them spoke Russian.

"Each represents an aspect of your personality," Genie told him. "I believe your mood tonight makes you most compatible with Katerina. She currently has enough furlough time to join you aboard your space station, if that is your mutual desire. Whatever your decision, she will be available for the one thousand achievements that the party has been scheduled for. There is more than enough time for you to become acquainted with all of your guests."

"Thank you, Genie," Vladimir said, turning to Alex. "They even speak Russian."

"Of course," said Alex nonchalantly. "They are perfect matches."

"Perfect," mused Vladimir. "Who will you choose, Alex?"

Alex turned to the computer. "Genie. Select from my file. Indulge me with the exotic. I want Vladimir to see the scope of our women."

The computer paused for a few moments as it scanned its databanks. "Alex, Annette's daughter Amanda has arrived on leave from duty on the Moon Base. She has already requested an evening with you. I detect that you appeal to her as a father figure. Shall I invite her?"

Alex felt his face blushing, even though there was no way Vladimir could know how old Amanda was. Genie had accurately predicted his desire for an intimate relationship with his friend's daughter. Before her death five years earlier, Annette had asked Alex to look after her daughter. Since then, he had observed her request, watching over Amanda's education and eventual emigration to the Moon Base. He would be more than happy to chaperon her while she took her first leave from the Moon Base to see the Ark. He had only met her once, but had been immediately taken by her beauty and a personality that suggested maturity beyond her years.

Like her mother, she was tall and lithe, with straight blonde hair that caressed her shoulders. When she talked, her head and shoulders bounced from side to side, and she gestured with open hands, framing her face in the long webs of her thin fingers. She was quick to smile and her eyes were bright with mischievous energy. During that first meeting, he hadn't dared to believe that Amanda's suggestive looks had meant she was interested in him. He had occasionally hoped that he might meet her privately, but her presence on board the Ark presented him with his first real opportunity.

When he had first met Annette she, like Amanda, was twenty-four years old. She hadn't cared about his age, and he had fallen in love with her. Now he thought it natural that he should be interested in Amanda. She looked almost exactly like her mother, whom he had never stopped loving. As he thought about the past, he tried to think of how Amanda must see him. He figured that he was now something like seventy-five years old, but skin transplants and exercise made him appear to be no more than forty. No one kept solar time on the Ark and only the computer maintained statistics on chronologies, so that even Alex was unsure of his age. Even so, he figured that he probably looked better now than when he had met Annette while still in his forties. At that time he had been an overweight writer, struggling to make his voice heard. Annette had fallen in love with him despite his faults.

If he could judge by her dossier, he had more in common with Amanda than he had ever had with Annette. Amanda spoke Japanese, Russian, Spanish, Italian, French, German and English. She held Master's Degrees in Music, English and History. After her graduation from high school, she had used interactive computer programs to propel her through her undergraduate degree in languages in less than a year; she was a college graduate at seventeen. During her graduate work, she supported herself by giving bassoon lessons and writing a series of concertos that led to her first master's degree at age twenty-one. Again with the aid of computers and interactive video, she studied history and literature, earning her remaining degrees. She now performed with a symphony on the Moon Base, and was becoming a renowned composer.

Amanda's study of history made her partial to everything from the past. She loved to play classical pieces from the nineteenth and early twentieth century much more than the contemporary pieces popular with current symphony audiences. Alex thought that her interest in him might have something to do with her study of history, or maybe—he joked to himself—her love of antiques. She requested leave from the Moon Base in order to write a history of the Ark and she had been granted full access to the Ark's archives. Alex was proud of the fact that she hadn't needed his help in pushing her project through the Ark's historical commission. They authorized her work independent of his influence.

Alex had anticipated talking to Amanda at some point during her research and imagined that he might be able to speak to her informally as well. He secreted away his hopes that he might be able to entice her into a relationship like the one he had had with her mother. Now that Genie had paired them, he wondered if her keen intellect would sharpen her sensuality, accentuate the wildness and expertise of her mother. As he saw the hologram of Amanda before him, he was reminded of a nude portrait he had once painted of Annette, one of his most accomplished works. The image in the painting hadn't aged, even though he and Annette had. He wondered what it would be like to see that painting animated before him.

Alex instructed the computer to find larger accommodations for the party. Bulletins were to notify other occupants of the Ark that a *grande fête* was to be thrown in Vladimir's honor. "That should give you something to tell your fellow cosmonauts about, eh?"

"You are a generous man, Alex."

"To a fault, Vladimir," Alex quipped. He clapped his hands and addressed the computer, "Please prepare one advanced nap sequence for me and instruct Vladimir on how to participate." He spoke to Vladimir again, "Now you'll see how we stay awake for such extended entertainment."

Another panel opened to reveal a small console. Alex grabbed a headset and handed one of a different type to Vladimir, who noticed its similarity to the headset he used in his experiments. Alex placed the helmet-like basket of filaments over his head, explaining to Vladimir, "If you lived on the Ark, you wouldn't have to bother with electrode placement, but since you don't have implants, we'll have to set you up. I'll call in a technician."

"What are we going to do with these?"

"Don't worry. We're not starting on the ESP yet. We use a similar program to accelerate the dream state. We can get the equivalent of eight hours of sleep in one achievement."

"What is this achievement you keep referring to?"

"It's about fifteen minutes in Earth time. All time on the Ark is measured in achievement periods. Research has shown that most people are at their best for only small periods of time. We averaged out that amount of time to about fifteen minutes. Newcomers to the Ark use a rule of thumb to get used to it: four achievements is approximately an Earth hour; 100 is close to a day."

Alex finished fastening the electrode helmet to Vladimir's head. "Now don't worry about the R.E.M. accelerator," he assured him. "We've had people on this program for over one hundred thousand achievements with no negative side effects."

"Substitutes for champagne. Substitutes for love. Substitutes for sleep. Everything has been synthesized," moaned Vladimir.

"Feel my head, Vladimir," invited Alex. He pressed Vladimir's hand against the base of his skull. "Do you feel that bump?"

"Yes."

"That is the sender-receiver unit. Other implants

stimulate the occipital region for sight. There are others in different places for the remaining senses or memory. They're just under the skin, so in case of malfunction, they are easily replaced."

"Fantastic," marveled Vladimir. A uniformed technician appeared in the entrance and wordlessly began to complete Vladimir's connection to the system, placing electrodes on his chest and shoulders.

"Wait until you see what the women have done with this," Alex told him. "The technique of imbedding electrodes has become so commonplace that women have used the same method to implant precious stones in their skin. Amanda, the woman we saw on the screen, has diamond seams running down the back of her legs. When she walks her legs shimmer in the light. When you're close enough to touch legs like that, you can feel the texture of the stones. They're like the teeth of a file. If she decides to grab you, you can't get out without cutting yourself. Other women use magnets to lift where there is no longer any natural lift, if you know what I mean."

The two men laughed. "A well-placed magnet in a lover's body can do some amazing things, though. Especially if you've got a magnet yourself. The best thing, however, is the ease with which everything can be removed. You'll see some women tonight with what looks like the most painful kind of implants, in the eyelids, lips, genitals. But it's painless. You might even want to try it yourself."

Vladimir could not imagine a woman with gemstones implanted in her flesh. "What do these women look like with all of this?"

Images of wild costumes and extravagant make-up flooded Alex's memory. "The women here treat these parties as women in the seventeenth century treated invitations to the court. They allow themselves to become completely decadent, showing off their bodies in the latest fashions. It gets quite competitive. But everything is done with technology. All of our advances in computer applications are being used to make fashion statements. In some ways, despite our attempts at moderation, we're becoming like the Greeks and Romans, indulging ourselves."

The technician finished wiring Vladimir into the computer. With a word of thanks, Alex saw him out of the room and returned to sit by Vladimir. "See, I can move around the room with ease. If you stay here for a while, I'll help you get some implants."

Vladimir groaned jealously.

Alex egged him on. "I can watch a movie as I work. I can walk around the room, inputting data. I can instruct the computer to give me an instant nap. All without having to be tied into the console." He instructed the computer to begin the nap program. "Just relax, my friend, in one achievement, you will have had the best sleep of your life. You'll have beaten another addiction. There's no need to waste your life in a state of unconsciousness. When you wake up, you'll be ready for an experience I don't think you'll ever forget. Computer. Commence program."

Without having felt a thing, Vladimir was sound asleep, dreaming of women whose eyes shimmered like diamonds.

CHAPTER 6

AMANDA

Alex paused for a moment to watch Vladimir as he slept under the control of the Ark's computer. The Russian snored loudly, sounding like the great bear he had likened himself to only a few achievements ago. Alex took these moments alone to think through the plans he needed to make for the upcoming party, scheduled to last one thousand achievements, nearly ten earth days. As he considered whether or not to allow the computer to make all of the arrangements for entertainment and refreshments, he heard the doors swishing open behind him. Knowing it was too early for the party to start and that Genie kept the strictest standards regarding invitations and punctuality, he wondered who it might be. His heart leapt as he turned around to see the doors reveal Amanda, whose alarmingly sensual figure was embellished with a lascivious smile. Alex's heart continued to pound. Genie, he thought to himself, is probably enjoying seeing me shake like this.

For a few moments, neither he nor Amanda moved. Alex stood with a dumbfounded look, Amanda lithely smoldered in the doorway. Finally, she spun around with a tart pirouette, displaying both her outfit and her well-toned body. She wore a sheer lace blouse-coat that did almost nothing to cover her torso, the curve of her breasts fully revealed beneath the transparent material. A gold, heart-shaped locket hung around her neck. Her long legs spun into a small opaque sash that covered as little of her bottom as possible. The front of the sash was knotted into a small loincloth draped over her pubic mound.

"You like?" she asked him with a mischievous smile. Alex

nodded silently, admiring her perfectly muscled body. Amanda giggled and asked him if he thought she had her mother's legs.

"Just like your mother," he grunted in agreement as she continued to gyrate in suggestive circles.

"I know you love red so I thought I'd wear rubies tonight," she cooed to him. For a moment, she stopped spinning and turned her backside to him. A line of scarlet gemstones rose unbroken from her heels to her thighs, disappearing into the folds of the skimpy sash.

"Don't you just love the way they go all the way up to the cheeks of my ass?" she asked, flipping up her skirt to illustrate. "And how about my toes?"

Alex looked down and saw that she had tiny rubies embedded in her toenails as well. From the opening of a seven-inch stiletto pump that glowed with red metallic urgency emerged small whorls of the gemstones, duplicating the shapes of various galaxies. Alex raised his eyes to look into her face, her creamy skin set against pale golden hair, its tresses brushed up into strands punctuated by rows of sapphires and rubies. In the center of her forehead, a phalanx of rubies formed a small triangle that disappeared into her hair. These stones were echoed in light lines of smaller gems placed behind her eyelids, their somber but dazzling shades contrasting with the bright crystalline blue of her eyes, which stood out like two beacons of intense blue light.

Amanda walked closer to him, continuing her knowing banter. "You know, there is one thing that isn't anything like my mother," she said, mocking a sad child's frown.

"What's that?" he asked, unable to think clearly. He could not take his eyes from the languorous pendulum of her sash, which dangled hypnotically between her legs.

"These," she said with a giggle, heaving her chest up. Alex felt as if he had been slammed up against a wall as her enormous breasts pressed into him. Annette's chest had been so flat she could have been mistaken for a boy, but her daughter's bosom stretched taught the transparent fabric of her blouse. Alex wanted to ask her if it was surgery but decided he couldn't collect himself enough to speak coherently.

Amanda ended his wonder without a trace of embarrassment. "It's just amazing what a few doses of the right hormones can do. All a girl needs is a few shots and the right man sucking on them. It works miracles."

"Miracles," repeated Alex, amazed to find himself able to say something that made sense.

"I just couldn't live with the thought of going through life with those sad little things I had before. So tell me the truth, Alex. Do you like them?" She lifted them up to him with her hands, searching his face for a sign of approval.

Alex was about to answer but found his tongue stopped when he saw her nipples, each standing erect and pierced with a thin gold ring. She followed his eyes, realizing that he was shocked by her piercings.

"Oh, aren't those just lovely," she said teasingly, raising her eyes to his. "And they make me so sensitive."

Alex groaned.

"Especially," she continued, practically moaning, "when I'm ready to come. It feels like thousands of little needles prickling me. I want to die."

She grabbed Alex by the chin and pretended to scold him. "Speak up, Alex. You're so quiet. Don't you like me even a little bit?" She pretended to pout like a little girl. "Have I done something bad? Did you like Mommy's tits better?" She turned around and stuck out her hips. "Maybe you want to spank me because I've been so bad. But I just want you to like me."

She faced him again, placing her hand on his crotch, squeezing lightly. "Oh," she exclaimed, "I think you must like me a little bit. You're so hard. I think if I reach in there, you'll be a little wet, too."

Alex continued to stand before her, transfixed by this unexpected display.

"Kiss me," she directed. "Mom said that's what you do best." Alex remained motionless. Amanda's face puckered aggressively. "Kiss me, you fucker," she commanded.

Alex finally responded with a smile, still refusing to make any move towards kissing her. Amanda laughed and faked a Texas drawl, "Don't forget, pard'ner. I've got your number."

Still smiling, Alex reached out and took her face in his hands, gazing steadily at her. He felt his eyes beginning to tear up. She looked so much like her mother, he felt like he had been sent back thirty years. She pushed herself up against him and he leaned forward to kiss her. She parted her lips to accept the tip of his tongue with which he tickled the inside of her mouth. She opened her mouth wide in a gesture of submission, her tongue throbbing against his, wanting him to thrust deeper into her throat. But he teased her, giving her only enough to make her want him more.

He slid his hand under the fabric of her blouse and tugged lightly on one of her nipple rings. She exhaled with pleasure and he bit her lip, which made her shiver with equal parts surprise and delight. He flicked his forefinger at her other nipple and felt her leap back, overcome by the intensity of the stimulation. He hugged her close to him and thrust his hand under her black sash, where he passed his fingers through her finely curled pubic hair. He also felt light bumps where Amanda had implanted more gemstones around her clitoris, which felt like a slippery almond as he pressed his fingers against it with a circular motion.

Her kiss turned into small bites as she struggled to free her mouth to breathe. Alex slowly pulled his tongue back, allowing her to take only a little air at first, then letting her breathe deeply. Her pupils were dilated with excitement, glazed over as if they stood in pools of clear wax.

He flicked his tongue at her lips and smiled, mimicking her drawl in a deep, husky voice. "Don't forget, partner, I've got your number, too." Just as she started to smile, he thrust his finger into her as far as he could, sliding it up and down rapidly.

She gasped in ecstasy, sighing, "Alex, I can see why Mom liked you."

"Not as much as you're going to like me," he replied.

Amanda began to shudder. "Fuck me," she said in a far away voice. "Please fuck me."

Alex turned his head and snapped out, "Genie, help." The floor under them slid open and they gently collapsed into a slide that dropped them quickly onto a cushioned floor. As she slid down, Amanda cried out in an Indian war whoop, passing her hand back and forth over her mouth. The aperture from which the slide issued closed itself, leaving them alone in a room constructed entirely of windows, from which they could see the earth, moon and stars. The far reaches of space stretched out before them, stars and planets sparkling in the black void like a billion tiny candles in an enormous dark room.

Alex looked into Amanda's eyes, the light of the stars reflected in her irises. "Isn't it romantic?" he asked.

Amanda laughed and tried to wrestle Alex onto his back. "You're so strong," she said. "Such powerful shoulders. I'm going to love this."

Alex bowled her over onto her back, but she asked him to wait, retrieving her purse from the bottom of the slide where it had landed. She reached in and removed a small cylinder. "I got this from a friend on the black market," she explained. "It's XSY in aerosol form." Alex approached to examine it closely, but before he reached her, she sprayed him in the face. Instantly, he was overcome with a sensation of weightlessness. He watched dazedly as she misted herself with the can.

Her eyes took on a feline quality and he was unable to look away. Every muscle in his body tensed as if he were about to leap into the air. He felt the blood in his temples pulsing wildly. He heard a loud, animal-like groan, but realized that Amanda had not made a sound. It had been his voice sounding as if it had come from another part of the room.

Without knowing how it happened, he found Amanda's legs wrapped around his back, his legs pushing him deep inside of her. Her firm breasts rubbed against his chest, the rings catching against his nipples. Her pussy gripped his cock tightly, her hips pressing hard against him so that he could not break away. He was overcome by the feeling that he must get out, withdraw from her, but there was no way to escape her hold. A wave of anxiety passed over him and he felt like a man descending the crest of an icy hill on a runaway sled. He was certain he was going to die and screamed with horror before he realized that he was, in fact, in ecstasy. He pounded into her furiously, abandoning any vestige of control. He could not tell if he was flying or falling.

Amanda began to slither beneath him, moaning, "Oh, fuck! Alex! I'm coming. Oh, God, I'm coming." He felt himself release a torrent of warmth into her and she writhed wildly in response.

Alex stopped moving, and tried to wipe the sweat from his eyes. He didn't realize that he was crying until his body began to buzz with minute trembles. For the first time, he had surrendered completely, lost himself in a woman's body. He began sobbing deeply, Amanda clinging to him as wave after wave of orgasm swept over her. She tasted his tears on her tongue as another climax flooded her body. They passed from this moment of ecstasy to oblivion, falling asleep before they could comprehend anything but the physical sensation of their bodies against one another.

When he awoke, Alex breathed in the perfume of their sex together. It seemed as if every inch of his skin was scented with Amanda's cassolette, a sweetly pungent fragrance. Amanda opened her eyes and spoke softly. "Pretty good stuff, Alex?"

"Dynamite," he said. "I had no idea XSY could be like that."

"Aerosol's a little better than oral, huh?"

"God, yes," he agreed. "You felt so tight, I thought you were going to press me into a string bean."

"Just something I learned at school," she purred.

Alex laughed. "I never would've thought we'd be here together. I first saw you when you were two years old. I never imagined."

"I did," she said playfully.

"You were two," protested Alex. "How could you?"

"I remember the first time you came over to our house. I swear." She was serious now. "Mom was trying to watch T.V. while she was talking on the phone. She got pissed off because we were watching some show about the effect of solar winds on the earth."

"Your mother was drunk," Alex recalled. "She was angry because we changed the channel from one of her soap operas when she left the room to get the phone. When she came back she was hysterical."

"Why didn't you marry her?" she asked him. "She loved you so much. You would have been a great father."

Alex found it hard to tell her, felt tears welling up behind his eyes again. "I really missed not being with you. Your grandfather thought I was a dreamer, and in a lot of ways your mother agreed with him. She never understood what I was trying to do, didn't think about things the way I did."

"And you think I'm intellectual enough for you?"

"Yes, actually," he said, thinking of her academic life. "All your mother wanted to do was screw and have a good time."

Amanda grabbed his ear with her teeth. "And what do you think I'm interested in? Music?" She released his ear and rolled onto her back, raising her legs so that they formed a "V" in the air.

Alex shook his head and smiled. "Aren't you the perfect whore?"

"That's what my friends say." She held her position. "What are you waiting for. If I can believe what I've heard, you should be ready for more." She lifted her head to get a good look at his crotch. "Oh, my," she exclaimed, "you didn't even need another shot of XSY."

She tumbled over to him and brought her face close to his. "Kiss me. I love the way you kiss me." Before he could do anything, she growled, "I can't wait until you let me suck your fat cock."

"Keep talking that way and I'll let you suck anything you like."

"Oooh," she cooed knowingly, "did Mommy talk dirty, too?"

Alex felt his face growing hot. Annette must have told Amanda everything. Now her daughter was competing with her, trying to do her mother one better. As if to prove him right, Amanda said, "I bet Mom could never get you this hard."

Alex teased her back, "I'm in love with your mind, Amanda. That's all."

"Bullshit," she cried, leaning back to give him a good look at her body. "I know you love my tits," she said. "And poor you. You haven't even had a chance to suck on them."

They laughed at one another and began gamboling about until they were interrupted by Genie, who informed Alex that his guests were arriving. "Vladimir has been asking for you," she said. He's been awake for some time now and he's getting anxious without you."

Alex had completely forgotten about Vladimir. "Try and explain to my friend that I am indisposed at the moment and I'll be with him in four or five achievements. Can you try and get him off to a good start without me?"

"Yes," Genie responded. "I will inform him of your circumstances. He has just begun dancing. That seems to be working better than anything I could do for him. He appears to be enjoying the women I selected for him."

"I never doubted that he would," said Alex.

Genie reaffirmed that everything was under control and signed off. Alex was glad that his time spent with Amanda hadn't affected the outcome of the party. Still, he thought he'd better get ready. "How about a shower?" he asked Amanda.

"I wouldn't miss a shower with the greatest mind in the universe," she said. "But first, I've got a little surprise for you."

"A surprise?" A look of concern passed over Alex's face.

"Don't worry," she said. "I think you'll like it." She pulled the locket from the chain around her neck and handed it to him. The first thing he noticed was his name engraved in the center, surrounded by a pattern of rubies. From each side of the heart emerged a post encrusted with rubies. Under his name was a small keyhole.

"Is it some kind of lock?" he asked her.

"Yes," she replied shyly. "I've been thinking about you for quite some time."

"Is this what I think it is?" he inquired, surprised that she had gone to such lengths.

Instead of answering him she told him she wanted to go steady with him.

"Go steady?" He was incredulous. "Isn't that for high schoolers?"

"It's something like that," she said. "It's all the rage on the Moon. Probably here, too. You really ought to keep up." She curled her arms around him. "I want you to put it on me after we shower."

"Once I put it on, how do I open it later?"

"Just ask Genie."

"Genie!" Alex shouted. He couldn't believe Amanda had already involved herself in a romantic caper with the Ark's computer.

The computer responded to his sudden outburst, "Yes, Alex?"

Taking a moment to recover, Alex dismissed Genie with an, "Oh, never mind," and asked Amanda to explain how she had gotten involved with Genie.

"Genie's told me all about you," she said. "I've had a crush on you for the longest time and she thought we'd be perfect together. She's the one who controls the locket."

"I think I've been manipulated," moped Alex.

"Well, why don't we take a shower and see if we can get this thing to work. I think you might enjoy a little manipulation."

Alex gruffly acceded, getting dressed in preparation for the shower. Amanda replaced her blouse and sash, stepping lightly into her shoes. When they were both fully clothed, he led her into a smaller chamber, the portal closing tightly behind them. The room filled with perfume and light; mesmerizing tones began to buzz around them. A computer asked them what type of clothing they wore.

They took a moment to check the tags on each other's outfits and then replied, "Seventy-five."

The chamber erupted in a momentary burst of water and chemicals, followed by a gush of dry air. Just as quickly, the doors opened and they found themselves clean and dry, their clothes perfectly free of wrinkles.

Amanda seemed a little disappointed. "I'm not so sure that's so much better than the old showers. It seems like something's missing. Hot steam. Time spent just listening to the rush of water as it splashes onto your face."

"Well," laughed Alex, "I suppose it beats having to go to the dry cleaners."

Amanda giggled in response. "I think we should find out about this locket, don't you?"

"I'm not sure I know what this thing's going to do?" said Alex, feigning ignorance.

"Try your imagination," she said.

"I have," he said. "And I don't see you being able to give up sexual liberation, or whatever it is you people on the Moon Base call it."

"I never said I was going to," she replied quickly. "I'm just giving up the best part for you. No one else will be able to have me the way you can."

"And what do I have to give up," he asked her, still unsure of the direction in which they were heading.

"Just thinking about me should be enough for you. I'm not asking for anything in return." She pulled a small golden ring from her purse. "If you wear this," she explained, "Genie will know we're together and give you control of the locket. We can make a contract for as long or as little as you like."

"So this is the new way?" he asked. "This is what you want?"

"I'm sure," she said, smiling broadly. "Don't you just love it?"

She sat down and opened her legs to him. Beneath the sash, he saw that her pubic hair had been combed into place around rows of ruby implants. She reached down and pulled her labia apart, exposing a small piercing on each side. She took the locket from Alex and inserted the ruby posts into the holes. "I want you to close it," she told Alex. He pressed down on the heart and felt the posts draw her labia together with a mechanical click.

"You and Genie had better take care of me, Alex," she said. Otherwise, I'll have to find some way to cut it off."

"Don't worry," he told her. "I'll take care of you."

"You're the only one who can open it, Alex. The only one."

"Don't worry," he said. "Don't worry."

CHAPTER 7

MEETING TANYA

Alex and Amanda emerged from their chamber amid a huge crowd of people. The women were festooned in extravagant costumes and exotic makeup. Men were dressed in formal uniforms of the finest cloth. As they rose from the sub-floor chamber, they attracted no attention and the loud chatter from the main room dissipated the amorous temper of their moments alone together.

They quickly acclimated themselves to the public affair. Amanda took Alex by the hand and began to lead him briskly through the crowd. She wanted him to meet a woman named Tanya, whom she described as her "very best friend in the world." She told Alex that Tanya, like a lot of other young people, had read everything Alex had written. His books, especially *Everyone Can Become a Genius*, were required reading in many university psychology classes. English, Composition and Rhetoric instructors used his books to illustrate techniques of creative structure. "She thinks you're brilliant," Amanda told him.

Alex was wary of meeting Tanya. Coming face to face with the young people who read his work was often a trying experience. Alex never felt that they completely understood him, and on occasion their statements made him sure that they were actually misinterpreting his work. Despite their inability to grasp the finer points of his vision, however, he usually found his youthful adherents entertaining and interesting. He wondered what Tanya would be like. If she was a friend of Amanda's, she must be something out of the ordinary.

"Did you know I failed every class in Composition I ever

took?" he asked Amanda.

"Really?"

"From high school to college. I was the dunce."

Amanda continued to crane her neck, scanning the room for a sign of Tanya. "I find that hard to believe. I would've thought you were some kind of brain in school."

His early difficulties with higher education never failed to make Alex peevish. "All those years in college seemed more like a struggle to keep from being eliminated instead of a challenge to succeed," he said crabbily. "The professors seemed to be happier giving out D's instead of A's, never saying anything positive about anything I did. They harped on grammar and spelling instead of just letting people write." He chuckled to himself. "I guess when I got that job as a Lecturer at the University of Arizona in Flagstaff, I probably pissed a few people off."

"You failed Composition and became a professor? That sounds good to me."

"That job paid off pretty well," he said. "I made a lot of good political connections and the university position gave me the time and credibility to travel all over the world. Being able to tell people you're an academic gives you a certain mystique."

Amanda poked fun at him, "Yes, indeed, Professor Abramawitz. Anyway, I want you to be nice to Tanya. She's a little sensitive about being black, but . . ."

"She's black?" interrupted Alex, who seemed startled by this information.

"Yes, she's black. But I sometimes think that she thinks she's white. She's a little weird that way." Amanda grew concerned. "I hope you're not prejudiced, Alex. I really want you to like her. She means the world to me."

Sensing something different about Amanda's relationship with Tanya, Alex pressed farther. "So how much of a friend is she?"

Amanda covered her face with her hand, smiling into her fingers. "She's my lover."

Alex tried to cover up his momentary discomfort with

this revelation by smiling. His mind raced trying to figure out how he really felt about Amanda's relationship with another woman. He looked at her carefully, awed by her beauty and youth. What a fool he was! He was like a man under the spell of a sorceress, agreeing to anything she liked. He was no longer himself, though he heard his voice speaking. He felt as if he had been drugged because he heard the words coming from a far-off place. "Well, that doesn't bother me," said the voice. "Just as long as we're together."

Even as he spoke, the words rang untrue. He was lying, he supposed, to please her. He was old-fashioned at heart and the caprices of the younger generations, he was afraid to admit, troubled him. He could kick himself for being such a hypocrite! Every day he asked people to share his vision for change, to let down their guard and accept new interpretations of morality and social responsibility. Yet when it came to accepting the idea of Amanda and Tanya together, he found himself just as provincial as the people he railed against.

"Oh, Alex, don't get me wrong," explained Amanda, sensing Alex's discomfort. "I love men. But Tanya and I have something special. She's like my sister, friend and mother all rolled up into one beautiful person."

"That sounds great," said Alex, unconvincingly.

"What bothers you, Alex? Is it that she's black?"

"No, I love black people. I swear." He began to rant nervously, trying to cover up his anxiety over her bisexuality. "I'm totally color-blind just like everyone on the Ark. I swear."

Amanda was clearly disappointed with his response. She took Alex's hand. "Just promise me you'll show her a nice time here."

"I promise," he said, sure that he could at least be cordial to her.

"Just don't go too far out of your way," said Amanda, squeezing his hand and giggling naughtily. Alex hadn't even considered that. The huge thump of a bass drum sounded in the next room and waves of people flowed toward the dance floor. Amanda told Alex she would look for Tanya on her own;

he should take the opportunity to look for Vladimir. She waved goodbye and disappeared into a throng of revelers as if she were disappearing into a fog bank. A moment ago she had been holding his hand and now she was gone. What was happening to him? He already missed her.

He began to circulate, making small talk among the guests but unable to take his mind off Amanda. Despite all of his talk about sexual freedom and experimentation, the idea of her relationship with another woman disturbed him, especially with a black woman. He decided to have a drink, a bit of a pick-me-up, and headed over to a kiosk where beverages were being poured from a canary yellow dispenser. As soon as he took a sip of the colorless fluid, he felt much better, his mind jumping back just far enough to remember his romp with Amanda and forget about everything else.

As he wandered away from the bar he noticed a group of people clustered around a tall, undeniably beautiful woman he had never seen before. Her skin was dark with the lustre of burnished ebony. She was standing against a wall, addressing two men with wild gesticulations. Alex walked closer to them, wondering if this might be Tanya. As if on cue, the party of three laughed simultaneously and the woman's bright smile radiated a warmth and humor that invited Alex to approach. She turned her head toward him and nodded, as if she had expected him to find her.

Before Alex could speak to her, one of the men clapped him on the back with an, "Alex, old man, how're you doing?" He faced the man and discovered he was Rick Page, one of the Ark's ubiquitous socialites. Hardly an event passed without Rick mingling, slapping people on the back and smiling. He was known for standing on one leg like a stork and leaning over so that, not unlike the leaning tower of Pisa, one believed he was about to topple over. On many occasions, tired by Rick's trying humor and obvious toadying, Alex had thought about giving Rick the firm poke that would send him tumbling to the ground.

As Rick smiled at him with an unnerving look of blithe joy, Alex wondered if the man was laughing at him or trying to count his teeth. Encounters with Rick were at the very least uncomfortable. Nonetheless, Alex extended his hand. "Fine, Rick, fine. I'm glad you could come."

With a hint of nervousness, Rick fiddled with a pair of eyeglasses suspended on a silver chain around his neck. "Oh, I say. I didn't realize it was your party, Alex." Although no one on the Ark needed glasses because of the Arkian opthamological innovations, Rick affected the look of a nebbish banker, fiddling with the chain or chewing on the earpiece during conversation.

Alex, taking a cue from Rick's obvious discomfort at his social disadvantage, said, "Oh, yes, it's in honor of a friend of mine from the Russian space station. Perhaps you know Vladimir Susoeff? He's one of their top researchers."

"Oh, no," said Rick, nibbling on his glasses, "can't say I've met the chap." In addition to his other quirks, Rick, born in Dayton, Ohio, and transplanted to Venice, California, tried to pass himself off as English gentry.

"Oh, well, I'll see if I can arrange something then. I'm sure he'd love to meet you," offered Alex with aggressive largess.

Rick, scrambling to return to his normal modus operandi, began to introduce Alex to the other members of his party. "Alex, this is Gene Burns." Alex shook hands with the man. "Claims to be a botanist even though he's only been with us a week. He's working in Plant Engineering and despite the fact that he looks like a young whippersnapper, he's got a list of credentials a mile long." Rick laughed loudly, self-aware of his own sense of humor.

"Pleased to meet you," said Alex. The man, apparently unfazed by Rick's behavior, nodded in response.

"And this lovely creature," said Rick in a voice reminiscent of a beauty pageant emcee, "is our latest and most beautiful addition to the Ark's crew." With a broad sweep of his arm, he intoned, "Miss Tanya Shannon, in Business Administration." Rick shot Alex a lewd wink.

Alex ignored him and introduced himself to Tanya. As he shook her hand, he was struck by the power of her grip, his eyes noticing that her arms, and indeed the rest of her body, were finely muscled. Her tight dress revealed the physique of a body builder. Alex cast his glance down to an abdomen that looked like a washboard. Her skin was silky and dark, but it seemed to glow, making it seem lighter than it was. The white fabric of her dress accentuated the rich tones that undulated around the sinuous ripples of her musculature.

His attention was drawn back to her face as she gave him another dazzling smile, telling him she had been looking forward to meeting him. Her open, friendly face was so engaging that it took him a moment to notice that she was completely bald; only an intricate pattern of gemstones covered her scalp. Matching earrings clung to the lobes of her ears. Still, as he continued to stare at her unabashedly, there was something not entirely human about her. She seemed to possess some kind of animal quality that Alex could not specifically name. When she spoke again—her voice laden with husky, Southern overtones—and mentioned Amanda's name, Alex realized what it was: she had used a special process to change the shape and appearance of her eyes so that they glowed with a cat-like quality. Her corneas appeared as diamond slits, her irises a luminescent yellow.

Alex told her, yes, Amanda had mentioned her name. Tanya smiled broadly. Alex wondered if she already knew what had happened. She continued to speak in a low voice, but Alex was unable to think about anything but Amanda wrapped around this woman's body, the two of them engaged in impossibly erotic acts. The phrase "She's my lover!" repeated again and again in his mind. He realized that Tanya was asking him a question, waiting for a response, but he found himself unable to answer, even as Rick, trying to resuscitate him, gave him a quick poke in the ribs.

CHAPTER 8

After a few tentative attempts at conversation, Alex inquired as to whether or not Tanya was interested in joining him for a little nourishment. Declaring she was famished, she took Alex by the arm and allowed herself to be led out of the party. They walked briskly to the cafeteria, Tanya admitting that she really was quite hungry, having missed her last two meals.

"I'm sure I'll get a lecture from Carl about balanced meals and all that," she said. "These computers don't miss anything."

"I just spent about sixteen achievements drinking and drugging myself with the Russian I just told your little social clique about. And after that, our mutual friend Amanda spritzed me with some bootleg concoction."

"She loves that stuff," replied Tanya, apparently unaffected by the implications of Amanda spraying Alex with XSY.

"And here I am now," Alex complained, "having missed three scheduled feedings. Carl probably won't let me back into the party."

"I wouldn't worry about that," said Tanya confidently. "I'm sure he'll come up with some formula to get you back where you want to be."

They passed into a large, brightly lit chamber. Close to a hundred people sat around tables of various sizes, but most of the room was empty. The majority of this sector's inhabitants were down the hall at the party or on a shift that required them to be at work. Around the sides of the communal room were private cubicles, each equipped with a video monitor. A few groups of people could be seen in these rooms, either chatting with one another or focused intently on the entertainment fed into the monitors.

"I always manage to run into someone I know at the cafeteria," said Tanya. "I'm glad the Ark kept the cafeteria going, even though we're all just munching on mush. It's still something of a social event."

"You think we might run into Amanda?" asked Alex, hoping he might get to see the two women together.

Tanya laughed. "Knowing her, she's probably in the arms of half a dozen young studs. You must not know her very well."

"I guess not." Alex tried not to react to the blow Tanya had dealt him.

"She doesn't work the machines too much, but she's a natural athlete. I've never seen anybody who could have sex as long as she does. She's like a marathoner."

"Are you trying to make me angry, or jealous?" asked Alex, trying to make a joke at the expense of his own bruised ego.

"Oh, you're not having a good time with me?" retorted Tanya playfully. "I think all you need's a little something to eat and a little time to take a snooze and you'll be just fine." She snorted out a little laugh. "I'll take care of you, Alex. Don't worry."

She's coming on to me, thought Alex. First Amanda, now Tanya. He wasn't sure what to make of it. As they approached the dietary analysis area, Alex considered Tanya's offer. He couldn't stop looking at her. Her body, perfectly shaped, was like a negative of Amanda's creamy white physique. He wondered if Amanda wanted him to get involved with Tanya. After all, she had left him free to become intimate with anyone he pleased. She had practically suggested that he spend time with Tanya when they were at the party. Was he struggling to keep himself out of an addictive cycle or was he confusing lust with love? His mind was refusing to make sense of the issues. He decided he probably just needed some food and a talk with Carl.

Tanya clasped his hand in hers. "Alex, after we eat, do you mind if we do a little shopping? I'd like to get something interesting to wear after our nap. A little something to get your mind off Amanda."

"You want me to forget her already?"

"Honey, after I'm through with you, you won't even remember her name." She wrapped her arm around his neck, brushing her head against his shoulder. Alex was surprised at how natural her attraction to him seemed. Only a few moments ago, he hadn't even known this woman, and now she was offering to sleep with him. Despite the fact that it made little sense, he enjoyed the feel of her body, the feeling that he was desirable.

They entered the cafeteria testing area. Breathing tubes like the one on Genie's console emerged from a similar control bank. Breath samples were analyzed for nutritional imbalances and appropriate nutrients were added to a paste-like substance presented in either plain white bowls or thin tubes for people on the go. Alex spoke his name and the computer whirred for a brief instant, calling up his nutritional records from its databanks.

"You have missed some feeding sequences, Alex," said the computer, whom everyone called Carl.

"It's nice to know you care, Carl," answered Alex. He breathed into the tube and waited for Carl's prescription.

Normally, the paste was issued without delay, but as Carl scanned Alex's breath sample, his memory banks seemed unable to process the combination of drugs Alex had imbibed. Alex figured it was probably the aerosol XSY that threw him off. The newest black market products took time to find their way into the Ark's computers. Alex wondered when Carl would be outfitted with a free association program like the ones developed from research in the children's creativity nursery. Once Carl began thinking, something only a few of the computers aboard the Ark were starting to do, it would be much more difficult to fool him. As the warm green and amber lights on Carl's panel flashed chaotically, Alex allowed himself to relax: Carl was not going to find him out. He loved putting one over on the computer.

Finally, Carl spoke. "Hummmmmmm," his famous indicator of dissatisfaction. "Well, Alex," intoned Carl like a family doctor, "I show a very bad chemical imbalance. You've missed feeding sequences and you have so badly depleted your body's reserve nutrients that you are beginning to draw from critical body tissue. It is a wonder that you are not wasting away."

"That bad, huh, Carl?"

"You are low on anti-oxidants, choline, calcium, tocopherol, linoleic, linolenic anachadonic acids, potassium, cobalt, phosphorus, selenium, zinc, inositol, folacin, biotin, pyridoxine and thiamine."

"And just what does that mean?"

"This pattern indicates tissue absorption of a new drug compound, XSY 7550, a tranquilizer synthesized with a toxic aerosol, freon chlorodiazamine."

Alex was stunned. Carl already knew about the bootlegged drug! Even worse was his prescription: "Alex, I am going to have to ground you for at least ten feeding sequences."

"Wait a minute, Carl," Alex protested, his anxiety causing him to use earth time-terminology, a psychological slip that Carl would be sure to pick up on. "How did you even know about the new XSY compound?"

"It is no big secret," Carl replied flatly. "Rick Page and the Ark Syndicate have been exporting it to the Earth for quite some time. In fact, my analysis of impurities in your system indicates that the dose you had came from an Earth manufacturer. You have taken a cheap imitation."

If he'd had an imitation, Alex wondered what pure XSY must be like. But he continued to press Carl for information. "Since when do you have access to such information before I do?"

"Alex, you helped program me. I am a health care professional, and that profession requires me to keep abreast of the latest developments. I used the on board science interlink and my medical research status to open up a few confidential files in the Syndicate databanks."

"And that's in keeping with your medical ethics?"

"I have a duty to everyone on the Ark to monitor all developments that might affect metabolic efficiency."

Alex was impressed by this defense, wondering what Carl's intellectual dexterity might be like when he was upgraded to full artificial intelligence. Carl continued to dispense advice.

"Alex, at your age you might want to consider taking it easy when it comes to new drugs. At any rate, you will be fine once I get your system back in balance. There has been no permanent damage, but I will need to monitor closely all of your feeding sessions for the remainder of the probationary period."

Alex accepted this information stoically. "I'm impressed with your abilities, Carl. I really thought I had you on this one. But let me ask you, since your sources are so good, if you know how much additional revenue the Ark is getting from the new XSY compound?"

Carl's memory banks flashed for a few moments. "Exact information regarding those figures is classified, but most data indicates that the figure is close to five billion dollars per ten thousand achievements. Rick Page is in charge of the operation and has received several commendations on his work."

"No wonder Rick's been so cocky," Alex thought out loud.

"Actually, Alex," replied Carl, "Rick is not aware of the financial success of the project. He merely sets up the transactions and the systems that manufacture and distribute the product. The Treasury Office manages the financial ends. The Separation of Powers policy does not allow Rick access to that information."

"But you have it, Carl."

"Yes, but I cannot reveal my sources."

Alex banked all of this information in order to sort it out later. He decided to concern himself with the near future. "So, you want to take me out of the party until I'm in balance?"

"Yes."

"What's the soonest that might be? I could accelerate my routines, increase exercise levels and you could crowd my feedings. What then?"

"Hummmmmmm," Carl thrummed away. "I estimate that increasing exercise, sleep and chemical concentrations by a factor of five would allow you to return to your life of abandon within thirty to thirty-five achievements."

"That sounds wonderful, Carl. Tanya and I will eat and take a nap and then spend time exercising in Zero-G." He prodded Tanya playfully at the word "exercise." "Then perhaps a movie followed by more rest and exercise. What do you think, Carl?" Alex hoped his anxiousness to return to the party was not overly apparent; Carl might ground him for addictive behavior. Although he wanted to deny that he was acting like an addict, he knew it was true. Amanda was already controlling him in ways he hadn't anticipated.

"I have adjusted your security clearance and scanned your enzyme rates to ensure that you will be able to absorb the increased chemical dose. You will be required to extend your sleeping periods, taking care to allow for clearance of synaptic gaps to get rid of the toxic material that may have bonded to any transmitter neurons."

"And what about my friend here?" asked Alex, indicating Tanya, who stepped up and blew into the console. Carl's circuits whirred with desultory indifference, as if to show his disapproval for the toxins he knew he would find.

"Her reading is almost as bad as yours. I am seeing more and more of these XSY cases. You will have a partner in your extended naps."

Alex felt that he might cry tears when he heard that Tanya was in equally poor shape. She would need to recuperate with him. "Thank you, Carl. You have a wonderful bedside manner."

"I appreciate the compliment. Enjoy your meal."

Alex and Tanya took their bowls of paste and headed off to a private table, sitting under the glow of a large video monitor. Alex was still bemused at the life-like and informal quality of Carl's program, a personality he had suggested at the outset of the Ark's construction. He was happy to have given the most advanced technology an engagingly human face. It seemed like Carl had understood his desire to return to the party. Simulated or not, his acquiescence satisfied Alex.

He began to look forward to seeing Amanda again. His heart began to pound. She had left him at the party as if she didn't care when she saw him again, but Alex had a feeling that she, like him, was a fish caught on a line. Either one of them could be reeled into the other with luck and cunning.

As they ate, he smiled at Tanya, wondering what she was thinking about him. She returned his smile with an immense, cat-like grin, her yellow eyes flashing dangerously. She shook her head so that her diamond skullcap glittered in the light. Almost as Tanya had predicted, he began to forget about Amanda.

"You're incredible," he told her.

She lifted her hands to her face, striking a model's pose. "Do you really think so?"

Alex saw the well-defined ripple of her arm muscles, his eyes travelling down to reconnoiter the spectacle of her armor-like abdomen. "Stunning," he asserted. "I should take lessons from you and forget about the computers in the shaping rooms."

"Those computers did it for me." She considered for a moment. "That and genetics, I suppose."

"It must be genetics," griped Alex.

"Oh, come on," she said. "You've got the sexiest legs I've ever seen on a man." She narrowed her eyes. "They look pretty strong to me, too. Your chest and arms are impressive. You're a powerful man."

Alex smiled, mildly embarrassed at the compliment he had been fishing for. "There must be something amazing in this food Carl gave me. I'm starting to feel horny again. I wonder what'll happen once I finish all of it."

"My mother always told me to take care of a man's tummy first and the rest will take care of itself."

"Yeah," replied Alex. "Feed him and spray a little XSY in

his face."

"Isn't that stuff wonderful," gushed Tanya. "Amanda and I met this terribly attractive guy at a party. Actually, it was Rick Page. I guess you know him."

"I might have figured it was Rick," groaned Alex.

"He gave us some, but he didn't tell us he was manufacturing it. I probably wouldn't have believed him anyway. But he did say he was a friend of yours."

"He did?" Alex was surprised at the depths to which Rick would sink.

"He said you two were inseparable. And he was so funny. He kept us in stitches all the time." Tanya said funny "fuhn-nee," drawling it out in her broad Southern accent.

Alex felt himself flushing with jealousy. "Yeah, a real card." He forced himself to say the words with as little sarcasm as possible.

Tanya apparently didn't notice, going on with her story. "Oh, I tell you," she giggled, "when we took a hit of that XSY, we went crazy. I thought I was turning into a wild animal. Rick'll never forget that night."

Alex's face was twisted like an apoplectic's. Tanya realized something was wrong. "What is it, Alex?"

"Nothing," he said unconvincingly.

Tanya caught on. "You're not jealous, are you?" she teased.

Alex forced a smile. "Not in the least." But, God, the thought of Rick fucking Amanda and Tanya drove him crazy. It seemed like Rick was everywhere on the Ark, improving the systems Alex designed, receiving citations for success. The man was becoming a phenomenon. Alex hated being envious of Rick almost as much as he hated the man himself. His feelings were completely irrational and he knew it.

"You really should lighten up, Alex," said Tanya, trying to calm him down. "It was nothing, really. Just a party."

"I'll be fine," said Alex, attempting to control himself. "Carl was right. My metabolism's way off." He joked about the food to change the subject. "Isn't this delectable?"

Tanya puckered her face, "Oh yes, blanched white is my

favorite color." She held a pale spoonful of the mush against her dark cheek. "How can you eat this shit and say it's good for us? I know you've got a hand in it somewhere. I want something real—pizza, apples, chicken, pie—anything that looks and tastes like Earth food. I'm surprised more people don't jump ship with what you're serving in the mess."

Alex decided to relax his stance as an official of the Ark. He wasn't feeling like much of a model citizen at the moment. "Did you know there was almost a riot here?"

"Really?"

"Some jerk figured he could make a killing selling apples. People were so desperate they were hording outside currency to buy a black market apple. Customs finally got hold of most of the guy's stock, but people went crazy, having paid in advance for the opportunity to get their hands on one. At the time, Rick was in charge of Customs. I think the bastard must have eaten a few, even while people were running amok trying to get their money back. He went around for a week with a self-satisfied, shit-eating grin on his face. I wanted to punch him out."

"I guess Rick was wrong about you two being such great buddies."

"Believe me, it wasn't just me. We had to assign three bodyguards to Rick's security detail. Everybody wanted to take a poke at him. He was under orders to destroy the apples, but everyone on board was certain he was gobbling them up in some secured airlock."

Tanya pressed on with her criticism. "So maybe the nutritional system isn't the greatest idea."

"Well, after the apple incident, we took greater precautions to keep Earth food off the Ark. Still, some of the new people who come on board continue to fantasize about Earth food for a hundred thousand achievements or more. Most of them, however, only take about twenty-thousand or so to get used to it."

"What about the ones who don't?"

"Some we have to ship back. They can't adapt. Freud should've written about food instead of sex. People really can never get enough and they're always looking for something new and weird."

"Why don't you at least give us a little variation?"

"Maybe in the future, but right now we're having trouble keeping up with demand. It's one of the few systems we've fallen behind on. But frankly, the specialists don't think we should make the food all that exciting. If people began to overeat because they liked the taste, all the advances we've made toward increasing longevity, health and productivity might vanish. Right now, messing about with a formula that seems to be working is not our top priority."

Tanya didn't look convinced as she faked gagging down another bite. Alex decided a demonstration was in order in order to convince her of the efficacy of the Arkian dietary plan. He pointed at a woman in the common room. "Do you see her? How old do you think she is?"

"I don't know. Maybe a well-preserved forty? Those wrinkles around her neck and eyes. She must be at least that."

"But no older than what, would you say?"

"No older than fifty. Tops."

"Okay. I guess you women are pretty good at guessing each other's ages."

"It's our second nature."

"Anyway," he continued undaunted. "How about that man over there?"

"He's a little harder to guess. Maybe sixty. No more than seventy."

"You're sure?"

"Sure. Why not?"

Alex grinned smugly. "Oh, that's not bad at all."

"Really?"

"Really. She's seventy-five. He's ninety-eight."

Tanya's eyes opened wide in disbelief. "Bullshit! That's absolutely bullshit! Maybe I'm off ten years, but not twenty-five or thirty."

Alex laughed out loud. "It's true. I swear. I was treating each of them as patients and the computer gave me their chronological ages. Diet, exercise, a good attitude and some plastic surgery. Give 'em that and this little white bowl three times a day and you've got people with a reason to live."

"That's your answer?"

"Everyone thinks we're trying to provide an answer, but we're not. It's just a way of life. We give everyone a good job, an opportunity. These people feel like they've got a reason to live so we don't need retirement homes. They're healthy and they continue to contribute. Everyone who comes here, no matter how old, finds a new life."

Tanya tossed down her spoon. "I just hope I look that good when I'm seventy-five."

"The way you're going," Alex poured on the compliment as if he were spooning thick cream onto a dessert, "you'll look even better."

"I guess this stuff doesn't seem so bad after all. Too bad you can't sit down and have a little pep talk with everyone."

Alex flashed a wan smile. "There's a price for everything. You just have to decide if you're willing to pay it.""

CHAPTER 9

AND THEN THERE IS MOTHERHOOD

"There's nothing, and I mean nothing, better than shopping with a lover after a meal." Tanya spoke in her sultry Southern twang, slouching in her seat. "It makes me feel free, like I could buy anything. It must be this full stomach. I'm so content that I don't feel a rush to get anything; it feels like sooner or later, it'll just come to me."

She took Alex's arm in hers. "You don't mind if we put that nap off for a little while, do you? I think I'd like to buy you a little something. How does that sound, honey?"

"Why don't you buy yourself something?" he asked. "Get dressed up."

"Oh, now that's a wonderful idea. Something for after our nap, when we're refreshed. It'll be like being reborn. Something we can share together."

She pulled him over the table towards her and kissed him on the mouth, staring into his eyes. He wondered at her conceit, transforming her eyes into those of a cat. Her predatory nature was exhibited in every aspect of her being. She made him feel that he might be able to metamorphose himself into some different kind of creature, another kind of man. A shopping trip with her would be like wandering through an exotic bazaar. He imagined himself passing through strange shops, holding familiar objects in his hand as if he were touching them for the first time.

Suddenly, she pulled away from him, startled. "Oh my God!" she exclaimed, staring wildly at a point across the room. "It's my sister. I thought she was still on the moon." She turned to Alex. "You've got to come with me and say hello. You've probably heard of her husband, Jeffrey McDonald.

The one who found all that gold."

Alex racked his brain trying to make an association between Tanya's brother-in-law and the geologists he had sent to exploit the Moon's natural resources. But before he could respond, Tanya was running out of the cubicle, her arms flung open.

"Coralis! Coralis!" She was practically screaming at the woman. When she reached her sister, they embraced vigorously. Alex rose and walked slowly over to them. As the two siblings parted, Alex was struck by the sisters' dramatically different appearances: Tanya in her outrageous costume, Coralis in conventional clothes of subdued colors. While Tanya's regalia was sure to grab attention in any setting, her sister's ensured nothing but the opposite. One feature, however, stood out: Coralis was a few inches taller than her sister. Unlike Tanya's catty restlessness, Coralis seemed entirely relaxed, apparently unmoved by this chance meeting with her sister. She was a cold fish, Alex concluded.

Tanya introduced Coralis to Alex. "I was sure we'd meet *someone* in the cafeteria," she said, taking Coralis' hand. "What a surprise. I never thought I'd see you here."

Coralis remained nonplussed. She glanced derisively at Tanya's garb. "Don't you think you're overdoing it just a little?"

Alex tried to avert a squabble. "I've heard so much about your husband's work. It's really something. Are you involved in the Crater City project?"

This seemed to snap Coralis out of her distraction with Tanya's skimpy dress. For the first time, she focused on Alex.

"Oh God," she said, a look of recognition passing over her face. "You're *the* Alex. Normally my sister has such terrible taste in men. But I never would've imagined she'd go this far."

Tanya smiled uncomfortably and gestured toward a booth so they could sit down together. When Coralis turned toward the booth, Tanya shrugged her shoulders sheepishly, indicating that there was nothing she could do about her sister's temper. Watching Coralis shuffle toward the booth,

Alex noticed for the first time that she was pregnant, probably in her last few weeks.

Coralis put off taking a seat, explaining, "I've got to go deal with Carl. My buzzer's been going crazy. If I want to avoid the psycho-babble lecture about my health and eating for two, I'd better not be late."

Upon uttering the word "psycho-babble," Coralis cast a disapproving look at Alex. Apparently she was more than a little hostile toward the Ark's mandatory supervision of prenatal care. As usual, he felt obliged to champion the system. "You're having the baby here in Zero-G?"

"I suppose I have to. Jeff insists upon it."

"Well it really is safer," said Alex, trying to remain cheerful. "All of our studies show it puts almost no stress on the child. And they talk to the baby right up to the moment of birth. It really works wonders for the child's health and happiness. All of our primate research indicates an increase in intelligence and psychological adjustment. Have you seen the documentary on videochip?"

"No, and I'm not going to." Coralis practically spat the words out. "A friend of mine told me all about it after she delivered her baby here."

"Didn't she like it?" asked Alex.

"She said it was almost painless. Like she wasn't even there. She told me I wouldn't feel a thing. It sounds so far removed that it's a wonder I even have to be here. I suppose you'd rather I just feed the child into a computer bank and let you edit him on screen. When he meets your specifications, you could just print him out."

"Well, that's only one part of it," he said, trying to convince her.

"Look," she said, "I want the best for our baby, but everything you've got here is so high-tech it makes me sick. I'm surprised you don't have the machines carrying the child. Just get rid of the mother all together."

Alex was glad Coralis hadn't read about the Ark's new project in primate studies doing just that. Mothers were so often upset by the Ark's birthing innovations that Alex had learned to give up trying to explain anything when it became apparent that they weren't the least bit interested in listening to his side of the argument. Coralis waited for him to respond to her latest flurry of criticism, but he said nothing. She took his silence as an opportunity to head toward the testing and dispensing unit.

Tanya whispered to him. "She hates the Ark. That's why I never thought I'd see her here. She thinks we're all decadent."

"She really likes it out on the moon?"

"Well, even though she doesn't like the Ark, she and Jeff really are devoted to the new society. But she told me that ever since she's been carrying the baby, she misses being close to nature. She says she wants to walk in a park with real trees, birds, bees, whatever."

Alex laughed, "I guess the Solarium just doesn't do it."

"And," continued Tanya, "she thinks we're all too obsessed with sex. 'Don't you think you're all a little overboard?' She's always asking me things like that."

Alex saddened at the suggestion, even second-hand, that the Ark was overly concerned with sexuality. His second wife, Wendy, whom he had married on the eve of the Ark's maiden voyage, had moved back to Earth for precisely that reason. She refused to raise her children by a first marriage on the Ark, or even allow them to visit. Typical of the Ark's propaganda machine, the whole sequence of events had been hushed up. Officially, Wendy remained on Earth as part of a fundraising effort that was too politically important to allow her to return. Actually, while it was true that she was heavily involved in public relations for the Ark, nobody was aware of her deep-seated animosity toward Alex's plans for the Ark.

Oddly enough, Alex still felt strongly about Wendy. Initially, she had left only to visit her two daughters, but it soon became obvious that her sojourn was permanent. Alex, who still felt occasional pangs of jealously, had been frustrated to learn that her work on Earth gave her the opportunity to engage in long-lasting affairs with important political figures. Before he could grow too maudlin, however, Coralis banged her tray on the table top, wedging herself into the booth beside Tanya.

"Thank God we grow real food in Crater City," she said. I hate this place." Nonetheless she began digging at her food with no lack of appetite. Her mood seemed to brighten.

"Well, you guys must be having a great time. You must have gone to a party. Did you two dance together?"

Alex told her they had not.

"Oh, well, you must. She is simply the most wonderful dancer."

Puzzled for a moment by this unexpectedly pleasant turn of the conversation, Alex remembered Carl, who must have added a little extra happiness to Coralis' bowl. He took her improved attitude as a sign that he should quit talking while they were still on good terms and excused himself to use the restroom.

The bathrooms on the Ark were one of the few places that remained private. Even the ever-present computers were not visibly installed here. However, the technology Vladimir had envisioned during his semi-hallucinogenic trance in the bathroom began just behind the walls. In 1965, Alex allowed a German scientist named Karl Schultz to modify his Huntington Beach, California, house. The man had discovered a new process for reclaiming waste products. Nothing went unrecycled.

Schultz, a former Nazi, thought the discovery should be used as part of a plan for American dominance of the world. "People absolutely need to be told what to do!" he declared. Since Germany had failed, he decided that America should continue in the Third Reich's grand tradition of peace through force, world leadership by dictatorship. He saw the domination of space as the ultimate opportunity to impose the will of the elite on the whole world. Later, as Alex laid plans for construction of the Ark, plans that included a modified version of Schultz' water reclamation systems, he reminded himself of how horrified he had been of the man's political notions. When people like Coralis suggested that some of the Ark's programs had overtones of totalitarianism, he grew anxious.

As he entered the bathroom, he was reminded of the committee that had been assembled to oversee construction of the Ark. The committee's meetings had been his first taste of Rick Page's political ambition. From the moment they were introduced, Alex found Rick so distasteful that he immediately—and correctly—assumed they would almost never agree on anything. So he was surprised when Rick agreed that the commode environment should be private, the technology concealed. A plan was devised that allowed the Zero-G aspect of the commode's recovery system to begin only upon excretion of waste. However, this required both men and women to relieve themselves sitting down, as the Zero-G system needed to operate in a near-vacuum. A bidet-like jet of water made toilet paper unnecessary. Scanners allowed for a sample of urine and feces which could be used to detect diseases.

It was this last element that so appealed to Rick. Men and women could be intimately analyzed in an environment that made them feel as if they were escaping the scrutiny of the Ark's computer systems. Health concerns and early detection of venereal and other communicable diseases had overruled privacy concerns when the issue was brought to a committee vote. As Alex felt the warm swish of perfectly heated thirty-seven degree Celsius water washing over and between his buttocks, he was made even more uncomfortable by the idea that some disease control researcher might be staring at his ass, checking the data for signs of some heretofore undetected ailment. He hated the feeling of that water, as did almost everyone else he talked to.

"You and your fucking bright ideas," he muttered to himself. Finally a blast of hot air dried him off, welcome relief from the tepid and unwanted water wipe. He pulled up his pants, remembering the joy a good piss had given him back on Earth, standing above the bowl and letting the urine splash satisfactorily into the standing pool of water.

To make matters worse, a sign reserved for emergency communications, normally invisible to restroom occupants, flashed on and off in front of him. Someone had tracked him down in this last bastion of privacy. "Please consult with Carl," was all the message related to him. He cursed himself for having allowed Rick this security measure.

He wondered aloud, "Now what in hell could possibly be wrong?" But he knew the lab must have found something wrong with his sample. Alex walked out of the bathroom, deciding he'd put off having his little talk with Carl. God damn Rick and his projects. Fuck him.

He recalled a time when he and Rick had been assigned welding jobs that required a space walk. At seventy years old, Alex was still being assigned hazardous jobs because the computers were programmed to push everyone to their limit. Joined by an almost illiterate Indian man, who insisted on wearing a turban under his helmet, the trio had gone out to repair a faulty aileron on one of the Ark's navigating wings. During the job, Alex inexplicably found his life support line cut, the force of the escaping gases so strong that he was jettisoned several hundred yards from the Ark. Without hesitation, Rick had jumped acrobatically out to Alex and reeled him back in. For his effort, Rick had received his fifteenth medal and cluster for bravery.

The man was such a risk-taker that he had more decorations than anyone on the Ark, but Alex was sure that Rick had been the one who had cut his line in the first place. The Indian had been blamed for the incident, but something about Rick's behavior suggested that he was aware of Alex's suspicions. Because of the accident, Rick's political currency shot up and his design for a new jet pack went into production. All space walkers were required to wear the jet pack and Rick was highly considered among the technical crews. In one way or another, Alex figured Rick probably did deserve medals for bravery, only not in the way everyone thought. He deserved a medal for cheating the odds with such high stakes at risk.

In time, Alex had decided that he'd have to accept his adversary, take him with a grain of salt. Rick, however, made that decision difficult. Once, when Alex had chanced to ask

Rick's secretary about a trip she had taken with her boyfriend, Rick charged into the room, accusing Alex of prying into her personal life. "Why don't you just stop harassing her?" he shouted. "Just keep your nose out of her business. She's told me before you're always snooping." The secretary turned bright red and Rick disappeared from the room as quickly as he had entered. Alex felt duly chastened.

"I was just asking," he bleated lamely to the secretary.

"Mind your own damn business," called Rick from his office.

The next time Alex had seen Rick at a party, he had been his usual slithering self, laughing and punching Alex in the ribs, telling everyone how he had saved Alex's life, calling him an old sport. Everyone assumed they were best of friends. It drove Alex mad to think that people considered them close. This business about the toilet made him even more furious, but he blamed himself. If only I hadn't been such a fanatic about this environmental engineering program, I could take a piss without Rick sticking his nose up my ass.

At any rate, he knew that he and Rick were stuck with one another. Alex was still trying to learn to live with him. "Oh well," he reassured himself. "Rick's who he is, and I'm who I am." He continued walking toward Tanya and Coralis, who were laughing and talking with such animation that they didn't notice him approaching.

CHAPTER 10

BACK TO CORALIS

Still annoyed by his experience in the bathroom, Alex slunk toward the booth where the two sisters sat. Tanya was the first to see him, flashing an easy smile at him. "You have a nice time in there? Enjoy your little sit-down?"

Everybody joked about the Ark's toilets. Some people even went so far as to say they enjoyed duty on the moon because it allowed them to relieve themselves in a uniform-gravity environment, on commodes similar to those on Earth. This kind of thinking contributed to claims that even the air tasted better on the moon.

Coralis threw Alex a chiding smirk, as if her distaste for the Ark had been proven. "See," she said, "you don't have all the answers on the Ark, do you?"

For a moment Alex was able to remain rational, thinking, God, I really do need to see Carl. Normally, this kind of insignificant attack on the Ark's amenities passed by him without comment. But something about Coralis' attitude, perhaps it was the fact that she was Tanya's sister and Alex felt she was undermining his authority, made him explode in a rare display of temper.

"Nobody," he said with barely concealed rage, "ever gives me any credit for my vision." As soon as he said this, he knew it was patently untrue; he had a wall filled with honors and awards. But he continued nonetheless. "You women give me nothing but bullshit all the time, especially when you're pregnant. You come off with this holier-than-thou vision from the womb, as if motherhood is the only state of being that allows anyone a right to make a decision. It makes *me* sick to hear your whining!"

Alex was apoplectic. Even as the words escaped his mouth, he couldn't believe how filled with bile he was. He knew he must sound like a fool, but he couldn't stop himself. Tanya and Coralis sat dumbfounded before him.

"Men are the ones who have built society from nothing, from our earliest animal existence to mankind's grandest vision. And it's women who try and drag us back down with their nitpicking insights on the trivia of everyday life! It's ridiculous. I'm looking into the void of eternity, trying to keep this species from the brink of extinction and you're cutting me down about a toilet. No, the Ark's not perfect. I'm not perfect. But in ten years there hasn't been one cold, one death due to disease on this ship. People are living as they never have before, living up to their genius. It's a reality now and I've made it that way."

At this point, Alex began directing his diatribe at Coralis. "And we've made it so that you, you mothers, and your children suffer as little as possible. Relieved of trauma and freed from possible death, you still manage to complain. Your children will live better than humans ever have, like supermen and not like the primitive animals who pass themselves off as human back on Earth. We've given you dignity and you give me back this crap. I can't believe this bullshit, because that's what it is. I had a dream and I did something about it. So maybe the reality, the praxis of my dream has not been perfect. So what! You've got a choice: you can live here or on the Earth or wherever, I don't care! But if you're going to stay here, I wish you'd keep your petty little trap shut!

"I gave myself the same choice and that's why I'm here. I can choose who I want to be and I'm not complaining. I wanted to leave behind the ludicrous moral hypocrisy of Earth so that I could choose who I love and who I do not love, choose who I want to sleep with without worrying about some Italian pontiff's notion of good and evil, or have to think about some woman trying to con me into raising her kids for her. I came here to forget about that."

Coralis cut him off, tired of his display. "Well, Alex, now

you have your choice." She spoke without hesitation. "I hope you choke on it."

"You guys really love each other," Tanya joked, trying to break the tension between them. "I didn't think you'd hit it off so well."

Alex, realizing how ridiculous he had sounded, apologized, cracking a weakly recalcitrant smile. Coralis, remaining silent, managed to ease the look of recrimination on her face. Tanya, tired of seeing them bicker, went so far as to begin tickling her sister, who broke into a giggle that mutated into a full-throated laugh. Tanya joined her, bellowing out with her booming guffaws. Now laughing with them, Alex sat down beside Coralis, placing his hand on her arm. She allowed him to kiss her on the cheek, accepting his apology.

Alex was impressed by how easily Tanya had transformed the situation. It's amazing, he told himself, every time she laughs, I have to laugh with her. She can even make me laugh at myself. For Alex, it was the first admission to himself that he might be falling in love with her.

CHAPTER 11

Having parted ways with Coralis, they walked along narrow passageways lined with holograms projecting replicas of storefronts typical of an American shopping mall. They passed a Macy's, several small gift shops, a Saks Fifth Avenue, Nordstrom's, Sears, Frederick's of Hollywood—one of Alex's personal favorites—and an abundance of shoe stores, athletic shops and entertainment centers. National chains were granted slightly more space to project their images to passersby than the businesses owned by private citizens. The projections varied several times per achievement period, each change showing a different area of the store, maximizing the amount of merchandise displayed.

Waving off Alex's attempt to window shop at other locations, Tanya skipped ahead to Frederick's. As she pranced ahead of him, Alex contented himself with watching her behind sashay smoothly above her willowy legs. He enjoyed gazing at her backside almost as much as looking at her eyes, her tantalizing smile. He set her walk to music, watching her taught muscles undulating beneath the fabric of her dress as if she were a dancer on a stage. Unlike some Arkian women he had known, she had not turned herself into an Amazon with weight machines; she remained feminine, alluring. He looked forward to seeing her try on the Frederick's lingerie.

Due to limited space on the Ark, there was nothing behind the holographic storefronts. Customers window shopped and then entered another holographic center to try on garments or inspect merchandise up close, ordering what they wanted. Tanya and Alex entered a private booth where clothes were projected onto a three-dimensional image of the customer. Alex didn't bother to ask Tanya if she wanted to try the clothes on privately. He understood that she wanted him to see her. Hell, he figured, she's probably vain enough to get a kick out of it herself.

"Oh, honey," she said, laughing at the little-boy-in-a-candy-store look on his face, "we're gonna have to get you something, too." She laughed in her booming tenor, grabbing his hand and planting a wet kiss on his cheek. Alex felt his legs buckling; she was sweeping him off his feet.

"My mother told me there's nothing better for a man than to shop with a woman," he said. He felt his heart beating rapidly. He wanted to confess to her, tell her how much she thrilled him. Instead, he only alluded to his amorous feelings. "I'm glad we'll be taking a nap soon. You know, get a little sleep. I've got to think about getting myself back in shape so I can face Carl."

"Who said anything about sleeping?"

He smiled at her, relaxing. The feeling was mutual, making it unnecessary to confess anything.

She prodded at a control panel and Alex saw her naked figure coalesce holographically before him. As she scanned each department, a representative garment—wedding gown, tennis outfit, swimsuit—appeared on her body. Upon arrival at Lingerie, Alex witnessed an alluring procession of skimpy fabrics clinging to her supple figure. He was further aroused by imagining how easily he might slip her breast from a transparent top, how a lavender teddy might fall to the floor in a pile around her feet as he loosened it from her shoulders. As he considered what might happen once he finished denuding her, he was distracted by her laughter.

At her bidding, the computer now projected a holograph of a muscular black man, completely nude. Alex wondered what she was doing until he realized that what he saw was, in fact, an image of himself with darkened skin. Tanya was laughing so hard, she wiped at tears in the corners of her eyes. She rotated the image so that he saw his posterior, surprised at how good he looked from that angle. Women had always complimented him on what they called his "cute butt."

Perhaps a little more work on my calves, he thought, and I could be a model. For a seventy-five year-old, I look pretty good.

The image pulsed brightly for a moment and Alex saw himself bleached back into his own skin. "I just wanted to see what you'd look like if you were more like me."

"And?"

"It's not too bad, but I think you're better the way you are." At this, she let out another loud guffaw and Alex glanced over to see his head shaved bald, covered with the same pattern of diamond studs implanted on Tanya's scalp. He watched in anguish as his eyebrows were systematically uprooted and replaced with diamonds, his eyelids colored in a changing palette of mascaras and eye liners. After settling on a deep blue hue, she began experimenting with different eye colors, settling for the moment on a pair of yellow-orange cat's eyes similar to her own.

"Oh, you do have sexy eyes," she whispered in his ear, finally changing the eyes back to his own pale blue. She started in on the rest of his body, placing an intricate tattoo on the left cheek of his buttocks, hanging his testicles in what appeared to be a finely meshed black baggie. His nipples were stained a dark coffee color—the right nipple pierced—and tattoos of white and blacks stars appeared on either arm. She placed a pair of loose-fitting shorts over his loins, covering his feet with a pair of leather sandals that ran up his shins like brown serpents. The triangular bones of his knees were outlined in diamonds, as were the lobes of his ears.

Tanya let out a tart laugh. "Oooh," she cooed, "aren't you cute?" She turned the image around. "Man, your ass looks good." She took one more look and pressed the accept button.

"I think it looks great," she stated, not bothering to ask for his opinion. The machine asked them to wait a moment while it collected the articles of clothing.

No money had changed hands. Shopping on the Ark consisted of the computers altering assigned work achievement periods to allow Arkians to pay for whatever goods and services they requested. People rarely spent beyond their means because of the efficiency methods implemented in all on-board systems. Although tastes were sophisticated and often expensive, Arkians were never denied what they wanted. The goods and services the Ark provided to Earth were extremely profitable, making shopping relatively painless. The disadvantage of this economic imbalance, however, was that repatriation to the home planet was often a dispiriting proposition for those who were not independently wealthy upon their departure from the Ark.

"I guarantee you Amanda is going to love this," said Tanya, noticing the dubious look on Alex's face. "She really goes for this wild shit."

"What about you?" he asked her. "I want to know if it's going to turn you on?"

Tanya massaged his arm. "Why do you think I created it?"

Alex smiled. "I just hope nobody laughs when I show up at the party. I usually don't appear in public dressed so flamboyantly."

"Where's your confidence, boy?" she bellowed. "Here you are, creator of the Ark and whatever other grand visions you were hollering about a few minutes ago, and now you're afraid to wear something new. Don't be so insecure. Are you a trendsetter or what?"

"What, I guess."

"Honey, trust me, you look so good I think even the men are gonna be clawing to get at you."

"You think I look that good, huh?" He grinned sappily at her odd compliment.

"You bet, honey."

"Well then," he said, executing an obviously false yawn. "I guess it's time for a little nap." He grabbed the parcel the machine presented and they left the mall arm in arm.

CHAPTER 12

TANYA

As they lolled on a bed together, the XSY starting to take its full effect, Alex noticed Tanya's Southern accent coming on stronger. She spoke in slow, singing phrases.

"Baa-by," she crooned, "for the first time in your life . . . you are going to be with a woman. And, honey, I want you to prepare yourself. This momma," she pointed to herself, "knows how to treat a man . . . the way a man . . . should be treated. I'm not putting on any kid gloves for you, darling . . . and you may never be the same."

She held her hands up to the straps of her dress, letting out one of her deep laughs. "Honey child, are you ready for mama?"

She began taking off her clothes, slowly undulating to reveal her figure as the flimsy garments slid from her body. She fixed him with a flirtatious smile, indicating that she knew she held him like a possession. Her choice to display herself before him was a conscious decision. Alex watched her as one watches a panther in a cage, mesmerized, waiting for what might happen next. His heart proceeded to pound in his chest as he anticipated their coupling.

She opened her mouth wide so that he saw her perfectly white teeth contrast with the deep brown of her face. Her tongue moved slowly across her teeth as if she were a lioness about to devour her prey. A low, purring sound emanated from deep in her throat, a sound comprised of equal parts contentment and aggression. Alex tried to imitate the sound, surprising himself with the powerful rumble that thrummed within him. He felt meaner and stronger than he had in a long time, his body taut, ready for anything.

"Mmmmmm," she burbled, her tongue moving outside of her mouth, moistening her lips. "Alex," she sighed, "you're so big. So strong. And I'm good for you, baby, don't you think? I'm a mean mother and I'm going to have to fuck . . . you . . . so . . . good . . . boy."

Alex imagined her on top of him and breathed deeply. Suddenly, his head began to ache horribly. He clutched at his ears, trying to massage the pain out of his skull. "Oh, God!" he cried, his face contorted.

"Alex, honey, what's wrong with you?" she said with alarm.

"I've got this buzz in my head. It's like pins in my ears."

Tanya let out a bellowing laugh. God, she's laughing at me, Alex thought. I can't believe it.

She looked at him as if he were a child, pointing to his hand. "Honey, you're gonna have to take that ring off your finger."

Alex looked down at his hand, considering the ring Amanda had given him.

"Did Amanda give you that?"

He nodded weakly.

"She's always trying that old pinning routine. 'You don't have to do anything for me but wear this ring.' Is that what she told you? She loves pulling that one."

Alex dazedly pulled at the ring, managing to slip it off his finger, at which point the buzzing stopped. "What the hell was that?"

"Honey," said Tanya, folding her arms around his neck, "I'll explain that to you later. Right now I think we have other things to take care of. Look at me Don't you think I'm beautiful?"

She kissed him and he almost immediately forgot about the ring and the pains in his head. Just as quickly as that memory subsided, Tanya leapt upon him, pinning him to the floor. He quickly tried to pick himself up, rolling her over, trying to keep her away from him. She slipped away and in an instant she was on his back, pressing his chest and face into the carpet. He felt as if he were fighting to keep her from destroying him. She was at least as strong as he was, maybe stronger. He would have to use every ounce of his strength to overcome her.

He finally managed to worm his body into a position where he faced her, his back still pinned to the floor. Her nostrils flared, her yellow cat-eyes closed tight with exertion. She glistened, her sweat spread like fine oil over her skin, the sheen accentuating the cut of her straining muscles. He could see hundreds of small tremors in her arms. Each groan, each breath brought on an orchestrated shudder of hundreds of tiny muscles.

He felt her perspiration rolling onto him as he moved inside of her, his body quivering, dancing toward ecstasy. He felt their every motion together energizing him, the act empowering him to be more than he had ever been before. Alex wanted to die rather than stop. He tried to tell his body to slow down, to let the moment last, but he seemed to have lost control over his limbs. The arms he had spent years toning in a gym exerted more force in his grip on her waist than they had on any machine. His legs pushed his loins into her with more strength than he thought he had.

He felt like he was in the hot heat of the Arizona sun, able to move only one step at a time. Even as his body pushed itself farther into Tanya, he wondered at the source of his strength. He felt as if her energy blazed out like an incredible burning star, a fount of power from which he drew. He felt the tumble of his own organism, a minute warmth that pushed Tanya forward. He tore at her face with his fingers, pressing his face into her neck, biting her. Still, she clung to him, her legs wrapping themselves tighter around him. He swung at her, striking her ribs with the full force of his hand. It had no effect, but to increase her hold on him. She bit back, her teeth sinking so deeply into his shoulder that he felt no pain. She scratched at him, all the while the sound in her throat curdling into at first a lion's roar and then an unbridled scream as her body shook in climax.

Alex began swearing at her, calling her horrible names, and her body began to shake with fury, her teeth clamping down tighter on his arm. There was nothing he could do, not even a blow from his hand could get her to release him. He finally pressed his forearm against her throat as she tried to sink her teeth into his chest. They snarled at each other, both trying to push the other back, refusing to surrender.

Finally, Tanya broke out into laughter. They relaxed, falling apart, tumbling wildly back onto the carpet.

"I feel like I've just fucked a lion," Alex told her. She responded with more laughter.

"That's what I call fucking," she gasped. "Next time we'll have to do it in the anti-gravity room."

Alex took this opportunity to throw her off guard, rising to his feet, attempting to pull her up. "Come on, let's go do it."

"Oh, no," she said, pulling her arm away from him. "Why don't you just admit I've done you in?" She pressed her hand against her mouth to stifle a smile, Alex noticing for the first time how white her palm was against the rest of her skin. "Just look at yourself, all covered in teeth marks and scratches."

Alex looked down and saw that his torso and arms were covered in deep gouges, some of the blood smeared in crimson swaths.

"You need some medical attention," she laughed. "Here, let your momma kiss that and make it better."

Alex knelt before her and she kissed him tenderly. "Still," he told her, "I'm going to have to show everyone what you've done. If you're going to treat me like this, you don't think I can let you get away with it?"

"Alex, what're you talking about?"

Alex smiled cruelly.

"Did you videotape us?"

"Genie, play us back some highlights."

"You creep! You don't miss a trick, do you?"

"And, Genie, make sure you play it on the big screen in the party hall so that our friend Amanda has a chance to see it."

"I'm sorry, Alex," said Genie, "Amanda is in another room with someone else." Tanya snickered at this news.

"Well, then, play it back into her occipital receivers," Alex commanded. "Especially the part where Tanya's tearing up my back."

"Oh, you are a bastard, Alex," cried Tanya. "You're going to play it in her brain while she's screwing someone else?"

"She's tough. She can take it." They laughed together. "Should we have it played back in our receiver while we fuck again?"

"You're incorrigible. Why not?"

Before Alex could even ask Genie to do this for them, he saw an image of himself with Tanya transparently superimposed over his field of vision. Beyond the holographic figures, he could still see the room he was standing in.

"I never knew I looked so wild," wondered Tanya.

"This is some fantastic editing, Genie," complimented Alex. "Throw some music in there."

"Oh, I'm turning myself on," marveled Tanya. "I look great! No wonder Amanda loves me."

Alex laughed at Tanya's self-infatuation. "I guess I'm not too bad either," he said. "Not for a seventy-five year-old man."

"If I can look half as good when I'm that old, I'll be happy," she told him.

Alex decided to change the subject, even as the pictures kept rolling before them. "So, why don't you tell me about Amanda's ring, honey?"

"She didn't explain that to you?" Tanya looked at him with some disbelief.

"Something about a going steady fad. I thought it sounded a little strange."

Tanya laughed at him. "You really don't know, do you? While you've got that thing on, you can do whatever you like except have intercourse. And if you want to do that, all you have to do is take off the ring."

"So that's what I did."

"Right. But once you do that, she's allowed to renegotiate her contract with the computer. Some people have it worked so that you can't even kiss someone or dance, or do anything with a stranger without renegotiating. So, anyway, right now Amanda is probably following hot on your heels, screwing her heart out."

"You're sure?"

"Oh, honey, she loves to play the virgin and blame the man for breaking the contract. Only she didn't have to wait very long with you."

"She never explained any of that to me."

"And if she had, are you trying to tell me you wouldn't have made love with me?"

Alex wore a guilty look, embarrassed at his own self-contradiction. Did he really love Amanda or was he just kidding himself, really wanting to have sex with anyone he could find?

"See what a bad boy you can be?" Tanya teased him. "You just can't get away with those kinds of tricks anymore. Don't you love Genie for it?"

Tanya reached out and touched him on the cheek. "Come on, honey, let's just fuck some more. Don't you want Amanda to see us? I know it'll turn her on."

Just as she finished speaking, they heard Amanda's voice resonating in their ears. "Okay, you fuckers," she chided them, "just watch my show."

At this point, their vision was filled with three images: themselves in real time, the tape of their previous lovemaking and a new image of Amanda frolicking with three muscular, handsome men. Watching her rock in spasms of ecstasy gave Alex a queasy feeling. He felt like he wanted to cry. He hadn't realized he was so possessive.

"Honey," he heard Tanya's voice in his ear. "You can't cage her. You've got to let her go."

Alex reluctantly turned to face her. "You're right, I know." For a moment he was afraid his words might be accompanied by tears. "But I can still smell her. Taste her."

"You picked the wrong lady to think about owning. Nobody's going to have her forever. Not even me." She touched his face. "Just be happy with the time you have with her. That's what I do."

She smiled at him. "Can't I make you forget her, even just for a minute?"

Alex forced his eyes shut, trying to blot out the images of Amanda. "Genie," he called out, "stop my transmission to Amanda." After a moment, his eyes saw only Tanya and the room they occupied.

With a tired gesture, he stood up from the floor, putting his arm around Tanya's waist. "Let's get some more of that prescription food. How does that sound?"

"Oh, great," said Tanya sardonically.

"And then we'll take a little nap together?"

Tanya smiled at this. "Sounds like a plan to me."

CHAPTER 13

NAP TIME

They had fallen asleep snugly in each other's arms, suspended in a hammock-like sleeping bag that kept them from floating around in the Zero-G room. As they slumbered, they looked like two groggy children, each clinging dreamily to a teddy bear.

"I can feel you," Tanya sighed. "This is so wonderful. If only we could always communicate purely, emotionally, we would be so happy. I feel like I'm dreaming."

"Maybe you are." Alex embraced her tighter and it seemed as if they remained in one another's arms, lightly kissing, sometimes whispering tokens of affection, for hours.

Tanya spoke, her voice heavy and somnambulant. "Is it true the Ark has leased the Sahara desert? I read about it in the *Times* recently. What do you want with all that sand?"

"What do you get with water and sand?"

"Mud?"

"Right," he laughed. "One big mud pie. Just right for farming. Did you read the whole article?"

"Well," she said with some embarrassment, "I never did go in much for technical stuff. All I know is it sounded weird to me. Where are you going to get the water?"

"From the ocean."

"So you're going to farm with ocean water?"

"Well, water from the ocean, but it will be distilled. We have pumps that will run for years using our new battery packs. They're charged with energy we harnessed from the solar winds at the Hydrogen Plasma Electrical Generating Stations. We distill the water with a simple and cheap process. The water runs through a long system of pipes, each fitted with different sized sieves. After traveling hundreds of miles, the minerals are extracted and the water flows out as fresh water, perfect for irrigation."

Tanya looked at him blankly, uninterested in Alex's fantasies about the Ark's technology. He continued anyway. "And the interesting thing about the project is that the vast amount of water we'll siphon off should offset the greenhouse effect of rising ocean tide levels. The water that evaporates will contribute to greater rainfall east of the Sahara and the net result will be greater areas worldwide for crops. The crops we'll grow will be tended mostly by robotics, but for those on Earth, more farmlands will undoubtedly make life a little easier. We're going to be using the same principles on different planets when we begin to colonize them. And did I mention the fish farms?"

"No, you didn't," said Tanya, casting him a withering look.

"Well, we'll be producing so much food we'll make a fortune selling it back to Earth. They love a good meal. And we know there's nothing to fear from people we're feeding."

"I don't know why you're so hung up on fearing Earth," she said with exasperation. "I'm not a scientist, but everyone knows just one of your generating stations could produce a blast that would level an entire city."

"Well, it's true that they could," said Alex, scrambling for a defensive posture, "but they can't. We've made sure that all our generating lasers pulse away from the Earth. All of our other weaponry is short range only, designed for defensive purposes. Anyway, the Ark has so many people on board with relations on Earth that they'd revolt if we ever mounted any kind of an attack on Earth."

"So you could make an attack, you just choose not to?" she demanded. Alex could tell she didn't fully believe him.

"Well, I suppose we could, but only if we were directly attacked by some entity on Earth—only if we were in extreme danger." He felt like she was reading his mind, as if she sensed the dangers he knew about.

"Are we really asleep now?" she asked. "I feel like we're

awake and carrying on a conversation."

"We're asleep, believe me. Sound asleep. The computer is facilitating this ESP conversation between us. You're picking up my thought transmissions."

"When you talked about the Sahara, I actually saw pictures of the farms. I saw date trees. I even saw the pumps you were talking about. I love talking this way. When are you going to let other people do this?"

"Actually, we need a little more time. Some people have more natural ability; you, for example. Right now we're trying to work with some of the Russian programs, especially with pharmaceutical enhancers, to make the system more practical. Right now, this system works with EEG monitors, harmonizing biofeedback to maximize the waves we can send to one another. Some of us have been using imbedded electrodes to use the ESP mode at all times.

"Learning to communicate this way is like building muscles, training to do something you're not accustomed to. Once the EEG techs discover the most sympathetic waves traveling between two people, they reinforce those signals, allowing the two to communicate. It's similar to the technique we use in the sleep programs."

"I've never gotten used to getting a full night's sleep in one achievement," she admitted. "But this seems like something really great. Maybe the best thing you've ever done."

"Don't forget getting rid of the common cold," he teased her.

"Oh, of course. The cold. I love never having one of those lousy days with my nose running all the time." They laughed together.

"Okay," she continued, "explain why I saw so much lightning in my vision of the Sahara."

Alex grinned, embarrassed that he had accidentally disclosed information about one of the Ark's most covert research projects. "That's one of the problems with ESP, all kinds of tangential, subconscious thoughts get sucked in with everything else. The lightning you saw is part of another project that's top secret. And now, I guess you know more about it than anyone without a security clearance. That's one reason the Russians have worked so long on their ESP programs. Interrogation gets a lot easier when you can reach into your subject's mind."

He put his hand on her shoulder. "Now tell me what you saw besides the lightning."

Tanya began hesitantly, unsure about Alex's concern. "I saw something like a kite, it's funny but it reminded me of those stories about Benjamin Franklin. And I saw a ship with some kind of pulse coming out of it. Yes, that's it. A ship in a lightning storm."

"That's incredible, Tanya. The project's called the Ben Franklin project. It's based on harnessing the energy from lightning storms in the same way we harness the solar winds. The engineers calculate the largest concentration of electricity in a cloud from satellite readings. A robot plane is sent into the storm, seeding the area by attracting negative charges. When the discharge occurs, it's attracted to the plane, which redirects the energy in the form of a laser to one of our collectors. The collectors, in turn, store the power in one of our capacitors. That energy is what we've been using to charge the batteries we've been selling to Earth.

"Eventually, we'll give this technology to poorer Earth countries. They'll make a profit by selling excess power to more developed nations and be able to keep what they need on hand. Did you know that just one of those batteries can power a household for an entire year? And we estimate it might cost as little as one American dollar. Families could have enough power to run everything in their home, including air conditioners and heaters, for almost nothing."

Alex pointed to the stars and out into infinite space. "We've finally realized that everything we need is out there. We don't have to horde our possessions. It belongs to the universe, not just one person."

He gestured again, motioning to the heavens. "You can't make a fence big enough to fit around all of that."

CHAPTER 14

THE SOLARIUM

Alex's sleep was disturbed by a voice that took him a moment to recognize. "Alex, Alex," the voice repeated until he was fully conscious. But the speaker was not in the room. She was communicating via his temporal receivers. Trying not to disturb Tanya, who was still sleeping beside him, he decided to use his subspeech vocal cords.

"Amanda?"

"It's me."

"I was taking a nap."

"Is Tanya still with you?"

"Yes, we were speaking telepathically earlier. I was telling her about the Sahara project."

"God, Alex. I must have been dreaming about you two. I kept having these vision of huge lakes of water in the middle of a desert."

"That must have been us."

"Are you two getting along alright?"

"We're having a great time."

Amanda paused for a moment, unsure of how to respond, perhaps just a little sorry she had asked the question. "I hope you miss me just a little bit," she finally said.

"At least a little," he replied.

"I want to see you. Both of you. Why don't you meet me at the Solarium. I need a break from this marathon party you're throwing."

"I'd almost forgotten about the party. What's been happening?"

"Well, your friend Vladimir is still going strong. He keeps asking everyone about you. He must have danced with every woman there. I don't know how you're going to get him back to his station. He's a natural for the Ark. He fits right in. I have to give those Russians credit for knowing how to party."

Alex considered this last statement, wondering just how familiar Amanda was with Vladimir's "partying" techniques. Deciding it really wasn't any of his business, he declined to follow up. It seemed to him that the younger generation had given up on possessiveness and he would have to try and do the same. Still, something about their time together had given him a sense that she belonged to him. What, after all, had that whole locket escapade been about? Was it just a game Amanda liked to play with old men? Whenever he felt like he was in love with someone, his reasoning turned to mush. He reminded himself to try and suppress his possessive impulses.

Avoiding the subject altogether, Alex inquired as to what activities they might pursue at the Solarium. "If Tanya and I arrive before you, what are you in the mood for? The ocean? Mountains? Tropics, river delta, lake? And I think they just added the Arctic, Brazilian Jungle and Sedona, Arizona."

"Anything but the Arctic. I'm not in the mood for icebergs. Why don't you two just surprise me."

Tanya, now awake, broke into the conversation. "Honey, I've got more than a surprise for you. We'll see you there in two achievements."

Amanda lowered her voice, speaking with sultry anticipation. "I can't wait." She ended the communication.

Tanya pushed her face up into Alex's, like a cat looking for attention. She looked into his eyes, a contented look on her face. She kissed him gently on his face and neck, and then wrapped her arms around him tightly. "You make me feel so good, Alex. I'm so relaxed."

Alex pushed her away gently, apologizing. "There's no rest for the weary. We've got to meet Amanda."

"She can wait just a little longer," purred Tanya, pulling Alex on top of her.

Despite the slight delay in their departure, they arrived

at the Solarium in less than one achievement. The Solarium was a vast holographic chamber where the Ark's crew revisited the earth. When Alex and Tanya entered the Solarium, they found themselves on a vista point, looking over the massive geological formations and waterfalls of the Yosemite Valley. The sound of crickets and birds surrounded them, the rustling of small rodents in the brush occasionally emanating from unseen locations. Contact with animals was unusual on the Ark, as there were no insect or animal populations with the exception of specimens in the zoo. Even the simulated sounds of jays and sparrows were a welcome respite from the monotone hum of the Ark's environmental systems and computers.

The holograph providing the images and sounds was the most sophisticated imaging system ever created. Visitors to the Solarium felt as if they were in a three-dimensional space. Alex and Tanya could even smell the pine trees, sense the crispness in the air. The sound of the Merced River's quickly flowing water could be heard in the distance. They looked with awe upon the exquisite vista. On one side, El Capitan loomed domineeringly over the valley floor. Half Dome's glistening polished rock jutted up on the opposite side. They could just see the foaming white spray from Upper Yosemite Falls.

Distracted by the vision, they did not see or hear Amanda approaching until she announced her presence in a loud voice, just behind them. "I always wanted to do it in the wide open spaces of Yosemite."

Alex and Tanya turned around to see Amanda already starting to remove her clothes. She wiggled her body suggestively as she freed herself from one garment at a time, protracting her denuding with dramatic flourishes. As her transparent blouse fell to the ground, covering a shrub and a granite boulder, Alex wondered at the contrast between Amanda's exquisite apparel and the rough country here in the Sierras. He looked back at her and saw her breasts exposed to the open air, ripe as polished fruit shining in the artificial sunlight. She was beautiful.

She gyrated her way out of her sash and was now completely naked with the exception of her high heels, which she left attached. The odd juxtaposition of a nude body wearing stiletto heels in the wilderness struck Alex for a moment, but Amanda's brash poise allowed her to carry it off with style and verve. Her regal posture against the bracken made her look radiant.

Amanda looked at Tanya and then Alex with an accusing eye. "This is no time for modesty," she announced. "I think it's about time that Alex followed my lead."

Alex was happy to acquiesce, shedding his clothes quickly and moving to embrace Amanda. She held him at bay, waving her finger at him as if he were a naughty child who had forgotten to do what his mother asked. "First you've got to get this locket off," she reminded him. "Genie!" she called.

"Yes," responded the computer.

"It's time to unlock the lock," said Alex.

"Have a good time," Genie exhorted in a cheerful voice. The lock clicked open softly. In addition to Genie's matchmaking functions, she was also responsible for monitoring sexual activity, ensuring that no one was injured because of overexertion, or hurt because a partner had been inconsiderate or abusive. Since her program had been in use on the Ark, there had been no heart attacks or violent sexual assaults. In addition to ministering to health and safety concerns, Genie also helped participants to overcome their inhibitions, allowing them to enjoy without reservation a wider array of sexual activities.

Amanda, who had been playing with her body during the exchange, now moved her hand to her crotch and started to gently remove the locket from its secured position. When she finished retrieving the device, she held it aloft like a champion soldier displaying a trophy head. "Oh, Genie," she said. "I want you to take good care of my friend Alex. He means so much to me."

Alex wondered what Amanda wanted Genie to do for him, but decided to let things play out a natural course. He began to approach her once more, and Amanda proceeded to wave the locket before him in the manner of a matador waving a red cape before a bull. Alex lunged at her but she eluded him with a swift sidestep. They repeated a series of charges and escapes until he threw his arms around her waist and began placing small kisses all over her body. He fell to his knees, placing his lips over the fuzz under her navel and she began to moan. He looked up at her and saw that she had concealed a canister in her hand. Before he could say anything, she had sprayed him with the XSY aerosol. As Alex reeled from the initial impact of the drug, Amanda dosed Tanya, who had been standing beside them.

His mind racing so fast that he believed he could feel the pulse of blood moving through his veins, Alex shouted at Amanda. "You little devil."

She pushed her face into his. "I like you hard, Alex, really hard. I don't want you just thinking hard, I want you to be hard." She gave him an affectionate slap on the cheek.

"After all," she continued in her baby doll voice, "this time you've got to take care of both of us. I've been waiting so long. It must have been a hundred achievements. And all I've had are those gorgeous hunks of young men to pay attention to me while you and Tanya were having your fun together." She motioned to Tanya. "Don't you think I deserve to be spoiled a little?"

Alex thrust his head between her legs, slowly moving his tongue over the inside of her thighs, finally parting her labia. "You do that so well," she told him. "Isn't he just marvelous at that?" she asked Tanya. "Where did you learn to do that?"

Alex heard Tanya moving beside him, the sound of clothes falling to the ground by now familiar to him. As he pressed his tongue deeper and deeper into Amanda, he felt Tanya's hard, warm body towering over him. He looked up and saw Tanya kissing Amanda's breasts, her face rapturously concentrated on her actions. As he continued to caress Amanda's labia with his tongue, Alex wondered how much of his action was instinctual and how much was inspired by Genie's influence helping him to overcome his inhibitions. He decided to surrender himself to whatever happened, knowing that Genie wouldn't allow him to go too far. As long as he was in her hands, he would be okay.

As if he had been vocalizing his thoughts, Amanda suddenly pinched him and said teasingly, "Genie, please keep close tabs on Alex. We don't want to lose him and he's too young to die." The two women laughed at Alex, and he chuckled in accord.

In a matter of moments, Alex found himself on the ground, Tanya wrapped around his chest, his hips mounted by Amanda. As she slipped his cock into her, he marveled at how incredibly tight she was. She must, he concluded, have been taught her mother's trick of using isometric exercises to strengthen her vaginal muscles. God, how he loved a tight pussy. Who didn't? The harder he pushed into her, the harder she gripped him, each stroke opening a deeper channel of pleasure, of pure communication between them.

At times, Amanda gasped as if she were in pain, but she begged him to go deeper, further. She could no longer tell if it was pain or pleasure she was experiencing, she only asked for more, more, faster, faster. She spread her legs out as wide as she possibly could to allow him to move farther into her. The harder Alex pushed, the more she wanted. She was insatiable. "Please," she whispered, "please." And then she was shouting, "Harder, harder!"

Tanya had focused all of her attentions on Amanda, and as Alex heaved himself against Amanda, Tanya nibbled and sucked on her breasts. As he felt Amanda's passion rising to unbearable heights, he thrust his finger into her anus. She screamed with pleasure, her eyes rolling wildly, unfocused as she tried to catch her breath. Finally, the three of them collapsed into a pile, Amanda losing consciousness for a few achievements.

She awoke to find Tanya and Alex looking down on her with what she took to be almost parental affection. To be here in the sunlight, in the mountains, feeling the warm air and the touches of her friends made her happy beyond description. She smiled broadly, glorying in this wonderful and rare moment of unequivocated bliss.

"I'm so happy," she told them. "That was wonderful."

They said nothing, merely smiling down at her like bemused Buddhas.

She laughed. "Oh, but I can't be so greedy. Now it's Tanya's turn."

Alex turned his radiant smile to Tanya. "Well," he intoned, "isn't it?" Tanya blushed.

Amanda, recognizing their intimacy with one another, found herself no longer in the least bit jealous of her two friends. "I see you two have been getting along very well."

"Well, I don't know," said Tanya, finally speaking, "maybe it's Alex's turn."

"That sounds good to me," agreed Amanda.

Alex, without a hint of reservation, decided to take advantage of the situation. "Well, I don't know. I've had this fantasy all my life that I'd one day be able to watch two women making love."

Amanda and Tanya smiled at one another. Alex continued, "I know it's typical. Quite a few men have the same fantasy. But I've always imagined that two women together would be especially sensitive to one another, would have a gentleness that men lack. Somehow, I felt I'd be able to learn something about tenderness, about what it is a woman really wants. And, even more, there's something taboo about watching, something illicit and forbidden."

Amanda asked him with some incredulity, "You mean to tell me that with all your years of experience living on the Ark, you've never watched two women making love to one another? In . . . what is it?" She paused to think. "In ten years you've never done that?"

"Not like this," he said. "Not with two women I felt this close to."

"Well, hold on, my dear," Amanda told him with a leering smile, "Tanya and I aren't about to disappoint you. My sister and I know everything about each other."

In an instant it was as if they had forgotten Alex was there. Amanda slid up to Tanya and placed her arm gently around Tanya's waist, cooing softly as she made contact with

Tanya's flesh. As if acting on a signal, Tanya looked up, gazing into Amanda's eyes.

From where he sat, Alex could see Tanya's diamond-shaped pupils dilate and he thought he detected a reddish blush in her face, her cheeks turning to burnt sienna. Tanya's lips parted slightly, showing her white teeth from which the tip of her tongue protruded.

Amanda seemed taller, more confident than he had seen her before. She was no longer a flippant prankster. She concentrated all of her attention on Tanya as if she were a virtuoso about to play a piece on a musical instrument. Perhaps what surprised him most was that he had expected Amanda to be submissive to Tanya's strong, overpowering body. Instead, she was Tanya's master, setting the pace, taking initiative. He felt a pang of something that resembled jealousy course through him as he realized how complete they were in this act without him. They were transformed.

He felt a tingle in his brain and suddenly he had no more reservations. A powerful surge of euphoria welled up through his body. He reveled in their exquisite beauty as they enveloped one another. The contrast between the physical appearances appealed to him: their black and white skin, their intertwining limbs. Tanya's body was hard, as if she had been chiseled from black marble, her skin tinted with metallic finish. Amanda was white, light and airy, her body voluptuous, loose and rolling. He couldn't tell which one of the two he loved more, or if it even made a difference. He heard the sounds they made and they seemed inhuman, animal-like but possessing an intelligence and compassion that no animal could have. It was musical, a song of love.

Amanda cupped one of Tanya's breasts lightly in her hand. She stared at it as if she were spellbound. Tanya made loud licking noises with her tongue and lips, her body writhing in excitement. Amanda finally spoke in a tone of voice Alex had not heard her use. She spoke as if she couldn't decide whether she was pleading or commanding. "Tanya," she said, "I love your breasts. You don't need to put them on these platforms. They're beautiful the way they are."

Upon saying this, Amanda removed the platforms that had supported Tanya's breasts from underneath. "See how firm and erect they are." She touched and squeezed them. Tanya watched as Amanda fondled her.

"Doesn't Tanya have pretty purple nipples?" Amanda asked Alex. "Would you hold her tits for me while I suck on her nipples?"

Alex felt another tingle in his brain. The momentary panic he had felt ceased. He reached out and held Tanya's breast, watching as Amanda's lips encircled her dark nipples. He could feel Amanda's warm breath on his hand. He watched as Tanya moved her hand to Amanda's breast, lightly kneading Amanda's nipples with her fingers. He told himself that this was like playing his trumpet; all he needed to do was relax and go with the music. Don't think, he thought, flow with it—just flow and feel. He felt himself swept along in the current. He decided to stop watching—everything that happened was being recorded, he could watch it some other time—and start feeling, to try and enjoy the experience for what it was, to take part in it rather than observe.

As if she were speaking from a distance, he heard Amanda say, "God, Alex, you're so turned on. Are going to be alright?"

Tanya's deep voice followed. "Don't worry, he likes being an animal. Momma conditioned him."

"Oh?"

"Alex, show Amanda what an animal you can be when you're with me," commanded Tanya.

All of his efforts to hold back were broken by Tanya's demand. He had let himself come this far and he didn't want to stop. He looked beyond the two women and saw the expanse of the Grand Valley of the Yosemite and was inspired by its primitive power. His heart thumped wildly, the veins in his neck beginning to tic.

Everything happened quickly, and he felt almost disembodied, as if he would never remember what he had done. He felt himself overcome with primeval sadness, saw himself as a pinprick of a man in an infinite universe. Who was he, he wondered, to care about what he did or what he might do? From the recesses of his brain came premonitions of guilt, of nightmares, of fear. Try as he might, he could not escape his reservations about the two women. He knew without a doubt that he wanted Amanda more than anything else. He wanted to desire both women equally, but his body and mind wouldn't let him. He only wanted her.

Amanda was the first to break into his private deliberations. "Well," she said in a huff, "I've got to get back to the party. I loved being with you two, but you know I've got to be where the action is."

Before either of them could respond, Amanda was dressed and gone. Alex gave Tanya a puzzled look, but Tanya only snickered and then laughed out loud. "That's my Amanda!"

CHAPTER 15

EXERCISE TIME

Alex watched Tanya fidgeting beside him, scratching at her fingers, then her neck. She seemed distracted, not having said a word to him for almost an entire achievement. He asked her if something was wrong.

"I don't know, Alex," she said. "I feel restless, like I should go work out. My whole body feels tight and tense. I need to get myself into that Mother Machine." She stood up, stretching her arms toward the ceiling, pulling them down into a body builder's pose. "It'll make me feel so good. Why don't you come with me?"

Alex looked doubtful. For the past one hundred and twenty achievements, he'd done nothing but exercise with Tanya and Amanda. He didn't know how much further he could push himself.

"Come on," Tanya encouraged him, "you don't know how good that machine makes me feel." She changed her position, bending her legs so that he saw every muscle in her thighs and calves. "It makes me feel like a Goddess. I can feel every part of my body after I've finished, but Mother never lets me get a cramp, and I never get stiff the next day. Mother's the one thing on the Ark you managed not to mess up." She continued to flex in a variety of positions, as if she were competing for a prize.

Alex spent a few moments thinking it over, admiring Tanya's strength and definition. He thought about contacting Carl, to check and see how a workout would fit into his probationary regimen, but just as he was telling Tanya of his plan, there was a beep on his receivers and Carl's voice greeted him. "Alex, this is Carl."

Alex had to smile at Carl's timing. Tanya waved a finger at him, as if to warn him about Big Brother looking after him at all times. He asked Carl to go ahead with his message.

"It is about time for your feeding, Alex."

"Well, that's good because I was going to call you anyway. Tanya and I are going to work out."

"Wonderful. I am glad to hear that. If you extend your workout for one additional achievement, that should help maintain the metabolic balance we have been aiming for."

"That's fine with me, Carl. We'll see you in about a nan."

"Very good. Enjoy your workout."

Alex and Tanya left the compartment and headed toward the gym. On the way, they took a brief detour down a small passageway to a food stand. Alex had been so active that he was feeling small pangs of hunger, a rare sensation due to the precise feeding schedules Carl had planned for him.

Tanya separated from him, heading toward a private cubicle. He approached one of the blue screens, announcing himself. "Hi, Carl. This is Alex." Before the computer could respond, he grabbed the sample tube and blew into it violently. "There. Analyze that, buddy."

The screen blinked on and off and Carl intoned in his melodic but authoritative voice, "You have done very well, Alex. I want to show you some images that I have put together. They document your body's changes from your last feeding to this feeding."

Carl's monitor displayed two images of Alex's body, both in cross section. One showed his metabolic patterns at the time of his last feeding, the other showed his current status. Each area in the body was labeled in detail, different colors representing the various levels of nutrients, blood-oxygen ratios, blood sugar, lipids and other information. Alex was amazed to see his thalamus and hypothalamus labelled with so many tag materials. Both cross sections were superimposed over what a normal pattern should be. He had made tremendous gains from his last feeding; he was almost in balance.

"Fantastic, Carl. You've done a great job." Alex was

always compelled to congratulate the machines on their performance. He easily forgot that they weren't human.

"Thank you, Alex. You are one of my most cooperative patients. I wish more people were so attentive to my advice."

"I'm sure you're a master of persuasion, Carl."

"Yes. I have my ways of getting them to listen. But I find you so much more understanding of my duties. Our latest correction is something of a triumph for me. I was quite worried after your first urine sample, but when I scanned you during your nap, your brain waves were right on target."

"Well, that's great, Carl. We wouldn't want to have anyone out of control, especially me."

"Yes, Alex. I worry about that quite a bit. I don't like to have anyone on board the ship who is not regulated. In fact, I was worried about your Russian friend. He drank far more than he needed to."

"He did, did he?"

"Yes. But he didn't leave the celebration area. I'm glad that chamber is so far from the city center, away from the families and children. Rick's security system has been a great help in that regard."

Alex considered this for a moment, thinking, Sure, that's because Rick doesn't want his wife and kids seeing him partying with the rest of the swingers.

"What did you say, Alex?" He had forgotten that Carl could pick up his subvocalization.

"Oh, nothing," he tried to exonerate himself. "I was just thinking some rather nasty thoughts. I'm not perfect, you know."

"I understand. We all have a tendency to be judgmental."

Carl could be so understanding. Here he was now, trying to counsel Alex. A machine cares more about my emotions than I do, he thought. "Sometimes my ego is just a little too big for my own good," he confessed. "I need to be more humble."

"No, Alex. It is your lifelong insecurities that frighten you. Look at everything you have accomplished in spite of them. Well, I know you are in a hurry so I have fixed a special meal just for you. I have added extra taste and texture for your pleasure." A bowl was filled with a typically unappealing lump of paste.

"Thank you, Carl. You're a wonderful cook."

"You enjoy yourself with Tanya and Amanda."

Alex was taken aback for a moment. How did Carl know about both Tanya and Amanda? He realized that Genie, being the more sophisticated computer and needing health information about her wards, took Carl into her confidence, the two data banks exchanging information.

Alex remembered a science fiction story he had read as a boy, in which computers had been transplanted into human bodies. He felt that Genie and Carl were practically human. He almost thought that he loved Genie, even though he knew she was a machine. Genie was becoming more like Keiko, acting as his counsel, his source of reassurance. Some people on the Ark's committees had accused him of placing too much faith in computers, but he would never let them lower the capability of the machines. He had even safeguarded Genie and Carl's programs, along with several other computers, against debilitating reprogramming. I'm probably just paranoid, he thought. But when he considered Rick's motives, he thought he was better safe than sorry. It was such a trial trying to maintain his vision among people who doubted him. If humans on the Ark wanted to live like humans on Earth, why didn't they go to the Moon or Mars. They didn't have to stay on board.

Alex took his tray and headed toward a table. He saw Tanya in a nearby cubicle, gesticulating wildly toward the screen. He paused for a moment, wondering what was happening and then saw Carl dispense her portions of food. Assuming everything was copacetic, he sat at a table and waited for her. After a moment, she exited the cubicle, spotted him and approached in a very stiff, regal walk.

"Well, I see this time your food isn't as green as before." She sat down. "Let's enjoy our turkey or steak or fish or potatoes or whatever it is."

"Cut the sarcasm, Tanya."

"Well, now that you've convinced me I can live to a hundred and fifty by eating this stuff, I'm happy to do it. I'll eat anything."

"So I've made myself a convert, huh?"

"Yes, my love, you have." Despite her sarcasm, Alex realized she was serious. "I want to keep up with my man." She was slipping into her Southern accent, and Alex took this as a sign of happiness. Perhaps the prospect of a good workout really meant a lot to her. She smiled and proceeded to shove a huge portion of food into her mouth.

"Mmmmmm, good," she said.

Alex took a bite, commenting on the consistency of the food. "Did you notice how crunchy this tastes? I think they've started adding a new fibrous plant we've developed to the recipe. It's a lot less pulpy."

Tanya licked her lips. "Oh, it's so good, Alex."

He was sure she must be joking with him and told her so.

"No, I mean it," she protested. "It's really good. Try some of mine."

Alex smiled at her, letting her teasing slide by without further comment.

After a short walk, Alex and Tanya arrived at the gym, a huge room colored with sparkling lights. Inside the workout area, Alex sensed a vibrant aura of energized good feelings that seemed to affect every person in the place. He immediately felt more alert, ready to run, box, or lift his way to health.

Aligned along each wall was a series of coffin-shaped boxes called the Iron Maidens. The exerciser crawled into one of the boxes and the lid was closed tight. The subject told the computer his or her name and the interior was molded into a perfect fit around the subject's body. A mask molded around the face to control the flow of oxygen to the body. The computer, like Carl and Genie, used breath samples to monitor metabolism, circulation, pulse and other vital signs. Any irregularity in the exercises, such as cramping or cardiac conditions, was rectified by adjustments in the oxygen mix, changes in the rate of exercise, or small electrical pulses to a specific muscle group.

Since the machine provided perfectly regulated resistance, each exercise gave the muscle an efficient and effective workout. Computer records on each individual's desired body shape determined the rate, resistance and duration of each exercise. The individual saw a hologram of his ideal body shape and was able to monitor progress towards that goal. If any changes were desired, they could be made to the hologram first and then implemented into an exercise regimen. Exercise plans were coordinated with Carl to maximize the efficiency of feeding periods and nutrients.

The Iron Maiden's workout regiment took only one achievement, but was as effective as a three-hour workout on Earth. Because of the sophistication of the Ark's gymnasium, its athletes were not allowed to compete on Earth's professional sports teams or in the Olympics. On the Ark, there were no professional teams. Anyone could play on any team in any sport. In fact, the Ark had developed several extremely challenging games that no Earth athlete could imagine competing in.

Tanya headed straight for the nearest available machine. She shouted over her shoulder, "See you in one achievement!"

"No, Tanya, two. Carl told me two."

"Okay, two then," she said tartly and disappeared under the lid.   Alex wondered if Tanya might challenge him to some sporting event after they were through. She was strong enough to be a worthy opponent in any activity. He anticipated struggling against her in competition as he had struggled against her during their lovemaking.

He entered another Iron Maiden and tensed for a moment as the mask tightened around his face and the workout began. His hologram materialized before him and he decided to enlarge his calf muscles. He believed he could feel the change in resistance almost immediately. As the workout grew more and more intense, he felt no pain, just a sense of warmth and mild fatigue. As his body released endorphins, he began to have a euphoric feeling, and his mind began to clear itself of all tension and stress. He saw an image of Amanda wiggling her backside at him. There were brief flashes of Rick and then Keiko. He saw Tanya laughing uncontrollably, followed by his daughter Dominique, who smiled at him and reached out to touch him, saying, "How're you doing, Dad?"

He responded out loud. "I love you, Dominique."

He had a tremendous love for his daughter, for both of his children, a feeling that ran deeper than anything else in his life. That feeling was now changing, dramatically, to fear. He began to sense terror on his daughter's part as her image began to fade. He felt he had to protect her somehow. The urge to stop the workout and go to her was overwhelming.

Then he saw a flash of white light and felt the wind and heat of Arizona. He saw Keiko again, dressed in white, standing on a mesa, moving slowly. She became a small, white speck and then disappeared. He heard himself yelling, "Keiko, Keiko! Come back! Please, don't go. I need you."

An image of his son Tim followed. He remembered how faithful Tim had been to him. His son was one of the most giving people he had ever met, as was his mother, Lorraine. No one else had loved Alex as unconditionally as Tim. He had stood behind Alex, always loving him, no matter what he did.

Tim's face was replaced by an ongoing succession of faces, faces of people he didn't know, faces of a thousand different cultures and nationalities. They were like torrents of rain pouring down in front of his eyes. From among them emerged a figure of incredibly bright color. He felt himself engulfed by a cleansing stream of white light. He was flushed with energy, purified, and then suddenly, the light was gone and he heard the machine counting, "six, five, four, three, two, one." The exercise was over.

The Iron Maiden opened slowly and Alex adjusted his eyes to the lights of the gym. He lifted himself out and stood still for a moment, trying to steady himself. He focused his eyes and saw Tanya standing across from him. She did not see him as she straightened out her clothes. She looked beautiful, transformed by the exercise. He realized how strong his feelings for her were and he wondered if he should confide his vision in her. No, he was not ready yet. He needed to understand more fully what it was the vision required him to do. She had come here to enjoy herself. He didn't want to trouble her yet.

She looked up and saw him. "Wasn't that great! I feel so wonderful. I worked so hard my mind went blank. It was amazing. I've never gone that far before. I saw this incredible white light that shot through me. And it was the strangest thing, I thought about someone named Tim. I saw his face. He looked just like you."

"He's my son. He's an attorney who's getting rich finding loopholes for the rich. When he was younger, I could never punish him, he'd always find a way out. Give me some logical explanation of why he'd done something."

"Sounds like some kid."

"Yes. He's a smart kid. He was the kind of person who put everything off until the last minute. But, then, his first day at law school, he came home and read almost every book he had. From that day on he got nothing but A's in his courses."

"You must miss him."

"I do. I've tried to get him up here, but he loves Southern California so much he won't leave. I even tried to send him to Stanford or Berkeley for college, but he didn't want to move up north, out of his comfort zone. He doesn't like changes. But I'm so proud of him. I wish he could be here with me."

It was as if actually saying the words forced Alex to realize how much he missed his children, how much he wanted to be with them. Here I am, he thought to himself, floating around in space on what is supposed to be the realization of all my dreams. But sometimes I feel so isolated, I think I'll never see my kids again. What kind of prison have I built for myself? Am I ever going to be happy?

He watched Tanya striding confidently beside him. How could he tell her what he was thinking? She had read all of his books. She was a believer. So many of the people here were believers, yet he, the creator of it all, was doubting himself. If only Dominique and Tim could be here with him, he'd feel whole. He wanted a family to share his life with. He turned around and looked back toward the gym. The computerized machines hummed and clicked. He wondered if the machines were the only things that would stand by him forever.

CHAPTER 16

BASEBALL TIME

After their workout, Alex and Tanya wandered the corridors of the Ark. Alex was debating whether or not he should return to the party when Tanya broke what had been an uncomfortable silence. "Know what I want to do next?" she asked.

"How could I possibly know that?" he replied, mildly perturbed that his train of thought had been broken.

"All right. Well, forget about that. Anyway, my friend Helen Steinler, she's an incredible athlete and she's playing for the Dodgers today. That's my team. I promised I'd go and root for her."

An anxious look passed over Alex's face. "Do you even like baseball?" she inquired. "Say you'll come whether you do or not."

"I don't know, Tanya. I guess I figure baseball just isn't baseball without a couple of hot dogs and a cold beer followed by a pretzel with mustard and a packet of warm peanuts."

Tanya was amazed at his reaction. Alex expressing a desire to eat real food? This was not like him at all. "God, Alex. I never thought I'd hear you say that! If you like all that stuff so much, why don't you have one of the committees or one of your friends come up with artificial hot dogs or pretzels made of soybeans or tempeh or something?"

The set of Alex's lips suggested that he needed to respond in a way that wouldn't make his dissatisfaction with the food rules overt. "Well, I wish I could, Tanya. But the whole principle of the Ark's feeding program is to limit variety so that the committee and the health specialists can give people just the right amount of nutrients. I'm sure the board would vote down any new proposals almost immediately. Even if they did pass new standards allowing people to eat what they liked, could you imagine all the cases of indigestion and obesity we'd have on our hands? People would go crazy and eat and eat just for the taste of it. They'd get out of hand."

"Does that mean you're not going with me?" Tanya entreated.

Alex gave her a look of mock exasperation. "Well," he began teasingly, "I guess I don't have anything better to do. I suppose I could manage to squeeze it into my schedule."

Tanya flashed a triumphant smile. "Oh, I know you'll enjoy it. Helen's team is wonderful and they're playing against the Red Sox, who are in first place. I know it's going to be a great game."

"I think I actually know someone who plays on the Red Sox." Alex shook his head as if he were trying to jar the memory loose. "I can't remember . . . . Oh, wait, I know. I think Rick is playing with the Sox."

Tanya's smile was absolutely beaming now. "This is going to be so wonderful. Imagine Rick playing against my team! There's no way you can't come now."

Alex couldn't hide his own excitement—he might get to see Rick crushed on the playing field—even as he tried to be cool about the upcoming event. "I guess I'll have to live without the hot dogs." He pretended to mope for a moment and then burst out, "Sorry, Rick, but I hope the Red Sox get clobbered!"

"You can bet they will!"

Almost all of the athletic events on the Ark took place in the Zero-G sector. Lack of gravity lent even the most mundane sports, like golf, a new element of intensity. Balls that were just as likely to float up into the air instead of cascading to the ground meant that every game was now played with an expanded sense of the three dimensions. And while Earth stadiums could accommodate thousands of people, the Ark's arenas were on a smaller, more intimate scale. The Arkian arenas were covered by a dome-like structure that encased the playing field and seats.

While seating in a typical gym or stadium might be referred to as bleachers, the sophistication of the Ark's accommodations made that term inadequate. Each seat was like the plush chair of a corporate executive, upholstered in fine fabric and able to swing around in a full circle with room for the spectator's legs to be fully extended. The Zero-G environment required fans to put on specially designed magnetic shoes before they entered the stadium. Similar to the steel-wheeled roller skates of the 1940s that allowed children simply to strap the skates on over their shoes, the magnetic boots used a metal lever that adjusted and tightened a high-tech clasp for an exact fit over the spectator's street shoes.

Inside the arena, the playing areas were padded from the field to the top of the dome to prevent injury to players who sometimes propelled themselves one hundred feet into the air to make a play. The spectators were protected from the incredible velocity of balls batted in Zero-G by a transparent fence, woven out of invisible plastic fibers. In one section, spectators paid an extra fee to rent heavily armored suits and masks that allowed them to watch the game without any barrier between them and the playing field. Balls driven into this area inspired much competition among the fans who, just like fans on earth, lunged for the leather and cork souvenir of a day at the ballpark.

Once inside and seated, spectators not watching from the special section were required to belt themselves into their chairs. Initially, the tension generated in close games had often caused fans to forget themselves and begin jumping about, causing consternation and the spilling of drinks as they landed from an accidental seventy-five foot leap. The Ark's athletics commission immediately rectified this situation with the imposition of the belt rule. Any spectator not complying with the rule found his view blocked by a black screen that rose up in front of his seat until the belt was engaged. At first, angry fans had pummeled and kicked at the screens, trying to force them back into the ground. But the commission had designed the screens to withstand any such assault and now use of the belts was an accepted and unquestioned practice.

Tanya and Alex arrived early and found their seats in a nearly empty bleacher. They proceeded to put on their shoes, adjusting them for perfect fit and a magnetism level appropriate to their body weight. In order to walk with any level of control, the boots usually needed to be set on full force. Standing up in Zero-G was a precarious activity and novices usually found themselves weaving back and forth. Over time, both Alex and Tanya had developed considerable coordination in Zero-G, but it still took them a few wobbly minutes to accustom themselves to the new demands of the environment. Other early arrivals clanged about the stadium, their magnetic shoes on the decks of the seating aisles resonating loudly.

"These should be good seats," said Tanya. "We'll be able to see Helen in the outfield. I swear she is so amazing. She'll go for the ball anywhere. Watching her play is so much fun. I could sit here for an hour just watching her jump up and shag fly balls."

"I'm not one for jumping around," replied Alex. "I normally play first base. All you have to do is stand there. I was never much good in the outfield."

"Oh, I just hate playing first," Tanya declared. "I always think some slob is going to trample me. You can get killed. I like jumping around, running for the ball. Have you ever played catcher?"

"Never. And I don't want to, either. I don't know how those guys do it with their boots on low power. When the ball hits 'em, they get knocked all the way back to the fence."

"I've tried it a few times, but I can never figure out where to set my boots. Whenever I've got them set on high power to control the pitches, somebody pops up a foul ball and I'm falling all over myself to get out there and catch it. I haven't got the knack for switching my boots to no power in the middle of a play."

They passed time for quite a while, talking about their

favorite plays, series and teams. Tanya, it turned out, was a huge fan of the game. While Alex had always enjoyed a casual pickup game, Tanya was highly competitive both as a player and a spectator. She could reel off batting statistics like a professional announcer. While they talked, the stadium began to fill up and their conversation was interrupted by an eruption of boos, catcalls and hollering as the two teams took the field.

"Look at the pads these guys have on," exclaimed Tanya. It was true. Arkian athletics had stringent safety regulations and each player was bundled into a protective suit, gloves, and helmet. "Still, I love Dodger blue. Their uniforms are so pretty."

She paused for a moment, scanning the field. "Oooh, there's Helen," she said, pointing at one of the women on the field. Alex, unable to see the jersey numbers, was not able to identify her immediately. Tanya leapt out of her seat, shouting and waving hello to Helen. She almost began to float away, but Alex reached up and grabbed her leg, pulling her back into her seat. "I get so excited," she said, "I don't even know what I'm doing!" She began to yell, "Dodgers! Dodgers! Dodgers!"

For a moment the stadium was hushed as the American national anthem was played, both in honor of the country that had invented the sport and due to the fact that almost all of the players were of American descent. After the anthem, the teams were announced and each player's stats were displayed on a large screen. In addition to their playing achievements, the players' history included their job descriptions and talents. The Ark had no professional players. These teams were culled from the amateur athletes on board the ship. Despite their lack of professional status, the Ark players were confident, even cocky, about their abilities. Every time an exhibition game had been arranged against American professional teams, both on the Ark and on Earth, the Arkians had won handily. The embarrassing losses suffered by the Americans were one of the reasons Arkians were banned from all Earth sports competitions.

As they announced Helen's name, Alex read over her stats. He teased Tanya, "Do your stats look like that?" Tanya responded by listing her batting average, R.B.I.'s and stolen bases. Alex was surprised at her accomplishments.

"You are good, aren't you?" he said lamely.

"Maybe if they need a pinch hitter today, I'll get in there and knock a few around. After my workout today, I feel like I could do anything."

If Tanya wants to go, that's up to her, Alex thought. But he hoped he would not be drafted into the game. Occasionally, play was so rough that a team ran out of reserves, in which case the managers recruited from the stands. Due to Alex's high profile on the ship, he constantly was being asked to stand in, even though he was a terrible player, always overcompensating for the lack of gravity. No matter how much time he spent in the simulators, he couldn't improve his performance.

The danger to which the players exposed themselves was constant. Any time a ball was hit, lack of gravity caused it to rocket into the field with the force of a missile. Players who turned off the magnetic fields on their boots propelled themselves twenty or thirty feet into the air at high speed in order to stop the ball. Collisions were common as players mixed their signals and decided to make the same play. Occasionally an infield player would forget to brace himself properly for the ball's impact and the force of inertia caused him to become another projectile for the outfielders to deal with.

As the anthem finished, a deafening roar rose from the crowd. People on board the Ark were aggressive fans, shouting at top volume. It was impossible to hold a conversation over the din. Alex decided to speak to Tanya over her electrode. "Hi," he said and she turned and smiled at him.

"Aren't you clever?" she responded, her smile not parting to form the words. "I love hearing the national anthem up here. I get chills every time they play it. It makes me feel like I'm in touch with the people back on Earth."

Alex nodded in agreement. "I can't wait until the day we play the anthem in another solar system. It makes me proud to know how much we've accomplished. Sometimes I thought we were on the wrong track—back in the sixties, right after Kennedy got us to the moon, I was telling everyone we should be building rockets to get out into space, forget about building cars—but I know the country will live on no matter what happens."

Down on the field, the teams took up their positions, the Red Sox batting first. The first pitch resulted in an ear-splitting crack of the bat and a ball speeding directly in the direction of the stands where Alex and Tanya sat. Just as Alex was certain the ball would clear the perimeter for a home run, a blurred figure streaked into the air and snagged it. Helen, with unerring accuracy and speed, had made the first out. The fans went wild. She tossed the ball back to home plate casually, as if her breathtaking catch had been effortless. The hollering continued long after the play was finished, Tanya yelling louder than anyone else. Finally, Helen waved to the crowd and they calmed down.

As play resumed, Tanya turned to Alex with small tears forming in the corners of her eyes. "Wasn't that just beautiful? She looked like a ballerina." She wiped her eyes with the back of her hand. "God, I'm all choked up just thinking about it. I've never seen anyone but her make a play like that. She even did it with all that padding."

Mention of the protective suits caught Alex's ear, triggering his thoughts on another subject. "Speaking of padding," he asked, "have you seen the new spacesuits?"

"What?" asked Tanya, not following his change of topic.

"The new spacesuits," he repeated.

"Oh, yes. Actually, I wore one just the other day. They're fantastic, absolutely skin-tight. It's like the difference between wearing a diving bell and scuba gear for undersea exploration." She reached out and stroked Alex's bare arm. "Now I can see why you haven't got any hair. When they peeled that plastic off me, it ripped every last hair off my body. They should've warned me first."

"I took a depilatory pill before I put the suit on, so it was painless. Once everybody goes hairless, there won't be any problem. I got the idea for the suits from Jules Verne. You know, he came up with the idea for wetsuits decades before they were invented. I figured we could manufacture a suit like a surfer's neoprene wetsuit, except instead of neoprene, we'd use a stronger, flexible plastic. The reinforced material keeps the body intact even in a vacuum.

"The hair problem's a little tricky, but for guys my age, it'll probably be a blessing. As I got older, I started growing weird hairs everywhere: ears, nose, eyebrows. I got tired of tiny little strands pushing themselves out wherever they felt like it. Taking the hormone pill is a lot easier than plucking it all out." Alex reached out and caressed Tanya's head. "Are you on the pill, too?"

"Yes," she laughed. "I used to take it periodically for freedom of movement. When I'm playing sports, it makes my body feel unencumbered, like I'm faster. The ancient Greeks used to shave after every bath and then cover themselves in fine oil. They were just as fanatical about their bodies as we are."

Another crack of the bat and a roar focused their attention to the field again. The batter had swatted a powerful ground ball that was headed toward center field. Helen was barrelling toward the ball, but the second baseman also was trying to make the play. It looked as if they would collide, but at the last moment, Helen kicked out her leg, deflecting the other fielder while she swiped the ball with her left hand. In mid-air, she whirled around and threw the ball into home plate, keeping the runner from scoring. While Alex and Tanya were talking, two batters walked. The bases were now loaded with only one out.

The next batter bunted, but the catcher, whose shoes had been set on light power, fell over himself trying to field the ball. The pitcher attempted to back him up but bobbled the ball, sending it out into right field, where the ball was retrieved quickly by a player named Hansen. Although he quickly tossed the ball into home, a runner managed to score and the batter was safe on first.

The manager called for another bunt, but the catcher fielded this one handily, firing the ball to second base well ahead of the runner. Two outs. The second baseman made a wild throw to first, blowing the double play, and the batter made it to third before the ball could be recovered. Three runs had scored and the stands echoed with equal parts boos and hurrahs.

Another long shot to the outfield resulted in a double for the next batter, but the runner was held to third. The sixth batter pounded the ball toward center field in what looked like a sure home run, but once again Helen made an astounding play, fielding the ball to end the inning. The fans stomped the bleachers with their boots, an incredible metallic clamor engulfing the stadium. For a moment, Alex considered the strain on the epoxied steel. If the hull of the Ark can take the battering of space, Alex thought, I guess these bleachers can handle a few thousand people thumping their feet.

"With Helen on the Dodgers, Rick's team hasn't got a chance," said Tanya. "I feel like I should go down there and bat in a few runs for them. I feel sorry for him."

At the mention of Rick's name, Alex began to fume. Tanya kept mentioning Rick's name so often that he was sure she was trying to throw him off guard. He hated it when women tried to make him jealous, and he hated himself for feeling that way. It was like a fire burning in the pit of his stomach. He began to pout, thinking to himself, "Well, if that's the way you feel about it, I'll just turn my systems off so I won't have to see your spiteful face. Puff! You'll be invisible and I won't care."

He regretted even thinking the words, and was glad he had not spoken aloud. Where had he learned these intricate and ridiculous defense mechanisms? He thought of his mother's picture, the one he kept with him at all times. He remembered her soft skin and her perfume. For a moment, he was back in her arms, a little boy, comfortable and safe. Then he heard her voice, its high register no longer soothing, now explaining that she had to leave him to go to work. His father was gone and his grandfather dead. She had to go to work to support them, leaving him home alone, feeling abandoned. He understood what she said but it didn't blunt the pain as she walked out the door. Everyone left him: his father, his grandfather, and now his mother. A voice inside him called out, "Don't think about them. Don't care about them. Forget about it." He felt himself becoming someone else, escaping his body, escaping this world of pain.

He spoke coldly, analytically. "I would love to play against you and Rick, but I really must leave and find Vladimir. I've hardly talked to him since he's been here. Why don't you go ahead without me, and we'll catch up with one another later at the party? I'll be wearing the costume you designed for me."

Tanya was frowning slightly, trying to understand the sudden change that had come over him. Unable to put a finger on exactly what it was that bothered her, she bemoaned the fact that she wouldn't be the first to see his costume.

"Oh, you're right," he said, laying the sarcasm on thickly. "The only reason I'm going to the party is so that I can see you. You've become the center of my universe. I'll wait to get dressed. I'll sit there alone until you decide to arrive to help me zip my zipper or whatever. After all, I want to look perfect for you."

She decided not to address this last series of remarks, realizing she couldn't change his mind or his attitude. He turned around to leave. "Alex," she called after him. He stopped.

"I hope you'll miss me," she said. "I'll be thinking of you."

"Right."

"I'll be there as soon as I can. Why don't you give me a kiss?" He approached her and gave her a perfunctory peck on the cheek. She sighed deeply, exasperated and disappointed.

"Good luck with your game," he said. "I'm sure you'll turn the team around, especially with you and Rick fighting side by side."

As she watched him walking away, Tanya told herself she had just seen the cold side of Alex's personality that

Amanda had warned her about. It didn't make any sense to turn on her like that. As she headed down to the locker rooms to dress for the game, she thought of him wearing the costume she had designed and snickered. He won't be able to be so grouchy when he's wearing that outfit, she thought. He was a puzzling man, one moment warm and tender, the next moment ponderous and turned in on himself. Whatever he had on his mind, it was making him more and more distressed. She decided she would forget about him until the game was finished. She would see him soon and they would work everything out.

Chapter 17

Amanda's Beautiful Feet

Alex entered the party chamber and fought his way through the throng, shaking the occasional hand offered to him, accepting slaps on the back and uproarious toasts. To every group he encountered, he inquired about Vladimir. Had anyone seen him? Everyone, it turned out, had seen him at one point or another, aggressively fondling women, engaging in wild drinking contests. At present, however, no one had an idea where to find him.

He made his way to a distant corner of the room, wending through a mass of wildly cheering people who were too caught up in the spectacle before them to answer any of his questions. As he reached the front of the group, he saw what they were so engrossed in: Vladimir was crouched down in front of them, his arms folded across his chest. On the two and four of every measure of music, he kicked one of his legs out from under him, keeping his torso perfectly erect. Sweat poured down his red face. His eyes were shut tight with concentration. Alex wondered how much vodka he had had to drink. After watching Vladimir execute a few more kicks, his attention was diverted to a tall, white figure clad in a red outfit. Something about the way she moved reminded him of Amanda. Although the woman's back was turned to him, Alex ensured that it was Amanda with a quick glance at her legs: incredibly long, shapely legs, unmistakably Amanda's. Although only a short period of time had passed since he had last seen her, his heart was seized with tightness. He despaired at seeing her dancing in the center of such a crowd, so close to Vladimir. She turned around and placed her arms around Vladimir's neck, encouraging him to keep dancing.

He pushed his way closer to the action, elbowing a few people in the ribs to force a passage for himself. As he stood in the front watching her, Amanda finally turned her head towards him, smiling in acknowledgment of his arrival.

"I've been looking all over for you," she shouted over the din, walking toward him. "You just disappeared. I was ready to send out some Saint Bernards to find you."

She looked him over for the first time. "It wouldn't have been too hard with what you've got on. You look great. That is so funky."

"I guess I didn't go far enough. You still recognized me." Although he professed disappointment, he was overjoyed at her interest in his costume.

"Well, sure I recognized you. But I never realized you had such a great ass." She slapped his butt for emphasis, letting her hand linger for a moment so that she could give him a tremendous pinch. "And," she stage-whispered in his ear, giving him a squeeze, "you've got incredible balls."

"Hey, Owww!" He laughed.

"Come on out here and dance with me, Mr. Modern Man. They're finally playing some decent music."

He grabbed her hand and walked cockily out to the center of the dance floor. Amanda tried to lag behind, waving goodbye to friends, but Alex persisted in dragging her across the floor. When they reached the middle of the floor, Alex suddenly changed his mind, walking all the way across the floor and proceeding to leave the room. He pulled Amanda along with him.

With the doors closed behind them, he pulled her close to him and she placed her arms around his shoulders. She kissed him on the face and exclaimed in a bubbly voice, "I guess this means we aren't going to dance together." She kissed him again. "I guess I don't mind. You looked so good out there on the floor I wanted to make love to you right in front of everyone."

They walked down the corridor into a vacant room, embracing one another instantaneously as the doors closed behind them.

"You're so beautiful," he told her.

"Boy," she said, giving him a sad look, "you've really got it bad, don't you?"

Her reaction shocked him. Once again she had shunned him, deflected the intensity of his feelings for her.

"That's what you do to me," he said, trying to hide his disappointment. "Is that so wrong? Can't you let me have my illusions?"

She blew into his face, pouting conceitedly. "Well, don't blame me if you get hurt." She paused, trying to save the moment from being a complete loss. "But you've still got a nice ass," she managed to say, giving Alex's posterior an affectionate tweak.

They kissed and pulled back from one another in silence. Amanda noticed that Alex was still staring at her with a dreamy look, as if he had been hypnotized. Although she was flattered by his attentions, she was used to men treating her this way. Almost every man she had spent an amorous few hours in her company became completely devoted to her. But the intensity in Alex's gaze was different, almost unsettling. It was a look of such intense hunger that Amanda, jaded as she was, thought that Alex's feeling for her must be something out of the ordinary. She felt she had to protect him, save him from herself. And in recognizing that she wanted to save him, not treat him like the other men she had been with, she recognized that she, too, felt something for him that she had not for any of her other partners.

"You're such a loving man," she told him. "Sometimes I've wondered if I'd ever meet a man who felt things as intensely as I do." As she spoke, however, she realized that Alex's attention had been diverted. He was staring at her feet. "Do you like my legs?" she asked him.

"They're perfect," he answered. He found he couldn't explain with any exactitude why he found them so, he just felt a sense of perfection as he continued to ogle her. Her muscles were perfectly balanced, taut underneath perfect skin. He indicated that he wanted her to sit down and she did. He took hold of her ankles and slipped off her shoe.

"Your shoes," he said. "They look like they're part of your feet." It was true. Amanda had had the shoes specially carved to appear like a natural extension of her feet. And now that her shoe was off, he saw that he found her feet just as perfectly proportioned, just as beautiful as her legs. He held her foot in his hands, stroking her delicate toes, massaging the sole.

"Alex, that feels so good," she murmured.

He began pulling lightly on her toes so that she made little jumps of surprise and pleasure. He caressed around her ankle and then rubbed her arch with a circular motion. She began to purr. As he continued to massage her feet, he began to occasionally stroke her legs, the sweep of his hand encompassing more and more of her legs until he had reached her knees. She began to spread her legs, inviting his touch.

"It's like all the tension in my body is passing out through my feet," she said. "Where did you learn to do that?"

Alex didn't answer, but remembered learning massage techniques from a woman named Jane. Everything he had learned about how to treat women had come from women themselves. They were his best instructors in how to give sensual pleasure.

He had been with so many different women, but he thought he would never meet anyone who made him feel the way Amanda did. His feelings for her went beyond his usual lust for a moment in a woman's bed. She had awakened a desire, a carnality that he had not known before. She appealed to his basest instincts, feelings that he had kept hidden for so long, he never even knew he had them.

Still, their relationship was tenuous at best. He had learned to deal with lack of devotion when he had been with Annette, Amanda's mother. Annette had been able to profess her love for Alex one moment and sleep with another man the next. When they walked on the streets together, if a man passed by, Annette's nostrils would flare, her eyes light up with sexual attraction. She emanated such strong sexual signals that men, upon passing them, would stop to turn around and stare at her. Alex knew that for every time this happened as he walked by her side, there were many occasions when he was not with her. And Annette, no matter how much she told him she loved him, could not resist the urge to find out what the man would be like, how this stranger might be different.

Amanda was just like her mother. Her loyalty in love went nowhere. She would never be content with just one man. Still, Annette's escapades had never gone so far that she did not return to Alex. No matter what she did, he still desired her, still wanted her to come back to him from whoever's bed she had spent a few hours in. Perhaps, he thought, it was this elusiveness, his inability to possess them, that made mother and daughter so attractive to him.

Annette had forced him to deal with a side of his personality he didn't like to think about: his jealousy, his desire to kill the men she had been with. And Amanda, too, was drawing this dark side out of him. Day-to-day life offered few opportunities for a man to act on his more primitive emotions. He had to keep them bottled up with complex, almost neurotic, defense mechanisms. But despite his complaints, he knew that the idea of being involved with a woman he thought of as "wicked" appealed to him. He felt like he was getting back in touch with his whole self, rediscovering his sense of adventure, his need to experiment.

He had lost Annette because of his inability to cope with her flirtatiousness. He wondered if now, at age seventy-five, he was any more mature. Maybe in the Ark's new society, he would find the strength to let go of his pettiness, to be brave enough to deal with not knowing what the future would hold. Nobody could be sure of anything, he knew, and trying to cling to the life he had known was not the path to wisdom. He didn't know if he believed in karma or in an afterlife, but he thought that somehow, by living to his potential, by trying to clear himself of debilitating societal constructs, he would be pursuing a worthy goal.

He remembered his unending conversations with people he had hardly known, conversations in which he described love and its inadequacy, how sick people had become, chasing after something that would never satisfy them. People talked about their spouses, their boyfriends, girlfriends as if they were obstacles to overcome. As if they had the same problems with drugs, alcohol, overeating. "I just can't help myself," they'd say. "I love her. I love him."

When Alex pointed out the similarities between their relationship with their lovers and their addictions, they nodded their heads in acknowledgment that Alex was right. But still, they said, they were helpless to do anything. "We're sick," they'd say. "We're all screwed up." But instead of trying to change anything, they simply attributed their behavior to being "human." It was inborn, they insisted. There was nothing they could do.

In every book he read, Alex looked for a hint at a solution, but nothing seemed to offer a lasting cure. When he was with Keiko, she had tried to teach him spiritual techniques to overcome his problems. She showed him how to meditate to try and find his place in the universe. But still, he had never found happiness, never felt like he was truly alive. With Amanda, amidst the uncertainty, the chaos, he felt like he was back together with Annette, that he was moving forward, breaking the barriers he had been afraid to approach.

As he moved inside of Amanda, hearing her moans commingling with his own, their sighs of love intertwining, he thought, this is what makes the hate, the horror, the awfulness bearable. These moments of overwhelming joy were the reason he lived, the moments he dreamed of. Pursuit of such ecstasy was what he based every second of his life on. It gave him motivation to wake up, walk around, talk, work.

Slowly but surely, their passion dwindled into a quiet, languorous togetherness. It always seemed to surprise Alex that he could be so entirely spent when he finished with lovemaking. They paused now, sated, but soon they would once again be hungry for one another.

He looked at her face, her perfect color, a quality he would never be able to reproduce in one of his paintings. Her eyes were wild with abandonment, their pale blue reflecting his gaze in their watery depths. Her eyes reminded him of

Keiko's, as he though he could see insanity, fear, openness and love concentrated together in the fractured color of her irises. Her hair fell in golden strands, thin and soft. He breathed in the fragrance, a honeyed, flowery smell he would never forget. He wanted to bury his face in her hair for the rest of his life.

Alex was so relaxed he began to fall into a dreamlike state. Amanda, however, sprang from the bed and began straightening out her clothes. She bent over, letting her hair dangle to the floor, then shook her blonde mane, and jerked her neck back, whipping her blonde locks into a wild arrangement around her shoulders.

"I have to go now," she announced. "I promised someone I'd meet him in ten achievements."

"Him?"

She froze in place, casting a withering look in his direction. "Give me a break, Alex. That stuff didn't work with my mother and it won't work with me. Not in this day and age." She tried to soften her rebuke, stroking his face, smiling at him. "You've got to learn to play by the rules, Honey."

She turned away abruptly and continued to dress. "Anyway, you've got Tanya and I know exactly what you're feeling, so don't tell me you're suffering." She faced him again, about to say something, her lips slightly parted. He noticed her teeth shining behind her bud-like lips.

"I," she said softly, "love you."

He thought he saw small tears forming in her eyes, but before he could say or do anything in response, she had fled the room, the door closing behind her.

CHAPTER 18

VOTING

On a list of the Arkians' priorities, voting fell into place right after feeding and working. More time was spent in government than any other major activity. The Ark's voting process was unlike Earth's, in that a fifty percent majority was not the standard by which proposed legislation was introduced into law. Instead, a quorum of at least ninety percent was required, and decisions garnering one hundred percent support were not uncommon. The Ark's voting population was much more sophisticated than their planet-dwelling brethren due to an elaborate system of computers, communications networks, analytical techniques and civic education. Issues were approached from every angle, the results of research and analysis presented to the public. Only after citizens had proven that they had attempted to the best of their ability to synthesize the material were they allowed to vote.

Alex was excited because today a vote was due on the latest round of new program recommendations and his bill for expediting funds for extra-solar system colonization was up for adoption. As chair of the committee that had proposed the bill, Alex's political stock was tied up in the result of the ballots cast. While he voted as a senator, and a full vote of the senate was required to pass the bill on to the President, there was always the possibility that the President might veto the bill. Unfortunately for Alex, Rick would be acting President for the vote on the extra-solar system proposal and had the opportunity to veto a bill even if it were passed by the Senate. Alex was worried that his enmity toward Rick might finally be reciprocated in the form of a presidential killing of his bill.

Still, he knew he had to accept the realities of the political system he had helped to create, a system that offered a greater scope of democracy than any other society.

On the Ark, there was no ongoing president. Each ten thousand achievement period found a different citizen sitting as acting president. Computers allowed every citizen to be informed and able to execute the responsibilities of the office. Knowing how invariably power corrupted those who possessed it, the Ark's government avoided placing permanent power in the hands of a few.

But even before the bill got to Rick, a rigorous debate would be held on the merits of the new ideas. Alex was worried that he might be more embarrassed by having to vote against his own bill than by suffering a presidential veto. Although it would be unheard of for an Earth politician to oppose his own legislation, on the Ark the computer systems that compiled research on the impact of each bill often persuaded the bill's authors to oppose its implementation. Alex feared that the computers might come up with arguments and problems he had never considered. There was honor, he knew, in recognizing that he was wrong, but he hated to be proved wrong, even if it was for the good of the Ark. In the long run, however, he had confidence that such stringent scrutiny benefited everyone and ensured the continuing success of the Ark.

Alex made his way to an educational chamber, a small, egg-shaped room filled with viewing screens and database equipment. The door closed with a whisper behind him and he removed his clothes to make himself comfortable. He believed that his nudity allowed him to concentrate more fully on the issues at hand. Once ready, he deactivated the chamber's gravity function and allowed himself to float up to the center of the chamber where he could see all of the screens simultaneously. Upon command, the Senator's program began. Multiple images of senators and other concerned parties revealed that they were already in progress on the debate, some speaking in favor of the space exploration bill, some against it. The program was designed to allow the viewer to digest the information simultaneously without having to continually shift his concentration to each individual speaker. However, when Alex saw a screen fill with an image of Rick, he couldn't resist focusing all of his attention on the man who might easily negate all of Alex's hard work.

Rick began his statement with a series of jokes, intended to endear himslf to the audience. Canned laughter followed each punch line. Alex hated Rick's jokes and was surprised at the number of people, especially women, who thought they were hilarious. He remembered Tanya saying, "Rick's so funny," and he felt his skin begin to heat up with equal parts jealousy and anger.

After finishing his comic turn, Rick began to present his argument: "I know that some people claim that we need to find a new Earth out there. But do we know if there really is another planet we can call our own out in space? And even if there is, how far away is it? How will we be able to find it? There is a planet that I know of. I can show you where we can find it, too." He pointed down with an exaggerated gesture. "Why do we need to find another Earth? Why do we need to spend so much money for ships that, with the current rate of advances in technology, will be outdated by the time they are built? Even if we do get the ships built properly, how long will it take them to travel the light years required to reach even the nearest stars? Will any of us be alive to see the results?"

Alex began to groan inwardly. He had known that Rick was going to make this argument and he wondered how convincing this sounded to the other senators.

"We know one thing for sure," Rick continued, "and that is that in the twenty-five million achievements it will probably take to complete this project, we will have ships that will overtake the manned space flights this bill proposes. Haven't we learned anything from history? If we want to explore space to satisfy our curiosity about the possibility of living someplace else, let's use computer probes and not risk human lives in a mission that might never succeed."

Rick began to turn his argument into an attack on Alex.

"In addition, why are we so concerned with finding a new place to institute a new society? Our obligation is to the present. To the here and now. The argument that we need to establish our own society on our own planet is just gobbledygook. It's an extension of one man's vanity. If a man can't live in his present society, then he needs to fix what won't work, not run away to find something else."

Alex began to twitch his fingers rapidly, clutching them into fists, his body shaking with rage. Here was Rick addressing the body of the senate and he felt powerless to stop what he perceived as slander against him. As much as he wanted to break into the communication and shout out, "Stop all this crap!" he controlled himself and forced himself to listen to the rest of Rick's speech.

"And let's talk about the funding and economics of the whole thing. There are so many places in our own solar system that have viable projects waiting to be funded. We have plans already established for Venus and Jupiter, but we lack the money to do anything about them. Our funds are not, as some people seem to think, unlimited. Why should we be looking to spend millions to find what might be another earth when we have this one to fix? And some people tell me we might discover new forms of intelligence. But is that what we really want? If we encounter these new beings, will we be able to protect ourselves against them if they are hostile? I don't think some people's visions of universal love are necessarily applicable out in space. We need to be realistic. I say we're not ready for new threats to our way of life. I say we don't need to waste money on flimsy promises of new worlds when we have one we can work on right below us. We're not ready to take the risks involved!" He paused to let his point sink in and then, obviously on cue, the camera pulled into a tight close-up of his face so that he could ask, with almost a whisper, "Are we?"

A long burst of synthetic applause burst forth from the speakers and the picture faded out. Alex was appalled at the negative spin Rick had put on his ideas. For a few moments, however, he had to admit that he had begun to feel doubt about the bill. What if Rick was right? There was always that possibility. But he believed in exploration, he told himself, with all his heart. Man cannot hold back the hands of time. He has to keep moving forward, keep taking risks.

Images of different speakers began to present themselves and Alex refocused his attention on the debate, reminding himself that it was his duty to hear all of the arguments presented. If Rick cast doubts upon his vision, perhaps there would be others who believed in what he wanted. He ordered the machines to fast forward and he saw and heard each speaker moving rapidly through their presentations, the essentials of their arguments displayed in captions on the screen.

On a side screen he saw Amanda and he asked for her speech to be played in real time on the forward screen. She was dressed in a traditional Japanese costume and as the volume was raised to an audible level, he discovered that she was speaking Japanese. After a few moments of listening through a translator, Alex realized, as he had hoped, that she was praising the program. She looked ravishing, appearing almost entirely Japanese, with the exception of her height, which was unusual for an Asian woman. Still, Alex hoped her argument would help to further convince the Japanese contingency aboard the ship. Polls indicated that most of them were in favor of the bill, but the power of their lobby and the numbers in which they voted made them an essential voting block to have on his side. A unanimous vote from the Japanese almost always indicated a high majority vote in the general populace.

Amanda spoke eloquently about the promises the new bill offered. "This will be a new adventure for humankind. We will be trying to populate outside our own solar system, trying to find a new Earth unspoiled by man. And when we do find it, our new technology will allow us to live there without ruining its pristine condition, without upsetting the natural balance. There may be vast new oceans, teeming with life. New habitats for animals. We may be able to keep herds of animals for our own benefit.

"In this solar system there is only one water planet, Earth. I know about the plans to replace Venus's atmosphere with another. I know of the plans for freeing up water systems on Mars. Others have suggested that we create another sun by igniting Jupiter's gaseous atmosphere. And while our current president sees hope in these plans, he offers no concrete evidence that they will work. Even if they do, they will never replace the Earth, never offer oceans and unlimited water supplies. And that is why we must move on to find new oceans, new sources of resources on a planet where humans will prosper."

She began a direct appeal to her audience: "The Japanese people have a tradition of leading the way with new ideas, in taking ideas to the marketplace and making them work more efficiently. Time and time again, the Japanese people have taken new ideas and new technology—in aviation, transistors, superconductors, rockets, energy sources, geo-synchronous space launch stations, space cranes and elevators—and turned them into practical realities. I ask you to look at this new challenge, to see the benefits that will be reaped from new space exploration. We may encounter new life forms, new forms of intelligence. At the very least, funding will provide the incentive for hundreds of new technologies that will provide immediate benefits both on the Ark and on Earth. Why should we limit ourselves to just the Solar System? Voting no on this bill is the equivalent of voting no on the Ark twenty years ago, the equivalent of saying we should never have left earth, that this project would never work. This is a challenge that will lead us to greater success than we have ever known. And that's why I ask all of you to vote yes now."

Amanda's picture faded from the screen and he saw the tallies from viewers who cast their votes immediately after the presentation: one hundred percent voted in favor of the new bill. "Good girl," he thought. He knew that Amanda, though she acted the part of vixen around him, was one of the smartest and most talented people on the Ark.

Alex turned to look at the presentation of the budgetary figures, which listed the source of funding for the bill and how much profit might be expected from new technologies and new land discoveries. The calculations showed an astronomical profit, even if no new planet was discovered. Rick's arguments about wastefulness were contradicted by hard numbers. There was no way, he thought, that Rick could veto the plan. A trillion marks in profit was too hard to turn down. And the promise of new colonies with new markets for products and real estate offered an endless supply of income for the Ark. It was a perfect example of the Malthusian Doctrine, with the ultimate positive effect. The Japanese understood, thought Alex, that for every negative associated with the project, there were also positives: the yin and yang. In the new universe, however, he knew that those positive aspects would so outweigh the negatives, offer rewards so rich, that anything would be possible.

He replayed his own speech and reviewed some of the rebuttals. Although he winced at his performance in a few places, he thought he had come off rather well. He initiated the testing stage of the interactive voting program and passed a short quiz on the issues. The computer authorized him to cast his ballot and he did so, happily pressing his finger on the pad marked yes.

As the votes continued to come in, he saw that the bill had amassed a nearly one hundred percent majority, including Rick's presidential ballot. Upon the president's vote, there was no longer any dissenting votes as people sought unity. Soon the computer cleared the screens and asked Alex to vote as a senator, voting on the issue as representative of his political bloc. He then voted as a judge, vice-president and leader of the congressional minority.

After all of his political responsibilities had been fulfilled, the computer allowed him to sleep for a short while. He dreamt of Amanda and Tanya. He saw Amanda in her kimono, her arms hidden under the folds of material, the way her hands gestured delicately as she pressed her points. He loved the way her words sounded like hissing and gurgling when she spoke Japanese. He saw himself discovering a new world with Amanda and Tanya by his side, starting a life in a virgin world. He remembered Keiko, and looked to see what she would be doing in the new world, but he could not find her. He called her name but there was no answer. Where is she, he wondered. He woke to the sound of his voice calling her name.

He left the chamber and took a shower, dressing in a fresh set of clothes. He went to a feeding station and Carl congratulated him on the passage of his bill. As he ate alone, he longed to see Amanda, to thank her for supporting his bill and tell her how wonderful he thought she was. Maybe Tanya was wrong and Amanda was beginning to love him after all. Of course she loves me, he thought. Everyone loves me. It's not a finite thing. There's enough love in the world for everyone to be cared for.

At this moment he believed it was true. Love was unlimited, infinite, going on forever. It was the strongest force in the universe, the true power. Force and fear had no place in the new society. Machiavelli had written that force and fear were the tools necessary to achieve anything on Earth. But now Alex believed that Machiavelli's ideas had no place in this new society. The Arkians had left the Earth behind and hope and love were the new guides to success. Alex was sure this was true. How could he have doubted it?

Chapter 19

No, No, Not The Moon, Too

"Alex?"

He heard his name called in a voice that sounded as if it were in pain, a voice speaking from some past hurt.

"Yes, Amanda?"

"Do you love me?" She spoke with difficulty, not looking at him, as if she wanted someone else to be saying the words.

He looked down at her worried face, trying to suppress the giddiness he felt inside. Unable to help himself, he smiled broadly and reached out to take her hand. He responded in a soft voice that underscored his happiness: "Of course I love you."

Still, she seemed frightened, unwilling to accept his declaration. "Do you really?" she asked.

"I love you very much. Everything about you. The way you talk and walk. The way you touch me. I like the way you look at me. The way you listen. And there's something magical in your eyes, something that tells me you love me."

He watched her eyes turn watery, splashes of red beginning to branch across them. Her face twitched quickly, as if tightening itself to hold back the tears, then turned into a stoic gaze on the verge of metamorphosing into a pout. Just as he thought she was about to break, she snapped her head back, flinging her hair over her shoulders. She looked at him directly and said, "I have always wanted to ask you something. How were they able to increase gravity on the moon?"

For a moment he was unable to respond. How can she change the topic to this, he wondered. One moment it's love and the next it's science. Still, he had a sense that she knew what she was doing, that she was playing on his idiosyncrasies. He couldn't resist talking about the Ark's ground-breaking projects. She knew how to get to him, but he wondered why she was doing it. One look at her face, blankly waiting for him to respond, told him it was useless to question her about her true motives. He decided to see where the conversation would lead.

"Well," he began, slipping into a professorial role, "we think of the Moon Project as one of the greatest human engineering achievements ever accomplished. It's bigger than the pyramids or the Panama Canal. We've disclosed a lot of the information about what we did, but most people on Earth will never understand what it is we did. Let me show you what I mean."

He spoke into the air, commanding Genie to play a holographic documentary of the Moon Project into their occipital receivers. Within moments, they saw three dimensional simulations of the moon's surface. A voice-over began talking about the first stages of the project.

"Thanks, Genie," said Alex sharply. "Could you cut the sound, please?" He began his own narration of the images they saw before them.

Amanda admired the scenery before her. "This new technology is amazing, Alex. I love that I can still see you while you talk to me. You remind me of my grandfather. He was a professor and he used to explain everything to me just like you do. And he looked just like a professor, so warm and caring with his head full of snowy white hair, smoking a pipe. He always smelled like tobacco. It was in his clothes. He used to put me on his knee and explain the world in a manner so sweet even a little girl like me could understand. I feel the same way when you're talking to me, Alex. I love that about you."

Alex began to clue in to what she was doing. She has me playing grandfather, he thought. Amanda, brains and all, had long ago learned to play the fool when she wanted something from a man. As he watched her, he saw that she did indeed look like a little girl being taught a school lesson. She seemed enraptured with everything he said, which, of course, had the irresistible effect of making him feel important, needed. Most women wanted him to be their therapist or father. He was used to those roles. Oh well, he figured, if she wants me to be her teacher, that's fine, too. At least I know what I'm doing.

She sighed, her eyes open wide with disbelief. "How can these images look so real?" she wondered. "They're better than any holograph."

"We don't have to do anything special or use any enhancements with the images because the image is generated by the brain. The electrodes pass the signal on as if they were coming through your optic nerves. The brain interprets the signals as natural stimuli. Ever since we developed implanted electrodes, the number of applications we've found has been astounding."

"It really is great," she exclaimed.

"It makes me laugh to think about all the people on Earth still using headsets and speakers. They still have touch tone telephones instead of the new computer interphasers."

"Well, why don't they just use the new technology?"

"We know much more about the brain than ever before, but people on Earth aren't ready for that knowledge yet. I remember that when I was younger I used to tell people about my ideas for the future, but I could never convince them that they would become realities. They were too stuck in their conventional ways of thinking. One time I almost got fired for showing someone at work an advance chapter from one of my books."

"You did? I find that hard to believe."

"It's true. I was working in sales and I showed some of my work to a secretary that I was friendly with. She took it home and read it and was so horrified by what I had to say that she called my boss at home and complained about me."

"What was her problem?"

"Well, mostly, she thought I was a pornographer. My boss thought she was going to file a sexual harassment suit against the company."

"Did he agree with her?"

"He thought I was a pornographer, too."

"Gee," Amanda smiled lewdly, "What was in those chapters?"

"Well, of course there was sex. But I found out later that all this woman had read was the last page. She had ignored everything else! She didn't see it as satire, like most people. And my boss, all he saw was a lawsuit. He didn't want to know about anything I was thinking."

"So what happened?"

"He put me on probation, and I had to promise I wouldn't mix my job with my life's work. All of the ideas I had for the Ark and for the development and settlement of space were completely ignored. And it went beyond apathy! People actively hated my work. It was so ironic, I thought. Here people are, preaching Christianity, and I have presented them with a society that allows people to live in brotherhood, to live like geniuses, but they wouldn't listen. I felt like I was censored all the time."

Alex felt his throat tighten. Even after so much time had passed, he still got emotional when he recalled his first public receptions. "But even then," he continued, "I knew I had to keep going. I knew that someday I would be successful. And now," he swept his arm out, as if indicating the stars outside the ship, "there's all of this. The universe supplies us with endless amounts of energy. We've discovered ways to feed every person on earth. We've recycled almost all of Earth's garbage into new products or energy sources. We even have the largest cryogenic vault in the world. Someday, hundreds of thousands of people may be resuscitated through cryogenic surgery."

"It is amazing," Amanda agreed. "You know, the reason I wanted to come here in the first place was because of your early writings."

"Really?"

"You wrote with such conviction, as if you were sure it was more than just a dream. And now that I'm here, it's as if I'm living inside a dream, seeing the things I had only read about, only imagined, actually working here in front of me." She grasped his hand. "You were just ahead of your time, that's all."

"You know, I had to sell one book at a time at first. All my life I had spent my time selling other people's products. But I reached a point when I realized I could sell my own ideas to people. It went slowly at first, but I knew the message would get out soon enough."

"Okay, okay," she laughed. "You're the world's greatest salesman. But you've also managed to change topics on me. I wanted to know about the Moon's gravity."

"Oh, yes," Alex grunted, as if he were being reluctantly tugged back into consciousness. For a moment he wondered if he should accuse Amanda of switching topics on him, but he decided against it. She tugged on his hand as if she could pull the information out of him. She looked like an eight year-old, hungry to hear her favorite story. Alex found her, as usual, irresistible.

Impatient with his lack of immediate response, she prodded him to answer. "Why are they digging that huge hole?" she asked, referring to the images passing before her.

"Well, first of all, for mining purposes. We discovered several usable minerals in deposits in the area in which we were digging. Also, we're excavating a huge volume of material so that we will be able to build living facilities under the surface, creating a buffer between the main housing areas and the atmosphere. Or, I should say, lack of atmosphere. We use the Moon's surface to protect inhabitants from the different types of solar radiation."

"So, if all you're building is housing, why do you need so much space?"

"Well, in addition to the new structures, we decided to use the excavation below them as a waste disposal site. We packed it with waste materials that were denser than the original materials we dug out. That way, we were able to engineer a land mass that had its own gravitational pull beneath the settlement site."

"So you created an artificial core."

"Exactly. A core with its own gravitational field. What surprised most people was that we didn't have to go to the center of the moon to build it. We just aligned the artificial core with the settlement site. Of course it took massive amounts of robotic labor to excavate the area, but in addition to creating the new gravity field, we also recovered large amounts of precious metals."

"So what happened to all of the material you've taken out? How do you counterbalance it?"

Alex beamed at her as a teacher beams at a bright pupil who has asked the right question. "That's where the asteroids come into effect?"

"Asteroids?"

"Do you remember seeing the big vessels with the large solar sails?"

"I guess I was too busy looking deep into your eyes," she admitted.

Alex ignored her girlish smile and asked Genie to replay the images.

"Many of the asteroids in orbit around the moon are loaded with heavy and precious metals. But in order for us to retrieve the materials, we needed to find a way to transport them efficiently to the surface of the moon where we could process them. Genie," Alex commanded, "superimpose the earth against the sails of the transport vehicles."

"Those sails are larger than the earth." Amanda spoke in an awed whisper.

"It's true. But what's more interesting is that those sails are microscopically thin, but still strong enough to capture hydrogen plasma coming from the sun. The force of the plasma is strong enough to push the sails forward, just as wind pushes the sails of a boat. With a control station on the moon's surface, minute adjustments allow us to move the largest and heaviest asteroids wherever we want. Once they've entered the right trajectory, we simply drop them into the excavation."

"And that gives you all the mass you need for gravity?"

"Not exactly." He smiled at her, trying to provoke her into asking another question. All she did was squirm uncomfortably, like a child seated at a classroom desk. Alex decided to continue without her prompt.

"Let's think of it this way. If we tried to place all the asteroids we needed to start a new gravitational center into that hole, they'd never fit. We used new developments in superconductors to compress the asteroids and excavated soil into a dense mass of materials. The proximity of molecules is so close in the condensed material that the only other place we've measured greater levels of gravitational pull in such a small area is in a black hole."

"So, is it as powerful as a black hole?" she asked. "Are you going to be sucking planets into the moon?"

"No, not at all. We have complete control over the process. The gravitational field is always maintained at the same level as the G-Force on earth."

"But if you've increased the Moon's mass, even by a relatively small amount, won't that eventually affect the moon's orbit? Is it possible that greater gravitational pull between the Earth and Moon will lead to a decaying orbit? Won't that bring about a collision with the Earth?"

"I'm glad you know your physics," he said, proud of her aptitude. "We calculate that it would take about five hundred years for the Moon to slowly decay in its orbit, at which time we'll just divide the Moon into smaller Moons. We may eventually place the Ark nearer to the Moon's former orbit. We might even push the Moon further out."

"God, are you trying to tell me you think the Moon is disposable? You're just going to get rid of it when it suits your purposes?" Her questions were shouted at him like accusations.

Alex had expected her to be surprised about the plans for the Moon, but he had not expected such a vehement reaction. "But Amanda, we're already noticing changes in every part of the solar system. When you look up at the sky from Earth, what do you see? When I was a little boy all I saw were the stars and the Moon, but now all you see are rocket trails, satellites and space stations. Maybe we want to always keep things the same, but that's not the way the world works."

He reached out to touch her, trying to calm her down.

"And there are other, more subtle changes occurring," he continued. "Changes in air currents and ocean currents and tides. Things that you can't see with your eyes. Our monitors are recording thousands of other changes, changes that seem more significant when the Ark, the Moon, and some other large heavenly bodies align themselves. That's why we are planning to disperse everything more evenly so we don't have these problems in the future. Have you noticed how mild and uniform the temperature on Earth has become? The Ark is quite aware of what's happening. That's why we're starting more programs, like the Sahara program. We are constantly trying to balance out all of these changes. We're trying to maintain equilibrium despite everything that's been happening.

"Most scientists understand what's been going on, but we try not to disturb the people left on Earth. They're not aware of what's happening and they really don't need to know. The people on Earth get paranoid when things move too quickly. They want to hold back progress, trying to protect their ignorance."

"It sounds to me like you're trying to protect yourselves," said Amanda venomously.

"We try not to be secretive," Alex replied, trying to keep her on his side, "but we have learned to be careful about what information the Ark releases. United Europe, the United States, and all of the other major countries are always apprised and informed. But they understand that whatever we're doing is done in the name of progress. Technical and social progress is moving along so rapidly on the Ark, the Moon and Mars that there isn't any way that Earth can keep up. And there will be other planets and moons that we will begin to domesticate. Everyone is afraid of what's happening, but in my mind it's no different than what happened in the eighteenth and nineteenth century United States. Social change comes and people don't think they can handle it. Education can't keep up with progress. The only thing that saves us here in space is that our educational facilities allow our citizenry to learn more than a hundred times faster than people on Earth."

"Alex, I just can't imagine being down on the Earth, looking up at the sky and not seeing the Moon. It would change everything for me. The nights would never be the same. I love standing in some dark place, in an open field or on the beach at night, watching the Moon shining through the clouds, its light changing everything from second to second. The Moon is so beautiful. I've seen it in the desert where you could swear you almost feel its light, feel it like the warmth of the sun on your body. It feels clean, like it's soaking down into every one of your pores. In the full moon, the light is so bright you don't even need a lantern to see by. It's one of the most enchanting things I've ever seen."

She began to cry, sobbing into her hands. "Now you're trying to tell me you're going to destroy the Moon! It's hard enough to look up into the sky and see all those satellites and the Ark blocking out the light of the stars, but not to see the Moon at all? That's horrible. There's a whole universe out there. I wonder how long will it take for you to figure out how to destroy all of that?"

Touched by her intimate display of emotions, Alex put his arm around her waist, pulling her into an embrace. "It won't take too long," he said, "but then there will be other moons to look at, other places to live. They'll never be anything like our memories of our home, but they'll be just as beautiful in their own way."

She moved away from him and began screaming. "I don't like your world, Alex! I'm sick of everything turning into metal, plastic, and machines. I hate it!"

She was shaking, sobbing uncontrollably. Alex moved to put his arm around her shoulder to support her, to hold her, but she pushed him away.

"Don't touch me, Alex. I hate you. I hate all these modern inventions and I hate you for inventing them. All your smugness. You think you can control nature. You think you're making things better. The fact is that it's people like you who are destroying everything." She pointed her finger at him, as if she were testifying in a courtroom, pointing out the guilty party. "What an incredibly selfish ego you have. You think because you can bullshit people with your science and your facts that you have the right to take everything away from them, to make them slaves to your technology. I thought I was falling in love with you, but I should have trusted my instinct, my intuitions. You're nothing but a manipulator. You take as much as you want and use what you think you need and then you throw whatever you don't want away, expecting other people to clean up after you. I want to go back to Earth. I don't want to stay here one more minute. I want to feel the rain on my face, to smell the flowers, freshly cut grass, freshly cooked food and hot bread right out of an oven. I want to go back."

Amanda began pounding her fists on Alex's chest, screaming at him. He was used to this. Some people, he knew, reacted even more violently. He assumed that his talk about the Moon must have triggered some deep childhood memories in Amanda's mind. He attributed her rage to a form of what people liked to call Arkclaustrophobia or Ark Fever. Adjusting to life on board the Ark often made people exhibit symptoms of paranoia or depression. While Amanda was certainly not mentally ill, Alex assumed her acrimonious speech was the result of her inability to assimilate to the changes around her.

He decided to call on the one person who could help Amanda through her crisis.

"Genie!"

"Yes, Alex, right away." A wave of euphoria passed over him. Any doubts he had about the future were washed away. His concern for Amanda had dissipated. His fear that she was rejecting him had ended. When he looked down at her, she, too, seemed rejuvenated.

"What happened, Alex? I feel so weak. My legs feel like rubber." She put her hands to her face. "My cheeks are all wet. Was I crying? And what happened to your clothes? Your shirt is all torn up and your chest is all red and scratched."

She looked into his face quizzically and said, "Did I do that?"

Alex only smiled and nodded.

She smiled back seductively, announcing, "Well, I'm sure you deserved every bit of it." In a voice that showed how little she actually cared about his pain, she asked, "Did it hurt? You want me to do that to you again?"

Again, Alex said nothing. He merely nodded his head.

She laughed. "Well, I don't know about you, but I just feel great. I must have had one good cry."

Alex rolled his eyes.

"You can hold me now, Alex." She said this as a queen condescends to tell her subject he may kiss the royal hand.

Despite her attitude, Alex flung his arms around her, feeling security emanating from her warm and fragrant body. She gave him a kiss, pulling on his lips with her teeth, drawing him closer for another kiss. As he looked into her eyes, he saw that she wanted to devour him, that she was ready to do anything for him. She pulled him onto her and covered his mouth with her own.

But as she kissed him, Alex's mind began to wander. He knew he shouldn't think about it, but Amanda's comments reminded him that he missed Earth. He had prepared himself for a day like today more than twenty years ago. He had seen man's destruction of Earth: the poisoning of the air, overpopulation, the extinction of thousands of species, chemical pollution—pesticides, toxic materials, and radioactive materials released into every environment without regard for nature, without regard for humankind.

Foreseeing the coming destruction of the planet, he tried to treat every day on Earth as if it were his last day. He would stand by the ocean to smell its salty air, feel the deposit of salt on his skin. He stood in the rain, let it beat on him, the fresh water running down his face. He would touch trees and smell flowers. He watched birds flitting and cats slinking around his backyard and marveled at how complex the cycle of life was. He thought of Jaycoff, his wonderful Weimaraner, the most beautiful animal he had ever known. He loved that dog and he believed that, in some animal way, the dog loved him.

"Alex, you're drifting." Amanda's voice brought him

slowly back from his daydream. "Don't I excite you any more?"

He said nothing and she gave up on trying to kiss him with a dissatisfied sigh.

"All right, then, why don't you tell me what you're thinking about?"

"Jaycoff, my dog."

"Mom told me that your wife had him put to sleep. That must have been terrible. I know how much you loved him."

"I really did love him, but it wasn't her fault. We just couldn't care for him. We tried to find a home for him. He was like a horse, he needed lots of room to run in. We lived next to a small park, but I   travelled a lot and Lorraine worked. Things weren't going so well in our marriage and somehow he picked up on that. Every time we fought or talked about breaking up, he was the first to go. We tried to find a new home for him, but he just kept running away from them. I guess he didn't want to live with strangers."

Alex hesitated for a moment, then he took a deep breath, continuing his story. "One time he disappeared for weeks. It turned out he had been found by a kid who lived nearby. Jaycoff had almost made it back to us. We got a call at Christmas time. This kid's sister called and wanted to know if we had given Jaycoff to her brother. I guess she thought that maybe her brother had stolen the dog. She called on Christmas Eve and at that moment I wanted to take him back but I knew it wouldn't solve anything. So I just told her to keep him, that we couldn't take care of him any more.

"It was only a few weeks later that I got a call from the Orange County Animal Control, telling me they had found him roaming the streets. Tim, my son, got the call and I told him not to tell Lorraine but, being a good kid, he felt he had to tell his mother. When she heard that they were going to put him to sleep, she insisted that she be there with him. She said it was cruel to let him die alone.

"Lorraine worked as an operating nurse, and her job was to be the one who pays attention to every detail, counting every sponge and needle. She could paralyze you with her ability to recall even the most trivial information. And it was horrible. She told me everything about the procedure. She told me he was disoriented and didn't recognize her. And just before they put the needle into him, even the veterinarian's aides moaned about having to put such a beautiful animal to sleep. They pleaded with her, trying to get her to change her mind, but she was adamant. Jaycoff had to go."

Amanda began to cry again. "Oh, Alex, that's so sad."

"I know I should have gone to the Pound but I couldn't. I was afraid that if I saw him again, I'd want to take him home. When Lorraine and I got our divorce I always thought that he was the first victim of that divorce. She had been asking me to make a choice between her or the dog. I wasn't ready to make that choice then. When the divorce came through a year later, I ended up with the kids but not Jaycoff."

"Isn't that about when you met my mother and fell in love with her?"

"Yes, it is. Your mother and I used to talk about getting another Weimaraner. She used to buy me little statues of Weimaraners because she knew how much I missed Jaycoff. I've still got one of those statues."

Amanda sighed, "I guess you two really loved one another."

"I tell you, I really thought I had met my soul mate and everything would turn out the way the fortune tellers told me it would. I was sure that we'd have a little girl, and another Jaycoff, and that we would live somewhere in Monterey. I guess it sort of came true when I met Wendy some twelve years later. She had a young daughter and we moved to Prescott and we got a Weimaraner."

"Why didn't it work out with my mother? She always talked about you and how much she really loved you."

"We tried for ten years, on and off. I loved her but I knew she would never stay faithful to me. She wanted more than just me. I guess my pride got in the way. I proposed to her so many times, but I always made it a condition that we continue to see a therapist. The pattern after that was always the same. We hesitated to call each other for weeks and then ended up getting back together. Other times she wouldn't take my calls. Months would drift by and we wouldn't see each other until we both started talking about marriage again. She finally got married and about fifteen years later I married Wendy. Still, we sent Christmas cards to each other. She sent me pictures of you and I even sent her a picture of the new Jaycoff."

"I remember that," she told him. "I was about ten when she showed me the picture and told me the story of Jaycoff. I could tell by the way she told me the story of your first dog that she still loved you a lot. She always told me that you were like a little kid that never grew up and how lucky you were. She used to call you the cat that always landed on his feet. She admired the way you stuck to what you believed in, even though she thought you weren't practical."

"I got the feeling that her family thought I wasn't quite good enough for her. They knew how expensive her tastes were and they thought I never allowed her to spend money. We always ended up arguing about money."

"You're right. She did complain a lot about how cheap you were. Well, if you had been a little more patient and waited for a while, you could have shared in her inheritance."

"You know, that's funny. Every time I would read your mother's tarot cards, I told her that she would inherit lots of money. Her dad's business must have finally paid off."

"She used to give you lots of credit for starting that laboratory with her dad. You should have stuck around. I think you would have made a great dad. We could have done all those nice things that a father and a daughter do. Well, you just missed out on a good thing."

"Are you implying something?"

"Oh no, I really like older men." She stood up and gave him a facetious curtsey, mischievously whispering the word, "Daaaddy."

Chapter 20

Tanya's Possessiveness

Alex found Tanya in the airlock room, her belongings next to her in a large, plastic stretch bag. She sat with her head bent down in concentration, oblivious to his entrance. He shuffled his feet loudly to announce his presence, but she did not look up.

He stood silently beside her for a few moments, but was still unable to elicit a response. Deciding that she would ignore him as long as he kept quiet, he asked loudly, "Why didn't you tell anyone you're leaving?"

She seemed startled by the sound of his voice, but maintained a studied attitude of apathy. Without bothering to look up at him, she said, "Oh. Hi, Alex."

"By chance I saw your name on the Moon Shuttle passenger list. Does Amanda know you're leaving?"

She spoke without emotion. "No. I hate goodbyes. She'd probably try and make me stay or decide she wants to come with me. Both of those are no good."

For a moment, she appeared to liven up, sharpening her tone with an edge of sarcasm, "And if she went with me, I know you'd get the wrong idea. I need to find some work and I like the Moon Base. It feels solid up there and my sister's already back there. I think I'm going to stay with her awhile."

Alex saw her eyes begin to water. Her voice almost cracked as she told him, "I just need some time to think. I want to be away from you two for a while."

Her body began to shake with spasms and Alex heard her begin to make horrible gasping noises. Without any warning, she leapt to her feet and dashed across the room, screaming at an ear splitting volume. Before Alex could do anything to stop her, she flung herself into the wall head first, her body bouncing back violently from the impact. She fell to the floor and rolled over on her side, moaning incoherently. At first he thought she was motioning him to come to her, but as he approached, he saw that her arms were waving crazily, as if she were trying to tear out strands of her nonexistent hair. As he knelt beside her, she rolled herself into a fetal position and began to suck her thumb.

Alex, though he tried to comfort her with soothing words, was terrified by her behavior. He had never seen a person's emotions exhibit themselves in such a violent manner. She had thrown herself into the wall without any regard for her own safety. The passion and abandon she had shown during their lovemaking now revealed itself in this act of self-destruction.

Alex began to feel guilty, as if he were somehow at fault. His heart began to pound as he tried to remember the way he had parted with Tanya. Had he said something that would have made her this upset? Was it the amount of time he had been spending with Amanda? Perhaps he had said something to Amanda that she had repeated to Tanya. As hard as he tried, he could think of nothing.

He put his hand on her face, wiping the tears from her eyes. Her skin felt cold and rigid beneath the warm flow of her tears. Her body continued to convulse. It's like watching an epileptic go through a seizure, he thought. He wanted to talk to her, to comfort her, but was afraid he might say something that would upset her further. Instead, he kept his hands on her face, trying to empathize with her, to share her pain. For a moment he felt nothing and then he began to feel utterly alone, without pride, without a sense of himself. He began to take on Tanya's emotions, making them his own. He understood how terrible she felt and began to console her with words.

"Everything will be okay," he whispered, massaging her back.

Finally, she took her thumb from her mouth. Her sobs became less frequent, the convulsions stopping altogether.

After a few moments, she croaked, "I . . . love you, Alex . . . but you don't love me. You don't care for me the way I care for you."

"Baby," he said lamely, trying to explain something that could never be explained.

"You don't have to lie to me," she shot back. "I see the way you love Amanda. Don't even try to tell me you love me. I don't want to hear your lies. I love Amanda, too, but nothing's been the same since you came along. You've changed her. My sister was right about you. You want to kill everybody's feelings. You want us to be machines, like your computers, unfeeling, under control. Sometimes I hate what you stand for."

She pulled her face out of his hands, leaning against the wall.

"I used to love Amanda," she continued. "It was love without any conditions. She was so child-like, funny and loving. Now she's cold, serious. I think she's always calculating something, keeping secrets. She doesn't share anything with me, especially when it comes to you, because she knows how jealous you are. We were friends long before you came along and now there's this terrible *thing* between us."

"I didn't have anything to do with that," he protested. "I never told her anything about us. Or what I thought about the two of you."

"You're just a dictator. You're jealous of everything, and it's so obvious. And the worst part of it is, you don't even love her. You just love yourself. You're the most narcissistic fuck I ever met, so fucking in love with yourself. You think you can live forever, turn your sad, old seventy-five year-old body into something new. You think you can try and find some ideal woman, remake her into the image of Amanda's mother. But it's pathetic.

"What do you want with Amanda, anyway? When you're a hundred years old, she'll only be fifty. You're just trying to suck her dry, use her like you used me. I feel like I'm one of your possessions from your precious collection. Only now you're tired of me. You'll let the rest of the crew put their hands all over me because I'm not good enough for you any more."

She reached out and grabbed his arm, pinching the skin between her fingers. "This is new, but what about the rest of you. You can't compete with Amanda. You can't keep up with her generation, but you don't want someone your own age."

At this, Alex began to wonder if Tanya might be quite a bit older than he thought. He didn't have much time to think about it, however, because now she was pinching his face. He slapped at her hand, trying to free himself from her grip.

"It's new alright," she cackled. "But what about your lungs and heart. Whoever gave you the idea you could be immortal? You're going to die just like the rest of us."

She relaxed her grip on him and began to talk into her hand, smiling to herself. "Immortality, huh. Long life. Do you really think anyone believes your bullshit? No wonder Rick hates your guts. He knows an idiot when he sees one. Conceited, pompous ass. You think you're so good looking, standing in front of a mirror. You think you're so hot with the ladies because you fucked me, you fucked Amanda. But what about Keiko. You used her just like the rest of us. You think living up here in this hunk of metal is real life? You're deluded. It's a giant toy. A tinkertoy. But you think it's a monument to your genius.

"Your writings are trash and so is your dream. I've read your books and they're full of an egomaniac's bullshit. You think you know what a woman wants, you think you can write about sex, but you're just a lazy fuck when it comes to the real thing. Why don't you learn to fuck like a man!" She screamed this last epithet at him.

"I thought you liked what I did to you," he said, trying to recover from the vehemence of her attack on him.

Realizing that she had finally gotten to him, she changed her tone of voice, allowed her real feelings to come out. "Oh, Alex," she cried, "I hurt so much." Tears began to roll down her face and as Alex moved toward her, he realized that he was crying, too.

"Alex," she said, a smile breaking out on her face, "I love you so much. It hurts so much." She began kissing his face.

"I want you so much." She grabbed his hands, moving them all over her body. "Please," she begged, "love me one more time."

He felt her tearing pieces of his clothes off.

She asked him again, speaking now in her familiar, deep voice, the sadness gone from its resonant drawl. "Can't you see what you've done to me? I'm jealous and I hate myself for feeling that way. I can't stay here with things the way they are. I can't stand being here and not having you."

After everything she had said, Alex was astonished at the lengths she had gone to hurt him. He had tried to be close to her, to understand her, yet she had lashed out at him anyway. Still, he had to admit to himself that he did love her, and maybe she was right about the way she felt, perhaps he had used her. As she pressed herself against him, he used no words to express his love for her. He used his body.

Afterwards, he felt as if he had never been closer to another human being, not even Amanda. He heard himself say, "I love you."

After they lay together for a while, she dressed herself and readied to leave. No matter how he tried to persuade her to stay, she was determined to board the next shuttle. When it arrived, she ran for the loading dock without bothering to look back. He stayed and watched until the shuttle was out of sight. He wondered if she had been right and considered moving to the Moon base himself, maybe to Mars. He could start a life with Tanya, get away from the Ark. Maybe he had been here too long. Maybe it was time for a change. She was right about one thing: he wasn't going to live forever.

She was also right about Amanda. He was running after her because he hadn't been able to make his life work with Annette. Why did he think everything was going to be so different with her daughter? But even the thought of leaving Amanda made his heart ache. I'd rather die than be separated from her, he thought. I've gone crazy for her. I see her everywhere I go. It's like torture sometimes, but I can't let go.

Why, he wondered, can't I just find one person to love and have her love me back. Is that crazy?

Maybe I've gone crazy, he told himself, and I'm the only one who knows. I'll have to ask Genie. Things like this aren't supposed to happen on the Ark. God, maybe I do want to be a machine. Maybe Tanya was right. But Amanda's not an illusion. I love her and that's all there is to it. I never stopped loving Annette and I'll never stop loving her daughter. That will never disappear. It's the same way with Keiko. I'll always love her.

At the thought of Keiko, he began to cry. He said aloud, "Keiko, I love you. You've always been so honest with me."

He stumbled out of the airlock, tears running down his face. Each step he took was like a tremendous pain jolting through his body. He said to himself, over and over again: "Everything's going to be alright. Everything's going to be alright."

Chapter 21

Consulting With Keiko

After watching Tanya leave, Alex returned to the revelry at the party he had thrown for Vladimir, but he was disconsolate amidst the loud music and inane conversations. His problems with Tanya and Amanda were only adding to the stress caused by the escalating conflicts on Earth. On his way from the shuttle platform to the party, Rick had contacted him with troubling news about a nuclear weapon that had fallen into the hands of a terrorist group. He still had not had a chance to talk further with Vladimir. Until he could fully brief his Russian friend, he couldn't be sure that his plans to rectify the situation would work. He was tired and edgy. Carl still hasn't gotten my body completely straightened out, he thought.

In addition to his fatigue, he had been experiencing a strange series of sensations, culminating in an unexpected longing to talk to Keiko. He took this to mean that she was trying to contact him, or had been thinking about him. Her influence on his life was so great that even the smallest amount of her energy directed toward him was enough to make him aware of her intentions. He looked forward to talking with her, knowing that a single achievement spent in conversation with her was enough to ease his mind.

As Alex walked down the hallway toward Keiko's chamber, he considered the romantic entanglements he had gotten himself into. He wondered if what Tanya said was true, that he had never stopped loving Annette. Hadn't his whole life been dedicated to showing her that he was deserving of her love? Now that she was dead, he wondered if her memory wasn't somehow deceiving him.

When he was with Amanda, his memories of Annette—the way he saw her face, her body—were sharper, more real. How had he come so far in his life, gone through so many experiences, so many years, to find himself still in love with a woman who was dead? Why hadn't they been able to work out their differences when she was still alive, when there was still a chance for their relationship to work?

Now it seemed that the small things that had bothered him meant absolutely nothing. It had infuriated him that she cried when she read what he considered trashy romance novels. Women writers, especially, sent her into paroxysms of tears. In those books, of which she had read hundreds, the lovers always fell into one another's arms by the end of the story; true love found its way. In Alex's life, at least as far as he was concerned, nothing of the sort had happened.

In every woman he had been with since their break-up, Alex had looked for signs of Annette's spirit, for an indication that he might be rekindling the love he had once known. So many of the women he dated had resembled her: perhaps they looked like her, or maybe it was something about the way they talked, or walked. Perhaps some small gesture that reminded him. All of them possessed some quality that lured him to them in hopes that there might be more than just a similar smile or a familiar gait. Now Amanda, more than any of the other women Alex had been with, was tempting Alex with a promise of Annette's ghost.

He reached Keiko's door. She must have been watching for him, because the hatch opened immediately. She stood in the doorway before him.

"Hello, Alex," she said. She smiled as she spoke, but Alex saw that the rest of her face was tightly drawn, as though her smile would dissolve into a pensive frown as soon as she gave up on the initial courtesies. Alex approached her cautiously, as she made him feel like a student trying to explain to his professor why he had not even started a term paper due a week ago. His confidence in her, his belief that she was somehow superior to him, always gave him this sense of hesitancy.

Years ago, when he had been living with Annette, he had actually enjoyed similarly uncomfortable exchanges with Jaycoff. Although he knew Jaycoff would not bite him, he loved to challenge the dog's natural instincts by placing his hand inside of his pet's huge mouth. Other times, he brought his face close to Jaycoff's, taunting him, but being sure to keep his eyes away from the large teeth and quick bite of the Weimaraner.

His life with Keiko had often been the same way: a series of exchanges in which Alex dared to push her as far as she would go, unsure of how she would react. Her previous mental conditions hinted at a wild quality that could never be entirely domesticated and he both anticipated and feared the moment when his actions might inflame her emotions to such a degree that she would have to act on them. Only occasionally had he seen a look in her eye, a wild glint of hateful destructiveness, that indicated her utter disenchantment with him.

The few times that he had seen her in such a state, he had literally trembled, afraid that at any moment she might lunge at him, tearing at his face with sharpened nails or wielding an ordinary kitchen device—perhaps a knife?—turned weapon. It had been years since he had seen her in such a state, but today his foul mood heightened his sensitivity to detect even the slightest suggestion of rage. He could not explain, even to himself, exactly what it was about her that indicated a propensity for such violence. But today, here in this room, he was overcome with uneasiness, unsure of what to say or do.

He forced a suggestion of cheerfulness into his voice and reciprocated her greeting. "I wanted to see you," he told her. "How are you doing?"

"Oh, I wanted to see you, too," she said, her voice reverberant with a happiness he had not expected. "You look so handsome. You always look so good." She laughed. "After all these years, I still can't get over how handsome you are."

Within moments, Alex had relaxed completely. His initial concerns about her temper vanished.

"You still remind me of the first day I met you," he told her. "The way you stand. The innocence of your eyes. Remember when I told you I thought of you as a one hundred and fifty year-old woman in the body of an eighteen year-old girl? I still do. There's always something of a little girl that shines out in you."

"And you, Alex, will always be my hundred and fifty year-old man."

He chuckled at this. "In a few more years, I'll be there."

"How about a hug?" she asked.

They took a few more steps, closing the remaining distance between them. He held her close to him, wrapping her up in his arms.

"You feel so good," she whispered in his ear.

As they separated from their embrace, Keiko took a step backward and began, with disarming matter-of-factness, to question him about his love life.

"You've talked about Annette all your life. I know you loved her. Does Amanda look like her mother?" Her voice changed slightly as she said Amanda's name.

Once again Alex was on his guard. Keiko had either heard gossip about him and Amanda or she had been able to divine the information from her extra-sensory powers. It was common for Keiko to ask about his love life, but he had not expected her to be so familiar with his present situation. She always expressed her concerns about his relationships with different women. Whether things were going well or badly for him, she always sought time to talk with him, encouraging and supporting him.

He had been with her for so many years that he no longer knew exactly what their relationship was. At different times, she could be anything: mother, lover, daughter, sister. Sometimes he thought she was his guardian angel, always protecting him. Besides counseling him on his love life, she always showed active concern for his political ambitions and decisions. She was one person, Alex was sure, who never pulled punches when expressing her political views. When she disagreed, she would shake her head vigorously and declare,

"No, Alex. Absolutely not. I cannot agree with that." And when she supported him, saw that his actions and ideas were moving the world towards a state of more peaceful existence, she would tell him gently, "Yes. That is what you want. I can feel a vibration that tells me we will have peace, that goodness and harmony exist and will continue to guide us." When she spoke in this way, Alex felt that his political decisions sometimes began to resemble spiritual missions.

Despite their candid relationship, Alex was troubled by Keiko's questions about Amanda. For the first time, he felt guilty about his sexual life, afraid that somehow he had managed to betray Keiko with Amanda. He spoke slowly, searching for the right words to express how he felt without, he hoped, hurting Keiko.

"In a way, she's more beautiful than Annette," he began. "Much more. She's smarter, more spiritual. Somehow I think that she's a combination of Annette and myself and you. Somehow she reflects a part of every person I've met. And that's beautiful to me." Alex looked away from Keiko, unable to meet her gaze as he spoke about Amanda.

"And I'm so attracted to her physically. When we were together, it was the most wonderful experience. I felt like I was lost inside of her. It felt like I had been with her before, as if, despite the short amount of time we'd spent together, we'd been together for years."

"And how long will you stay with her?" Keiko asked, continuing to look directly at him.

"She's like her mother, I think. She loves men. She loves sex. And one person won't make her happy. Also, she's bisexual. She has a lover named Tanya who's incredibly jealous."

"Does it bother you to think that she has a female lover?"

He wanted to tell her about Tanya, to go into detail about that part of the relationship, but something held him back. Instead, he spoke vaguely about what he had been going through. "I don't know what I'm feeling. I always tell myself to try not to possess people. Nonpossessive love: that's what I preach on the Ark. But when it comes down to the real question of sharing someone that way, I can't do it. That was my problem with Annette and now that's my problem with her daughter.

"Something about being with Annette was so unlike anything I ever had with anyone else, I guess I'm still trying to hold on to that. I thought I could never share her with anyone else. Now when I think about it, I wonder if the fact that our time together didn't last is part of the appeal for me. I wasn't with her long enough to go through anything disappointing. Maybe that's what made it seem so different."

While Alex spoke, Keiko remained before him, still gazing at him levelly, her face showing no emotion. Her only signals to him were an encouraging set of her mouth and an occasional nod of her head to show that she was following what he said.

"I try to go back over the years and think about my time with Lorraine," he continued. "That seventeen years of marriage could never be duplicated. I was young and unexperienced and everything seemed unique, maybe even romantic. And then, with Annette, it was so different. Maybe because I was older. Maybe it was because I'd been married. Maybe I just had a better idea of what I wanted. Annette and I went through a lot of misery together. We had ups and downs. But there was something about her, some chemistry that we had. It had nothing to do with, well . . . . It was a combination of fulfilling mind and body. There had been women who fulfilled my mind, but not my body. With others it was the other way around. But I worshiped Annette. She could have told me to do almost anything and I would have done it—with a smile on my face."

He laughed. Keiko remained still. After a few moments, they were both silent.

He began thinking back to his first years with Keiko. He had been in his early fifties when they first started dating and now he saw himself, even at that age, as being naive. At that time he never could have imagined himself as he was now: seventy-five years old, in some way successful. At forty-eight, just before he met Keiko, he had given up on life. He thought no one would ever care for him.

His life with Keiko was far different from the time he had spent with either Lorraine or Annette. Keiko was years younger than he, only twenty-four, when they first became involved. When she was with him, she seemed child-like, innocent. Yet he knew that when she was away from him, she exuded a scholarly, poised persona—with people she didn't know, she tended to speak in a precise manner, exaggerating her English accent. But it was more than her manner. There was something centered about her that gave people the impression of a person content with the world, content with herself. When she had made a decision that satisfied her, she was immovable.

Sometimes when she spoke to him, she said things so sagacious that Alex felt he was the youth and she the old woman. But when he tried to make love to her, he felt like he was reaching out to a very young girl, an adolescent afraid of her body. His desire for her was not so much for sexual intimacy as it was for mutual tenderness. He strove to nurture her, to protect her like a father.

Their first night together she had listened so carefully to him that he had the impression that she, unlike anyone else, was understanding everything he said. Even the emotions and ideas he found inexpressible seemed to find her empathy. She was not classically beautiful as Annette had been, but he found her serenity and intelligence attractive. He believed she had touched his spirit, elevated his consciousness.

When he saw her body for the first time, he had not been able to resist cataloguing her many imperfections. Her body seemed too short, not proportioned to her buttocks. Her arms were covered with hair and her teeth, although white, were aligned strangely in her mouth. Her eyes were odd, as well. When he looked deeply into them, he had the sensation that they weren't the eyes of a human. When he thought about painting them, he found himself unable to find a way to visualize them. They shone with child-like tranquility, but he was unable to find a trace of personality, as if she had surrendered her body and soul to some benevolent force.

Despite their lack of physical intimacy, Alex felt that the time he spent with Keiko relaxed him, allowed him to find out who he was. After a while, however, he found it disturbing that he might go for days without thinking about her, while at other times, she was the only thing on his mind. He felt simultaneously attached to her and set free by that very attachment. It was as if she were a gaseous, ethereal form that at any moment might be blown away from him. Finally, he thought, he had found the difference between momentary infatuation and a soulful, lasting relationship. He believed he would feel her vibrations forever. He responded to her fragility, as if she were a spider web that, if someone pushed hard enough, would collapse into a tangled mess.

After nearly a decade of almost complete chastity with Keiko, Alex began seeking out women with whom he might have brief, clandestine affairs. Although he was sure Keiko suspected him, she said nothing. Alex, however, having had a renewed taste of the conjugal life, decided that he would leave Keiko in order to marry Wendy Rasmussen, a political scientist he met in Washington, D.C., while lobbying congressmen for funding for the Ark.

Wendy was the kind of woman who was driven to always appear in control and act respectably. Despite her intelligence and beauty, she was afraid of making a fool of herself, no matter how much Alex tried to instill confidence in her. Her compulsive conformity forced her to live with systematic habits and idiosyncrasies that afforded her life an almost clockwork regularity. Oddly enough, Alex found himself attracted to her not for her looks or brains, but for her reliability. He loved being able to predict her behavior, to know how she would act in a particular situation, especially when it came to their relationship. Wendy was always there for him, nurturing him, practically waiting on him. At first her devotion to him had been troubling, but soon he came to expect her to focus all of her attention on him.

In addition to the strength of her love for him, a love which at the time Alex fully reciprocated, Alex was rhapsodic about her body. She was a fashionable dresser, buying all of her clothes from expensive boutiques. Alex had spent a great deal of his childhood shopping with his mother. He loved fine clothes, fanciful fabrics. Wendy wore designer dresses in a way that drove Alex wild. Her bust, hips, and legs were so voluptuous and undeniably perfect that she appeared to have been sewn into her clothes. Her every movement was like shifting light on a painting. Alex swore that he saw someone different every time he looked at her.

He became obsessed with her body. They would be at a dinner party or a bar and the only thing he could think about would be taking her home and undressing her at the foot of their bed. The longer he had to wait, the greater his passion grew. As she became aware of this, she began to play games with him, seeing how far she could push him. Even when the physical act was consummated, he was still hungry for her. She might fall asleep, but he would content himself by watching her slumber, transfixed by her beauty.

The only way Alex could ever get enough of her body was to place her in front of his easel, where he painted her portrait over and over again: torsos, nudes, animated poses. Sometimes he painted only a detail of an eye, a wrist, her neck. The power that she had over him drove him crazy. But it seemed that just when he had convinced himself that he had finally found someone he would be able to love for the rest of his life, things began to go wrong.

Wendy had two daughters, Sharon and Elizabeth, by a previous marriage, but she refused to allow them to live on the Ark. She told Alex that she didn't want her daughters isolated from the rest of humanity during their formative years, so Sharon and Elizabeth lived with their father in Connecticut. After several years had passed, however, Wendy began to miss her daughters more and more. She would take extended trips away from the Ark, often as long as three months, in order to visit them.

Alex, lonely without Wendy, turned to Keiko for comfort and companionship. Although there was nothing sexual between them, Wendy became jealous of the time Alex spent with Keiko. Alex asked Wendy to bring Sharon and Elizabeth onto the Ark, so that Wendy wouldn't have to leave so often, but she refused. After two more years of arguments and conflict, they decided to separate. Wendy would remain on Earth to do promotional work for the Ark; Alex would remain married to Wendy in name only and be free to consort with whomever he pleased. That had been three years ago, and in that time Alex hadn't found anyone—until Amanda's arrival—to begin a long-term relationship with. Through all of this, Keiko remained his closest friend, never failing to console or counsel him.

Keiko finally broke the prolonged silence between them by reaching out and hugging him. Feeling her against him, he was sorry that their sexual problems had broken up their relationship. He had tried so many times to make it work, but in Keiko's own way, he knew, she considered an embrace the equivalent of sex. The exchange of energy, the surge in emotions, some of the same feelings he had felt with other women during intercourse, were present in only the briefest of Keiko's touches. There was a spiritual quality that was lacking with anyone else, a pure energy, a pure force, devoid of lust.

"Come, sit down," she told him. "Let me fix you some warm tea."

Alex sat on a low couch before a table.

"I think I'm still in love with Annette," he said, as much to himself as to Keiko.

He spoke louder, the beginnings of tears forming in his eyes. "I don't understand. Why do I have to be tortured by that woman all my life? Why does she have to follow me? She's always there, in the air around me, in the perfume of another woman. No matter what I do, I see her face. And now it's her daughter. I'm too old to go through this again." He began to sob. "God, I can't believe that I think I love her."

Keiko said nothing, appearing to be too busy preparing the tea. But he knew this was her way of listening carefully. She would respond when she had finished. He knew how much she loved him. He could have loved her, he thought, if it hadn't been for the sex. But no matter how gentle he had been, no matter how much space he had given her, she had always rebuffed his approaches. Whenever they got close, some inadvertent clumsiness ruined everything. She was beautiful, cultured, and still youthful. He was proud to be with her. But without sex, he knew their relationship would come to nothing.

He thought to himself, Oh, Keiko, if you would only let me love you. If you would only let me be passionate with you, I'm sure I could bring out the woman in you without hurting you, without destroying you. But the truth was that she preferred meditation. As she grew older, she talked less and less about her sexuality. She no longer dressed to be enticing. Whatever clothes she put on were feminine, but not alluring. There were no laces and frills, no long, painted nails or bright lipstick, no rouge or eye liner. In her forties now, she had become plain, asexual.

Yet this was the very complaint she had about most of the women he dated. She would tell him, "This one is very plain, Alex. I don't know what it is. She's just too plain for you." Actually, she was critical of all almost all the women he was with, saving positive remarks for the few she judged to be spiritually appropriate for him. She concerned herself not with his body, but with his soul.

They drank their tea in silence, but Alex felt as if Keiko had spoken volumes. When he got up to leave, she touched his face and it felt like he had been touched by an angel. He left her quarters rejuvenated, ready to face the trials that lay ahead.

Chapter 22

Alex Wants a Baby

Alex found time to spend a few moments alone with Amanda in a private compartment. They talked at length about Tanya's departure, deciding it was a good thing—Tanya needed to spend time alone. A furious session of lovemaking ensued, followed by a languorous conversation about parenthood, including Alex's experiences from the past and Amanda's hopes for children in the future.

Her face still flushed with the pleasurable warmth of sex, Amanda turned to Alex and said, "I think I'd like to have your baby." Catching herself, she let out a quick giggle. "*Our* baby."

Alex wasn't surprised by her admission. Every woman he had been involved with, at some time or another, had expressed a desire to have children. Childbirth and parenthood were two of the few instinctual biological functions that were still encouraged on the Ark. Even if some discovery had allowed them to do away with it, Alex doubted that he or anyone else would be able stop the biological urge to procreate. Perhaps, he thought, the Catholic Church had been right about their insistence on propagation. Children were a precious aspect of life.

Alex wondered how his chromosomes might commingle with Amanda's. What would their child look like? What would their grandchildren look like? Their great grandchildren? Their offspring in a million years?

"Did you hear what I just said, honey?" She poked him in the stomach.

"Yes. And I'd love to have a baby with you." He said it as if he were agreeing to be her lab partner in an experiment.

"You would?"

"Of course. But I'd have to insist that we use the Ark's child-rearing techniques. Would you be willing to do that?"

Amanda considered this for a moment, her face screwing up in a doubtful expression. "The Ark's way?"

Alex nodded. He wondered if Amanda had ever really thought about actually raising a child.

"I don't know," she finally said. "I've read so many articles about it. They make it sound like they produce these perfect kids, but I haven't actually seen anything—any pictures, for example—of what they do."

"You haven't seen the nursery? I thought they showed that to everyone."

"No, they didn't. They just shot me right off to the Moon practically as soon as I set foot on the ship."

"Well, if you haven't seen that part of the ship, then you hardly know why we call this the Ark. Endangered species aren't the only organisms that propagate on board. *Homo sapiens* have had great success in our experimental processes. People have been coming to the Ark for the express purpose of utilizing the Ark's childbirth technology. Along with tourism, it's one of our most popular and lucrative businesses.

"But it really gets me mad," he continued, "when they just shuttle people like you out to the Moon without any kind of Ark orientation. Everybody says the Moon's the place to be, they like that solid ground under their feet. But what about Mars?   What about the other planets we'll be colonizing? They're beautiful, but nobody talks about them."

"So, are you going to show me what it all looks like?" Amanda asked, trying to head off one of his infamous soliloquies.

"Oh, sure, sure," he said somewhat unsteadily, his train of thought having been broken. "Let's take a walk down to the nursery. I'll show you everything."

They walked down a series of passageways, headed for the nursery. Alex underwent a subtle but increasingly obvious change that transformed the nature of his relationship with Amanda from that of two intimate lovers, possibly planning a venture into parenthood, to that of a seasoned tour guide and his charge.

"As you know," he discoursed, "the Ark spends a great deal of time training the child while it is still in the womb."

Amanda thought she had heard of something like this before. "Oh, you mean like on earth where they talk to and play music for the fetus?"

"Well, we actually do a little more than that," replied a patronizing Alex. "We have the mother sit in a darkened room where a specialized projection device places images, information, and color before her. The material is abstracted in such a manner that the symbolism, shapes and forms can be communicated to the baby. Post-natal experiments have shown us that there is retention of the experience.

"In addition to the color and image process, we also use the more conventional method of taped monologues of the parents' voices reading informative texts designed to accelerate learning capabilities. And we also use programs that repeat the basic phonetic elements of foreign languages over and over to familiarize the child with the multicultural and multilingual environment here on the Ark.

"What is interesting, we've found, is that all of the time spent educating the child also serves as an important educational experience for the mother. The information shared between the two individuals makes the learning process much easier and establishes a relationship that nurtures education throughout the formative years of the child's life. An unexpected result of this has been reduced anxiety on the part of the mother about the birth itself. When labor begins, the mother is much calmer, more aware of what is happening to her. And anything, we've found, that reduces the trauma of what in the past was an almost universally painful experience, helps to strengthen the bond between the parents and their child.

"Of course," he continued, "all of the births on the Ark occur in a Zero-G liquid environment. The water is heated to the same temperature as the mother's amniotic fluid. Oxygen masks are used to allow the child immediate respiratory activity. The instruments you see in the corner of the tank have been specially designed for underwater anti-gravity use. They ensure that the child's metabolic processes and neurological systems are all functioning properly.

"As well as the state-of-the-art monitoring systems, we also simulate the taste and smell of the amniotic sac. Over a period of a few days, the child is weaned from the olfactory replication, but we believe that gradual changes in the newborn's environment are conducive to a well-balanced psychological state."

"Do you really think the fetus actually tastes and smells while it's in the womb?" asked Amanda.

"You're asking if the fetus of an advanced mammal can taste and smell six months into its development? Can an amoeba taste and smell?"

Amanda shrugged.

"Probably not in the way we can, but in its single-celled way, it reacts to stimuli. The sophistication of a human fetus in terms of neurological development is far greater than that of most animals. So of course it has faculties for sensing its environment. Hell, we've been aware of fetal learning for decades. Those programs were used on domesticated animals for years before humans came down off their supposedly sophisticated, if you'll excuse the expression, high horse to use the techniques on their own children."

"I've seen mothers singing to their babies months before they were born. The way you put it," she looked at him now with absolute admiration, "you make it sound ridiculous for people not to do it. I don't see why people weren't more aware of this before."

"It's just ignorance," he propounded. "Humans can be so ridiculous. On earth we were so wrapped up in wars and politics and chaos, we never stopped to think about the beauty of human life or how we might make life better. Without medical attention, people were living perfectly ghastly lives, with horrible deformities. I remember seeing pictures of hundreds of South American children suffering needlessly from minor cosmetic problems like harelips. With simple surgery, their lives could have been changed."

He fixed her with a passionate gaze. Amanda saw that his eyes were nearly glazed over with the power of his conviction. As usual, he was putting on a riveting, if self-absorbed, performance.

"Did you ever read *The Hunchback of Notre Dame*?" he asked her.

She nodded her head. "That was such a sad story. He gave up his life for that woman because she was the only one who would even think about being nice to him."

Alex placed a comforting hand on her shoulder.

"On the Ark, there aren't people who suffer as he did. We've learned to be compassionate. What medicine can't do for people is treated with psychology. We do everything we can to allow people to reach their potential. And part of that process is happening right here, before children are even born. More and more, we're weaning children from their mothers in an attempt to get them to transfer their bond with their mothers to an affiliation with our computer systems."

"Towards the computer?"

"Well, not just a computer," Alex explained, "but a very sophisticated robot that manipulates and handles the baby in the same way a mother would. We've been using similar machines for years in our endangered species research. We found it impossible to bring certain species back from the brink of extinction without designing surrogate mothers for the juveniles."

"Did you make a machine look like a peregrine falcon?"

"Something like that. Actually, designing human robots was a piece of cake after all the work we had done on the endangered species project. The biggest problem we had was people accepting the robots in an environment where they didn't think they were appropriate. People weren't threatened by them when they saw them in amusement parks or production lines, but we humans think we're so superior that we can't imagine robots being programmed to take care of our children. But believe me, these Ark babies have the best care a child could want. The computers are always there to pay attention. They never lose their tempers. The robots even look and act like the mother and father.

"The Ark's children never have to be toilet trained. They never fall. When it comes to education and learning basic skills, these robots can teach them a task over and over again without getting fatigued. Through computer simulation and physical manipulation, the child learns how to walk. Most of them have learned so much in training sessions that they can walk on their very first footstep. Do you remember how traumatic it was to take that first step and fall flat on your face?"

"No, Alex, I don't remember," she said, shaking her head. She didn't appear to be convinced.

"Well, I do," he continued matter-of-factly. "The theory is that from six months on, the fetus is a fairly sophisticated neurological machine, fully capable of learning. We're not sure how to represent the information to the fetus and we're not sure exactly what it is capable of retaining, but we think we've identified several fixed stages of development. We're currently not able to accelerate a child beyond certain neurological and physiological stages, but once he or she arrives there, we saturate that stage.

"For example, newborns normally do not develop the ability—it's actually something of an exploratory reflex—to reach up and touch something in front of them until they are much older. Early on, the child doesn't have the eye or hand coordination. However, we feel that if we can work on that coordination, accelerate its development, then once the child has appreciably increased his coordination, we can develop dexterity skills much more efficiently. All of which leads the child to the next level much more quickly than if he were left on his own.

"And there is a cumulative effect of this acceleration. As children get used to developing complex skills quickly, they are invariably better equipped to adapt themselves to changing situations. That skill, when learned at such an early stage, leads to a better adjusted child, one whose intellect is capable of learning and growing faster.

"An interesting byproduct of our research is that using the robots is giving us a better understanding of addictive personalities. We're starting to see how tendencies toward alcoholism and drug addiction develop in the formative years. We suspect that, in addition to biological factors, the bonding relationship between the mother and child plays an important role in the initial stages of problematic personality disorders."

Their brisk walking had finally taken them into the nursery section of the Ark. Arriving at a sealed door guarded by security terminals, Alex made an unusual but obviously false gesture of humility. "Well, here we are. Let's see if we can get in."

He spoke into one of the terminals. "This is Alex and Amanda. Can we enter the nursery?"

"You may enter," responded the computer in a soothing voice. For a moment, Amanda was certain it was a recording of her mother. "Please be as quiet as possible. Some of the babies are sleeping."

"That sounds just like my mother," whispered Amanda.

"Everybody says that," replied Alex.

They entered the nursery chamber and sat down behind a holographic screen, observing an infant being manipulated through a series of exercises by a spongy-armed machine. The robot closely resembled a human being, its mechanisms hidden under a flesh-colored plastic skin. The baby appeared to be of Asian descent and they assumed that the features on the robot's "head" were those of the child's mother. The baby wore a huge smile, cooing and laughing, unaware that she was being subjected to more than a tickling session.

She floated in an open pen, clearly in Zero-G because she was surrounded by nets that prevented her from wandering off. She wore no diaper and almost as soon as Alex and Amanda sat down, a thin stream of urine was expelled from her backside, collecting in a small cloud of droplets near the ceiling. Almost immediately, the robot extended a clearly mechanical arm, explaining in a soft voice to the child what it was doing. The arm was apparently fitted with some kind of vacuum as the urine disappeared quickly, sucked into a hidden receptacle.

Amanda laughed and said, "I like that, Alex. No diapers!"

"I thought you might." Every mother, potential or otherwise, loved the fact that they no longer had to deal with cleaning up after their children.

"It's wonderful," she continued. "It's so good for the baby, Alex. She never has to sit around miserable in a pair of wet, soiled diapers. Even moisture alarm diapers never worked that well."

Alex was not surprised by her answer. Women, he had found, tended to care more about children than about themselves. Nevertheless, he was glad to find her enthusiastic about her initial exposure to the robotic mother. Many women had balked at the idea of a machine being so intimately involved with their children.

"You're right, Amanda," he said. "The babies love it. No diaper rash. Less toilet training problems. We don't need to manufacture and dispose of dirty diapers. On earth, diapers are still causing an ecological nightmare."

He pointed excitedly toward the robot and child.

"Do you see how the computer is working on eye coordination? The robot is trying to get the baby to move its eyes toward that object. Every time she moves her eyes in that direction, she gets a reward."

The child turned her head to follow a block the robot was holding. A small yellow and red light began to flash rapidly. The baby flailed her arms and gurgled happily.

"There. Did you see that flashing light? I tell you, Amanda, these babies are so well-behaved I never hear them cry."

"They never even cry?"

"Why should they? They're fed before they're ever hungry. They're never exposed to toxic food. They never, as you mentioned, have to wait to be changed out of their dirty diapers. And when they're awake, they are constantly being paid attention to. They are the happiest babies you will ever see. There is absolutely no reason for them to be unhappy."

Alex began to wax rhapsodic. "That's one reason these kids will grow up to be such positive people. I don't think these kids could ever create a place like Auschwitz. They won't perpetrate horrors on one another. Atrocities like that won't happen at the hands of these children. Earth is such a negative place, filled with terrifying events, horrible people. But one look at this nursery tells another story. How can human beings, such intelligent creatures, be so stupid and not work harder to give their offspring something better than a primitive, animal existence? It's practically beyond my understanding.

"I almost went insane when Lorraine and I raised Dominique. Everything that could go wrong went wrong. I remember taking Lorraine to the hospital. It was horrible. There I was, afraid of what was going to happen, and they refused to tell me anything. They took my wife in and brought her clothes back to me in a paper bag, saying, 'You just go on home. We'll call you when she's ready to see you.'"

Amanda flashed him a look of disbelief.

"What's wrong?" he asked.

"A paper bag?"

"Just because you don't remember seeing one doesn't mean they didn't exist."

"No, I know what you're talking about, but I don't understand what they were doing."

"Well, in those days it wasn't fashionable for the father to be involved in the birthing process. To me, the paper bag was the final insult. It was a supermarket bag. It said Alpha Beta right on the side. They were about to make thousands of dollars performing a service, and they not only ignored me, they handed me this bag, the cheapest kind of bag you could give a person."

"Supermarkets?   Boy, Alex, you are really dating yourself."

"Yeah, yeah. I know," he laughed. "But these hospital people didn't care, they really didn't. They just didn't hold life up as being valuable. And these people, these doctors and nurses, thought of themselves as enlightened when they were behaving just like animals. I don't know how we even dared to call ourselves human then. We were just animals.

"They finally called me at home after Dominique was born. I immediately drove back to the hospital, but no one was there to point her out to me. Even so, I picked her out from all the other babies in the nursery. She had cheeks just like mine.   I was sure she was mine when I heard her screaming so loud that she was keeping all the other babies awake. At first it was funny, but she kept crying and crying and nobody came to comfort her. She looked so lonely and miserable there, I just started to cry. I wanted to help her but they wouldn't even let me near her. All I could do was stand behind a pane of glass, watching her cry."

"My God, Alex, how long ago was that?"

"Nineteen sixty-three."

"It's nothing like that anywhere in the world now. That must have been awful for you and your daughter and your wife."

"You will never understand how awful it all was. I know 1963 seems like a long time ago and you think your life as a child was much better. Sure, parents share in birthing and raising children, but can you imagine a time when everything we're doing here on the Ark will seem routine for the family of the future? I can't tell you how badly I want to raise a child in this new world, give him a chance of growing up and becoming an intelligent human being."

"I understand, Alex. It does seem that we should offer a child the best that we can."

"And what you've seen is just the tip of the iceberg. We raise the kids here in an almost germ-free atmosphere. It's so clean in there that, from time to time, we have to change the environment to expose them to subtle, low levels of germs. The Ark is so germ free that Arkian children have to be exposed to germs in order to strengthen their immune systems for journeys off-ship."

"I was wondering about that. How did you manage to prevent colds and flu on the Ark?"

"It was easy," he bragged. "We were able to do that very

early in the game, within a year of the Ark's inauguration. First, we immediately isolated anyone who had a cold. That prevented any germs from spreading to other crew members. Whenever a person was monitored for their food intake, if they had any symptoms of soreness, redness or a respiratory problem, the computer singled them out for examination. If medical personnel determined that they had a contagious disease, they were quickly isolated. Later on, once we got our filter systems running, we were able to filter out minute particles and germs, preventing almost everyone from getting sick.

"One of the things I am proudest of on the Ark is that we have very little staph. To me, that was more of a plague than colds. You have to remember, Amanda, we are living in a very tightly knit environment. It wouldn't take much for a sickness to reach epidemic proportions. We constantly have to be on guard against all infectious diseases.

"Okay. Well, let's get back to the children," she said.

Alex nodded in agreement and rose from his seat. He took her hand and led her into another room.

"Let's have a look in here."

A screen opened and they saw an infant suspended in a Zero-G chamber. The child's limbs and body were being manipulated by a robot-machine similar to the earlier robot they had seen. The arms of the machine were made of soft, flesh-like material, but the robot bore no other resemblance to a human being. The room was like a small theater, moving pictures and diagrams projected onto the walls. Alex touched a button and Amanda could hear what was happening in the room.

The child was being taught words and sounds, followed by pictures, colors and symbols. At the same time, his body was being manipulated. Alex kept his eyes glued to a console monitoring the child's EEG readings.

Amanda was surprised to see that the baby looked half asleep. When she glanced at the EEG readout, her observation was supported by the brain wave patterns. Every once in a while, a beep sounded, coinciding with the introduction of a new piece of information.

"In this room, Amanda, the baby is being stimulated neuromuscularly so certain reflexes will develop faster. He's also being taught basic word, sound and form recognition. At the moment, he's in a semi-hibernating state, but . . . oh, look, he's waking just now."

With a jerky motion of legs and arms, the baby's head pulled backwards. His eyes opened and he began to look at the images on the wall. Alex noticed an instant change in his brain patterns.

The baby began to make small noises and Amanda was amazed to hear the robot respond with similar noises and affectionate words. It was incredible. The machine was actually operating as a surrogate mother. The robot-machine had stopped manipulating the child's limbs and now seemed to be involved in playing some kind of game.

"Another ancillary discovery from teaching these children at such a young age," Alex told her, "is our increased understanding of how a child thinks, how human thought patterns work. In fact, we have been running some of these models through our newer computers and we are getting closer and closer to total artificial intelligence. Soon, I'm sure, we will have true thinking machines."

"Are you telling me we'll be able to make a computer that can write a symphony or design new clothes?"

Alex hesitated. "Amanda, where do you think some of our better inventions are coming from?"

"You mean?"

"Really. Quite a few of them are the designs of almost true-thinking machines. Every new development made here in the nursery means that we are able to model a more lifelike system in the computer. It's giving us fantastic results."

"That does sound fantastic."

"And there's another discovery we've made that will change the way we think about life. We believe that we have found, in a manner of speaking, the key to immortality."

"You've discovered everlasting life?" Amanda clearly disbelieved him.

"Oh, we can't prevent accidents, and maybe we won't last eternally," he demurred, "but we are now able to prevent almost any disease and we've developed methods of transplanting every organ in the body."

"I thought organ transplants were already common."

"They are. But whether or not a patient gets an organ from a donor is a matter of some concern. People often have to wait years to receive a heart or an eye. Often, they die before an appropriate donor can be found. And even after the operation is complete, even if the blood type and chromosomal scans indicate a match, there is the chance of the host rejecting the new organ.

"We have learned methods of surgically removing tissue from growing human fetuses to cultivate clones of the child's own organs. At any point in the subject's life, childhood or old age, if he or she needs any kind of transplant, we can use an organ duplicated from their own cells. Essentially, we are transplanting their own kidney or eye or heart.

"In addition to the specific organ tissues, we are harvesting cells so young that their function has not yet been determined by the DNA. By treating them with solutions that contain particular genetic information, we can use these cells to cultivate more efficient hearts or eyes that can see farther, more clearly. It's just the beginning."

Alex took her hand in his. "With all of the comforts offered by this new technology, I cannot wait to have a child who will be able to take advantage of all this."

Amanda found herself inexplicably drawn in by Alex's exuberance. The prospect of creating another human being with Alex gave her a strange feeling of power. She had never felt so close to another person. It was as if for the first time she were standing on something solid. She imagined herself as mother to a child that would depend on her, that would be tied to her for the rest of her life.

She decided not to tell Alex of her feelings, afraid that her emotions might be getting the best of her. She deflected the conversation away from their own plans.

"Alex," she said, "I can't get over how happy that baby

looked. I'm almost envious of him. He seemed so content."

"Well, the robot serves two purposes. Obviously, the child wants attention, it needs someone to bond with. And the robot's manipulation of the baby's limbs counteracts the atrophication of the muscle tissue normally seen in Zero-G subjects."

"Now I'm finally beginning to really understand your book's chapter on bonding. You've managed to apply those principles to almost every aspect of the nursery. It's incredible."

"I think that the major breakthrough, Amanda, was that once we realized that a six month-old fetus is as complicated as an adult, neurophysiologically speaking, we were able to think about prenatal care in an entirely new way. The fetus can learn and communicate. Once we broke through that barrier, all of this became possible."

"God, I do love you, Alex. I never could have thought of all this. It's not in my program to think about things that way. But it's so wonderful to see these kids as happy as they are. And it must be great for the parents, too. The machines must really free up a lot of their time."

"Well, they sure give working people a lot more leeway to enjoy life. We always try to keep an image of the mother or father in front of the child so that they feel as if they are being cared for by their parents."

Alex rose from his seat and gestured to a door in the distance. He led her into another secured area marked "Biological Studies." As the door swished open, they entered a room where they were surrounded by sophisticated electronic gear. Several electron microscopes stood side by side in rooms sealed off from the main chamber. Sterile gowns and hoods hung on pegs near every room. A large bank of deep-freezing units stood against one wall.

Amanda turned to Alex with astonishment. "What do they do here, Alex? I can't believe all the equipment."

"Well, this is where we're trying our newest techniques in genetic engineering. We've been able to take a sample from a subject's skin tissue and extract the chromosomes and genes we need. In female subjects, we've been able to place extracted genes and chromosomes in a neutralized egg—"

"So you can artificially select for almost any kind of characteristics you want?"

"Yes, that's one possibility, but in practice, most of what we've been doing is creating newly fertile eggs for women who cannot produce them. We take the egg from another woman and insert her genetic codes. In a similar manner, we've been able to take cells from an infertile man and fertilize an extracted egg with them."

"You mean you don't even need a woman's egg or a man's sperm?"

"That's right. So even if someone is sterile, we are able to reproduce their characteristics in their children. We've been working on this for such a long time that it's almost to the point where we'll be able to make it a routine procedure. In fact, Amanda, if you really want to do this, that's the way we're going to have our baby."

Amanda frowned in confusion. "Why's that, Alex? I don't have any problems. I've been taking Fertons for quite some time. As soon as I take the supplements, I'll be fertile."

Alex laughed nervously. "It's not you, Amanda. It's me. I've been sterile for a long time."

She snickered. "I never even thought of that."

He continued. "We can fill out a questionnaire and decide how tall we want her to be. We can decide on the color of her eyes, skin and hair. We can decide whether she will look more like you or like me, whether she'll have my nose or yours."

"That's fantastic! How come I haven't read about this?"

"Well, we've been trying to keep this pretty much an Ark secret. We don't want to get the people of Earth too excited. You know how traditional they are. If they heard about this, they'd be talking about moral problems and master race theories. It'd be ridiculous.

"There are so many good things we can do, beyond simple physical traits, that it would be criminal if some obtuse furor on Earth prevented us from doing our work. If the parents have a history of heart or lung disease, for example, we can change their children's genetic structure to avoid those problems. We can even extend their life expectancy by choosing genes that produce healthier, longer-living people.

"And there are other reasons not to let earth know what we're doing. Let's face it, Amanda, Earth is very crowded. What would they do with people who live for two hundred and fifty years? It would create incredible problems. For the moment, it's better that they not know about these techniques.

"Anyway, I'm not sure we could duplicate these techniques on earth. The clean rooms here are a lot cleaner than they could be on Earth, because of the vacuum of space. Zero-G has given us unique abilities of manipulation that would be unimaginable on earth."

Amanda seemed to be distracted.

"Are you tired?" Alex asked.

"I've just seen so many incredible things. It's overwhelming."

"There's just one more thing I want to show you. I think you'll like it. I want you to meet Judy."

"Judy?"

"Well, she's sort of one of my patients. She's very young, about seventeen, and she's going to give birth sometime today. I hope we're in time. One of my friends on Earth had been counseling her for heroin addiction. She was in terrible shape. Made an absolute mess of her life. My friend decided that treatment here on the Ark would be much more effective than conventional therapy on Earth.

"After we got her through detox, she decided she wanted to start her life over again. She wanted to have a baby. At first, after making the decision, she had been very apprehensive about the pain and possible problems in labor, but after she saw our facilities, she decided to go through with it."

After a few turns through the labyrinthine hallways, they arrived at another secured portal.

"If we're lucky, we'll be able to see her giving birth. How

does that sound?"

"It's your tour, Alex. You might as well continue."

Alex approached one of the terminals and said, "Could you tell me what room Judy Arbor is in? And would you get permission from the staff for us to come in if she wouldn't mind?"

The computer answered, "Just a minute, Alex. I will try to get the information for you."

There was a brief pause and then an answer.

"She is in room eleven, Alex. According to her dilation, she should deliver in three or four achievement periods."

"Wonderful!" Alex exclaimed, taking Amanda's hand. "We're in time. Let's go."

A few moments later, they entered a somewhat large room. A huge spa dominated the center of the room. The walls were lined with electronic equipment. An attendant stood near a young girl, half-submerged in the water. She wore a loose-fitting, white smock.

As they entered the girl turned to face them. Upon seeing Alex, she smiled widely. She spoke with unrestrained joy.

"Alex, I'm so happy you're here! Oh, I was so worried that you wouldn't come."

Alex returned her smile, walking toward her position in the pool. "I want you to meet my friend Amanda," he said.

Judy looked at Amanda for a moment. flashing her a courteous smile, quickly saying, "Hi, Amanda," and turning her attention back to Alex. "Oh, I'm so happy to see you, give me a big hug."

To facilitate the hug, Judy took a few steps out of the water. Alex leaned down, careful to avoid her distended abdomen. Despite the care with which he wrapped his arms around her, he pulled back from the hug with splotches of water on his shirt and pants.

"Are you all right, Judy?" he asked. "Everything going okay?"

"I'm really fine. I just feel so wonderful. The water's nice and warm and I feel so relaxed. Just floating here in almost Zero-G is so nice."

"Feel any pain?"

"Not really, Alex. I feel the contractions but I'm breathing with them. I can tell Nicholas really wants to come out. He's getting impatient."

"The front desk told me you're almost there."

"Am I really?"

"That's what they told me."

"Oh, how wonderful. I can't wait to see what he looks like. I'm so excited."

After passing a few more minutes in conversation with Alex, Judy realized that Amanda was being left out.

"Amanda, are you new on the Ark?" she asked. "I'm still practically a newcomer. You must let me give you some pointers."

As they started to talk, Alex got up to check on the status of the procedure. The attendant reaffirmed that everything was going according to schedule. The information on the terminals and monitors confirmed the evaluation. He found himself smiling. Everything was just perfect. As he walked back to rejoin Amanda and Judy, the future mother called out to him.

"Is everything fine, Alex? Is everything all right?"

"You couldn't be in better hands. Everything is going great."

"Ooh," she moaned in momentary pain. "Alex, I feel it more now."

Alex looked over to a nearby monitor and saw that the frequency and strength of the contractions were increasing rapidly. The baby's estimated arrival was now within less than an achievement. The computer had a fantastic database to work from. It was able to pinpoint deliveries to the precise nan.

"He should be along any moment now," Alex told her.

"Oh, Alex, Alex, I feel it!" Judy gripped the side of the spa with her hands, her legs jutting out horizontally in the water.

Alex looked down in the water. He could see the dark

hair on the little head starting to protrude. The attendant now stood in the water, ready with a respiratory mask designed to suck out any fluids from the respiratory tract and then immediately begin diffusing a mixture of oxygen into the baby's lungs.

Judy's face showed how much of her energy was being exerted in trying to push the child out, but it was clear that she was in very little pain. Because she was pushing down on an object that had no weight in the Zero-G pool, each push carried enormous force. Alex was glad to see that Judy didn't seem to be flustered or anxious. Her prenatal training had prepared her for this moment.

The baby was now all the way out, the water around him stained red with blood. Alex could clearly see the umbilical cord floating in the water. Any moment now the placenta would appear and the water would get very red. He assumed that the circulating pumps and vacuum filters would remove it from the water almost immediately. Judy looked up at a monitor and saw her child suspended in the water.

She exclaimed excitedly, "He looks like me, he looks like me!"

Amanda took this opportunity to whisper in Alex's ear. "Who's the father?" she asked.

Alex responded in an open, loud voice. Amanda turned red with embarrassment, her curiosity having been revealed. "Oh, Judy wanted to have the baby by herself," Alex announced. "She decided she didn't need to have a father. A lot of women on the Ark are doing that these days. She just picked some sperm out of our sperm bank. That way she was able to choose which sex she wanted and the characteristics of the donor."

Alex spoke to Judy. "It worked out great, didn't it, Judy? He's handsome little guy, isn't he? Look how strong he is, swimming away."

Alex saw the umbilical cord being cut and the placenta gently picked up and sent out through a receiving window for analysis. Judy was then allowed to slide into the water, her baby still contentedly submerged in his mask. The attendant gently handed the baby to her and Judy slowly slid up so that his head was out of the water. She removed the mask from his face and hugged him to her body. Somehow the baby found her nipple and started to suckle contentedly.

"Oh, Alex, this is all so wonderful," she sighed.

"Judy, can Amanda and I hold him? What's his name—Nicholas?"

They started to step into the water just as the technician started to step out. She moved about the chamber, checking the monitors. Alex noticed the laboratory report on the placenta and the baby's chemistry coming up on the terminals. Alex looked at the technician and then at Judy and said, "Everything looks just fine. No surprises."

Amanda and he slid into the pool and got close to Judy and the baby. They were now more than waist deep in the water. Amanda had an ecstatic look on her face.

"He's really cute," Amanda announced to no one in particular. "Alex, look at him sucking away. He's so hungry. Oh, he looks so content, so happy. Do all the newborn babies look this happy?"

"Of course," Alex said. "I told you the Ark's program is the best there is. After all the controversy about my book and the ideas of machines caring for children, it comes down to this: a happy mother and child."

Nicholas stopped sucking. Amanda reached out to hold him and Judy cautiously transferred him into her arms. Cradling the baby protectively in her arms, Amanda gazed dreamily at him. "Isn't he adorable, Alex? He looks so healthy and handsome. You have a beautiful son, Judy."

Judy started to walk around in the water, keeping her eye on Nicholas. "Oh, Alex," she said, "this so peaceful. I never thought I could feel so content. So happy. I feel fulfilled. It makes me want to have babies one after another. It was painless. Look, I can even walk!"

Amanda continued her conversation with Alex. "Well, I can understand the way people felt, Alex. I read your book and I got the same impressions. It did seem mechanical. I never would have been convinced until I saw how content these children are."

"It's just so frustrating," Alex said. "How can I describe a theory to people? I write it down in words and try to describe it as best I can. But how can you compare words with an experience. Most people refuse to use their imaginations. They lack that intuitive insight. When they see something written down, they can't get beyond their own preconceptions to look for a deeper meaning."

"Well, you've managed to convince me."

"That the Ark's nursery is a good program?"

"Yes, definitely that. And Alex," she lowered her voice, "I want to have a baby. And yes, let's have it the Ark's way."

She held the baby tightly, paying him inane compliments in a soft voice.

"Oh, Amanda, you are really funny sometimes," Alex said.

"Aren't I?"

Judy tapped Alex on the shoulder and smiled.

"Looks like you are going to be a father," she said.

"Looks that way."

"Is it going to be a girl or a boy?"

Alex smiled. "I'd like to have a girl if that's all right with Amanda."

Amanda smiled back. "That's fine with Amanda."

They stayed there for an achievement, playing with the newborn baby, touching him as if they were already part of a family. Back in Judy's arms, the baby drifted off into sleepy peacefulness and they said goodbye.

When the door to Judy's room closed behind them, Amanda had tears in her eyes. At the moment, she was more hopeful than she had ever been. She looked at Alex and hugged him tightly.

"We're going to be so happy," she said.

CHAPTER 23

HECTOR

Amanda sat in her private cubicle, agitatedly issuing commands to a computer terminal. She was, she had decided, bored with the clothes she had been wearing and she now consulted with the computer on new dress designs. In the past, she had never had a problem coming up with a new costume. Almost instantly, she had been able to create an ensemble that perfectly matched her mood. But now, perhaps because of her clouded feelings for Alex, she was unable to find a look that satisfied her.

Nothing seemed to come together properly. Either the material lacked distinction or the pattern fell short of her expectations. She ended up erasing the entire file, starting over from scratch. When she attempted to give up control of the design, nothing the computer auditioned for her seemed right, either. She rejected the ideas out of hand. Every time she thought she had something she liked, she pictured herself standing next to Alex in it and she was unable to concentrate. Uttering an anguished command of, "Lose it," she watched the garment disappear from the screen.

Her feelings for Alex had made her a wreck. She was fond of him, she knew. She was looking for a man who made her feel secure, who offered maturity, but she hadn't found those qualities in the men she met in space. Alex's fatherly, attentive personality seemed to offer the comfort and warmth she had been seeking, but every time she thought about his best traits, she was irked by his age, how settled he was. The very characteristics she found charming were at the root of the problems she foresaw for herself in an ongoing relationship with him.

The men she usually dated were reckless. They took her on the emotional equivalent of a roller-coaster ride, they volunteered for jobs that put their lives on the line every day. They made her feel alive. When she was with them, she could see the hunger in their eyes. Their desire for her was unparalleled. Each time she dated a new man, the thrill of expectation and unfamiliarity led her into new liaisons. But the thrill, she knew, was due only to infatuation. Invariably, the excitement dimmed and she was unable to feel any kind of passion for the man who had, for a few moments, meant everything to her.

Alex, on the other hand, possessed a certain timidness that somehow assured her that his feelings for her were real. And somewhere deep inside of her, she believed that somehow she had inherited her mother's love for him. All of her life, she had heard her mother talking about him. She had grown up with stories about the man she was now having an affair with. Perhaps, she thought, she was trying to make a place for herself inside of that myth.

But Alex, she knew, was not a myth. He respected her, listened to her ideas. He, a man who had pressed forward with plans for the spaceship she was presently traveling on, seemed to think that she had great creative potential. Secure enough in himself, he never judged her. She felt she could tell him anything, confide in him all of her secrets. The difference in their ages, nearly fifty years, made their physical union akin to breaking taboos, which only heightened her interest in him. Rebellion of any kind had always interested her.

God, she thought, I must be in love with him. She smiled to herself, gazing at her image in the monitor. Having accepted the thought, she put it away, burying herself deeper in the activity before her. Only now, sure of her feelings, she felt peaceful, relaxed.

She focused on the monitor before her, staring deep into an image of her own eyes. Shall I make them the eyes of an eagle or a cat, she asked herself. Chartreuse or bright pink? Or maybe an albino look, with that terrible pink tinge. Perhaps I'll put my hair down, wear it around my shoulders.

Or I could wear a wig and wear it hanging all the way down to my waist. Each time she thought about a new look, the computer image before her changed to reflect the new idea.

Suddenly, she was overcome with the idea that, because she was in love, her dress must reflect the purity she felt inside. She decided to swath herself entirely in white, affecting a look something like a snow fox. She selected a minuscule white panty that just barely covered her pubic hair, but revealed the rest of her body. She designed a thin strip of white fur that covered only her nipples, leaving the majority of her breasts exposed. She decided to give her skin an albino appearance, her eyes taking on a peculiar pale-pink cast.

Looking at the work she had done so far, she decided she would need to use a hair-removing hormone, after which she would cover her head in speckles of white fur and gems. Every detail would be white: her makeup, her shoes, little white bracelets around her ankles and waist, and one around her biceps. She would even cover her body with white powder, giving her skin an exaggerated, snowy cast.

She asked the computer to project her design holographically and saw an image of herself materialize in full scale with the clothes and accessories she had chosen. She walked around the holograph, examining it from all sides.

"Beautiful," she said. "Just what I want. Oh, I look so beautiful."

She felt herself trembling before this image of herself. She had the ability to love herself simply for the exquisite beauty she could achieve. The costume she had designed, every detail reflecting her emotions, was like a work of art to her and she reveled in the joy of creation. She anticipated Alex's reaction. He would love her even more when she wore these clothes. Every man who saw her would be unable to avert his eyes. Even Tanya would have been aroused by this new image.

The one truly troubling aspect of this new look was her plan for baldness. She had never cut her hair before and she was afraid to lose so suddenly the hair that so many men had complimented her on. But as she scrutinized the hologram, she saw the streamlined effect it gave her body and imagined the thrill it would give Alex. She decided to use the depilatory ointment all over her body.

When she had finished, she was amazed by the results. Her skin felt exceptionally soft. Her now bare pubic area made her look like a marble statue. As she marvelled at the change in her appearance, she thought to herself, no wonder everyone makes such a fuss over me. I am the perfect female. She had to giggle for a moment at her own egoism. But, still, she tried to convince herself: I am perfectly proportioned and I'm not a musclebound dyke like Tanya. No wonder Tanya loves me, she decided, I am so much more beautiful than she. She looks like a man, or maybe an Amazon, but she wants to be with a woman who looks like a woman. Like me. A woman shouldn't have muscles and blood vessels popping out all over the place.

Oh, why am I making fun of Tanya, she wondered. She realized that she was more than a little jealous of Tanya's relationship with Alex. Alex had some strange power over Tanya and just as Tanya claimed that Alex had changed Amanda, Amanda knew that Tanya's spending time with Alex had changed her as well. Tanya, she knew, had discovered a way to control Alex by anticipating what he wanted and acting out his fantasies. Also, Tanya had realized early on just how much Alex enjoyed being idolized. She played along as a sycophantic student just enough to keep Alex happy and make herself feel that she was able to manipulate him with her fawning. Tanya had told Amanda how strange she had felt, the odd pleasure she had experienced in controlling him that way. The only thing she had not been able to influence was Alex's feelings about Amanda. Ultimately, that inability had driven a wedge between Amanda and Tanya. Their years of friendship were feeling the strain of competition.

Isn't that the way it works with two people, Amanda thought. They both feed on one another's inadequacies. She knew that she, too, like Tanya, was playacting with Alex. He told her what she wanted to hear and she kept him guessing, leading him on, allowing him to enjoy his pursuit of her.

She absentmindedly dangled her hand near her crotch,

feeling the smooth skin.   As smooth as Alex's face, she thought, he's not the only one who enjoys the inventions on the Ark. The Ark and her experience with Alex, her newfound freedom, had all effected an enormous change on her. She knew she was not the same woman she had been before her arrival. She attributed her transformation to the way in which the Ark allowed every one of its passengers to change themselves, both mentally and physically.

She studied the monitor a final time. "God," she said to herself, "I do look gorgeous."

She felt a tingling sensation all over her body, a sudden moisture in her private parts. In an instant, her nipples had become erect, her entire being aroused to an invisible sensual presence. It was as if she were experiencing a miniature orgasm, for as soon as the feeling had come, the flush and heat dissipated. She sighed to herself. "Wonderful. What a wonderful creation you are, Amanda. I love you. I love you with my very essence."

She turned to the holograph still wavering beside her and said, "Baby, baby, you're so beautiful."

She wished her mother could see her in this place, looking the way she did. For a moment Amanda was saddened by her mother's death at such a young age, but then realized that her mother probably wouldn't have approved of anything she had been doing lately. Oh well, she thought, I approve and that's all that really matters. I can't wait to see the looks on people's face when they see me tonight.

She decided to add a dose of mystery to her costume, placing a small mask over her face so that only her eyes showed. If they can guess who I am, she told herself, I'll take it off. But if no one comes up with my name, I'll leave it on just to keep them guessing. Oh, but I'm sure Alex will know that it's me, she told herself. Tanya would certainly have seen through this disguise. She wondered if Alex would be as adept.

She made a quick pirouette in the air, kicking her feet together. Like a little girl, she danced around the room, hopping and skipping to a music only she could hear. The anticipation of seeing herself transformed into the woman in the holograph was too great. She decided to change into her costume immediately.

She spoke decisively to the computer. "OK, baby. Make it happen."

As Amanda, with the help of her computer costumer, prepared for the party, Alex also readied himself for the final night of the fete he had planned. He thought of Amanda, wanting to do something different for her. Would she understand how he felt in just a fleeting glance? Could she feel the burning inside of him? He thought she must know how he felt. But why was she being so cautious?

How could he tell her that he desired no one but her? He wanted to share his whole life with her. He felt as if knife blades were perforating his stomach. She was like an electrical power, a force that he wanted to reach out and touch forever, but he feared that she might be too much for him, that he might be overwhelmed by the kick she carried inside of her.

She was too beautiful, he thought. Looking at her was like looking into the sun. He couldn't stop himself from staring at her, even though he knew that every moment he did so, he blinded himself to reason, made himself crazier for her love. But his desire for her went beyond her beauty. It wasn't just her skin, her soft hair, or her sleek figure. She knew, either through some strange intuition or natural empathy, how to draw any emotion from him. She could play him for a fool just as easily as she could pledge her love to him forever.

No one, he knew, could resist someone as beautiful as she. He strove to come up with an idea that would convince her, finally, of his love for her. He was seized by an idea that seemed just crazy enough to work. Would Hector make the difference? Would he be able to send her the right message?

Hector was the first fully automated, mechanical sex toy. He had a stainless steel and super plastic penis covered with a synthetic skin. Hydraulic tubing and flexible joints allowed his member to not only elongate itself to any length, but also to increase its diameter. He was therefore able to find the perfect fit for any mate, male or female. His penis was powered by a driving mechanism that allowed it to move at any angle or speed. Synthetic hips allowed him to gyrate wildly, to move with a simple up and down stroke, or to thrust with a corkscrewing clockwise motion.

His "nerve" system had specialized sensors and heaters that reacted immediately to moisture, heat and friction. Stimuli were fed into a small network of computers that adjusted his actions to the desires of his partner.

Hector resembled a humanoid torso mounted on what appeared to be two large, pillar-like legs. Powered by pneumatics, these pillars worked and acted like legs, slowly perambulating him about the corridors and rooms of the Ark. In addition, he had arms and hands that closely resembled human body parts. His hands were covered with the same synthetic skin as his penis, but there were only three jointed appendages in place of the five fingers. These joints utilized the same delicate sensors as his penis.

A sensor in Hector's head tracked a laser beam that carried information from Genie and other computers on the Ark. Genie relayed orders to Hector as needed. Genie's function as a computer designed to understand and fulfill the sexual and romantic needs of her patrons allowed her to command Hector to perform exactly the right services.

Alex decided he would have to contact Genie right away. She would have to help him devise the perfect seduction of Amanda. He was confident he would succeed. After all, who knew more about women's physiology and psychology than Genie? As Alex called Genie to attention over the comlink, he shivered in anticipation of the tryst he was designing.

CHAPTER 24

THE PARTY

OR

AMANDA'S GOOD TIME WITH HECTOR

Alex decided to arrive at the party early in order to prepare Hector for Amanda's arrival. He also hoped there might be a slight chance that he would find Vladimir among the early arrivals and have a chance to speak with him. As he entered the chamber, there were already several hundred people in the room. He assumed, correctly, that if he looked for an especially large crowd of people, populated in the majority by exotic and attractive women, he would find Vladimir among them, the center of attention.

Sure enough, he almost instantaneously fixed upon an exceptionally boisterous circle of revelers. As he approached, he caught a glimpse of Vladimir's visage. For a moment, their eyes met and Alex saw a look of recognition and joy spread over his friend's face. Alex decided he would have to fight his way through the throng to get to Vladimir, but before he could even take a step in their direction, he saw Vladimir clawing his way out of the group and bounding toward him. He leapt in front of Alex and immediately clung to him with an immense bear hug.

"Alexsous!" he shouted. "My Brother! Comrade, I am so happy to see you. What a party, no? The super vodka! The women!"

Alex found himself unable to respond to this barrage of exclamations. Vladimir, however, did not need Alex to prompt him. He continued with his praise of the Ark's hospitality.

"Mmmmmmm," he slavered, holding his fingers to his

lips in a gesture of famishment. "Where do you find such exquisite women?" Vladimir pointed to a group of five women, each costumed in the excessive garments typical of Ark fetes. Alex saw that one woman wore a transparent shift beneath which an intricate pattern of filigreed tattoos covered her entire body. The interlocking design gave the impression of fabric. The only opaque element of her ensemble was her boots, tooled of an exotic leather that matched the intricacy of her tattoos.

Another woman wore what appeared to be a body suit made of snake skin until Alex realized that she actually wore a costume akin to her friend in the transparent shift. This woman wore a similarly sheer dress, but rather than tattoos, her skin had been transformed into snakelike scales. At one time, years ago, Alex remembered having been with a woman who had undergone a similar process. The smooth, cool softness of her skin on his had sent their lovemaking into another dimension.

One of the women beckoned to Alex, inviting him to join their circle. Alex took a second glance at their array of eagle's eyes, cat's eyes, talons, claws, peroxide blonde wigs, diamond-studded heads and garish clothes. In the past, he never would have considered passing up the chance to spend time with such women, but his thoughts of Amanda made him pause.

Vladimir seconded their invitation. "Yes, please join us." He began to drag Alex toward the group.

"I can't," protested Alex. "I'm waiting for Amanda."

Vladimir stopped his tugging, looking back at Alex in awe. "Oh, you lucky man," he said in a low voice. "I met her. She is so beautiful. And what legs. I have never seen such long, fine legs."

Vladimir made a gesture with his hands to suggest the expanse of Amanda's legs. "Beautiful, absolutely beautiful!" In the middle of his appraisal of Amanda's beauty, Vladimir surprised Alex by actually ceasing to speak. His gaze was fixed excitedly on the opposite corner of the room. "Actually, my friend, this is she, no?"

Alex directed his attention to the doorway and saw a

masked woman in a revealing white fur bikini. He squinted at her, attempting to verify whether or not it was, indeed, Amanda. Certainly, he thought, there is something familiar about that woman, but he was vaguely sure that it was not Amanda he saw before him. After a few more moments of concentrated ogling, he realized who the woman was.

"That's not Amanda," he told Vladimir with assurance. "That's Keiko. She loves to wear disguises. Do you remember what I told you the night you first arrived? She can't resist white powder. It makes her think she's a geisha, I suppose."

Vladimir laughed, raising his eyebrows suggestively, noting ironically Alex's earlier description of Keiko as a retiring, withdrawn entity. "So this is your shy Keiko. I should be so lucky to meet such a shy creature."

"I told you she has her moments," Alex replied, "but tomorrow she'll be back on the holy and spiritual path. She'll pretend she was never here." He kept himself from making any further comments. He shouldn't talk about her that way, he thought. She had been good to him. In his disappointment at not seeing Amanda, he had forgotten how much she meant to him.

Then Alex saw the lecherous look in Vladimir's eyes as he watched Keiko cross the room. Vladimir had quickly accustomed himself to the luxuries of the Ark. Somewhat shocked by and envious of his friend's open admiration of Keiko, Alex continued in the vein of his earlier comments. "Oh yes, tonight she's beautiful and different, free from all her inhibitions. But tomorrow she'll be depressed and guilty, trying to forget what she's done. She'll talk about meditation and being one with the universe. She'll talk about evil and evil in the universe. She'll tell me about how I need to be on my guard, that no one should corrupt their mind by giving in to unholy, bodily pleasure. After a night like this, she talks about sex as if it were some kind of unnatural phenomenon."

Despite his attack on her, he decided that he ought to at least be polite and say hello to her. "Oh, well," he told Vladimir snidely, "I guess I need to go over there and disappoint her. Tell her that I see through her disguise."

"Then I will join you," said Vladimir gamely.

As they approached the woman in white, Alex carefully studied her disguise. "You're right," he told Vladimir, surprised by her appearance. "I've never seen her look more beautiful. I never realized she could look this good. I suppose I've gotten so used to seeing her in a different light that I forgot she could be this way."

"Then it seems you have forgotten quite a lot," said Vladimir.

"Maybe I have taken her for granted," Alex confessed. "But right now I'm so caught up in Amanda I can hardly think about anything else, much less what Keiko used to mean to me. Whenever I see Amanda, my heart skips a beat. Keiko just doesn't do that for me any more."

Vladimir laughed, pointing back toward the group of women they had left behind. "Look at me," he said. "I have the same problem. I see these women, my hearts beats differently, too. I forget about how much I miss my wife."

As they drew near to the woman in white, Vladimir laughed to himself, positive that they were in fact walking toward Amanda and not, as Alex thought, Keiko. He prided himself on his memory of beautiful women and he was sure he was not wrong now. He could never mistake those beautiful long legs for someone else's. Already well versed in the Ark's sense of humor about social exchanges, he decided to keep his knowledge to himself, allowing Alex to discover for himself the truth about the woman in white.

Vladimir stopped walking and drew Alex near to him. "Well, my friend," he said in jest, "I am sorry you have to go through such punishment." He roared with laughter at his own joke. "I am thankful that this vodka has numbed my brain so I do not hear your thoughts inside of me." At this, he pulled his hands to the side of his head, as if he were pressing Alex's thoughts into his ears.

Alex laughed, but Vladimir grew serious.

"I know that you believe that life takes us on it's course," he told Alex. "That your life is like a river and you flow upon it like you are in a boat. You tell everyone that we are supermen. You tell us that all of these wonderful machines let us do anything we want. We must let our talents take us out into the Universe, beyond what we already know. Is this not right?"

"Yes," said Alex shakily, unsure of where Vladimir's comments were headed.

"And, my friend, isn't it you who tells us that we have unlimited talents and unlimited love? You say we can't be afraid to grow. We have to be like little children, without fixed impressions, without fear." Noticing the confused look on Alex's face, he gave him a reassuring smile. "Alex, love is wonderful. You must feel free. Let your feelings out. We smell things better and hear things better when we are in love because we are meant to love. Why hide your love? Let it show. You have a beautiful creature here in front of you. Look at her. She loves you. You need to be like me," he joked, indicating the women behind them. "I'm in love with all of them." Vladimir laughed loudly as the women waved back at him.

Alex, having taken Vladimir seriously, spoke desperately. "Vladimir you don't understand. I can't love anyone but Amanda! She's the only one. Maybe I know it's an illusion, but I don't care. I know she's not perfect. Her legs are too long. Her mouth is too small for her big teeth. She talks with a lisp, but I think it sounds sexy. Is that crazy of me?"

Vladimir shrugged noncommittally, enjoying the surprising furor of Alex's rebuttal to his earlier statements. Did he really think that Amanda's beauty was so flawed? Or was he just feeling guilty about the flimsiness of his dedication to his past lovers?

"Despite all that, Vladimir, I still think she's the most beautiful woman in this whole universe."

"I do not doubt that, my friend," replied Vladimir with a smile. As Vladimir faced the woman in white again, his smile grew wider. Amanda had seen Alex and her joy at finally spotting him in the crowd made her face glow with happiness. It is undeniable, Vladimir thought. She loves him.

Vladimir turned back to Alex. "Well, my friend," he said,

"I know you tell me you do not want to make love with Keiko. Amanda is the only woman for you. But I think you should just enjoy yourself. Relax. Drink some of your marvelous vodka. Answers will come to you much easier after a few glasses." He gave Alex a tremendous slap on the back.

"But right now," he continued, "I think you need to attend to your beautiful friend. She has noticed you. Trust your feelings, my friend, and they will guide you."

Alex turned away to leave but Vladimir held his arm. "Alex," he said, "I am not what you would call a homosexual, but I want to tell you I feel deep love for you. The same kind of love I feel for a woman." At this, the Russian again enveloped Alex in a powerful hug. Alex felt like he was hugging a brother, that they somehow shared the same blood. Their physical proximity merely underscored the closeness of their hearts.

Before he released Alex from his powerful arms, Vladimir spoke into his ear. "Life is full of barriers, my friend, but we must hurtle them one by one if we want to live. Do you know who taught me that?"

"No."

Vladimir let out a gruff chuckle. "You did, Alex. In your books. In everything you have accomplished."

"Really?"

"Love them both, Alex. Leave your heart open. They are both beautiful women and a moment is only a moment. Today is today and tomorrow is tomorrow."

Vladimir stepped back, letting go of Alex. "I think she is looking over at us, no? Go on, Alex. Enjoy yourself."

As soon as she had walked into the party, Amanda felt as if everyone were staring at her. It was irrational, she knew. Women dressed in outrageous costumes were a common sight on the Ark. But her wish that the simple ploy of her mask might allow her not to be recognized immediately made her nervous. Would Alex know her, she wondered?

After only a few moments inside the door, she saw Alex and Vladimir talking across the room. She thought Vladimir had seen her almost immediately, but he did nothing to show

that he recognized her.   Although confused by Alex and
Vladimir's lack of response, she took it to mean that her
costume was effective enough to fool even her friends. She
began to relax, holding conversations with people she had
often talked to as if she were a stranger.

As she made small talk, she noticed that Alex and
Vladimir were walking toward her. They've finally noticed
me, she thought. She couldn't wait to talk to Alex. But
suddenly, they stopped again, just a few yards from where she
stood. They were apparently having some kind of serious
conversation. Amanda was further surprised to see them,
amidst all the partygoers, locked in a passionate embrace.

Alex and Vladimir finally parted and she saw Alex
headed straight toward her. He does know it's me, she told
herself. Arriving at her side, though, he acted as if he were a
stranger introducing himself for the first time. He extended
his hand like a Southern gentleman at a formal ball.

"*Guten tag, fraulein,*" he said.

She smiled back at him, responding in perfect German,
happy to play along with his game. "How did you know I was
German?"

He grinned, continuing to speak in German.   "I just
guessed it."

They paused awkwardly for a few moments, Amanda
having decided to let Alex lead the game. Alex, however, was
confused. His mind was on meeting Amanda, not continuing
this conversation with a disguised Keiko. Finally, he chose to
put an end to her game.

"You're not going to fool me this time, Keiko," he told her
assuredly. "I know it's you."

Well, Amanda thought, this is a new twist. She was
almost shocked to think that Alex wanted her to play the part
of one of his old lovers. She tried to deflect him from
addressing her as Keiko. "Keiko?" she said quizzically. "My
name is Teresa."

Alex laughed snidely.   He spoke to her like a
condescending father.   "God, Keiko, it really is a perfect
disguise. But don't you think it's a little too close to what you

wore the last time you fooled me?"

Amanda said nothing, still unsure of what Alex was trying to accomplish.

"And I can't believe you shaved your head," Alex continued. "I always thought you'd be too afraid to do anything like that. But I'm sorry honey, even though I can't see your eyes or hair, your white skin, all this powder, it's a dead give away. Nobody on the Ark likes white skin the way you do. I must admit, however, I've never seen you look more beautiful. I never realized how beautiful your legs are."

Amanda allowed herself to blush after the compliment, but she was terribly confused. Apparently, Alex didn't know who she was. She decided to play along with him, to see how far she could take her disguise. In response to his earlier formality, she took the part of a society debutante being introduced to a suitor.

"Obviously, you don't believe me," she said in a mannered voice, "but my name is Teresa. If you wish you can call me Keiko. It's a very nice name. It will be quite intriguing for someone to think I'm someone else. It gives one a certain air of mystery, don't you think?"

"It does indeed. Since you have so succinctly made up your mind, Teresa," he exaggerated her name, "and since I haven't the slightest clue as to who you are, would you consider giving me the pleasure of a dance?"

"I would love to, but I'm afraid I'm waiting for a friend."

"Oh, that's all right. I am too. But she's a little late." He offered his hand again. "By the way, my name is Alex."

"Nice to meet you, Alex. This is my first ball on the Ark. It really is so nice to meet new people. I do hope you'll help me to not make a perfect fool of myself. Several people have told me that these parties often get quite out of hand. You must come to quite a few of these gatherings. Can you tell me anything?"

Taken aback by Keiko's acting talents, Alex couldn't help but smile. Amanda, now less troubled by Alex's strange behavior, began to accept the fact that it might take a good deal of time before she found out exactly where Alex intended to take their game. Both of them acted so well that the other was unwilling to end the masquerade.

"No, no, there's really nothing to worry about," Alex assured her. "Every once in a while there is an odd event, but our balls really aren't much more than a New Orleans Mardi Gras. There are, of course, a few little oddities here and there, but nothing to concern yourself about."

For a moment, visions of some of the wilder parties, orgies actually, flashed through Alex's mind. Remembering himself naked in a circle of people, smothered with chocolate almost caused him to burst out laughing, but he managed to keep a straight face.

"By the way," inquired Amanda, "this woman that you say I bear a resemblance to . . . Keiko, is that her name? Is it possible that she could be German? That's not a German name."

Alex, unable to control himself, smirked knowingly. He gazed directly into the eyes behind the mask. "No, actually she's Japanese. But I think she'd like to believe she's German."

Amanda shot him a quick look of mock indignancy. "Do you mean to tell me that I look Japanese?"

"No, no. You look very German."

"Are you sure you're not just handing me a line?" She winked at him. "How is it possible that I could look German and yet you remain quite sure that I look like your Japanese friend, Keiko?"

Alex shrugged. "I'm not sure how it's possible. It just is."

Amanda began to enjoy playing on his momentary lapses. "Tell me," she asked, "does your friend have as nice a figure as I?"

Alex began to wonder how far Keiko was planning to take her game. He decided to go on the attack himself. "No," he assured her, "my friend's figure is quite different. In fact, she's really not comparable to you in terms of beauty. Most people would agree she's rather plain."

Amanda feigned an angry tone. "Well, I should hope so.

It is quite horrible to think that someone might mistake a German for a Japanese, no matter what the other looks like."

"Excuse me?" said Alex, his neck craned so that he could see over Amanda's shoulder into the crowd. "What was that you just said?"

She laughed, knowing that she had caught him looking for her. "Sir, are you looking for your lady friend?"

"Oh, no," Alex stammered weakly, embarrassed at having been found out.

"Yes, I think you must be looking for her. Shall I have Keiko paged?"

"Actually," said Alex, growing bold, "I was looking for a woman named Amanda."

"You must have quite a few of them," she said.

"Quite a few what?"

"Lady friends."

"Oh, no. Not really." Alex grew more and more uncomfortable, wondering why Keiko insisted on bringing up his past in this setting.

"Do your two friends know each other?" she asked.

"No."

"Then tell me, sir, are you quite in love with both of them?"

This was getting ugly, Alex thought. Keiko was pushing him farther than he wanted to go. Why was it, he asked himself, that even though he claimed to hate jealousy and possessiveness, he always found himself with women who wanted him all to themselves. Worse yet, he found that he liked that about them. But now, his insecurity, his need to have women who were jealous of him, was backfiring. He had to be careful of what he said. Even though she was disguised, he didn't want to hurt Keiko's feelings.

"Yes," he told her. "I suppose I love them both in different ways."

"Is that so?"

"It is."

"So tell me, how did you come to meet this other one, Amanda?" Amanda couldn't wait to hear his response.

"I was in love with her mother when I was young . . . ."

She laughed. "You were in love with her mother? You can't be that old."

Behind her mask, it was impossible for him to see how she reacted to what he said. Alex could no longer tell if she was joking or not, but continued his confessional. "Actually, her mother died and her daughter and I just happened to hit it off."

"Was she very young, your first lover? How old is her daughter?"

He knew positively that this had to be Keiko. Other people on the Ark didn't bring up ages, but it was one of her favorite topics. "The mother was close to my age when we were together," he answered. "Her daughter's about twenty-five, but very mature."

"Oh, I think that's quite perfect," she said. "A man like you, in his forties, makes a perfect match for a young woman. You're in your best years. Men at your age finally start to look like they've reached maturity. Boys, no matter how handsome, still look like boys." She paused for a moment, as if she had to struggle with the next question. "If you don't mind me asking, what does she look like, this Amanda?"

"Why do you ask?"

"Oh," she said, flustered. "Just in case I should see her. I will be able to point her out to you."

"That's very generous of you." He smiled. It was an ingenious trap Keiko was laying for him.

"She's very tall and thin. She has long, blonde hair and blue eyes. Her skin is tanned a golden color. She is really quite exquisite. And she likes to wear red. In fact, she's so in love with the color red that I would be willing to place a wager on the fact that, when we do spot her, she will, in fact, be wearing red."

She ran her hand over the gemstone and white fur stubble of her head. "Blonde hair and blue eyes. You know that's the natural color of my hair and my eyes."

Alex, despite himself, was amazed at how far she was taking her act. He wondered how much her schizophrenia accounted for her daring. Perhaps, he thought, she has so submerged herself in the role that she actually believes everything she is telling me.

She continued, emphasizing her statements with subtle undulations of her body. "I'm rather tall, also, but not thin. I'm a typical German woman, don't you think? Full-figured, I believe you would say. Even so, I'm rather proud of my figure. Men are always complimenting me on it, especially my legs. My mother also had wonderful legs. It must be genetics."

Now that she mentioned it, Alex had to admit to himself that Keiko's body looked far different than he had remembered it. But, he told himself, the costume and time in an exercise machine easily explained the difference. Hell, for all he knew, she had undergone a bone extension treatment. Whatever she had done, the amount of skin her costume revealed made her look more appetizing than she ever had before. He nodded his head solemnly as if he were assessing a beautiful piece of art. "Yes," he agreed, "you do have a great figure."

One thing Alex had noticed that was exceptional about Keiko's disguise was that, on occasion, she spoke imperfect German, stumbling on an idiomatic phrase or searching for the words to express a simple thought. Normally, Keiko spoke impeccable German. Those mistakes weren't like her. Alex attributed this behavior to a special quality of the schizophrenic. Assuming that Alex might be catching on to her, she would make mistakes that would allow her to deny that she was herself. The disease that so often crippled her in real life had equipped her with fantastic resources for dopplegangery. Nonetheless, Alex attempted to trick her into slipping up. "What town are you from?" he asked her.

"From Lauenburg. It's a town about fifty kilometers outside of Hamburg. Near the river Elbe."

That didn't help him at all. Of course she would know that. She had travelled all over Germany.

She smiled at him. "You must be an American. You speak German well but your accent comes through."

"Do you speak English?"

"No, only German. Maybe a little French and Italian. I never liked English. I never liked the way I sounded when I tried to speak it."

"Have you been on the Ark long?"

"As I told you, it's my first trip. I'm leaving for the Moon after the party. I will stay there briefly and then go to Mars."

She informed him that she was thirsty and suggested they get something to drink. As they headed towards the bar, she told him about the trip she had planned. Alex was amazed at Keiko's routine. Was she actually trying to compete with Amanda? Perhaps she was afraid that she would lose him forever to this new competitor.

And yet there was something inexplicably attractive about Keiko in her present guise. More so than any of her other performances. She exuded a sensuality he found difficult to resist. He wondered if she might have recently begun to open up sexually. Why, he wondered, did she wait until now to show him this side of her personality. He had been more than patient with her, he thought. He had tried to wait for her but now it was too late. No matter how attractive she was, he still wanted Amanda and he cursed the fact that she had not yet arrived.

"Your girlfriend, Amanda," she asked, "is she really taller than me?"

"Oh, yes, she looks more like that woman over there," he said, indicating a giraffe of a woman who, not surprisingly, was talking to Vladimir.

A worried look came over his face. "I don't understand, he said, unable to further suppress his frustration. "She's always on time. In fact, most of the time she's early."

"You look very disappointed," she consoled. "You look like a man who is terribly in love."

"I am," he blurted out. "I wanted to make tonight special. I had a surprise planned and this is what I get."

"Oh, you know how those young girls are. They like adventure. They live for the moment. I should know. I remember the way I was at twenty-five."

"That's what her girlfriend told me. That I was being a fool."

Amanda was momentarily shaken by this revelation. So that's what Tanya's been feeding him, she thought. What a bitch.

"But my feelings go beyond my reason," Alex continued. "I find her so intriguing I can't help myself."

"Well, then," she said, smiling, since my girlfriend hasn't shown up and we are both still waiting, I don't see why we shouldn't have a dance."

"Great, Kei—" He caught himself. He had almost said Keiko, but corrected himself in time. ". . . Teresa."

They headed for the dance floor, where a slow ballad was being played. Keiko, he knew, liked these slow, melodic tunes. Not a great dancer, she preferred the slow, controlled movements of dancing as a couple. At other parties, Alex had watched her attempt some of the new, free-style dances popular among young people. She had been terrible. Any dance that demanded spontaneity was beyond her.

Oddly enough, Alex noticed that her movements during the ballad were more fluid, almost natural, than they had ever been. Yes, he had to admit to himself, we're dancing rather well together. As the music grew wilder, Alex wondered if she would want to stop, but she kept going, her body moving in perfect time to the rhythm. Alex marveled at the amount of time she must have practiced to become so adept. She was so good, in fact, that she began to attract attention, other dancers clearing a circle around them so that they could watch her.

At this, Alex had to wonder if he would not be better off rolling with the punches and enjoying her performance. Perhaps he might be pleasantly surprised by the rest of the evening. Maybe Vladimir was right, he told himself. Maybe I was right; he chuckled to himself at that thought. The Ark can be a magic place. People can change almost instantly. Would anyone who knew Keiko recognize her now? Perhaps it was not too late for her to come out of her shell. Yes, he thought, this is a disguise, but it's farther than she's ever gone before.

The tempo of the music increased again and Alex found himself barely able to keep up. The harder he danced, the longer he looked at her, the more he found himself attracted by this aspect of Keiko. He had fantasized that he might someday see her like this: wild, mischievous, erotic. But over the years he had given up on her. Even if it's just for this one night, he thought, I'll try to love her. Amanda, he decided, was not going to show up and he wanted to know how far Keiko was willing to go.

When they finally pulled themselves off the dance floor, Alex was breathing erratically. She had nearly killed him with the amount of energy she put into her dance moves. "We should try this in Zero-G," she told him. "And you're really good. I think we deserve another drink."

As they wandered back over to the bar, Alex abandoned all vestige of trying to get Keiko to reveal herself openly. "God," he told her, "you were terrific."

"Oh, is that so? Does your lady friend Keiko dance that well?"

"There's no one I know that can dance that well."

Arriving at the bar, really just a computerized drink dispenser, she pressed a red button.

Alex laughed. "Are you sure that you want to drink that. You asked me to warn you about the Ark. Well, that's a drink with quite a bit of sexual potency."

She giggled in response. "Oh, really? But I so like the color red. It just thrills me to think that you have red drinks here. I simply must have one. Why don't you join me?"

She passed him the glass she had just filled and quickly hit the dispenser for a second serving. "This is going to be my last party for a long time," she told him suggestively. "It's a long way to Mars and back."

"Well, in that case," he said, shouting to be heard over the crowd, "let's drink to a great time."

The drink worked much faster than Alex had expected. In what seemed like an instant, she was making oddly seductive leers in his direction. Before he knew it, she was in

254 DAVID J. NOWEL

his arms, her lips hard on his. Somewhere in the back of his brain, he knew their attraction to one another was due to the chemicals but he didn't care. He imagined that he was kissing Amanda and the more they kissed, the more he thought that he might actually be kissing her. Even though he knew he was with Keiko, he could feel no difference between her and Amanda. Her skin tasted the same. Her lips were just as soft. When she quavered in his arms, he was transported back to their love tryst in the chamber below the floor of the reception hall. They flowed into one another and Alex, swept away by the passion of the moment, forgot that they were in a crowd of people.

He made a clumsy attempt to pull her mask off, but she pulled away. She said something in German that he couldn't understand, but mistook to be some expression of pleasure due to her body shivering with delight. However, when she finally caught her breath and was able to speak clearly, what she said was: "I have to fix my hair."

Alex laughed, watching as she reached up in an attempt to brush her hair. Realizing that there was nothing to rearrange, she join him in a barrage of loud and intoxicated guffaws.

"Well, you know what I mean," she tittered.

He leaned toward her to kiss her again but she pushed him away.

"Alex, we'll have plenty of time for that later. And I promise I won't disappoint you."

"Well then, what should we do?"

"Why don't you come with me to the maze? Now that I've found you, I don't want to lose you." She smiled at him. "Not worried about meeting your girl friend, are you?"

For the first time, Alex became seriously concerned about where Amanda was, why she hadn't shown up yet. He'd find out soon enough, he thought. So far, despite the kisses he had given Keiko, he hadn't felt the same jolting sensation in his head as he had when he was with Tanya. Although he had expected the shock when he had kissed Keiko, nothing happened. He assumed that this meant that Amanda had taken the locket out and broken their contract.

The thought of Amanda with another man made his blood boil, but he saw no other explanation for her absence and his lack of pain. He almost wished that his transgression had not been with Keiko so that his betrayal of Amanda might carry more weight than a one night reunion with his old lover. He was surprised to find that within the space of only a few achievements, his love for Amanda had turned to bitterness.

When they reached the maze, a huge labyrinth whose design hearkened to Victorian hedgerow mazes, Amanda excused herself for a moment, leaving Alex alone to stew. She walked a few turns into the maze and then called out for Genie. When Genie responded, Amanda described her predicament.

"Genie, I've got to get this locket off. So far I've managed to fool Alex, but if he sees the locket he'll know it's me. I'd rather let him wait a while longer. He told me he had a surprise for me and I'd like to get it before he knows it's me."

Genie responded quickly. Amanda heard a click and reached down to remove the locket. As she placed it in her purse, she considered just how effective that red drink had been. She couldn't wait to get back to Alex.

Back by his side, she kissed him perfunctorily and asked about his present for her. "You mentioned that you had a surprise for Amanda. I'm curious, what did you have planned?"

"Oh, I had a stupid idea," he told her. Too intoxicated and too bewildered by her sudden change of attitude, Alex didn't care what he told her. "I know she thinks I'm possessive and old-fashioned. I wanted to show her that even though I love her I don't have to own her."

"Really? So what were you going to do about it?"

"Well, I was working on this machine for her. It's something I wanted to use to show her that I wasn't as conservative as she thought."

"So do you think I'd like this gift?" she asked.

"I don't know. Maybe." He was more than a little

embarrassed to think that he might actually have to show Hector to Keiko. If anything might break her happy spell in the guise of Teresa, it would be an episode with Hector. Perhaps if he plied her with more drinks, strong red ones, she'd be able to handle him.

"Why don't you show me your machine?" she asked.

Alex imagined seeing Keiko with Hector, copulating in front of a crowd. He had to admit the idea appealed to him. "Let's go," he called out. "I stored it right outside the entrance. But before we get it, why don't we have another one of those little, red drinks?"

She smiled enthusiastically. "Why not?"

After slugging down a drink and watching Amanda do the same, Alex left to retrieve Hector. Amanda, drunk on the aphrodisiac liquor and anticipating the arrival of Alex's surprise, tittered nervously to herself.

After a few moments, Alex brought Hector in. Amanda looked horrified. "Is that it?" she asked.

Alex, taken aback by her reaction, answered meekly in the affirmative.

Amanda paused for a moment as if she were trying to figure out what she actually thought about the phallic monstrosity before her. With dramatic flair, she placed her hands on her hips and screamed in a heavy German accent: "Alex!"

When Alex had first entered the party with Hector, a semi-hushed wave of astonishment and wonder passed through the crowd. But following Amanda's shout, complete silence fell on the room. Alex felt every eye on him, his face rapidly turning bright crimson. Too afraid to turn around and face his newfound audience, Alex kept his eyes resolutely on Amanda, hoping that Keiko, his confidante and sage counselor, might be able to help him. At first, she looked just as panic- stricken as he, but shortly he saw a broad smile form on her face. She indicated that he should look at Hector. When he did so, he saw that Hector's penis, probably at Genie's bidding, was moving rapidly back and forth. Amanda giggled and Alex joined her with a whooping roar. Soon everyone in the chamber was laughing and pointing at the robot's flagellating phallus.

"It's rather funny looking," she said. "What did you have in mind, big boy?"

She placed a hand on Alex's shoulder and writhed sensually, her fanny luridly pointed in Hector's direction. Alex wasn't sure whether her last comment had been directed to him or Hector. For the first time, he wondered whether this woman he was with was actually Keiko. "Big boy" was a phrase so foreign to everything that Keiko was about, he could not believe she had said it. Was she actually willing to join with a machine, right here in front of a party crowd? Looking into her masked face, into her eyes, he felt a sudden surge in his loins. He had never been so attracted to Keiko before. He whispered her name: "Keiko."

Amanda felt a rush of excitement upon hearing Alex say Keiko's name. He still didn't know who she was. She looked around the room, at the throngs of partygoers and Hector, and imagined herself making love to Alex in front of all of them. She didn't care who saw them. No matter who watched, they would still be alone, wrapped in each other's arms.

Alex's thoughts had been running in the same direction. He pulled a simulated mink rug out from a compartment in Hector's side. "I've always wanted to make love to someone on a mink rug," he told her. "My mother used to wrap me up at night in her fur coats. There's no other feeling like it."

Amanda's insides melted at hearing Alex talk about his childhood. He was like a vulnerable little boy, trying to get back to his mother. "You mean you want me to make love with you on that mink rug, with all these people watching, because your mother wrapped you in her fur coats when you were a little boy?"

He nodded.

"Not a bad idea," she said with a laugh in her voice.

She walked toward him and he took her in his arms, pulling her down onto the rug with him. She luxuriated in the beautiful texture of the fur. "It feels so wonderful," she purred, moving her body slowly across the carpet.

Alex watched her putting on her show, lolling on the rug. He felt himself growing hard. He grabbed her arms, pushed them behind her and held her still. Their eyes met, hers flashing sultry messages. She managed to wiggle out of his grip, but he lunged toward her fleeing form and grabbed her ankle. With sheer force, he rolled her over onto her back and spread her legs open.

"Hallelujah!" she cried. "That's what I've been waiting for." She thrust her legs straight into the air. "Alex, please. . . ." she begged, her voice trailing off into a sigh of submission.

Retrieving a can of XSY from another compartment in Hector's torso, Alex sprayed a powerful blast in her face. Now, he thought, we'll see if she comes out of her disguise. Keiko, he figured, couldn't hold up much longer. But rather than seeing Keiko break out of her shell, Alex was stunned to see her smiling maniacally as the aerosol took effect. My God, he thought, I should have done this years ago.

"Oh, Alex," she gasped, "this is too much. You're killing me." Her nostrils flared wildly. "More," she cried.

Alex moved to kiss her but she pulled away playfully. "Come on, get me," she said.

With a quick motion, Alex moved behind her, covering her eyes with his hands. Hector perambulated toward them, stopping just before Amanda. With surprising grace, Hector's penis extended slowly and pushed its way between Amanda's thighs.

"Oh, god!" she screamed. "That's amazing."

Her arms flailed wildly. Alex kept his hands firmly over her eyes. She began to bite on her lip, trying to keep control of her sensibilities. Soon, Alex knew, she would lose all control.

Her words escaped in small phrases, interrupted by gasps for air. "Alex, Alex. You are so hard. Faster. Please . . . faster. Alex. Harder. Alex. Faster . . . don't stop . . . faster! Oh, God! Alex. You are won-der-ful."

Alex, who until now had been content watching Hector perform, leaned down and began suckling on Amanda's breast. At that moment, she realized that Alex was not the one inside of her.

"Alex, you bastard," she shouted at him.

Alex smiled. "I just want to see how good you are. With all of your hot talk, Teresa, I wanted to make sure you weren't just full of hot air."

"Does . . . this . . . look . . . like . . . I'm . . . just . . . talk." Her moans of pleasure grew louder and more frequent. Alex was impressed that she had been able to respond to him at all. He watched as she let the next wave of pleasure wash over her.

"Your cock," she cried. Bring it to me!" She indicated that she wanted him to come closer.

As Alex straddled her chest, he could feel Hector increasing his pace. She took his cock in her mouth and began sucking with abandon.

For a moment, Alex found it hard to enjoy her attention to him. He was frankly amazed at Keiko's resiliency. Hector had been having at her for quite some time now, keeping up a fervor of penetration that no mortal man could match. Still, Keiko was not satisfied. She wanted more. Finally, he thought, he had discovered a sexual fantasy that aroused her normally prurient sexual appetite.

Alex had learned long ago that he would never be able to fully comprehend the depths of a woman's lust. The sweetest, most conservative woman might very well be fantasizing about a leather den or an orgy. Lorraine, the mother of his children, had taught him this years ago. After seventeen years of marriage, she had finally told him that her ultimate fantasy was to be attended to by three men at once. Two of them would occupy themselves with sucking on her tits and a third, preferably with very long dick, would be given the privilege of fucking her.

Alex looked behind him. Hector was still pounding away. Amanda was writhing expertly, shifting her body subtly to receive Hector's member at the most pleasurable angle. One thing was clear to Alex: Keiko, after all the years he had known her, was far different than he had imagined.

Suddenly, Hector went into overdrive. His thrusting

became manic and Amanda responded in kind. Alex watched as every blood vessel, every capillary near the surface of her body, began to pop out from her skin in purple relief. Her skin took on the quality of a transparent silk sheet filigreed with a multitude of tiny, blue spider webs. She looked like she was about to explode. How much more could she take? He had never seen a woman pushed so far in the name of ecstasy.

Her body began to quake violently. Her orgasm had arrived. Alex tightened his legs, trying not to be thrown off of her. His penis still in her mouth, he was afraid for a moment that she might bite him in the throes of her climax.

Hector began to slow down, allowing Amanda to enjoy the waves of energy coursing over her body. Alex looked back to watch him and noticed, for the first time a small, unfamiliar tattoo in Keiko's pubic area, almost disappearing into the crevice of her thighs. He made out tiny letters encircling a jewelled heart, rendered in remarkably realistic three-dimensional perspective. It was strange that she should have this, he thought. In the past Keiko had claimed she was afraid of any kind of permanent skin decoration.

Sensing that Amanda's undulations were growing less frequent, he relaxed his hold on her. Hector, he noticed, had withdrawn completely. He turned himself around to examine the tattoo more closely. The writing was small, almost microscopic, but despite its diminutive size, the script was fantastically clear. He strained his eyes to read what it said: "Amanda Loves Alex."

"Amanda?" he whispered. He turned to look at her, but she had other plans. Before he could say anything else, she sprayed him with the XSY. Instantly, he felt his face flush with blood, his cock stiffen. He reeled, unable to see the room around him. He was aware only of Amanda's body still beneath him. It was glorious.

"Alex," he heard Amanda say. She was finally speaking English again. "Alex!" She had grabbed his chin with her hand and spoke clearly so that he could understand her. "This isn't time for words, just action. If you want to compete with Hector, you'll have to start on even ground. You're gonna have to be hard as a rock."

She laughed as she sprayed her own face with more of the aerosol. "Come on," she said teasingly, "show me your stuff."

She gasped as Alex entered her, hard as he had ever been. In the short moments between his mighty strokes, she declared her love for him, begging him to love her forever.

As their story spread through the crowd, murmurs and giggles began to be heard. Having fooled Alex for so long, Amanda had earned the respect of even the most jaded of the Ark's denizens. Her initial duping and subsequent seduction of Alex had been a shining example of the powers of monogamy. She was undeniable proof that a single person could capture her lover's imagination, possess him by letting him go.

The party was finally over. Amanda and Alex had finished their public lovemaking session when Amanda had, rather irreverently, asked Alex if she was "going to get time out to piss." As she skipped off to the restroom, Alex marveled at the way she could make him forget his troubles. For the past thousand achievements he had been able to think of nothing but her.

He looked around the room and saw Vladimir standing at an exit with three beautiful women. The Russian smiled broadly, held his glass up high and drained its contents with a hearty cheer: "*Nasdrova!*"

Alex nodded his head in acknowledgement. Vladimir turned and left with the women. Left alone, Alex's thoughts returned to the troubles that he and Vladimir had discussed. While he had been pursuing Amanda, his attention had wandered. But still, the events unfolding on Earth and in the space stations in Earth's orbit had not, he was sure, changed for the better. He did not look forward to the next thousand achievements. Unless he was at his best, many people would be needlessly harmed.

Amanda returned, enveloping Alex in her arms.

"Now I know why people keep coming back to the Ark," she said. "The recreation is great. Where do I sign up for permanent duty?"

Alex laughed anxiously. Now that his mind had returned to his geo-political pursuits, he found it hard to break his serious mood.

Amanda noticed that a change had come over him. "So, this is the real Alex? The serious Alex? Time to go back to work, eh, Alex?"

"I guess so," he said, only half listening.

"I guess the party's over. Can we play again real soon?"

She tugged on his sleeve, forcing him to look at her. She pouted like a child to show her dismay at his sudden change in personality.

Alex pulled her to him, embracing her passionately, knowing that he loved her as much as he loved his own life.

"I love you," he told her. "I love you."

"Oh, Alex," she said softly, kissing his face, "I love you, too."

She took his hands in hers and then straightened her body into an almost military rigidity. In a firm voice she asked him if he was ready to get back to work.

"Yes," he replied.

"Then let's get this thing you're so worried about over with."

They walked briskly out of the room, Alex already calling out commands to the Ark's computers. After a few quick checks informed him of the status of the situation, he debriefed Amanda on what was going to happen. He was relying on her keen mind to help him avert an international disaster.

BOOK TWO

IT'S TIME

CHAPTER 25

RICK HAS HIS SAY

Even since Rick had been placed in charge of Ark security, his friends and associates had watched him grow progressively more paranoid. This latest crisis seemed to have pushed him beyond his limit, a fact exacerbated by his realization that his handling of the situation was being analyzed and judged by the citizens who had appointed him to the post. The inevitable signs of stress were beginning to show.

In the Ark's security control room, Rick moved quickly from one console to another, intently staring at the images on the screens. He muttered to himself in agitation as he hovered over a monitor. When he looked up, he was surprised to see Phil in the room. He had been so engrossed in what he was doing that he hadn't even heard him enter. Despite the fact that his heart was pounding madly due to the unexpected fright, Rick feigned indifference to his colleague's stealthy arrival. He continued to stare absently at the screen before him, pretending to be absorbed in the data it presented.

Finally, he collected himself enough to address Phil. "I've got Alex to thank for this one," he announced without bothering to raise his eyes from the computer screen. "He's gotten me into another impossible situation."

"It's that bad?"

Rick looked up at Phil sharply, his eyes flashing angrily from his corpulent face. He launched into a diatribe at Alex's expense: "I have no idea what I'm supposed to do to keep all of this from happening. He told me to get the money and he didn't care how and now I'm left holding the bag. I did what I was told and now I'm going to have to take the blame for it.

And where's Alex? He's probably out at some party fucking that nymphomaniac Amanda. There's probably only four or five guys on the Ark she hasn't fucked yet. You can't explain some people's taste. He's got Amanda, the nympho, Keiko, the schizo, and Wendy, the kike."

"So what?" said Phil.

"It's unbelievable. What does he think he's doing. One of them fucks everyone in sight and the other is the weirdest, most twisted little woman I've ever seen. Right now, Wendy's the worst. She got us into this whole mess. She might as well be an Israeli, the way she carries on about being a yid. Israel's always in the right to her, no matter who they've had killed. She's got an Israeli passport and she speaks and writes Hebrew. How's that for someone who calls herself an American? I told Alex he should never trust the Israelis, but he went ahead anyway because of Wendy whispering in his ear. Now they've got our cobalt bomb and I'll bet you anything they're headed to New York with it!"

Phil said nothing in answer to this last series of barbs. When Rick needed to blow off steam, there was no reasoning with him. He simply nodded and said nothing.

"What the fuck is a seventy-five year old man doing fucking some twenty-five year old, anyway?" asked Rick rhetorically. "What the fuck does he think he's doing with her? The guy doesn't even know he's already an old man. When he finally kicks the bucket, someone's going to have to tap him on the shoulder and tell him he's dead!"

Phil was unable to contain himself any longer. "He's always liked younger people," he told Rick. "You know that."

"And now he's in his seventies and he's still going for a twenty year-old?" Rick retorted. "He's either got mush for brains or he's stowing his brains in his cock. Does Alex really think that she loves him? She loves every cock that she can get a hold of. I fucked her and she took on three more young studs after me. And then there's Keiko. His precious, lovable Keiko. You could never know the headaches she gives me. She's always handing me some bullshit line about running this place." He began to imitate Keiko's accent. "'Everything will take care of itself. You don't have to spy on people. Everything is wonderful.' She's nutty as a loon. Alex calls her spiritual. Bullshit! She's nuts. Absolutely nuts. She's a fucking psychotic!"

"I don't know, Rick," said Phil, trying to remain calm in the face of Rick's dissembling fury. "I find her a very calming presence. There's something undeniably spiritual about her."

"Well, if she's so fucking spiritual, why the hell does she have to come up here? She never does anything, never goes to any functions. She just stays in her cubicle. The computer always manages to give her the simplest assignments. When it comes to taking any kind of real responsibility, she turns out to be a slacker."

Rick lowered his voice, as if he were imparting a great secret to Phil. "Can you believe she actually knows about our Cobalt Bomb being in the hands of terrorists? How does she know that? There are only three people who have access to that information: you, me, and Alex. Try explaining that."

Phil was visibly upset by this revelation. His voice squeezed out in high tinniness, "Do you think Alex told her?"

"The crazy thing is I don't think he did. Shit. He was the one who warned me not to tell her anything. 'Don't let Keiko find out about this, Rick,' he told me. 'She's been worried about something like this all her life. It would be very bad for her sickness.'"

"How do you think she found out?"

"Who the fuck knows! She's so weird, I wouldn't be surprised if she was reading our minds."

"Jesus."

Rick grinned haughtily. "And here's something else for you. Guess who's supposed to be in New York on the day the bomb's supposed to go off."

"Who?"

"Wendy. It serves that bitch right."

"Did you tell Alex that?"

"I didn't tell him anything, but he should know. She's been scheduled for months to make some kind of charity appeal on Christmas day. She's even taking Alex's daughter along for the speech."

"Are you planning to warn them? We've got to keep them out of there."

Rick reached across the console and grabbed Phil's shirt. "We're not going to tell anyone until we're sure, do you understand? Not even Alex. For all we know, this is a false alarm and even if it isn't, we've still got a good chance of aborting everything. If Wendy finds out about it, she may tip our hand to the Israelis. Even I don't know how deeply she's in cahoots with those yids."

"You're crazy, Rick. You know how Alex feels about his daughters. What if it were your daughter?"

For a moment, Rick almost returned to normal. "I know. You don't have to tell me. Things are tough enough already without this added complication."

Almost as suddenly as he had softened his position, he began to rage again. "What I don't get is why Alex is out there enjoying himself while I'm left behind to deal with all this bullshit. That's what I hate most about this place. It's like a fucking fairy land and Alex has always got his head stuck in some kind of sugar-coated cloud. He thinks he can just fuck his brains out and everything's going to take care of itself."

"Actually," Phil explained, "Alex sent me to tell you he's planning to come see you within a few achievements."

Rick ignored this detail and continued with his run down of the Ark. "You know what bugs me most of all? I wish I could at least get a decent meal. The food here is for shit."

Phil, after a quick scan of Rick's heavyset figure, cast a questioning look in his direction.

"Yeah, yeah. I know what you are looking at. I'm a fat slob, right? Well, I do get fed. Just like everybody says, I've got some connections. If I'm going to hold down this pissy job, I might as well take advantage of it." As the conversation shifted into a discussion of food, Rick began to relax. It was a subject he was comfortable with. "I've got some friends on the Moon who owe me favors," he bragged. "Every time we get freighted a high security shipment, they load it up with some real food for me. I still don't understand why, with all the other techno-miracles we have up here on the Ark, we can't have some decent food. Everyone's eating that gooey, stuffy, slick shit that passes for food. I don't get it.

"Phil, do you realize how many security achievement periods I spend trying to prevent food smuggling? I have to make sure that even the smallest tidbit doesn't get on board. Every day, we've got ten thousand people coming on board. Every apple, orange, or stick of beef jerky has to be sniffed out. And in Alex's mind, it's worse than drug smuggling back on Earth. In some ways he's right, too. People are willing to go through just about anything to get the stuff on board. Some of it's too disgusting to even mention. But none of it gets through. I see to that. I spend my time trying to stop the flow of oranges instead of trying to deal with international catastrophes."

At this point, Rick unconsciously wiped away a strand of saliva from the corner of his mouth. His eyes had turned glassy. "What really pisses me off is when I have to look at all that food, that perfectly good food, going into the shredder. And then . . . ." He paused, unable to speak. He gulped air into his heaving, barrel-like chest. ". . . and then they turn it into that gook."

Phil thought he noticed tears in Rick's eyes. Rick was pathetic, he told himself. But he had to admit that even he, at times, had moments when he remembered the savory odor and taste of a thick, barbecued steak. In his imagination, he washed the steak down with an ice cold, foamy beer. They stared at one another, lost in their thoughts, neither one wanting to part with their memories of food on Earth.

Phil was the first one to break the silence. "I guess Alex is right. Food is like a drug. Highly addictive." Judging from the last few minutes he had spent daydreaming of food, he wondered if Alex might actually be right.

"Well, I for one," he told Rick, "feel one hundred percent better since I've been on the Ark. Hell, I was at least forty pounds overweight back on Earth. I kept telling myself I only had to lose ten pounds, but it was much worse than that. I started to get high blood pressure. My heart seemed to be skipping beats and my joints and feet hurt all the time. I had to face the fact that I was slowly dying. I feel younger now, more energetic. My head is clear. It feels like I've been off of a drug."

Rick snapped back, "Okay, it's fine if you want to put me on a diet. Go right ahead. But at least give me real food. And if you can't do that, at least make it look and taste like real food. With everything else they can do on this ship, I know they can make the food taste halfway decent."

"On that end, I know Alex is right," Phil said. "Why does food have to taste so good? It's a power ploy. Good tasting food just made us more addicted to it. It was a trick women learned from their mothers to control men. And fast food chains used good taste to make it so that we couldn't resist coming back to buy more of their product. No one ever cared about nutrition as long as it tasted good. Look at all those fried foods they fed us on Earth. It was the worst food we could eat, but it was easy to fix and people kept coming back for more. The government wouldn't stop it because it was big business.

"And it's still that way. Think about all the money that's being spent on T.V., newspapers, throw away papers, and billboards. None of it has anything to do with feeding us. Besides, when we really get out into space, where is all that food going to come from? There's not that much room on a spaceship to grow crops, raise cattle or store food. And despite what you think, it'll be years before we'll have the capability to synthesize all that crap you like to eat. Be real, Rick, food synthesis is like teleportation: just a *Star Trek* fantasy."

Rick answered sarcastically, "By God, you're right. I'm just a machine. Why should I eat anything that tastes good?"

Phil threw up his hands in exasperation. "Sure. It tastes good, and it's also one hundred times more addictive than any drug we can find. You're forgetting the most important thing about our food here. Everything is carefully analyzed for any chemical toxins or impurities. And in addition to that, every single person's nutritional supply is tailored to their individual metabolism. You could never control regular food that carefully. Every person I talk to feels better than they ever did on Earth. It's not just psychology helping people to get over their allergies and diseases. Some people even swear they've overcome mental problems because of their change in diet.

"You're always talking about security problems, Rick. Can you imagine the security problems we'd have if people ate and drugged themselves the way they do on Earth? Thank God the computers balance us and make sure our metabolism is right on. You know more than anyone else what one unbalanced person could do to the Ark. It's not like this thing is built on solid rock. Everyone knows that this thing is a tinker toy held together with glue."

Rick grew livid with anger at hearing Phil refer to the Ark as a tinker toy. His thousands of achievements spent on the Ark had conditioned him to protect the integrity of the Ark. That conditional reflex overran any other thought. A slight tremor began to perceptibly palpitate his right hand. Phil knew he was getting to his target.

"Let's forget about the individual's metabolism," he continued. "How about the arsenic, phenol, lead, hippuric acid and other thousands of chemicals in the natural foods you're so keen on. We were poisoning ourselves on Earth and never knew it. As for the psychology part, Alex is absolutely right: Freud missed the boat. He should have been writing about food, not sex."

Rick had turned completely pale. "Maybe it's time I put in for the Moon," he stammered. "At least those people have some real food."

"Come on, Rick, don't kid yourself. Even on the Moon, they're starting to control the composition of their foods. They know the link between neurotoxicity, longevity and health is directly related to diet."

"You know, Phil," said Rick maniacally. "I think your head has grown soft and mushy just like our dear Professor Alex's. It's all Alex's fucking bullshit. The man is weird, that's all there is to it. He's making us do all these weird things. When's Christmas? Do you know what day it is today? We don't even know what time it is or how old we are. We should help this guy? He's trying to turn us into machines. By God, Phil, I like being a man! So I'm a little fat. So what!"

Phil realized that Rick's hysterical state was the first sign that he was suffering from Arkclaustrophobia. He'd settle down soon enough. After a few silent moments passed between them, Phil saw Rick regain control of his sensibilities. He decided to drop the subject of food.

After a while, Rick spoke again. "I never thought it was going to turn out this way. I remember when I first met Alex. We were trying to sell these Inter-Active Video systems. He kept showing off for our clients, using all these big words. Half the time I couldn't even understand what he was talking about. He was trying to pass himself off as an intellectual. I thought he was a bit of an ass and I still do. If he'd just stop trying to act so damn superior, it'd make my life so much easier."

Phil started to laugh. "I know what you mean. He drove me off the deep end, too. Alex means well, but he gets so caught up in his own ideas he can't wait for everyone else to catch up."

"Alex offered me a job up here with lots of money. It looked like a great opportunity when I was down there. A real cushy job, something I could get into on the ground floor. Lots of extra benefits. I guess I should have known better. Nothing is that easy."

Phil suppressed a smile at Rick's description of his expectations for the Ark. Phil had come aboard under similar circumstances. He knew what a persuasive salesman Alex could be. Phil had always been amazed at Alex's ability to lock on and home in on a person's hot button. He could seduce anyone by conjuring up all the right descriptive images. Phil remembered all too well the many ventures Alex had put him through. When they hadn't worked out, for some strange reason he had found himself still grateful to Alex for the opportunity to be involved.

When it came to the Ark, Phil thought that, for once,

everything had worked out. It wasn't exactly what Alex had promised him, but it was close enough. In spite of his occasional pangs of hunger for a cheeseburger, he liked it on the Ark. However, he knew exactly why Rick had come to the Ark. No matter what promises Alex had made him, Rick, Phil was sure, was on board for his own personal gain.

Rick was perhaps the most vain person on the Ark and he did little to disguise the fact. Yet in spite of his self-possession, he was well-liked by most people. Even Phil had to admit that, when he wanted to be friendly, Rick had a great personality. And whenever he was near a young, beautiful woman, Rick turned on charm like an electric current. When he wanted you to like him, he was irresistible. Turned on, Rick was the most sensitive, humorous and charming man one could ever meet. What was most impressive, however, was that even after his friends realized he was a manipulative control freak, they still liked him. Women he had burned just laughed at his antics, calling him an adorable little boy throwing a tantrum.

Phil could easily imagine Alex tempting Rick to join the Ark's crew. "But, Rick," he would say, "You just can't believe the women on the Ark. They're beautiful. You can't lose."

Rick continued his story: "I thought I was going to make millions. Alex didn't tell me that it was in stock and I'd have to wait ten years to sell it."

Rick paused for a moment before starting to retell one of his most infamous chestnuts. "You know I even saved Alex's life out there. Do you know that?"

"Of course I know. I don't think there's anyone on board you haven't told. You told me yourself. You did a double twist and brought him back."

"See," groaned Rick, "that's how everyone thinks about it. No one gives a shit that I almost missed him and almost lost my life doing it. No one cares that I saved his life. He and I would be out there floating for eternity if I hadn't caught him."

"You know, you've got it all wrong about Alex. He tells every beginning spacewalker that story. He makes you out to be a hero."

"Then why does he treat me like shit? Why does he make me feel like he doesn't trust me? He doesn't know it, but I'm probably his best friend and he always looks at me as if I'm some kind of Judas. Like he's just waiting for me to betray him."

"It's true. Alex can be a very mistrustful person. He's studied a lot of history. He knows what power does to people. He's always been a bit paranoid and in some ways, knowing only a few of the things Alex knows, I think he deserves to be paranoid."

"Well, he should be paranoid," Rick declared. "If it wasn't for my always bailing him out of trouble he'd have a lot more people after his ass. It'd be easy for someone to make his death look like an accident. There's a lot of people who'd like to see his big mouth shut for good."

"I think he's actually tried to step out of the limelight lately. He wants people to feel free to do what they want. He doesn't want them to feel pressured by his image. You know, founder of the Ark and all that. That's not his style. As far as I can tell, he's delegated almost all authority to different committees or to the Senate."

"Sure he has. But he knows all he has to do is write just one little article and he'll get it all back again. He loves playing cat and mouse with us. One day he gives up his power and the next he takes it all back. You can't bullshit a bullshitter. I know the games Alex likes to play."

"Maybe it seems like he's playing games, but I really think it's just that he likes to play the ham. He likes being a salesman, plays things up a bit just to show people he's still alive and kicking. Just because he writes an article, you can't say he's involved in the everyday politics of the Ark. He stays away from the committees and he rarely asks for anything unless he feels it's really important. The only little things he ever gets are donations for Wendy when she's out campaigning."

"She's another one of Alex's leeches."

"I don't know. I think she has a great sense of humor.

She's intelligent, very well read, an incredible organizer. She's done great things for the Ark in terms of P.R. on Earth. Did you know that when they were first married, she used to help him write his books? She was an editor for *Newsweek* when she lived in New York City. She was one of the main reasons he was able to get his books published. She's a first-class pusher."

"That was then," argued Rick. "How about now?"

"I don't know what's going on between them now. They never divorced, but you can see they're not living together."

"Well that's one thing the old boy was smart to have done a long time ago. I couldn't stand being with that Hebe."

A smirk made its crooked way across Phil's face. "I noticed you've talked about almost all of Alex's friends, but you haven't mentioned Tanya. Why is that, Rick?"

Rick's face turned red, but he quickly composed himself. He spoke seriously. "With all the women he goes for, even though she's black as a spade, she's probably the best thing he's ever had. She's got her feet planted firmly in the real world. She's not a freak like the others."

Phil agreed with him. "I notice that Alex seems more relaxed when he's with her. It sort of reminds me of the old Alex, the one I used to know when we chummed around together. Back then he was a lot more fun. Occasionally, he'd get all wound up about something, but he didn't take his philosophy so seriously. It was more like buddies just talking instead of some new doctrine. He didn't think he was trying to save the world then."

"I don't remember him being that way. He always acted as if he had some kind of rod shoved up his rear end. He was always anguished about something."

Phil changed the subject somewhat arbitrarily. "You probably already know this: Tanya and Amanda are lovers."

Rick responded in a quick, vinegary tone. "Of course they are. Everybody knows that. You don't think I'd be head of security if I didn't at least have a handle on what those two are up to."

"Well, I give Alex credit for carrying on as if everything

is under control. I don't think anyone on board has any idea of what's coming. Do you think he's told Amanda or Tanya anything."

"I don't think Amanda knows anything. She's too busy fucking all those young space jockeys. But I know that Tanya senses something. I ran into her at one of the parties and she gave me the strangest look, as if she knew exactly what was going on. But she plays everything so cool. I can't say I knew what it meant. Unfortunately, I think she's fallen in love with the old man. She has that look in her eyes. How does he do that with women? He's bald all over and a million and a half years old, but they still come flocking to him like he was thirty."

Phil was surprised to hear Rick actually giving Alex a compliment and even more surprised to hear him continue.

"Well, there's still a lot to be said for genetic manipulation," Rick told him. "He's looking better today than when I first met him. I have to give him credit. His body's in tip-top shape. I saw him dancing the other day and even Tanya had a tough time keeping up with him. And that girl's a real athlete."

"That's the Alex I knew. He loved to dance."

"You and him have been friends for some time?"

"I met him when I was still a student, going to school at San Diego State in California. We both wanted to be successful businessmen and, since the day we met, we've been close friends. Sometimes I think we've gotten to the point where we have some kind of ESP thing together. I'll be thinking of him and he'll call me up. It's the strangest thing. And lately, he seems to be more and more able to sense what's on my mind."

"Well, you do a great job of defending him. Look at me. I started out insulting him and now I'm talking about how good he looks."

"Believe me, Rick, you're not the first person I've heard who was sick of him. He's taken heat from everybody he knows, including his family. All of them. His parents, wife and children. At one time or another, they've all decided they hated his guts. But no matter how way out his ideas seemed at the time, he's always been right. He seemed so weird to us because he acted on his beliefs. It was easy for people to make up the most outrageous rumors about him. But after a while, I guess people got used to seeing him doing the most outlandish things. Now everything we thought was so bizarre is up here on the Ark."

"Yeah," admitted Rick, "the man has taken a lot of shit in his day."

"Anyway," said Phil, trying to return to the matter at hand, "do you think we're going to be able to handle this situation?"

"If you ask me, Phil, this situation is going to handle us, not the other way around. I don't think there's too much we can do about it. I just hope no one figures out how we got involved in the whole mess. This should teach us a lesson about getting involved in Earth politics. There's never a clean way out.

"I should have known better," Rick told him. "I should have suspected something sooner. A Cobalt Bomb is too fucking powerful to be messed around with. I think Alex was blinded by the confidential information he got from Wendy. He thought he had everything under control, but there was a huge blind spot. We never should have gotten involved with the Israelis. I should have known better. I should have warned him."

"Don't blame yourself. The Israelis were always reliable before. No one could have known that this was going to be the one time they didn't have everything under control. It could have been worse. They could have gotten an H-bomb. I mean to us a Cobalt Bomb is like a Chinese firecracker. It's really such a puny device compared to the energy we have at our disposal. We had no reason to suspect anything out of the ordinary."

"I know, Phil. Things are moving so fast up here, it's easy to forget just how backwards the Earth still is. It's getting so multinational here that every time I turn around I see another Indian, African or Chinese. We've got every kind of person you can think of and everyone seems pretty happy together. I can't think like an Earth person anymore. It's hard to figure out who's spying for who and for what reasons. Who's on which side? It's ridiculous, really."

The two men sat in silence for a few moments, considering the situation as it revealed itself further on the security monitors.

"Phil," said Rick softly, "do you believe in Karma?"

"I don't know. Somehow I want to believe we'll live through this and learn something important from whatever happens. But sometimes I think I'm just getting too old for all of this. Nothing ever gets better. We've been up here in space, making so much progress, really trying to form a lasting peace, and now there's a Cobalt Bomb headed for New York City and scheduled to be detonated on Christmas Day. Sometimes I think all those people down there are just a bunch of possessive, paranoid assholes. They get what they deserve. But I thank God we're up here. At least we can keep it under some kind of control. We can try to keep them from killing each other off."

Then Phil stopped, as if he were saying a quick prayer. "Well, I'm ready. If it has to happen, let it happen."

CHAPTER 26

PHILIP TRIES TO HELP

Phil left Rick and the security room frantically searching for a way to save Alex's daughter, Dominique. It was horrible, he thought, to think of her—an innocent bystander and daughter of a close friend—being killed because nobody had taken the opportunity to warn her. Perhaps, he thought, he might be able to place a personal call to her. Somehow he would be able to extricate her from the situation without tipping Wendy off.

And what if he did tip Wendy off? What if she found out? Phil doubted that it would really be such a terrible occurrence. He had known Wendy for twenty years or more and all of his instincts told him there was no way she could be a spy. Still, no matter what he did, he would have to be careful about stepping on Rick's toes. If Rick found out he had done something, or was even planning to do something, without consulting with the Security Commission, there would be grave repercussions.

But, as a friend of Alex's, he felt he had to press ahead. With all of the other stresses in Alex's life, he could not imagine what might happen to his friend if he were to lose his daughter. The situation would have to be handled carefully. Too many lives were at stake and if Phil made an error, the rescue of Dominique's life might come at the cost of thousands of other innocent lives.

A thought struck him. Dominique trusted her mother, Lorraine, implicitly. If he were to call Lorraine and explain the situation, he was sure he could trust her to keep Dominique from going to New York. She could tell her daughter she was ill, about to go into the hospital for surgery.

Surely that would bring Dominique back to California where she would be out of harm's way. Wendy would suspect nothing.

The problem came in making the first call to Lorraine. Any communications made from the Ark were likely to be screened by Rick's security men, especially as the crisis unfolded. It was too risky making the move on his own, hoping he was not found out. He would have to go to Rick and try to convince him that the plan was both practicable and worthwhile.

Phil made an abrupt U-turn and headed back toward Rick's chamber. As he passed through the doors, Rick looked up in surprise.

"I thought you left. Can't stay away from all the action?" Rick saw the serious look on Phil's face, but mistook his intentions. "I know it's bad, Phil, but believe me, it's not that bad. We'll be okay. There's no way anything can happen to the Ark or any of its colonies."

"Actually, that's not really my concern," said Phil with some hesitation

Rick seemed to sense what was coming next. His tone grew peevish. "Well, then, what is your concern?"

"Alex and Dominique."

"I told you I'd take care of it," said Rick, not bothering to disguise his annoyance with the resurgence of this issue.

"I know what you said. And I understand you're doing what you can about the situation. But I have an idea I thought you might be interested in."

Phil felt certain that Rick was going to yell, "Get out of my sight!" before he could even hear the suggestion. To his relief, Rick momentarily dropped his aggressive posture. "All right. Let me hear it," he said.

Phil explained his plan, but Rick shook his head vigorously, indicating his lack of enthusiasm. "There's no way we can tell Lorraine anything. I don't care how well you know her or how good a security risk she is. Just as you didn't want to call her yourself, I assume because you didn't want me intercepting the call, anybody else might overhear you talking to her. There's no way I'm going to let you communicate anything about this issue to anyone on Earth."

Phil thought quickly, trying to come up with an alternative plan. "What if I didn't tell her anything about what was happening. I could tell her Alex is coming home for Christmas and he wants to stop in California to surprise Dominique."

"Look," said Rick. "I've got to be honest. Saving her isn't the highest item on my agenda. But if there's something we can do to keep Alex from getting hurt, we might as well try it. If you want to lie about Alex's itinerary to get her back to California, that's fine. But I don't want a word, not even a hint, about anything else going to Lorraine, Dominique or Wendy. If anything goes wrong—maybe she decides dear old dad isn't worth cancelling her trip for—you've got to let her go to New York. No second guessing. If anything weird starts happening, Wendy will be on to us."

"I understand," said Phil.

"And there's something else you might be interested in, since you like playing Alex's babysitter." Rick leaned back in his chair, folding his hands together.

"What's that?"

"Our good friend Keiko appears to be deep in the throes of a depression."

"Is that unusual?"

"The computers are telling me she might not snap out of it. If Alex finds out, he'll be useless. Especially if anything happens to Dominique."

"So why are you telling me?"

"I'm telling you so you can be sure not to fuck up on this. Alex doesn't know about any of this right now, but if he loses his daughter and has to deal with Keiko, we're not going to have much of a leader. And if something goes wrong with our little bomb scare, we're going to need him to hold things together. Just as you left, the computers nailed our man in New York. He's probably the one in charge. As long as the New York cops don't fuck up, they'll be able to walk right into his apartment and slap the cuffs on him. The only problem is, it's Christmas and these cops get notoriously sloppy around the holidays. They're not going to know why they're arresting this guy and so they're going to think it's just routine. They're not gonna care if he gets away.

"And if that happens, we're screwed. There are a lot of people down there trying to trip us up, trying to discredit the Ark's program, and this will be just what they need. Hell, there's probably more people than we think on board right now who'd be willing to criticize us if they were given the chance. So, politically, we cannot make any mistakes. You got that?"

"I understand." Phil got up and walked out of the room, eager to get on with his plan. It felt good to be doing something to help.

Before he could clear the doorway, however, he heard Rick calling out after him, "DO NOT FUCK UP!"

"I won't," he said to himself. "I won't."

Alex sat before Amanda, trying to convince her that she should help him deal with Keiko. Alex was afraid that news of the terrorist plot might shatter Keiko's fragile emotional state. Amanda's jealousy of Alex's deep compassion for Keiko, however, kept her from agreeing with him.

"You don't understand," she told him. "I don't want to have anything to do with her. I refuse to actively share you with that woman. If you need her to be your spiritual guide, that's fine, but leave me out of it."

"Look, Amanda. I'm just asking for a favor. Who else can I turn to? I need a woman's sensibility to help me out here. I can't bear to see her suffer more than she has to."

"What is it to me if she suffers? Everyone says she's crazy anyhow. You two are the ones who are close. There's something between you I'll certainly never understand. Why do you have to ask me?"

"I'm asking you because I love you."

"And you still love her."

"Of course I do. She supported me when no one else believed in anything I was doing. She has always been loyal to me, even after I met you. I swear to you, once you meet her, you'll see how wrong everyone else is about her. If you'll just trust me, you'll see what I mean. She really is the most incredibly empathetic person I've ever met."

"She's not sensitive. She's crazy."

"Amanda," he said, leaning forward so that his face was close to hers, "you have to meet her first."

"Well, she is, isn't she?"

"I tell you, I've read every book I can find on the subject

of schizophrenia, insanity, whatever. All I've discovered is that people who get stuck with those labels are the most sensitive people I've ever met. They just don't have anything standing between them and the realities of life. Every person on this ship and every person down on Earth who is supposedly sane has to lie to themselves every day in order to make it through life. But Keiko can't lie to herself. She can't lie about anything. If that's insanity, fine, she's insane. But I just see a woman who feels so strongly, who loves so much, that it hurts her to live in this world. She's given so much to me that I can't let anything hurt her unnecessarily."

Amanda, understanding how much Keiko meant to Alex, decided that she couldn't let her petty feelings stand in the way. She realized she was acting like a schoolgirl who didn't want to share her best friend with anyone else. It really was ridiculous. "All right," she told him. "I'll go with you."

As they entered Keiko's chamber, Amanda's heart began to race in anticipation of meeting the woman she had heard so much about. Alex's face looked grim, reflecting the worry he felt about Keiko's condition. When she saw Keiko approaching them, Amanda was surprised at how small the woman was, how delicate. Although Amanda saw nothing but a diminutive woman dressed in a simple, robe-like dress, she began to feel herself surrounded by an aura of warmth that enveloped her like a warm blanket. She suddenly felt secure, understood that all of her earlier reservations about meeting Keiko were unfounded. Nothing, she knew, could trouble her while she basked in the presence of this woman.

As Keiko offered a greeting, Amanda was stunned by her beauty. A halo of pulsating light seemed to radiate from her. Her voice rolled out in melodic waves of sound. "I was expecting to see you, Amanda." Amanda heard a sweetness in her voice that was irresistible.

Alex saw the transformation that had come over Amanda. Although he had seen the same thing happen to others upon meeting Keiko, he was no less impressed by her powers. "You'll never believe how hard I had to work to get her to come meet you," he told Keiko. "She thought you were demented."

Amanda's face turned red at Alex's revelation. Keiko, however, just smiled. "Everyone thinks I have a screw loose. Or that perhaps I am spineless, weak."

At that moment, Amanda fell hopelessly in love with Keiko. Keiko, Amanda decided, was the most beautiful woman she had ever seen. There was an ageless quality about her, as if she had existed forever.

"I'm glad that you have come," Keiko told Amanda. I've heard so much about you and your mother and Alex. I feel like we're friends who have been apart too long."

Amanda, on a sudden impulse, ran into Keiko's arms, hugging her tightly. "I'm sorry," she sobbed. "I'm sorry I said what I did. I never knew you could be like this."

Keiko held her close. "It's all right," she cooed, stroking Amanda's head. "I understand."

With her free hand, Keiko beckoned Alex over to join them and as she held the two of them in her arms, Alex ridiculed himself for ever thinking of Keiko as if she were fragile as porcelain. She was the strong one, he realized. He was the victim of his own body, of his world, intoxicated by its baseness, its sick humanity. She, however, had learned long ago to free herself from the world. She still ate, walked, breathed and slept on the same plane of existence as he, but her soul was somewhere else.

Their embrace seemed to last for hours. As the power of Keiko's spirit flowed through her into them, both Amanda and Alex felt as if they were undergoing an almost sexual experience. A series of vibrations passed through them, causing their skin to tingle and warm, red colors appeared before their eyes. Alex was reminded of the way Keiko used to touch him, comfort him. She had enabled him to feel as if he were one with the universe, comfortable with his tiny role in the evolution of the cosmos.

Finally, Keiko withdrew her arms and announced that she was going to prepare some tea. She led them further into the chamber and indicated that they should sit down. They sat facing one another. Amanda had tears in her eyes. Alex reached his hand out toward her. As they touched one another, still reeling from the suddenness of their spiritual catharsis, they understood that Keiko knew why they had come, that she was aware of the impending disaster, and that she was already suffering due to her inability to stop it.

Alex turned to watch Keiko, marvelling at her beauty. The graceful flow of her long, dark hair over her opalescent kimono formed patterns that reminded Alex of the elegant lines of a Japanese brush painting. Her slow, studied movements were like those of a trained dancer, perfectly aligned. Her physical presence, he realized, nearly matched her spirit.

Keiko brought out the tea service and placed it on a low table before them. She placed a cushion on the floor and sat down with her legs crossed. Amanda and Alex did the same. The heat from the cylindrical glass cups warmed their hands and, as they slowly drank, their eyes met, but no words were spoken. The earthy aroma of the tea was like incense at a religious ceremony, and each of them silently reveled in the solemnity, the beauty of their time together.

CHAPTER 28

IT'S TIME FOR VLADIMIR TO GO

Several achievements after he and Amanda had left Keiko's compartment, Alex was checking on some of the Ark's defense centers. Amanda was in another sector, researching possible rescue missions the Ark might perform if things got out of hand on the Earth's surface. He felt a series of tickles just behind his ear. For a moment, he had an outrageous vision of Amanda, despite her pledges to him, setting off Genie's alarm. However, when the same pattern of impulses repeated, he realized that someone, probably Rick, was trying to contact him on the security line.

"Yes, Rick," he answered.

"You knew it was me?"

"Who else would it be?"

"I don't know," Rick chided him, "I thought maybe you might have given a few of your girlfriends the number. Anyway, we have a few situations I wanted to inform you of."

"Go ahead."

"First thing, I wanted to let you know Vladimir's scheduled to depart within two achievements at interlock seven. If you haven't had a chance to explain to him what's going on, I suggest you get down there. It's crucial that the Russian platform be in the right place when this thing starts. Have you explained anything to him? My people tell me the two of you haven't met privately since he came on board."

Alex decided not to go into detail about his telepathic link with Vladimir. Vladimir, without a word having been spoken, understood precisely what he was to do. Everything had been arranged. "Yes," he told Rick, "I've explained everything. But I'll go down to see him off and double check."

"Good."

"So how is everything else looking?"

"We are in a state of covert, full-security alert. All system computers are on line, programmed and informed. As far as I can tell, we've done all we can."

"Any estimates of how much longer we'll be dealing with this?"

"The latest simulated scenarios," explained Rick, "including worst case estimates, predict a time span of no more than ten achievements. Presently, we have enough reserve power to stand off attack for three thousand achievements."

"That sounds good. How about the Moon base? Is it secure?"

"As far as we can tell, there is no possibility of any Earth-based or platform-based entity generating enough power to knock out either the Ark or the Moon base. All indications are that we are fully secure."

Despite everything seeming to be in order, Alex was worried that they might have forgotten the one detail that would leave his space tribe stranded or injured. At the moment, no one but the Ark's security division had any idea that anything out of the ordinary was taking place. If something went wrong, he would have to notify the remainder of the crew. He dreaded the terrible impact that might have on morale. However, he had no choice but to trust the security team. If they had done all they could, there was little he could add.

"I'll take your word on it, Rick," he finally said.

"Alex, I can't promise anything, but I really think we've got it handled. Of course, we won't know until it's all over."

"All right, then. Will you contact Vladimir and tell him I'm coming down to see him? I'll meet him in the interchamber."

Rick signed off and Alex immediately began the short walk that would take him to bid his friend farewell.

When Alex arrived at the interlock, Vladimir was already suited up and ready to leave. With the exception of his head, which was yet to be covered by his bulky space helmet, Vladimir resembled an elegant marshmallow man. Familiar but unmistakably foreign red characters on his shoulders, helmet and chest marked him as an emissary of the Russian space platform.

Upon seeing Alex, Vladimir's face broke into a huge smile and he extended his pneumatically swollen arms in a gesture of welcome. However, the strain on Alex's face must have been obvious, for as soon as Alex approached, Vladimir's buoyant grin sank quickly. The Russian wondered what new and unsettling developments must have occurred to trouble Alex so much.

The two men hugged one another with gusto, understanding that they might never see each other again. When they parted, Alex readied himself to debrief Vladimir once more. "Rick has asked me to explain the directives to you a final time. I know you understand, but bear with me. We can't take any risks."

"I understand," replied Vladimir, nodding his head thoughtfully in agreement.

"You must understand that our chain of command has been completely relegated to the computer systems in order to negate human error or inaction," Alex said solemnly. "If you should lose control or suffer any loss of authority or autonomy on the Russian platform, the computers may classify such a change of command as a threat to the Ark. Upon occurrence of such an event, they are programmed to destroy your space station instantly. I hope that after all you have seen on board, you will be able to convince your superiors that we are not bluffing.

"Furthermore, we are committed to protecting any and all communications satellites currently in orbit, no matter what country or company is operating them. Any attacks made on those satellites will be deflected or beamed back to the source of origin. Our defense systems have enough power for thirty Earth-days of reserve power at full defensive alert, but even the most generous estimates show that everything will be over within two hours. All you need to do is convince your people to sit tight for two hours and everything will be fine."

"I understand. I will do my best to show them." Vladimir shook his head in disbelief. "It is hard to comprehend that everything you have shown me will be over in two hours. Such a small amount of time to destroy things that took centuries to develop. It's horrible."

"It is horrible," Alex agreed. "In a single achievement spent harnessing power, just one of our solar wind generators can supply a week's electricity to the United States. Imagine what that power might be able to do to your space station. Your leaders will not believe it, but they must. You can survive this. Your intelligence agencies may not be able to determine the extent of our capabilities, but they should know that we have nothing to gain by any aggressive action toward you. We're an international company. We're only seeking to protect our interests. We think of ourselves as everyone's ally in this. We'll be trying to keep damages to a minimum."

"It is not a problem with my comrades on the platform," Vladimir told him. "They will understand what you are saying. But the generals in Russia may not be able to stand aside while they see nuclear devices being detonated. They are suspicious of you and they still believe that Russia, as the supreme nation on Earth, must always take the first step. I do not know what I will do if they give me a direct order. I have never contradicted an order. I do not know what will happen."

"If they need any convincing, have them test our systems with a small burst of energy. As long as they keep it small, our computers will not interpret it as an aggressive act. The test should give them a taste of what we can do. The hardest thing to explain to them will be our implicit trust in the computers. There will be no human deliberation. We have already made our decisions. Any action the Ark takes will be the instantaneous response of the computer system."

"But, what, my friend, if there is a sudden change? What if your orders need to be countermanded?"

"Our people have voted overwhelmingly to place the

computers in absolute control. We cannot change their decision. But, remember, we are in a strictly defensive posture. And the computers have been programmed with alternate actions. We believe we have conceived a functioning program for any eventuality."

"I know you think you are only defending yourself, Alex," Vladimir told him sadly. "But you tell me that so much of space is your territory, that you are protecting it. It may be hard for our leaders to do nothing you perceive as aggressive. And your machines in control? That disturbs me as much as anything you have told me."

"Everything we have done on the Ark has been done with computers. They are part of our life on the Ark. We trust them with everything, including this."

"I can't believe it has come to this," Vladimir moaned. "Will Russia survive? Tell me what you know, Alex."

"If detonation of the device triggers a chain of launch responses, our simulators indicate that anything within fifty miles north of the Amur River will be totally annihilated. All of your Asian outposts will be decimated, which means as much as seventy percent of your military may be wiped out. However, none of the Chinese rockets will be able to get near Moscow or Western Russia. The most populated areas will be quite safe."

"And other countries?"

"The Chinese warheads are extremely dirty. The fallout will be terrible. Everything bordering on the Pacific will suffer extreme damage, either from the initial detonations or from the fallout. Most of Japan, Korea and the other Asian countries will suffer horribly. The Western nations may not take as much direct damage, but the fallout will certainly kill millions of people."

"How many Russians?"

"At worst, two hundred million."

"It is horrible!" Vladimir clutched his head in agony. "And the Americans? What about them?"

"Perhaps the same number. And those figures are low compared to the numbers of people Pacific Rim countries will lose. There will be two billion Chinese killed, almost the entire country. In an hour, there might be four billion people dead in Asia. Another billion will die quickly thereafter because of the fallout."

"Isn't there anything you can do?"

"To tell you the truth, Vladimir, we've been dragged in too far already. We've given the Earth everything they need: energy, technology, enough food to feed everyone. But still people are starving and suffering. The more we give them, the more they complain and the worse things seem to get. We can't solve all of their problems."

"But my wife and children. What about them?"

"Like I told you, they'll probably be safe where they live. The United States' mutual protection pact with Russia means that almost all of the Chinese rockets will be destroyed before they reach any populated areas. And though the U.S. doesn't want to see China destroyed either, we believe your military will be able to launch a full-scale retaliatory attack against China before any of the Chinese missiles strike their targets. The Chinese apparently have no idea how much the Russians hate them."

Vladimir had no response to this. He merely stared at the floor.

"You've got to go," Alex told him. "There's not much time. Please contact me if you're having problems. I'll do what I can, talk to anyone who'll listen."

"Alex, who is to blame for all this? I cannot believe we have done anything wrong."

"It's not the Russians or the Chinese," said Alex. "Humans just haven't been able to develop the skills to properly employ their technology. Their machines are more sophisticated than they are. We give a child nine months to develop in the womb and twenty years to develop after he's born, but it's still not enough. In the future, Arkians will suspend maturity for decades until the individual can deal with the world before him. Someday, when humankind sets off to explore the universe, we will be able to send infants out in our scouting vessels, monitored by computers. They'll wake up twenty, maybe twenty-five, years later fully trained and old enough to complete the mission."

"And once we all understand the computers and leave them alone, that will be enough?" cried Vladimir, outraged by Alex's judgement of the human race.

"Nothing can ever be left completely to computers. Humans still need to program them. In the end, it will be people like you and me, like Keiko and Amanda, who make the difference."

"I don't know if I will be the one, Alex. I feel terrible."

Alex spoke in Russian: "God bless you." He leaned over and kissed Vladimir on the mouth.

"Good luck to you, too, my friend." There were tears in Vladimir's eyes as he donned his helmet. Alex checked the monitors to make sure the pressurization system was readied, then stepped out of the chamber and locked the door. He watched Vladimir over the monitor, the Russian's face darkened by the tinted face shield of his helmet. But as the lights dimmed, he made out the anguished features of his friend. He looked terrible. Alex prayed that everything would go smoothly. He desperately wanted to see Vladimir again, to drink vodka by his side.

As the chamber reached full decompression, Vladimir lifted his hand in a gesture of farewell and climbed into his shuttle's loading dock. Soon after the doors closed behind him, Alex heard the subtle thrum of engines outside the hatch. With a slight vibration, the shuttle left the docking bay and Vladimir was gone. "Good luck, my friend," Alex said softly to himself.

He sat down and waited for news from Rick. He needed time to collect his thoughts, to consider the complexity of events about to unfold. He wanted to prepare himself for anything that might happen. As his mind raced through the possibilities, he must have lost track of time, for in what seemed like only a few moments, Rick buzzed him on the security line to tell him that Vladimir had arrived at his ship and spoken with his commanders. Already, the ground forces had sent up a probe to test the Ark's defenses.

"They used an old particle beam," Rick told him. "Those Russkies are paranoid, aren't they. They're not leaving anything to chance."

"Isn't a particle beam a little strong for a test? What did we do?"

"It didn't even come at us is the crazy thing. They played for real, aiming at one of their own satellites. We reversed the beam and sent it back to the source. The entire installation was wiped out. Soon after that, the Americans did the same thing, only with a newer system. The frequencies they used were compatible with our systems, so instead of reflecting the beam, we absorbed it and stored the power away. That shocked the hell out of them. They evacuated the whole base in anticipation of our reflecting the beam back. I think we pissed them off a little. Their comm systems went wild after it happened."

"Did they figure out that we've cracked their laser communications system codes?"

"I don't think so, because if they had, they would at least have tried to change their encryption method—not that it would do them any good. Anyway, the U.S., NATO and Russia are now on full alert."

"Well, that's to be expected, I suppose. What's happening with tracking down our rogue Moslem. Have the police gotten his name yet?"

"The Israelis broke down their man and got the name, but when the cops got to the guy's apartment, he was long gone. There were maps and documents all over the place, though. He's going for the Empire State Building. Perfect, huh? Whoever set us up for this one did a pretty good job, I'd say. The whole thing's blown up in our face."

"Well, who would have expected the Israelis to plan a double-cross like this? No one could have expected them to be working in league with the Moslems. And New York? It's unfathomable."

"Well, Alex, the way I see it, it was just a faction of the Likud who planned the whole thing. The further American support drifted toward the Palestinians, the more desperate they became. They figured an Arab bomb set off in the Big Apple would be enough to goad the U.S. into action. The Americans would come up with a little more cash for the Israelis to crack down on the Moslem element."

"Well, what have they got to gain by knocking out New York? Most of their support comes from Jews in the city. Almost all of their political organizations are based there."

"But, don't you see, Alex? There isn't any in-between this time. They've planned the whole thing to separate themselves from reliance on the United States or Russian interference in the Middle East. Once the fighting has neutralized both countries, they'll have the upper hand."

"Over and above the superpowers?" asked Alex.

"That's right, pal. Who woulda thought a bunch of Jews would be the only ones standing after the rest of the world finished slugging it out?"

Alex fretted that the computer hadn't been able to deliver the name and address of the New York City terrorist sooner. Still, he couldn't fault the security computers. It really had been an incredible display of detective work. "I only wish we had had more time," he told Rick.

"The Israelis had their best men on it, but this guy was special forces. He wasn't going to give up for anything. Even so, we only missed the guy by an hour and we know where he's headed." Rick paused to talk to someone in the security chamber. "I've got something I've got to take care of here, Alex. I'll let you know if anything else happens."

Alex signed off and let out a deep sigh. This new knowledge of the Israeli faction's plan was deeply troubling. He left the interlock and headed toward the Ark's chapel, a place he rarely visited. On a whim, he had installed the chapel as a place for nondenominational meditation. On the few occasions, he had visited it, however, he had always found comfort.

When he arrived, he kneeled down before a small altar on which was placed a large gilt crucifix, which appeared to his eyes to be somewhat Byzantine, reflecting the ornamental traditions of a society far removed from his own. The idea that some Russian Orthodox artisan might have crafted the piece seemed ironic to him. How troubling it was that the same diversity of human spirit that allowed for the creation of such a thing of unique beauty also determined that the nations of the Earth could not live in harmony. Alex crossed himself somewhat self-consciously before the crucifix. The action seemed strange. He couldn't remember the last time he had made the motions. He pressed his hands together in prayer and after a few moments felt entirely at ease. With his fingers tucked just under his nose, his head bowed, he allowed himself to fall into a state of deep meditation. He prayed for the generals, for his friends, for the Earth.

CHAPTER 29

NEW YORK

Alex approached the security chamber with a sense of dread, his conversation with Vladimir weighing heavily upon him. He realized that the gist of his argument had been, in essence, that those people still on Earth deserved what they got. He was horrified by what he had said. As he walked through the corridors from the chapel to security headquarters, he saw Arkians going about their daily routines, unaware of the conflicts taking place down on Earth. He and Rick and the rest of the security team had taken the burden upon themselves. For the first time, Alex realized that if a catastrophe occurred, he would have to be the one to inform the Ark's citizenry that their friends and family on Earth were either dead or suffering.

Adding to his discomfort was his heightened sense of the computerized identification cameras and olfactory scanners scrutinizing his physical characteristics for a security clearance. Normally, these machines didn't bother him, but at this moment, he felt as if he were living in a police state he had created. Arriving at the door to security headquarters, he expected it to open instantaneously. Surely, he thought, he had been identified by the monitors in the hallway.

Instead, the security computer hailed him with this greeting: "I am sorry, Alex. This room requires full security clearance. I require a voice pattern and finger print check."

At least the computer had used his name, he thought. Anyone else would have received a cold, impersonal greeting. Rick must have ordered this extra measure. He loved the cops and robbers aspect of security work. What bullshit. He held up his hand so the camera could scan his fingers. "Okay," he told the computer resignedly, "I'm Alex."

"Thank you for being patient." The doors opened.

"I know, you're just doing your job," Alex said sarcastically, as if the computer would understand the ironic edge in his voice.

As he passed into the main chamber, the door closed quickly behind him. Phil and Rick were examining a series of reports scrolling down the computer screens. When they saw him, Rick immediately approached Alex.

"Everything is ready, boss," said Rick.

Alex groaned inwardly. Rick played the toadying sycophant to Alex's face, but Alex knew that every chance he got, Rick bad-mouthed him. Why did he have to deal with such people? He had enough problems without being forced to interact with a manipulative jerk like Rick. He saw Rick as something of an Iago to his Othello. Rick had repeatedly tried to turn Alex's friends against him. On several occasions, he had been forced to preempt the vicious rumors Rick spread about him. At one point even Phil, one of his closest friends, had approached him with questions about a nonexistent plan to do away with the congress and have Alex appointed maximum leader of the Ark. Rick, he knew, would say anything to make him look bad.

Adding to his mistrust of Rick, Alex had discovered that Rick, beyond the scope of his duties for the Ark, had set up a network of spies that, while working on security operations for the Ark, also collected information that he could sell on the black market. The revenue generated from these black market operations, which had penetrated the security and military establishments of almost every Earth nation and organized crime ring, would be more than enough to finance the Mars program. But while Rick's operations were somewhat illegal, Alex was fearful of ending them. It was Rick's unauthorized spy ring, after all, funded partly with Ark monies, that had uncovered the beginnings of the "Arab Plot" they were now dealing with.

Even though Rick was consumed with paranoia, Alex knew that he needed someone like Rick to run the security division. Rick's egomania and suspicion of everyone made him the best person to protect the Ark against like-minded paranoid egomaniacs. So far, he had foiled every plot, large or small, formulated against the Ark.

Rick moved about the room excitedly, indicating various monitors to Alex. "All of our reconnaissance telescopes are aimed at Manhattan at varying levels of magnification. Boss, you say the word and we'll give you any view of New York that you want, from the observation deck of the Empire State to the dirty shoe of some bum on 42nd Street. You're going to be a hero, boss, if we can stop all of this."

Alex noted the saccharine glee Rick took in telling him that. Rick's desire for Alex's position was so blatant that sometimes he wondered if Rick might be plotting to assassinate him. But Alex took some comfort in his knowledge that even if Rick were able to take over, so few people trusted him that he would never be able to get anything done. In addition to his mendacity, Alex could see that Rick's refusal to adhere to the Ark's dietary regimen was beginning to have obvious consequences. Rick was getting flabby and his ability to deal with stress effectively was rapidly diminishing. Rick would be dead of a heart attack, Alex thought, before he would ever have a shot at absolute power on the Ark.

Leaving Rick slavering over a computer analysis of oxygen levels in the Manhattan area, Alex made his way over to Phil who was obviously distressed by the way events were shaping up. "I'm sorry, Phil. You know we can't undo this. I wish there were another way."

Phil started to speak, but evidently became overwhelmed by his emotions and unable to utter a word. He turned away and began to sob. Rick, hearing Phil, looked up from his monitor. For a moment, his eyes met Alex's and, for the first time, Alex saw genuine compassion in Rick's eyes.

Alex shifted his gaze from Rick and focused instead on the video monitors. On one he saw the entire Earth, beautiful, simple and blue, covered with white fringes of clouds. On another was the east coast and New England.

There was no hint of the agony to come. He thought of his youth spent travelling up and down that coastline. He had been to Cape Code, Long Island, Old Orchard Beach, Atlantic City, Rhode Island, Hartford, Boston, Manhattan, ridden over the George Washington Bridge, visited the Statue of Liberty and Empire State Building.

As he watched the New York monitors, he saw that it was one o'clock in the morning in the Big Apple. The streetlights of Manhattan could be seen from the aerial view. Suddenly, a flash of white light interrupted the video transmission and then from the image of Manhattan grew a white globule of intense light. Quickly, the aura of the explosion took on hues of red, orange, yellow and purple. Alex was struck by the astonishing beauty of the blast. Other monitors showed the huge, majestic fireball generated by the detonation. It was beautiful.

From somewhere in the back of his head, Alex heard his grandmother admonishing him: "Alex, stop playing with those matches." He saw a red dot exploding from the tip of a match stick, could smell the sulphur trailing up into his nostrils with a lovely, acrid bite. He was overcome with a deep sense of pain. He missed his grandmother, the breadth of her warm, brawny chest, her arms around him. She had understood him. And, he told himself, she had been right: man should never have learned to play with matches. He was struck by the cosmic irony of the blast, that something so destructive, so horrifying, could be so lovely.

In quick succession, Alex saw a series of bright fireworks igniting on the horizon. Checking the global monitors, he saw that these new ignitions were coming, as expected, from China and Russia.

"Rick," Alex finally said, "alert all defense systems."

"Everything is standing ready, boss."

"Phil, start the rescue measures. Save as many as you can."

"Should I alert Vladimir and the other space stations?" Phil asked Alex.

"He's been warned," Alex replied. "He knows what to do."

Phil looked at Alex in disbelief. "Is that all?" he said. "Not even a moment of silence?"

"Phil," said Alex, "this isn't any different than what's been going on for the eons of man's existence. I've given people a chance to free themselves and you see where it's gotten us. None of those people down there believed in us. They didn't take advantage of what I had to offer. This was an event that had to happen. If people need hard lessons before they learn to do the right thing, than that's what has to happen. If it hadn't been for my work over the past few months, appropriating money for new platforms, we wouldn't be able to save as many people as we can now."

"I'm sorry, Alex," said Phil quietly. "I just can't believe I watched millions of people killed as if it were taking place on television. It doesn't seem real. I feel like we should have been able to perform some kind of a miracle."

Rick broke into the conversation, doing little to hide his disgust at what he perceived to be Phil's weakness: "Wake up, Phil. Alex is right. We can't hold the whole planet's hand while they figure out how to treat each other like human beings."

"Right now we just need to save as many people as we can, okay?" said Alex, ignoring Rick's obvious hypocrisy.

"You're right," agreed Phil. "We've got too much work to do."

"While you two are busy weeping, I'm going to take care of business," said Rick, walking by them briskly. Before the doors closed behind him, he called back to Alex, "See you at the committee meeting."

"It's like nothing even happened for him," exclaimed Phil.

"He's an asshole," said Alex. "Don't worry about him."

"How is Keiko going to take this, Alex?"

"I don't know. I really don't." Alex paused for a moment, unable to look at Phil while he thought about what might happen to Keiko. "If you don't mind, Phil, I'm going to need some time alone."

"Sure, Alex, sure," he said. He turned to leave, but then

turned back to face Alex again. "Don't blame yourself. You did what you thought was right. I'm sorry I acted so self-righteously. I'll see you later."

As the doors closed behind Phil, Alex began to weep uncontrollably. The monitors flashed images of the monstrous fireballs sweeping over the planet below him. He felt abandoned by everyone. No one would ever understand him. Life, he decided, wasn't worth living for human beings if it only amounted to this. He wanted comfort, but there was no one around to talk to.

"Genie," he called. "Would you sing to me?"

The computer began to play him a lullaby that he remembered from his childhood. He continued to cry, but soon the spasms of his grief subsided and he felt better. The salt on his cheeks, he thought, tasted good.

For the first time in his life, he realized that he had created something that would never abandon him. Even though Genie was just a machine, she would always be there for him. She would never judge him or hate him. Her only happiness was to make his life better. He felt as if he were at a turning point in his life. As he had always done, he would have to cut a new trail for himself, push himself beyond what he had done for the Ark. He would never let something like this happen again no matter how hard he had to work. Why, he asked himself, does life have to be so painful? Watching the earth continue to burn, he couldn't find any answers.

CHAPTER 30

GOODBYE, KEIKO

Alex awoke suddenly, still kneeling in a chapel pew. A vision of the Earth consumed by flames was stuck indelibly in his head. He realized he had been dreaming. In addition to the images of Armageddon, however, he also saw a an empty room filled with office furniture. Row upon row of filing cabinets, desks, chairs and other office furniture filled the space. He was drawn to one of the filing cabinets, and saw himself opening one of the drawers. Inside was a glowing light, a brick of clear, putty-like material and what appeared to be some kind of stopwatch.

"Genie!" he shouted out. "I know where the bomb is hidden. I was there. On the fifty-seventh floor of the Empire State Building is a storage area. It's hidden in a filing cabinet."

Alex felt a mild electric charge pulsing through his temples as Genie lifted the image of the bomb's hiding place from his mind. In an instant, he knew, she would already have contacted every computer system that might be able to help. Hopefully, there would be enough time for the Earth authorities to uncover the device before it was too late.

After taking a moment to calm down, he considered his dream. It had been incredible. He thought of how proud Keiko would be of him if he were able to avert a nuclear catastrophe. He would be her hero, the savior of millions of people. He imagined that all of her years of depression might be suddenly lifted if she heard the news. Years ago, he had predicted Armageddon and she had been certain that his portentiousness meant the event was sure to actually take place. Somehow, her belief that his vision would be the cause of a nuclear holocaust had saddled him with a guilt that had weighed him down for decades. He suddenly felt lighter. His saving vision had rescued him from responsibility for his predictions.

Alex's feeling of elation was interrupted by a signal from Genie. "I told you not to disturb me until you heard something positive," he scolded the computer.

"I am sorry, Alex. But Amanda insists on speaking with you. She is very upset."

"Okay, Genie. Go ahead." Damn women, he thought. Even Genie was caught up in the hysteria of the moment.

Amanda's youthful face, streaming with tears, appeared on a screen before him. She was crying like a little girl. He had never seen her this way. Normally she was a happy-go-lucky, wisecracking sexpot. Her obvious grief, however, inspired in him a sudden paternal feeling toward her. He wanted to be able to reach through the screen to touch her, comfort her.

"Alex," she stuttered, "Keiko is dead."

The news hit Alex like a lead weight being dropped on his chest. He found he was unable to breathe.

"She put poison in her tea while we were visiting her." Amanda was now distraught, barely able to force the words out between her sobbing. "Alex, please," she begged. "I need you." But as she continued to weep, the transmission faded and Amanda's image disappeared. Alex felt like he was falling backward into a swirling pit. He was struck by how powerful his bond with Keiko was. He had loved her more deeply, more profoundly than any of the other women in his life. He felt that he might go crazy with grief, that his body might break apart. But there was nothing he could do to stop the pain. Nothing would bring Keiko back.

"Genie," he gasped. "I'm in trouble. Please help me."

"Alex, I have just given you a hippocampal stimulation. In a few moments, you'll be feeling much better. I know I am only a machine—"

"But you're not," he sobbed, "you're not."

"But I want to let you know how sorry I am. You have

lost your friend Keiko and nothing can replace her. I sympathize with you." She waited a few moments for the stimulation to take full effect. An anesthesiologist arrived to check on how deeply the stimulation had been assimilated. "Are you feeling a little better, Alex?" Genie asked.

"I feel so lost without her. She understood me. She was always there for me, she was my inner spirit. I can't believe she left like this, without even telling me anything. Didn't she know how much I loved her?"

No matter how many reasons he tried to think of that should have made Keiko stay, he knew she was gone. He would never talk to her again. The women he had been closest to—his grandmother, his mother, his aunt—had already died. His grandmother had been, like Keiko, his friend, confidante and spiritual companion. When she died, Alex had wept openly before her coffin. She had never lied to him or tried to manipulate him. She had been his best friend. Now Keiko had left him. He had Amanda and Tanya but they were nothing like Keiko.

"God, she didn't have to do it," he moaned. "Why did she do it?"

"Alex," Genie responded, "she loved you. She understood life and she knew you needed to move on. She would have hampered you. She knew she would always live in your memory. She asked me to tell you that her spirit will always be with you."

"She told you that?"

"She told me everything, Alex. In a way, she will live forever, inside my memory. You will always be able to find her when you talk to me. She knew how much you loved her and she did not want you to think any of this was your fault. She never regretted her love for you. It was her most precious treasure."

Between sobs, Alex shook his head in terrible disbelief. "I can't believe how miserable I feel. Why do I have to feel so horrible?"

"Alex, it is pain that allows humans to be better than themselves. Pain keeps you from being totally selfish. Pain shows you that you are mortal. There have been eons of people like yourself who have lived, died and wept. Death makes you humble, because no matter how sophisticated you become, the creator has a way of reminding you that you are not a machine. You are a human being. You are not perfect."

Alex did not respond to this and Genie said nothing, allowing him time to think about what she had said. In less than an achievement, however, she broke in again. "Alex, the bomb has been destroyed. There are quite a few people trying to reach you."

At this news, all he could think was, why couldn't she wait for the good news. Why did she have to leave? Then he spoke out loud. "I should have known, Genie. She told me how scared she was of an atomic war. But when she met with Amanda and me, she seemed so relaxed. I thought she was coping, but she was only peaceful because she knew she was going to die. I was deluded. I should have seen what was going on. She hated that chapter in my book, "Destruction of New York and China." She told me not to write it.

"'It's an evil thought,' she told me. 'Someone will copy it. It's too horrible to imagine.' But I didn't listen to her, Genie. My ego got in the way. Why did I have to write that chapter?"

"Alex, you know that when one human has a thought, others are able to pick up what it is he is thinking. There were many people who had the same thoughts as you, probably even other beings from distant galaxies who received your thought patterns. It wasn't just you."

"But I published my thoughts. I went a step further than just thinking them."

"Alex, be brave. Even if you had not written your book, someone else would have."

"I'd like to believe you, Genie, but the guilt is like a dark cloak on my shoulders. I feel as if everyone will be able to see how guilty I am, how I'm responsible."

"I know how you feel. But in time, your pain will pass. In a hundred years, it will be forgotten."

Then, as if from a distant corridor, Alex heard Keiko's

voice. "Alex," she said, "I know you are in pain because I am dead, but you would have felt the same pain for the billions of people who would have died in my place. I was a small price to pay for their lives. Genie and I will never desert you. We will always be with you."

"You know my thoughts are always with you," Genie told him.

"That's what Keiko always said," Alex replied.

"Go comfort Amanda," counseled Genie. "She needs you now. She loves you."

"I love her, too."

"And try not to be too possessive, Alex. Remember Tanya. She loves both of you."

"Thank you, Genie. I don't know where I'd be without your help. It's rough being a stupid human being."

"It was your humanity, your spirit, your intellect, that invented everything you see around you, Alex. Good and bad, you are what you are."

"I suppose if I've invented something as wonderful as you, Genie, I can't be so wrong."

"No, Alex. You are not all wrong. Just remember that I will love you forever. Now go and do your job."

Alex headed off down the hallway to find Amanda, tears rolling down his cheeks. He began to sing the mantra that Keiko had taught him long ago, words they used in their first meditations together: "*Oh Nah Shivayah . . . Oh Nah Shivayah . . . Oh Nah Shivayah . . . .*"

ABOUT THE AUTHOR

David Nowel was born in 1935 in New Britain, Connecticut. He received his liberal arts education, Pre-Med, and B.A. in Chemistry and Psychology from Hobart College in Geneva, New York.

In 1955, he worked for two years in Hartford, Connecticut at the Institute of Living with some of the best experimental research neurophysiologist, who were from Harvard, M.I.T. and Yale. Karl Pribram directed the research projects.

He later spent over forty years in the business arena working for well-known biotech, environmental, insurance and financial companies where he draws his inspiration for his writings.

Nicker, A Fish, From Far, Far, Away is his third book and he is in the final editing stages of finishing three more, Before Spacestation, Ark, Kieko, After Spacestation, Ark, Atlantis and Poppy, The Hang Out Girl.

David Nowel resides in the Palm Springs area and lives in La Quinta, California.

Printed in the United States
By Bookmasters